C000186613

Someday, Maybe

by

Jenny Piper

SOMEDAY, MAYBE

Copyright © 2013 by Jenny Piper
Cover design © 2013 by Susan Justice (Sveva)
Back cover design © 2013 by Fairytale Backgrounds

The right of Jenny Piper to be identified as the author of this work has
been asserted by her in accordance with the Copyright, Designs and
Patents Act 1988.

This is a work of fiction and should in no way be construed to
represent any individual or place unless otherwise stated.
Any correlation with real people or events is coincidental.

All Rights reserved. No part of this publication may be reproduced,
stored in a retrieval system, or transmitted, in any form or by any
means without the prior written consent of the publisher and copyright owner, nor be otherwise circulated in any form of binding or
cover other than that in which it is published and without a similar
condition being imposed on the subsequent purchaser.

ISBN # 978-1-907984-13-6

First published in Great Britain in 2013 by Sunpenny Publishing
www.sunpenny.com
(Sunpenny Publishing Group)

MORE BOOKS FROM THE SUNPENNY PUBLISHING GROUP:

Blue Freedom, by Sandra Peut
Brandy Butter on Christmas Canal, by Shae O'Brien
Breaking the Circle, by Althea Barr
Bridge to Nowhere, by Stephanie Parker McKean
Dance of Eagles, by JS Holloway
Don't Pass Me By, by Julie McGowan
Embracing Change, by Debbie Roome
Far Out, by Corinna Weyreter
Going Astray, by Christine Moore
If Horses Were Wishes, by Elizabeth Sellers
Just One More Summer, by Julie McGowan
My Sea is Wide, by Rowland Evans
The Mountains Between, by Julie McGowan
Uncharted Waters, by Sara DuBose

With thanks to M.

'Someday Maybe' *is based on a true story, though the characters and the settings have been completely changed and are entirely fictional. The title comes from 'The West, a Nest and You,' the theme song of Mart Kenny, Canadian music icon and radio pioneer, which was one of the songs that Mary used to sing to the little Patricia.*

A second novel, **'Moving On'**, *will be published shortly. It tells of a happily married retired couple who excitedly move from their dilapidated seaside town to share what is supposed to be a wonderful house in delightful country-side with their daughter and her family. The move turns out to be only the first of many, each one more dispiriting than the last, but their love for each other upholds them and carries them through to the end.*

Chapter 1

1935

There were some things a man had to do, and this was one of them. Closing his eyes and gritting his teeth against the early morning cold, Jim plunged across the frozen yard.

It was no warmer in the lav. The wooden seat was icy cold and he could hear his teeth chattering. *By the cringe!* His fingers were too numb to tear off the sheets of newspaper cleanly, but at least the cistern wasn't frozen up this time. The chain worked, even if reluctantly. Not waiting to button up his trousers, and fastening his braces as he went, he hurried blindly back to the kitchen.

Mary had filled up the kettle and set it on the stove before going down to the hens, but the fire that he had banked up in the small grate the night before seemed to have given up the ghost, or very nearly; only the smallest fragments here and there still glowing red. She must have forgotten to see to it before going out – his job at night, hers in the morning. Crouching and taking a sheet of newspaper from the basket, he unfolded it and pushed it up against the fireplace opening. Twice he released a corner briefly and peered behind it hopefully, but only smoke escaped. It made his eyes water.

At last, the relatively steady glow and flicker of flame behind the newsprint told him that the chimney was beginning to draw and he crumpled up the charred paper, though he stayed crouched for a moment, despite his hunger, willing the feeble warmth of the fire to thaw him out round the edges. *Bloody hell! Roll on summer.*

He had brewed up a pot, wolfed down a bowl of porridge,

drained two cups of tea and hacked off and buttered two doorsteps of bread by the time Mary got back from the hens. A blast of wintry air entered with her small figure and a gust of smoke billowed from the fireplace as she slammed the door.

He glanced over his shoulder. "Fire'd nearly gone out."

She had her knitted hat on, pulled down over her ears. He wanted to pull it off so he could touch her hair. "Eh?" She glanced guiltily at the hearth.

"Caught it in time. 'S all right now."

"I'm sorry. Too cold to think."

Too cold and too bloody tired, poor kid. He watched, chewing, as she carried the clanking hen buckets over to the sink and rinsed them. Reaching for the small cardboard tub of Wintergreen on the windowsill, she rubbed some into her hands, wincing. It worried him.

"You want to make sure you dry them properly, you know. That's when they get chapped, when you don't dry them properly." He meant it kindly, but it made her cross.

"I know, I know!"

He took another slurp of tea. "Only saying ..."

He continued to study her over the rim of his cup as she stowed away the buckets beneath the heavy, chipped sink and then unravelled her long woolly scarf and hung it on the peg. *Not bloody right, poor kid.* Still chewing, he pushed back his chair and crossed to help her as she began to tug ineffectually with numbed fingers at the knotted bit of rope that held a man's mac, old and dilapidated, about her slight body. "Here ..."

She was shivering. "Did you drink all the tea, or did you manage to leave a drop for me?"

He grinned. "Needs a drop of hot." As he hung the old mac on the peg she topped up the pot and then poured out a mug, cupping it between her cold hands and sipping it gratefully with her eyes closed. He frowned again. The familiar black cloud of depression drifted about his head, but he shrugged it away. Moving quickly behind her, he drew her tightly into the hard curve of his body. She felt fragile, like a little feather, though she acted as if she was tough as old boots, and she smelt of warm bran mash, cold air and Pears soap. Lord, he did love her!

"I missed you, again, last night," he told her, trying not to sound resentful. "So what was it this time? Earache, or a bad dream?"

She sighed. "She can't help it, you know, she's only a baby."

"She's five years old!"

"She gets nightmares. She can't help it if she gets nightmares." He could sense her getting prickly and his frustration was getting through, too. "Can't you get her a nightlight or something?"

She was bridling now. "I don't like to leave her with a light, she's too young, she might knock it over. Besides, she gets earache. Sometimes it's earache. I can't leave her with earache, can I? It'd be too cruel."

He squeezed her waist, put a tease in his voice. "I reckon it's just an excuse. Likes to have you at her beck and call."

"And so do you!"

He was taken aback. "No, I don't!"

"You do!" She turned in his arms, her grey eyes flashing with merriment. "Yes, you do. You're a bigger baby than she is!"

Now that hurt. His grip loosened. "I miss you, that's all," he told her, sulkily. "You never seem to have time for me these days."

"Ah, diddums!"

She giggled, and it made him smile. He could eat her up. Sweeping her into a big bear hug, he crushed her closely to him. "One of these days, I'd like to wake up and find you there," he told her huskily. "In my bed. By my side. Like it was in the old days, remember?"

Her arms tightened about him reassuringly and she nestled her head affectionately into the crook of his shoulder. "She'll grow out of it."

He cocked his head to listen for any sound from Patsy's room. It was worth a try. "She's still asleep. D'you want to come up to bed now?" he murmured hopefully.

"No!" She shook her head firmly and for a moment, he was hurt again, but she sounded rueful, which heartened him. "There isn't time, love."

He sighed resignedly, knowing that there wasn't. "Give us another kiss, then," he murmured grudgingly, pulling off her woolly hat. When he'd first seen her, a neat, spriggy little thing, she had worn her hair in tight, dark pigtails, and he'd liked that. When she had grown up and had it cut in a fashionable sort of style he'd been a bit disconcerted, but as time had gone on she had let it grow a bit and sometimes put it up so that it sat on her head like a plump, soft, scented cloud, and he had loved it. Today, so early in the morning, it was tousled, unwashed and unbrushed and smelled of the cold morning and of chicken feed, but he didn't care. He adored it. It was her hair. *His* hair. He could have stood there with the feel of her and the taste of her and the smell of her forever.

All too soon, though, she broke away, pushing at him firmly. "That's enough. Let go, you idiot! I want my tea!"

3

She took a moment to pull herself together, putting her hands to her cheeks as if to cool them, and then hurried to take her pinafore from the hook. "Right then – what's today?" she asked, all businesslike.

Reluctantly he pulled himself together, reached for his ledger from the old wooden dresser and sat at the table with a sigh. "Got to get this into some kind of shape for a start."

"Let me get the cloth off first." Mary whisked away the crockery and the tablecloth. The tablecloth was precious and not for Patsy to play on; one of three, pure linen, though not new, smuggled out of her aunts' house by Nancy, along with four sheets – only one of which had been sides-to-middled, three pairs of pillowcases and two tray cloths, both embroidered prettily. She liked this one for mornings. It was cheerful – white with a broad pale yellow band about the edge.

"Couldn't you do that tonight?" she asked, filling up the kettle and a heavy pan with water, and setting them on the stove to boil. "I really need you to make a trip into town. I can't get on with the Wooller funeral without more wreath wire and we need to order some paraffin." A thought struck her. "Oh, and could you pop into the chemist and get me a bottle of glycerin and some Ipecac? Some nights Patsy can't seem to stop barking and I'm sure it's the catarrh that's giving her the earache."

He tapped his teeth with his pencil. "What time have the wreaths to be delivered?"

"Three at the latest. Funeral's at four. One large yellow, one smaller mixed and a cross – all white, the cross."

"Have we got enough chrysanths?"

"I think so, just about."

Sighing heavily, he scraped his chair back from the table and crossed to take his jacket from the door. "Better get a move on, then, I suppose." He opened the door, and then hesitated, frowning. "Glycerine and what?"

"Ipecacuana." She hurried to him, reaching up to throw her arms about his neck and planting a big kiss on his lips. "He'll know what it is. Thanks, lovey. You are a sweetie-pie, you know."

He grasped her by the waist, his eyes narrowing. "I'll expect some kind of return, you know, if I'm to get frozen half to death."

She was puzzled. "Like what?"

He growled, furrowing his brow meaningfully. "Like no more midnight treks tonight."

She grinned. "We'll see."

"Give her some bloody knock-out drops or something."

She laughed, knowing he didn't mean it. "Don't be so rotten!"

"Cheerio!" As he hurried off, grinning, icy raindrops hit the back of his head.

E lsie Glassbrook opened her back door a crack, letting out a gleam of light and a gust of warm steam, just as he was stacking the last of her logs in her woodshed. Her broad face was red and shiny; must be washing day. He couldn't help noticing, in the unforgiving light of morning, that she was going grey already. *How old is Elsie, then?* he wondered. *Thirty-seven? Thirty-eight? Same class as me in school. Same age as me. Must be.* He felt a pang. *Don't let me do that to Mary. In ten years' time, don't let her look so old.*

"Cup of tea, Jim?"

He rubbed his cold hands together appreciatively. "Aye, that'd be grand, Elsie!"

"Bitter out there today."

"Not half!"

She pulled the door to. "I'll keep this door closed till you're ready, Jim. There's measles about and a couple of the little ones with runny noses. I don't want to let the cold air in."

It was warm and humid – almost too hot – in Elsie's kitchen, which would have seemed crowded even without the clothes-horse standing draped in front of the small range and other drying washing strung above it and across the room. It wasn't a bad sized room for a cottage, quite a bit bigger than theirs, but Elsie had seven children, and a table big enough for all and all the chairs took up a great deal of the room, even when the children weren't there. A faded armchair and a sideboard as well as a dresser took up more space, and today, with the big wooden washing tub stuck in front of the sink, the table laden and several of the children squashed in round about with their bits and bobs, it could only be described as cosy. The paraffin lamp on the table was lit and a storm lantern hung from a hook above, together making the kitchen bright and welcoming after the gloominess of the lowering sky.

Elsie, up to her elbows at the sink, glanced over her shoulder as he stamped his boots and ducked inside, closing the door again quickly. He slipped off his jacket, shivering. "By the cringe, it's miserable out there today, Elsie."

She nodded approvingly. "That's it, take off your coat. You'll need to feel the benefit when you get back out." She glanced at her eldest daughter. "Cath, a cup of tea for Mr Norris and take that wet coat from him," she ordered briskly. "Sit down, Jim."

Cathy, fair haired, round-faced and blue-eyed like her mother, jumped up from the table where she had been sticking pictures into a scrapbook with the little ones, and hurried to the teapot. "I expect you'd like a piece of cake, too, Mr Norris?" she offered hopefully.

"I would!" Mary hadn't the time to be making cakes that often, and he couldn't blame her for that, so he always looked forward to Elsie's, where there was always cake and where they never failed to offer him a slice.

"There's parkin or caraway seed, Mr Norris." Cathy hovered with the tin. "Which one would you fancy?"

He was about to plump for the parkin, when she told him, reddening a little with pride, "I made the caraway seed. It's very nice."

He grinned, ducking beneath the washing to lever himself into the easy chair wedged in between the clotheshorse and the range. "Oh, well, I'd better have a bit of that then, Cath!"

Elsie dropped a wrung-out shirt into a basket. "There you are, Cath – another lot ready for the mangle. Get that cake for Mr Norris, though, first. Sorry about the washing, Jim – no point putting it on the line just yet."

He held his hands to the fire. "You've got your hands full, Elsie, with all this lot to wash for."

"You won't mind if I get on, then, will you? Don't think I'm rude – you have yourself a rest."

He was glad to do it. The bottoms of his trousers were steaming dry already. He sipped with relish the hot, sweet tea that Cathy gave him and balanced the plate of cake that followed on his knee. "That looks grand!"

She hovered, clearly waiting for him to try it, so he took a large bite and chewed reflectively, pretending to consider, then took a second bite appreciatively. "You know what, Cath? I think caraway seed's my favourite and I believe this is your best one yet!"

She was pleased as punch. He could see that as she blushed even more deeply. "Just say, Mr Norris, if you want another slice."

"Mr Norris, here, look at my plane!" Tommy, Elsie's seven year old, dark haired and sturdy, held up a wonky creation of cardboard and rubber bands. "It flies really well, see? Do you want to see it?" Taking aim, he launched it into the air, where it held up long enough to travel right over the table, narrowly missing Jim's head before fluttering down dangerously close to the fire. Jim rescued it just in time.

"That's grand, Tommy!" Putting down his plate, he fumbled

in his pocket. "That reminds me ... Where's Chrissie?"

"I'm here!" Sniffing, the little girl looked up from her scrap-book. She did look a bit peaky. Jim hoped she wasn't going down with measles; he didn't want to take it home to Patsy.

"And Pauline?" Chrissie's twin emerged enquiringly from beneath the tablecloth. He grinned.

"Ah, yes – there you are!" He held out a small brown paper bag. "Here, Mrs Norris sent these for you, girls. Pictures, see," he added, shaking out a few colourful fragments of shiny paper. "For your scrapbook – that's a kitten, see, there's a pansy, and an elephant ... and there's a forget-me-not. All sorts of things, I don't know what else. I think she found them in her old schoolbook."

"Let me see ... let me see!" The children scrambled for them gleefully. Pauline, whose pink nose was running badly, threw her arms about his neck and planted a damp kiss on his cheek. "Ooh, thank you, Mr Norris!"

They were nice kids, he thought, pulling back just a little and hoping that she wouldn't notice. Elsie had brought them up well.

"They're a bit crumpled, I'm afraid," he added guiltily. "Been in my pocket a week. I forgot to leave them last time."

He took the last mouthful of cake as the children hurried back to the table with their treasures. "Really good, Cath!" he repeated, rescuing the last crumb from his chin and popping it into his mouth.

Elsie nodded proudly. "Oh, yes, she makes a good cake!"

He winked at her broadly. "How're you going to manage, Elsie, when she's wed?"

Cathy, pleased but clearly embarrassed, busied herself with the scrapbook. "Oh, I've no plans for that, yet, Mr Norris!"

"I should think not!" Elsie dried her hands on a tea towel. "Not for a long time, I should hope! I need Cathy here with all this brood."

He stood up regretfully, disentangling himself from a pair of clinging long johns that were dangling over his head. "Better go, Elsie. I've to get some wires for Mary – she's a lot of wreaths to make this afternoon."

"Let me get my purse ..." Elsie paid him for the logs, then held the door open just enough for him to pass through as he buttoned up his jacket. "Shall you be delivering to the house?" she asked. "'Cos if you are, Nancy said to be sure to call in because the frock is ready for you."

"Good grief!" He was startled. "She's finished it already? She must have been working her socks off. She needn't have, you know – it's not our anniversary for another three weeks, not till the seventeenth of December. I didn't mean her to do it in such a hurry. I hope she hasn't worn herself out."

"Well, she did say she had been burning the midnight oil doing it, but she didn't want *them* to see it, naturally. I think she was just pleased to be doing something for Mary."

"*Eau-de-nil,* it is, Mr Norris, with a pattern all of tiny daisies," Cathy joined in eagerly, forgetting her embarrassment. "Rayon crepe, with a gored skirt and little ruffle sleeves ... isn't that right, Mum?"

Elsie nodded. "That's right, that's what our Nancy said. She got the material in the market, quite a bargain, only had a tiny hole near the selvedge, and the buttons –"

"Mum gave her the buttons, Mr Norris." Cath looked down at her hands.

Elsie nodded. "Like little tortoises they are, Jim. Whalebone, I think. I'm sure she'll like them – Patsy will too. I had them in my button-box, always meant to put them on a blouse for Cath."

He smiled his gratitude. "Ah ... that's very good of you, Elsie." He felt a little awkward. He could see that Cath had wanted them. He cleared his throat. "I am sorry you've been done out of them, though, Cath."

She looked up with a shy smile. "Doesn't matter. So long as you like them, Mr Norris."

"Me? It's not me that's to be pleased, Cath, it's Mary. She'll be wearing them!" Cathy looked back down quickly at the scrapbook. He hoped he hadn't hurt her feelings. "And I'm sure she will, Cath," he added hastily. "Be pleased, that is." He pulled on his damp jacket. "Mary will be really pleased." Cathy nodded.

"You're managing to keep it a secret?" Elsie asked, as he turned up his jacket collar ready to face the rain. "She really doesn't know?"

He shook his head, excited. "Hasn't got a clue."

Elsie chortled conspiratorially. "Probably thinks that you've forgotten." She patted his arm. "It'll make a lovely surprise. She's a grand needlewoman, is Nancy. Used to make all us kids' clothes for our Mum once she'd got good at it. Takes a real pride in her skill with a needle, always has."

Jim frowned, musing. "If it's ready, I've got to think where to hide it."

"Well, don't go putting it in the potting shed or anywhere like that where it might get damp."

"Somewhere Mary wouldn't look ..."

Elsie, holding the door ajar, was growing impatient. "Come

on, Jim, you're letting all the warm air out!"

He hurriedly stepped out through the gap. "Sorry." Once outside, though, he hesitated again, frowning. "You're sure it'll be all clear?"

Elsie clicked her tongue. "Just stick your head in at the back door, she won't keep you a minute. You won't see *them*, especially if you can get round there about eleven o'clock. Nancy says they've got the vicar calling."

Chapter 2

I t didn't take too long to drop off the morning's logs and veg and to call in at the chemist and the ironmonger, so it was bang on eleven when he turned the cart into Broad Street, hitched up Meg's reins and made his way round to the back of the house. As always, he found himself dilly-dallying at the back door of the house, scanning the back windows, brushing himself down and running a finger nervously round his collar before stamping the mud off his boots. Nancy was very faithful to him in her ordering for his sake and for Mary's, but being caught at the back door, shabbily dressed in his working clothes, delivering sacks and boxes of vegetables made him feel ten times as guilty about Mary as he usually did.

Looking down their thin, pink noses, her aunties might have seemed to have been moaning about his cabbages or Brussels sprouts, but what they really meant was that a man who was married to the only niece of the Misses Buckley should have been smartly dressed and confident, going somewhere at the very least if he hadn't yet arrived, and should have been ushered into the morning room by Nancy with a polite bob. *That* man would have been welcomed into the family, not left shuffling at the kitchen door, cap in hand. It was a difficult position to be in.

Don't be so bloody stupid, he told himself, pulling himself together and rapping firmly at the door.

Nancy opened it smartly, peering up at him, her small, wrinkled face breaking into a welcoming smile. She always reminded him of a little grey mouse; you could almost see her whiskers twitching.

"Oh, there you are, Jim! Glad you popped in. I told Elsie – saves me traipsing over to the cottage." He glanced guardedly at the inner door but it was tightly closed. She frowned at his

11

hesitation, impatient with creative pride. "It's all ready. Come in, come on in, do."

He stepped into the flag-stoned kitchen, its air pervaded with the lingering smell of something sugary cooking. He could see the old blue dress of Mary's that he'd brought lying on a chair. "It's very good of you, Nancy ..."

"Now then, let me fetch it." Dusting off her hands, she bustled self-importantly off into the larder, and emerged with her handiwork on a hanger. She held it up proudly with a flourish. "Well, there it is then. What do you think?"

He gazed at it, anxious to please her by saying the right thing, but what should you say about a lady's frock? It looked all right, nice, soft material. The colour, a pale, muddy, greeny sort of thing, was unusual, but probably fashionable – he wouldn't know about that. Mary'd probably like it. It reminded him of the rainwater in the barrel, or the leaves of fading snowdrops when the snow had turned to slush. What had young Cath said the sprigs of white were? Oh, yes, daisies.

"Very nice material, Nancy. Green." She looked pleased, but was still waiting. "I like the daisies." Beyond that he was a bit stuck for words. "Oh yes, oh yes, indeed! It's very nice, very nice, Nancy." He gestured ineffectually. "Nice blouse. Nice, er ... thingummy. Pretty colour. Oh, yes, very nice."

Satisfied at last, Nancy spread the frock on the table and began to fold it carefully. "I'll put it in some brown paper, then it won't get all mucky in your cart. Oh, and I must give you the blue one back," she added, glancing at it. "Though, I must say, the material's gone, really, been washed too many times. I have tried to mend it but it's not –"

She caught his anxious glance at the door. "Oh, don't worry, they're tucked up nice and cosy with the Reverend. I've just taken in the morning coffee and some nice fresh ginger biscuits. I'll just get the blue frock." She nodded at a biscuit barrel on the table. "Do you fancy one?"

Jim opened the barrel eagerly. "I don't mind if I do."

"Oh, go on – take a couple, lad. Take three." Nancy fetched some brown paper and picked up the old blue frock of Mary's. "Do you want this separately, Jim?"

He nodded. "Please, Nancy." He pulled it towards himself so he wouldn't forget it. If he tried to open up the parcel to take it out and then wrap it up again, he'd make a pig's ear of it.

Nancy finished making a neat parcel of the frock, then tied a piece of string around it and patted the package with satisfaction. "There. I think Mary'll be pleased with that, Jim, don't you?"

"Mary'll be thrilled! Oh, yes, Nancy, you've done us proud, you have – really." He stood up and put an arm about her shoulder, giving her soft cheek a kiss. "I'm really grateful to you, Nancy. I appreciate your hard work, I really do, and so will Mary." He put his hand in his pocket. The wires and the medicines had taken quite a bit of the cash customers had paid on his way round, and he was supposed to be paying for paraffin, too, on the way home, but he had to offer. "Now, then, did I leave you with enough cash?"

She waved her hand dismissively in the air. "Oh, don't be so silly. You gave me more than enough, more than enough, Jim! Just hope it fits." Flushed with pleasure, she pushed the biscuit barrel towards him once again. "Go on – have another biscuit, do."

One of the bells in an array on the wall behind him started noisily into life, making him jump. Nancy frowned with exasperation. "I thought I'd got them settled. Whatever do they want now?"

Glancing warily at the hall door, he reached for the package. "I'd best not stop, anyway, Nancy – I've got to get back for Mary to get on."

"Right you are, Jim." She patted the package in Jim's arms. "I'm looking forward to seeing Mary in the new frock. D'you think she might wear it on Tuesday when you come to tea?"

His heart sank. "Are we coming to tea?"

"Tuesday teatime. You're all expected to tea at four o'clock sharp."

He rubbed his cheek apprehensively. "Are we?"

"I've to make some maids-of-honour."

He frowned, thoroughly disheartened. "You sure they're expecting me, too?"

*S*hould *I give her the dress now, then, instead of waiting?* he wondered as he made his way back to the cart. No, keep it till the anniversary proper, he decided. With a bit of luck, they'd not be stopping long enough to take off their coats, so it would be wasted Tuesday.

Bloody hell, a tea party with the aunties! Bloody hell.

The shrubbery was heavily overgrown; he noticed it with irritation each time he walked to or from the back door. Hardly any daylight could be getting into the house now. It was an elegant house, or must have been when Mary's mother was a child; he'd been ever so impressed when he first saw where

Mary lived, though even then he'd thought it a very gloomy place – and it had got gloomier over the years. The Misses Buckley liked their privacy, so they had thick net curtains hung at all the windows and had let the hedges and the shrubbery grow, and very little light fell inside the house. Poor little lost soul Mary must have been, when she found herself come to live with them.

Forgetting for a moment that he didn't want to be spotted, he paused, gazing in distress at the state of the shrubs; laurels like great trees now, not bushes; same with the osmanthus, and they took long enough to grow. Skinny, twisted branches of skimmia and ilex of one kind or another, kerria and syringa with suckers thrown and grown up into more bushes all over the place, the whole lot choking with the remains of the summer's bindweed. It was a right tangle; it almost broke your heart. Mary's aunties had the money to have it all seen to – they had old Tom Martin, after all, who came in to see to the lawns, but they never seemed to get him to do anything about it.

"Maybe I should offer to prune it for them," he'd suggested to Mary several times, wanting to see the shrubbery as it ought to be, but she had advised against it with a chuckle.

"No, no, they like it like that, Jim, tall and gloomy. It keeps the rabble at bay."

It was almost twelve by the time he got back and, despite Cathy's piece of cake and Nancy's ginger biscuits, he could feel his stomach rumbling. He left the package in the cart whilst he checked where Mary was. He'd have to put it somewhere in the house, but where? If he didn't look sharp, Mary'd fall over it very quickly.

He could hear the creaking of floorboards and the patter of footsteps on the floorboards above his head, but the kitchen was empty. It smelled of a pungent mixture of whatever was cooking on the stove – stew by the smell of it, he decided with satisfaction – and of the acrid scent of the yellow and white chrysanthemums which Mary had brought in and which were standing in buckets of water on newspaper laid over the old brown linoleum. The wire-cutters and the secateurs were laid out on newspaper spread over the tabletop, too, and the wreath frames had been mossed already, and were propped up against the chairs. She must have been listening to the wireless whilst she worked; the pips were just coming up to the twelve o'clock news. It was battery operated, and she'd been pleased as punch when he got it for her.

Dropping the packages of wreath wire onto the table, he pulled the chemist's bottles from his pocket and set them carefully on the dresser, then went quickly back outside and got the package. Clutching it to his chest, he picked his way between the chairs and buckets towards the inner doorway.

The steep wooden ladder that led up through a trapdoor into the half floor-boarded attic, where he and Mary had made their bedroom, took up much of the space in the small hallway, but he stepped round the base of it with the ease of long familiarity and let himself into Patsy's cramped bedroom. Crouching by the narrow bed he pushed the package as far underneath as he could, hoping that the dress inside wouldn't get too creased, then slipped back hastily out of the room. Moving to the foot of the ladder and peering up through the trap, he raised his voice. "Anybody at home?"

"Ooh – Daddy's home!" Mary sounded happy. That pleased him.

"Daddy! Daddy! Come and have a look!"

Something slammed shut. There was more movement up above, gales of laughter, the creaking of floorboards and then two laughing faces crowned with silver Christmas tinsel appeared at the trap, peering down at him.

More tinsel hung about Mary's neck. She wore a pair of mismatched dangling earrings, and a black silk shawl embroidered with crimson roses was draped about her shoulders. "Hello, sweetie-pops!"

An assortment of beads, just as mismatched, hung about Patsy's neck and from her crown of tinsel an ostrich feather, black and glistening, dangled. A diamante clasp hung above one eye. "Hello, Daddy! Hello, Daddy! Hello old Mr Mushrooms, you!"

He laughed, wrinkling his brow in mock mystification. "Who?"

"Mummy's Mrs Mushrooms and I'm – who am I, Mummy?"

Mary shrugged. "Mrs Pollyanna Wigglenose Dumplings, of course!"

He shook his head, grinning. "Well, you're a fine old pair!"

Patsy shrieked with laughter. Mary winked at Jim. "We're coming down, now, love." She straightened up, slipping out of the shawl and folding it carefully. "Down we go now, poppet. Careful as you go."

Patsy stood up, turned, and backed towards the ladder, feeling for the top rung with her feet. The old pink satin slip of Mary's that she was wearing over her dress and cardigan was much too long for her, hampering her movement. Jim reached up to her. "Hang on – you'll break your neck done up like that!"

Swinging her carefully down to the floor, he climbed onto the rungs again and waited for Mary to descend. He trapped her between his arms. "What are you supposed to be? The Christmas Fairy?"

Mary giggled, her face flushed. "Something like that!"

Grinning, he pinned her fast against the rungs, "Come on – give us a kiss, then, under the mistletoe."

It was late evening before he got round at last to dealing with his ledger. He sat at the kitchen table, frowning and resting an aching head on his hand, filling in columns by the light of the oil lamp. This was the part of things he liked least, because it always particularly brought home to him how badly he was doing for his family. It brought out the black dog on his shoulder, as Mary called it, and then he got moody and didn't want to talk to anybody, and it wasn't fair.

Lost in temporary depression, he wasn't aware that Mary had come into the kitchen with her candle, and jumped when he felt her leaning gently behind his shoulder. She slipped a hand beneath the collar of his shirt, running soft fingers over his chest.

"Hello." She brushed his head with her lips. "Come on, lovey. Come to bed."

He rubbed his eyes wearily and frowned. He really ought to get this damned accounting finished.

"Bed! I'm not waiting any longer."

She smelled of the Yardley's Pink Lilac talc he'd given her for her birthday and he glanced up at her, still frowning. Her dark hair was loose and she had her pink dressing gown loosely draped about her shoulders in spite of the cold night. He felt a flicker of hope. "Is she asleep?"

She laughed softly. "Fast, fast asleep."

The black dog jumped down from his shoulder, vanishing. Breaking into a broad grin, he reached to turn down the wick. "Then I'll not keep a lady waiting."

In summer, when it was hot so close under the roof, almost too hot to breathe, he and Mary threw off their clothes and Mary found the thinnest, oldest sheet to pull over them in case of later draught, and it was sort of romantic and daring making love in nothing but the moonlight streaming through the small window. At this time of the year, though, it was bitterly cold up there in the attic.

"Jim?"

"'Mm?" He strained to make out her pale face beneath him on the pillow, but on such a night, with the rain lashing down upon the roof tiles and the heavy clouds obscuring the moon, he would have had difficulty making out her features even if the thin cotton curtains hadn't been tightly drawn. He felt drowsy, replete with lovemaking, full of contentment, a thoroughly happy man. He could stay like this forever. In fact, Jim thought, with the thick eiderdown tucked tightly about his neck keeping out the draught and the glow of her soft body warming up his skin, he almost preferred the winter. It felt quite exciting being snuggled up together in their eyrie while owls hooted from the chimney top, vixens on the hunt for dog foxes on the hillside let out their wild and compelling screams and the wind howled round the ridge tiles. He smiled into the darkness of the pillow. "What's that, my love?"

"Jim?"

Bless her. She was his little pet. "Yes, my little duckling?"

"Could you move now?"

He frowned. "You what?"

"Move, please."

He frowned, drawing his head back a little, puzzled. "What?"

Mary pushed at him and giggled. "Get off me! Move, you great lummox, you're squashing me to bits!"

L ater in the night, sensing an empty space beside him, he reared up, and became aware of the muffled sound of Patsy sobbing down below and the faint creaking of the ladder. From the direction of the trapdoor a faint light flickered. He heard a soft murmur down below, "Sh, hush, ssh ..." and then the light disappeared.

He blinked into the lonely darkness. Outside an owl hooted, then again. The bedside clock ticked impersonally.
Bloody hell.

H e slept badly after that, and got up feeling quite groggy and just a bit feverish. He was later than usual, too. Mary must have already seen to the hens. She was eating a bowl of porridge and when he walked into the kitchen Patsy was happily crooning to herself and spoon-feeding her doll, her fair hair done up in bits of rag. Catching sight of Jim, she tugged excitedly at one of them. "Look, Daddy, look! I'm getting ringlets!"

His head ached but he tried to sound interested. "Oh? Ah ... yes."

Mary moved to dish him out some porridge. "Ready for this, sweetheart?"

"Getting a blasted cold." Pulling out a chair, he poured himself a cup of tea and gulped it gratefully, hoping to soothe his rasping throat.

She scanned his face anxiously as she set down the bowl in front of him. "Oh, dear, poor you! And it's cold out again, too. Take your time; don't rush. There's more water in the kettle ... Wait a minute, poppet, Mummy's just got to fill the teapot."

Over the top of the cup he saw Patsy clamber over her scattered tea set and trot over to the stove, reaching up to grasp the kettle. He rose quickly to his feet, but Mary had caught sight of her, too, and had reached out to arrest her. "No, no, NO, Patsy! You must never, never, NEVER touch the kettle!"

Jim sank back with relief, and sneezed. He fumbled for his handkerchief and blew his nose, groaning. Last thing he needed was a bloody cold.

Patsy looked genuinely puzzled as she withdrew her hand. "Why?"

Mary pushed the kettle further onto the stove. "Because you might scald yourself, silly!"

"What's *scald*?" Patsy stood on tiptoe, peering over the top of the stove.

"Burn yourself. Hurt yourself – badly. Boiling water is very, very hot." Mary directed her away from the stove, patting her bottom firmly. "*Away,* I said, Patricia. Now!"

Jim sneezed again. Head aching, he finished the last spoonful of porridge, drained his cup and rose unwillingly from the table, crossing to pull on his jacket. "Can't sit around, better get going. Got a lot to do today."

"Wait." Taking a small bottle from the dresser, Mary mixed a few drops of its contents in a small glass of water and held it out to him. "Here."

He took it from her warily. "What is it?"

"Essence of cinnamon. Just drink it. Sip it."

He did so, gingerly, and grimaced. "'S horrible."

Sighing, Mary rummaged again in the dresser, taking out a bag of barley sugar. "Here." She unwrapped one. "Sweetie for after."

Closing his eyes, he drained the glass, and she swiftly popped the sweetie in his mouth, chuckling, "There you are. That's a good boy!"

Chapter 3

He straightened, holding his aching back, watching Patsy as she offered a muddy spoonful of torn-up leaves and water to an invisible playmate. "Here you are, my dear. This will make you better."

He usually enjoyed digging, but today the task seemed to demand a great deal of effort. He mopped his brow. He was perspiring heavily.

She scanned the invisible one's features sympathetically. "You're a bit of a tired toad today, aren't you?"

He laughed. "Tired toad!"

She was indignant but dignified. "Well?"

Grinning, he turned back to his spade. "Nothing. Just wondered where you got that from, that's all. You're a funny lass."

"Cooee!" Mary was calling, high-pitched, from the kitchen door. "Cooee!"

He shook the soil from his spade, feeling his heart sinking. "Come on, pet. Time to go."

Patsy was reluctant as well. "Aah, why?"

He fumbled in his pocket for his handkerchief and blew his nose once more. "Got to see the great-aunties, haven't we?" Sighing, he shouldered his spade and started to walk towards the cottage.

Patsy's face set in a fearsome scowl. "No, no, Daddy – I don't want to go!"

"Come on, we won't stay there long, I promise." He held out his muddy hand. "Come on, there's a good girl, we've got to have a wash and things. Mummy'll be cross if we're late, won't she?" She began to trail slowly and sulkily towards him. "That's it." He squeezed her icy fingers as she slipped them into his.

"Why? Why have we got to go, Daddy? They smell."

He stifled a grin. "Sh, shouldn't say that." He was curious, though. "What of?"

She couldn't explain it. She grimaced, wrinkling her little nose. "Funny."

"They're old, that's all, Patsy. They can't help it." He squeezed her hand again. "Tell you what – don't tell Mummy this 'cos they're her great-aunties, aren't they – but Daddy doesn't want to go, either."

He was annoyed with himself though. How the hell could the thought of two old ladies still make him tremble in his boots? He was a big strong fellow, he could have reached out and snapped either of them like a twig. Mary's Great-Aunt Louise was just a silly, spoiled woman, and he could more or less cope with that, although she was very snippy and rude – even when he was done up in his best, she looked at him as if he'd come visiting in his gardening boots and muddy trousers and smelling of manure. The elder Miss Buckley was far worse. Mary's Great-Aunt May, with her wire-rimmed spectacles and icy, gimlet gaze, reminded him somehow of the first teacher he'd had in school, who used to crump you on the knuckles or box your ears and sit you up on the mantelshelf with a label round your neck saying 'I AM A BAD BOY' if you disobeyed. Queen Mary, he always thought, Queen Mary, only smaller and scrawnier; same sort of bosom, like a shelf.

Patsy was a traitor. "Ah, I'm telling!" Tearing away her hand, she set off, giggling, racing through the apple trees. "Mu-mmy ...!"

Jim screwed up his eyes and rubbed his forehead. *Bloody hell.*

I tell you, Mary, I don't feel up to this." The bus jolted over a particularly rough surface of the road, making him feel quite queasy. "Can't you tell them I've gone down with a cold and I don't want to risk either of them catching it?" He ran a finger round under the tight collar of his best shirt, trying to loosen it. "It's the truth, anyway. Hope it's not the measles. Might have caught it from Elsie's kids. I feel bloody lousy. Ache all over ..."

Patsy looked round quickly from the seat in front. "So do I, Mummy. I feel bloody lousy too!"

Mary glanced quickly, embarrassed, at the other passengers. "Ssh! Honestly, Jim!" She straightened her felt hat crossly. "Look, you're both coming in with me and that's that! They may be a couple of old dragons, but they're the only family we've got left between us, so just you be good, both of you."

He sighed heavily, unwilling to give up. "But, Mary ..."

She leaned towards him pleadingly. "Jim, you didn't come in with me last time. They've only just got to the point of accepting me back in the fold. I want them to get to accept you. However are they going to do that if you never come in with me?" Taking his big hand in her small, gloved one, she squeezed it earnestly. "We won't stay long, I promise."

Jim could see her own trepidation in the stiffness of her back, the tilt of her head and the way the firm tip-tapping of her high-heeled shoes slowed down as they walked down the path. At the heavy front door, she drew in a deep breath and quickly brushed invisible crumbs from Patsy's coat.

"Patsy, pet, try to remember your P's and Q's and don't speak unless you're spoken to – and if you are, if Aunty May or Aunty Lou say anything to you, remember to say their names when you answer them."

Patsy pouted. "Why?"

"Because it's polite, that's why," Jim told her. "And don't forget to say 'thank you for having us'," he added.

Mary rang the bell. "I still don't think I should be coming in," he told her, having one last try. "I'm sure I'm getting the measles, or the 'flu. I'm feeling bloody rotten."

"And you remember not to swear," she responded sternly. She peered intently at him, though, and her eyes softened sympathetically. "Ah, you do look a bit poorly ..." Slipping off her glove she felt his forehead, and her brows narrowed anxiously. "Just bear with it for a short while, love. You can go up to bed if you like as soon as we get home, I'll see to things. I'll make you some chicken soup if you like and you can have it up in bed on a tray. Just do this for me, eh?"

Patsy tugged at her hand eagerly. "Can I have soup on a tray, too, can I?"

"Sh!" They all pulled themselves together, straightening nervously, as the door swung open. Jim pulled off his hat. Mary smiled warmly. "Hello, Nancy! How are you?"

Nancy's face broke into a welcoming smile as they stepped into the tiled hall. "Very well, thank you, Miss Mary!" Jim saw her glance at the skirt of Mary's coat and then at him. He shook his head faintly, with a smile. Not wearing it today, no, not yet. She nodded. "Come on in then."

She led them down the drab, echoing hall. Jim saw Patsy wrinkle up her nose at the smell of boiled cabbage and floor polish that always seemed to pervade the house, and drew his brows together in warning. He grinned and winked reassuringly at her when she straightened her face.

"Miss Buckley and Miss Louise are waiting for you in the breakfast room," Nancy said over her shoulder. "We've had to move a bed in there for Miss Louise; her legs have got so bad she can't use the stairs at all well."

Mary frowned, but not with too much deep concern. She was inured to Aunt Louise's ailments, which were mostly feigned. "Oh, dear."

Jim squeezed Patsy's hand as Nancy knocked on the breakfast room door, but she pulled free and hid behind Mary's skirts when the peremptory response came: "Come!"

He gritted his teeth as Nancy pushed open the door. "Miss Mary, ma'am – and Mr Norris and little Patsy."

Though cold, the room was very stuffy, the general odour of the house strongly overlaid with medicinal smells. Aunty Lou, overweight, pink-faced, with thinning hair, was propped up on pillows in the bed which had been set up in the corner. The table beside her was littered with medicine bottles, water glasses, handkerchiefs and books.

As the family entered, the aunts both laid down their books and Aunty May rose from her upright chair by the unlit fire, her back ramrod stiff, her expression and tone both icy. "Ah, Mary."

Jim hovered warily near the door, twisting his hat between his hands, as Mary pressed her lips to the proffered cheek. "How are you, Aunty May?"

Aunty Lou pulled her pale pink knitted bed jacket more closely round her chest, frowning. "Do hurry and close the door, Nancy! There is a terrible draught."

"You may bring the tea in now, Nancy." Aunty May resumed her seat. Nancy bobbed. Jim winked at her as she hurried out of the door.

Aunty May peered sardonically over her wire-framed half-spectacles. "I am pleased to see that you have managed to find the time to join us, Mr Norris. Kindly bring that chair over for my niece."

He fetched the chair she indicated, setting it near hers, then returned to his post by the door. She sighed impatiently. "Sit down, man."

He felt a flash of anger but saw Mary glance at him anxiously as she took the chair, assessing his response. Taking out his handkerchief, he blew his nose loudly and then found himself another upright chair near the door. No point in making things even more awkward than they were.

Aunty May had turned her attention to Patsy, who was still clinging to Mary. "Stand up and let me look at you, child."

Mary gently nudged Patsy into an upright position. Aunty Lou clicked her tongue disapprovingly. "That child has very bad posture, Mary."

Aunty May frowned. "Hold up your head, Patricia," she instructed sternly. Patsy grudgingly obeyed. "That's better! Now you may give me a kiss." Patsy glanced at Mary and then back at Jim, who nodded reassuringly and winked. He saw her wrinkling her nose again as she complied, and grinned.

Aunty Lou anxiously fluttered a podgy hand clutching a lacy handkerchief. "The child had better not kiss me, May, she may have a cold." She turned her worried gaze on Mary. "I hope you don't allow her to play with the children from the village, Mary? You never know what nasty germs she might pick up." Jim swallowed his irritation with an effort.

Clasping her wrists firmly at her waist in a gesture of expectation, Aunty May drew herself up still further in her chair and nodded graciously. "Now, no doubt you have a little poem to say to us, Patricia? Come and stand here, at the mantelpiece."

Patsy glanced at Mary for help, but Mary seemed to be casting about equally blankly, momentarily lost for inspiration. Aunty May clicked her tongue in disparagement. "Come, come, a great big girl like you! You must be able to give us something."

Patsy looked dangerously close to tears. Reading and poetry and stuff like that were Mary's pigeons, really – Jim didn't get involved, so it wasn't easy, but for once memory came to his aid and he leant forward hurriedly.

"What about that one you were saying in the garden this morning, Patsy? The poem you were telling to your doll? *I once had a – once had a ...* That was a nice poem. Come on pet, how does it go?"

Relieved, Mary clapped her hands. "Oh, yes, lovey, you know that one!"

Shyly, Patsy took up a position in front of the mantelpiece as instructed, but with her hands clasped awkwardly behind her back and her eyes fixed firmly on the floor. She drew in a quavering breath.

"I once had a sweet little doll, dears ..."

Aunty May sighed with exasperation. "Goodness me, head up, head up! That's right, come along!" Patsy began again, but the impetus was lost.

"I once had a sweet little doll, dears, the – the –" She frowned intently, screwing up her eyes. *"I once had a sweet little doll, dears ..."* Twisting her skirt in her fingers, she ground pain-

fully to a halt once more.

"The prettiest doll in the world ..." Mary prompted hastily.

"The prettiest doll in the world ..."

Mary leant forward earnestly. *"Her cheeks were so red and so white, dears ..."*

Dumbstruck now, Patsy shook her head. To his amazement, Jim found himself calling out the next line: *"And her hair was so charmingly curled!"*

In his excitement and to his dismay, a violent sneeze caught him unawares and he fumbled in his pocket for his handkerchief. It drew Aunty Lou's horrified attention.

"Oh dear!" She twittered, dramatically clutching at her pale blue bed jacket.

"Has he got a *cold?*"

Enough was enough. He made great play of blowing his nose, and then rose to his feet with what dignity he could muster. "I have, actually, er – Aunty." He mopped his nose hard for good measure. "Perhaps I should go. Don't want you catching my germs, now, do we?" Avoiding Mary's eyes, he turned to open the door. "I'll wait outside in the garden if you would prefer."

Miss Buckley's tone was frosty. "I think it might be better. Very well."

Thank God for that. "Right, then." He almost touched his forelock, but stopped himself in time.

S it down, child." Patsy dismissed, Aunty May gazed at Mary disapprovingly. "I should have thought the man would have had more sense than to visit when he has a cold, Mary. Such inconsideration. Such bad manners! No example to the child at all."

Aunty Lou fluttered her handkerchief weakly. "Only what one might expect."

Mary drew in an irate breath. "But Aunty May –"

She was cut off, abruptly. Aunty May held up her hand. "No, Mary. The man demonstrates the kind of thoughtless behaviour that is typical of his sort. No concern for others! No knowledge of basic hygiene. This is precisely the kind of thing we were afraid of when we heard you were intent on marrying the man."

Aunty Lou was disintegrating into tears. "Why on earth you had to take up with such a very common person I shall never know! Oh dear! Oh dear ..." Blowing her nose noisily, she enquired, "Does he wash properly?"

Mary jumped to her feet, her voice shaking with anger.

"Stop it! You mustn't talk about him like that! That's disgusting, Aunty Lou, to say a thing like that. You're the one who should have better manners – in front of his daughter, too!" She grasped Patsy's hand. "I'm ashamed of you."

She crossed furiously to the door, throwing it open just as Nancy arrived with the rattling tea trolley. "We shan't be staying for tea, thank you, Nancy". Pushing roughly past, she strode furiously a short way down the hall and then hesitated. There was more to be said. Cheeks crimson with anger, she marched back past Nancy to the breakfast room door. "It was my idea he should come. He wanted to stay away but I wouldn't let him. I'm sorry if it was the wrong thing to do, but quite clearly, I am not as well bred as he."

Aunty May gasped in indignation. "Don't be ridiculous!"

"Oh! Oh, my!" Aunty Lou was disintegrating once more into tears.

Mary threw her a disparaging look. "I hope you haven't caught Jim's cold, Aunty Lou. I shouldn't think you have – he stayed well enough away from you and I don't blame him. In future, I shall be doing the same."

There was outrage in Aunty May's voice. "You will apologise to your aunt at once!"

Mary stamped her foot. "No, I will not! I will not, Aunty May! Not until she – until you *both* apologise for the way you treat my husband – like – like the gardener's boy!"

Aunty Lou sniffed coldly. "I thought that was precisely what he was!"

Mary felt ice-cold. Controlling her voice carefully, she drew herself up to her tallest extent. "Good afternoon, Aunty Lou. Good afternoon, Aunty May."

Aunty May rose from her chair. "If you go like this, my girl, don't expect us to receive you back."

Frightened, Patricia started to cry. "Want to go home ..."

Mary drew her closer to her side. "We're going now, poppet, we're going. Come along."

Aunty Lou pitifully raised her hands to her ears. "Oh, May, dear, stop that wretched child snivelling!"

Mary knew she was shouting like a fishwife. "She can damn well snivel if she wants to!"

There was satisfaction in the slamming of the door.

Squeezing Patsy's hand, she pointed her at the front door. "Go and find Daddy, Patsy. Tell him we're going home."

Patsy made for the door, hesitated, then turned back. Pattering quickly to the breakfast room, she opened the door timidly. "Thank you for having me," she mumbled tearfully.

Sitting closely side by side on the bus, she held his work-roughened fingers tightly in her own. He squeezed her hand. "Don't worry about it." She shook her head, staring furiously out of the window. "They're worried about you and they're set in their ways, that's all, you know," he added.

She shook her head. "There's no excuse for them, none at all."

He felt the black dog creeping closer. "I can understand their point of view. I've not been much of a catch."

She tightened her lips. "Stop feeling sorry for yourself. You're all I want." She rested her head on his shoulder. "I really don't mind, you know. About there not being any money."

"Don't you?" He continued staring out of the window. She could feel his chest rising and falling.

"You know I don't." He was silent. "I don't mind if there isn't ever any."

She lifted her head. He was staring ahead, set-faced. "Don't you, Mary? Don't you? Well, I do."

She made a great fuss of him for the rest of the day, packing him off to bed early and finishing off the chores herself. Though he went up apparently reluctantly, she could sense that underneath he was glad to go.

"Here we are, sweetheart," she murmured a little later, waiting to set a small tray on Jim's lap. "A nice drop of chicken soup and a bit of bread."

The candle at his bedside flickered as he struggled to prop himself up against the pillows. "I don't know if I can eat it, Mary."

She sat down on the bed at his side. "You better had, I made it specially." She held out a spoonful encouragingly. "Come on, it'll do you good." He sipped it weakly, and then opened his mouth for another. She smiled. "That's a good boy!"

"I'm sweating cobs," he told her miserably.

She felt his forehead, frowning. "Golly, you are a bit hot."

"Feel my pyjamas." They were wringing wet. She threw her arm about him.

"Ah, you poor old thing!"

"Hang on!" He clutched at the endangered tray.

"Oops! Sorry!" She giggled, leaning forward to cuddle him. "Who's my precious, then?"

His expression turned even more woebegone. "Thought someone else was?"

She was puzzled. "Who?" He nodded towards the trapdoor and the penny dropped. "Oh, I see ... Patsy." She giggled teasingly. "What's the matter? Want me to sing to you? Don't be so blooming daft!"

He grinned. Worthwhile being poorly, having her make a fuss of him. He pulled himself up against the pillows a little, but not too much. "Can I have some more soup?" he asked.

Wiping her hands on her pinafore, Mary crossed to the hall door. "Jim? Do you want a drink before I do anything else?" There was no answer and she called louder. "Jim? Do you want a drink?"

He sounded very sorry for himself this morning. "Oh! Oh – yes, please," he called back faintly, his voice heavily nasal with catarrh.

"Tea, or something cold?"

"Um – something cold, please."

She smiled to herself. He was enjoying this, great big tinker. Well, no point in spoiling the ship for a hap'orth of tar. Taking out her favourite tray cloth, the one her mother had embroidered with cornflowers, she spread it on the small tray and then poured a glass of lemonade and set the bread and butter on one of her best china tea plates. As an afterthought, she snapped off a flower from one of the buckets, and put that on the tray, too, in a small glass of water. She carried the tray to the hall doorway, dodging the drifting Patricia. "Patsy, poppet, you're in my way!"

"Can I carry the tray?"

Mary shook her head. "No, lovey, it'll be quicker if I do it. You get your dollies put away and that table cleared and then you can help me wire the flowers up. You can make a little posy yourself, if you like, a little present for Daddy," she offered as an inducement. "Do it quickly, now. I won't be a minute." Balancing the tray carefully, she climbed slowly up the ladder.

Jim, half asleep against the pillows, was jolted rudely awake by a muffled but very loud crash and the splash of spilling liquid from down below in the kitchen, followed, fractionally later, by a rising and wavering wail. He heard Mary call out in the hall, her voice hoarse with panic, "Patsy?" The ladder creaked heavily as she started to descend again. "Patsy!"

"What's happening?" he called out anxiously, hastily disentangling himself from the bedclothes and tightening his pyjama cord about his waist. *Not the kettle. Please God, not*

27

the kettle.

He stumbled round the bedpost. "Mary? Mary, what's going on?"

"Mummeeeee!"

Mary cried out, agonised: "Coming, I'm coming, darling!"

There was a slight pause, then an even louder rattling and shaking from the ladder, followed by the clatter and tinkle of broken glass or crockery as something hit the ground. She gave a frightened cry. There was a heavy, bumping, rattling noise, then a horrible, solid thud. Then silence.

His heart pounding, Jim hurried over to the trap. "Mary? Mary?" He peered apprehensively over.

She lay, silent and crumpled, at the foot of the ladder. A slow trickle of blood seeped from beneath her forehead onto the floor of the hall. Jim drew in a breath. His voice was barely a whisper.

"Oh, Mary ... oh, Mary, what've you done?"

Chapter 4

I 'll take these away now, Mr Norris, to the sluice room. We don't want flowers in the ward overnight, do we?" Bearing the huge bunch of chrysanthemums, Sister Roberts bustled off briskly through the door.

Mary giggled weakly. "Jim, honestly, chrysanths! It's not my funeral, you silly!"

Jim looked sheepish. "Well, I had to get Jim Taylor in town to do the wreaths for us, didn't I, and we had all those cut ready." She could see the worry imprinted on his brow. "Anyway, I thought it might be, for a while!"

She squeezed his hand. "I'm sorry, clumsy of me, I was just in such a panic! I'm sorry I gave you such a fright. I gave *myself* a fright! I really thought Patsy had pulled the boiling kettle over."

"Bloody ladder." He was deeply distressed. "Have to do something about it. Have to find a better place to live."

"One day." Oh, God, he was going to get moody. Seeing that his mouth was setting in tight lines she struggled to cheer him. "Oh, come on, Jim, all's well that ends well! I'll be right as rain. Ah, look, Jim!" She squeezed his hand. Standing on tiptoe, Patsy had pushed aside the flowered chintz panel that covered the glass of the door, and was peering in, with her nose pressed close to the pane. "Poor Pats. She wants to see me." Mary gave a little wave, raised her aching head a little from the pillow.

He craned his neck to see. "Why won't they let her in?"

"Hospital policy, I suppose. Children might carry in germs."

He grinned. "You sound like your Aunty Lou." His nose was dripping. Sniffing, he hunted once more for his handkerchief.

"You probably shouldn't be in here either, with that cold."

Patsy's face disappeared suddenly, and the door opened.

They saw her peeping through the half-open door as Dr Humphreys, their family doctor, bustled into the ward. Crossing over to Mary's bed, he bent over her forehead. He smelled very strongly of cigars. "Just check that dressing for you before I go, Mary."

She winced a little as he removed the bandage around her head and prodded gently at the wound just beneath her hairline, examining the stitches "Yes. Yes, good – well, that seems fine." He wound the bandage back. "Bit of a nasty cut, more blood than damage, may leave a bit of a scar, but nothing to worry about, soon clear up and the ribcage is just bruised. Nothing broken. Head hurting?"

Mary nodded, closing her eyes.

"Sister'll bring you something for that before she tucks you up. We'll keep you in the Cottage Hospital for a day or two, though, just to be on the safe side." He smiled, adjusting his cuffs. "Know it was only a bit of broken glass, but we can't be too careful, can we? No."

Jim nodded. "Thank you, Doctor."

"No harm in her taking a bit of a rest." Mary opened her eyes and glanced quickly at Jim. Oh dear, he'd take that as a criticism. She reached for his hand again.

A bell rang loudly and Sister appeared sternly at the doorway, hands clasped over her crisp white apron. "Time to go now, Mr Norris. There's a young lady out here who is getting very anxious."

Dr Humphreys clapped Jim on the shoulder jovially. "Marching orders! Time we were all off."

Mary gripped Jim's hand. "You can manage, can't you, Jim?" she asked, panicking. "I mean, with Patsy? I always read her a bedtime story, and then sometimes I sing her a little song."

"I'll call in and see you tomorrow." The doctor whisked himself off to the door.

Jim stood up, but Mary wouldn't let go of his hand. "You will listen for her in the night? If she has earache, warm up some olive oil, and if she starts coughing, give her some lemon and honey, or a spoonful of glycerine mixed with Ipecac, but not too much because it'll make her sick –"

He smiled and bent to kiss her. "You just rest now, like the doctor told you. Don't worry, Mary, I can cope!"

It'll be great – it'll be like you were a proper nurse!" Jim tried once again to slake his thirst, but the tea had gone stone cold.

"Want my Mummy ..." Tears dripped from the end of Patsy's nose.

"Oh, Patsy ..." Sighing, Jim pushed her boiled egg closer to her. "She's a very lucky Mummy to have a proper nurse like you to look after her when she comes home. Isn't she? Eh?" He set a thick slice of bread on the plate beside her. "Here."

Patsy sniffled. "When's she coming? When's my Mummy coming?"

He ran his fingers through his hair. "Soon, Patsy, soon!" Picking up a spoon, he held it out to her. "Come on, Patsy – eat up, there's a good girl! I've got to go and do the hens yet, pet." To his surprise, she opened her mouth and swallowed the mouthful of egg.

"Can I have a uniform?" she mumbled.

"Eh?"

"Can I have a uniform like a proper nurse? Can I?" She took the spoon from his grasp and dipped it into the shell. "When, Daddy? When? When can I have a uniform?"

Jim pushed himself away from the table. "You'll have to ask Father Christmas."

"When's he coming? When's he coming, Daddy?"

He sat down again to pull on his Wellington boots. "Eh? Oh – soon, Patsy." When the bloody hell was Christmas? He'd lost all track of time. "Soon, in a few weeks. You'll have to be a good girl, won't you?"

She scowled. "Ah, I want him now, Daddy!"

"Well, you'll just have to wait."

"Now, Daddy!"

This was bloody exasperating. He needed to get on. How did people cope with half-a-dozen kids? He could hear the impatience in his voice. "You'll have to wait, Patsy!"

Patsy buried her head in her arms. "I want my Mummeee!"

He managed to get his chores done and got her into bed at last, though it took a lot of doing. She was quite good while he was seeing to the hens, darting about and noisily shooing them into the henhouse, but then it started to pour cats and dogs while he was hauling the sacks of vegetables out of the shed and loading them into the cart ready for the morning, and she got very muddy and soaking wet, jumping in and out of puddles and babbling to her make-believe friend. He had to get the tin bath out and heat up enough water to give her a bath, giving up after he'd achieved about three inches of warm water. How on earth did Mary manage? It was no good; they'd have to get a copper.

Whilst struggling to unravel Patsy's sopping plaits, he tried to work out if there would be enough room for a bathroom off the kitchen if he roofed over part of the yard. The lav would have to stay where it was, off the yard, too big a plumbing operation and too costly, but a bath with a Calor Gas geyser or something and a wash basin ... It would be an improvement to Mr Harfield's property, so he ought to be happy to give him the say-so to do it. Mary'd be ever so pleased if he could get it done.

There was water all over the linoleum floor by the time the bath was finished, but Patsy wouldn't let him leave her on her own in bed, so he sat her in the armchair with a mug of cocoa and a picture book whilst he mopped it up, and then carried her off and tucked her under the blankets.

"You have to read to me, now, Daddy." She scrambled over further, making room for him. "This book!" Tucking the edge of the blanket over him, she snuggled down by his side. Reluctantly, he opened the book she thrust into his hand. It actually felt quite good to stretch his legs out in the warm bed. Already he could feel his eyes closing, but he manfully soldiered on.

"Soon he was safe home
Dry as could be.
Soon woke the dormouse –
Good gracious me!"
She wriggled restlessly. "No, Daddy. Not like that, like this!" Jarred by her sharp elbow digging into his side, he came fully awake, blinking.

"What?"

She struggled to sit up. "Not like that, like this! *Good gracious ME!"*

He attempted it again. *"Good gracious me!"*

It wasn't good enough. Frustrated, she showed him again, raising up her voice and widening her eyes dramatically. *"Good gracious ME!"*

He put his all into it; should have been in Music Hall. *"GOOD GRACIOUS ME!"* It seemed to pass muster this time, so he carried on.

"Where is my toadstool?
Loud he la- he lamented –"
Bloody hell that was a big word for a little one! He ran through the last lines rapidly.

"And that's how umbrellas
First were invented!"
He closed the book with relief. "There."

She opened the book again. "No, Daddy, no! Another one, another one, please! Mummy always reads me another one!"

"No, she doesn't."

"Yes, she does, she does!" She threw her soft arms round his neck. "Please Daddy, please, please, please!"

He groaned. "Will you go to sleep then?"

She kicked her legs in delight. "Yes, yes, yes, yes, yes!"

Sighing, he fumbled for his handkerchief. "Hang on, let me blow my nose ..."

She wriggled impatiently. "Come on, Daddy."

He opened the book with a sigh. *"Grasshopper Green is a comical chap –"* He paused, frowning, feeling her scramble from his side. "Now where are you going, Patsy?"

She pattered across the floor. "I'm going to get my dolly."

"Aah, *Patsy!*" Allowing his head to fall back against the pillows, he stared up helplessly at the low ceiling. "Come on home, Mary, love – I'm going crackers!"

They only kept her in at the Cottage Hospital for forty-eight hours, but all in all it seemed a very long time to Jim and Patsy. Mary looked pale and was a little bit weak, but apart from the bandage about her head – soon to be replaced with sticking plaster – and the fact that she held herself a little stiffly because of her bruised ribcage, she seemed as right as rain.

"I have to tell, you, I did enjoy the rest, though, Jim!" Mary admitted as he lifted her down from the cart.

"I'm glad!" He put his arm around her, leading her up the path. "It's what you needed. And I'm not having you running yourself ragged now that you've come home," he told her sternly. "You take it easy, now, do you hear? You're not to try to do anything yet in the garden – and Patsy and I'll see to the geese and the hens."

Patsy hopped around them in excitement as Jim led her towards the door. "Mummy, Mummy, I counted up to fifteen eggs this morning!"

Jim nodded proudly. "Fifteen eggs without a single mistake!"

Mary beamed. "Oh, well done, darling!"

Patsy tugged at her coat. "Come and see what I made you, Mummy!"

Jim nodded. "Let Mummy get inside now, pet." He paused with her on the doorstep, looking down at her with a soppy grin. "I feel as if I should carry you in!"

"You big silly!" She started to laugh, and then winced.

"You all right?" he asked anxiously.

"Mm ... fine. Bit of a headache, that's all."

He gently laid his hand beneath her breast. "How about the – ?"

She winced again, but smiled. "Bit sore."

He drew her closely to him and sighed heavily, careful to avoid the tender places. "Love you," he murmured softly.

Closing her eyes she squeezed him back, sighing with contentment. "Mm. Me, too. I love you, too."

Night-night, Daddy!" Patsy went off to bed happily, now that her mummy was back home.

"She hasn't woken at all for me," he whispered proudly to Mary. "No nightmares, no earache, nothing." He thought better of telling her that he'd slept all night in her room – and he'd do it again. Whatever happened; if he had to get up in the cold and go trailing down himself, Mary wasn't going down that ladder in the dark tonight. He wasn't risking that.

Whilst she was singing softly to Patsy he stoked up the grate, dragged out the tin bath and set it close to the fireplace, then put a lot of water on to boil. Rummaging in the dresser and the cupboards, he retrieved her store of candles and unwrapped a fresh packet, setting them about the room on saucers before lighting them. She might think it extravagant, but what the hell! Then he climbed upstairs quickly and found some towels and her soap and bath things, and collected her clean nightie and the warm pink dressing gown. He draped the nightie over the chair to warm, and spread the towels around the bath and on the fender.

When she saw his preparations and found the small kitchen softly flickering with the candles and with the fire's glow, her hand flew to her mouth. "Oh, Jim."

He ran his hands sheepishly through his hair. "Just thought."

She moved to him, reaching up to cup his head in her hands and kissed his lips. "It's lovely." He felt proud as punch.

Taking her hand, cold from sitting in Patsy's bedroom, he led her to the side of the bath. Her fingers went to her buttons, but he moved them away. "No, let me." He undressed her tenderly, if clumsily, at times, fumbling awkwardly with her bra strap and suspender belt. There was a dark bruise just beneath her right breast, and he brushed his lips against it very gently. "Little love."

When he had bathed her tenderly, he helped her out of the tub, wrapped her in a warm towel and sat her in the armchair while he dried her feet carefully. He bent his head over each toe as he came to it, kissing it, and she smiled, tangling her fingers in his tousled hair.

In their eyrie in the attic, the blood beating thick in his throat, he leant on one elbow, looking down at her and touched the skin above her breast lightly with one finger. "Are you sure it's all right, love? I don't want to hurt you."

She smiled up at him, her eyes gleaming in the candlelight. "Of course it's all right."

He brushed his lips gently to her forehead. "I wouldn't hurt you for the world."

"You won't hurt me ..."

"I'd never want to hurt you."

Her eyes glimmered in the candlelight. "You old softie!" Her lips were warm and soft and welcoming. He pulled himself over her with a groan of hunger, but heard her gasp, and drew back instantly, worried.

She reached for him quickly. "No, no, love. It's all right!"

He hesitated. "You sure?"

"Of course." He could hear the laughter in her voice. "Just don't squeeze me too hard, that's all!"

The wind blew hard in the night, howling in the trees round the little cottage. Jim thought it was that which had woken him, and he lay for a moment, staring sleepily into the darkness, listening and worrying, visualising the glass in the greenhouse caving in. It needed re-puttying, really. Should have done it a long time ago.

"Mu-mmeee!"

He groaned, catching the faint sound from below. Mary stirred instantly, turning awkwardly onto her back.

Bloody hell.

"Mummeee! I've had a bad dream!"

He felt her push back the bedclothes and groaned once more. "No, Mary, stay there. Let me go." But he was very tired.

Her voice was soft and reassuring. "I'm all right. No, I want to. No, I'll go."

He was relieved. "You up to it? You sure?"

"I won't be long. Go back to sleep, sweetheart."

He heard her light the candle with a match and watched through half-closed eyes as she pulled on her dressing gown and made her way softly to the trap. He ought to be insisting. He knew it was wrong.

"Take it easy, Mary."

The ladder creaked and the flickering of the flame grew weaker as she climbed carefully down.

The light from the candle she was carrying shone first through the small light above the door and then cast dancing shadows on the walls as she creaked open the door. "What's the matter, sweetheart?"

Patsy whimpered, reaching for her. "I had a bad dream ..."

Sobbing, Patsy clutched at her dressing gown, entwining it in her fingers as Mary set the candle down on the chest of drawers next to the bed and sank down beside her, stroking her hair. "Ssh. Shh ... Mummy's here ..."

The crying was giving Patsy hiccups. Raising the eider-down, Mary slid into bed beside her, drawing her very close. "What was it this time? Brer Fox and Brer Wolf again?" Patsy hiccupped. Mary stroked her arm. "Only a dream, sweetheart, only a silly dream ... Hush now, close your eyes." She began to sing softly.

Upstairs, Jim listened, only half-dozing.

"I have dreamed my dreams ...
And I have schemed my schemes ...
And I have built my castles in the air."

Castles. Mary should have a castle, that's what she should have, not this – this cowshed!

He should have got up, not her. He turned over, pummeling his pillow angrily into shape.

Chapter 5

Patsy, not there, lovey!" Exasperated, Mary ran her fingers through her hair as Patsy dropped her colouring book and pencils amongst the clutter of small chunks of log, dried flowers, glue, white paint, tufts of cotton wool, bits of fir, twists of ivy, and sprigs of holly on the newspaper-covered table. "I need the space, sweetheart. Go and take them over there on the floor."

"Where, Mummy?"

Mary looked around the cluttered kitchen. "Oh, I don't know! Go and do it in your bedroom. I'll light the paraffin stove for you in there, but you'll have to be very specially careful." She had so many orders for Christmas centrepieces and wreaths to hang upon front doors, that the kitchen had become a permanent workshop.

Dropping the gold ribbon she was trying to twist into a smooth bow, she pushed her chair away from the table. "Come along – there's a good girl." Lighting the round paraffin stove in the tiny bedroom, she settled Patsy with her colouring things under the eiderdown and then hurried back towards the kitchen. "Stay there, poppet, don't play over by the stove."

She hesitated at the bottom of the ladder, wondering if she should keep a hot water bottle in their bed all day. In this weather, it didn't take long at all for the bedclothes to get damp. She and Jim had started wearing woolly socks and jumpers on top of their nightclothes, and only that morning they'd woken up with little icicles on the edge of the eiderdown where their breath had frozen on it during the night.

As she deliberated she heard the back door opening and the sound of Jim's boots being stamped hard on the step.

"Mary? Mary?"

Now what? Running her fingers through her hair, she hurried into the kitchen. "What's the matter, pet?"

He was bending down, calmly pulling off his boots. "Eh?" He looked up at her, puzzled.

"It's only half-past ten. Is there something wrong?"

He looked at her a little oddly, she thought. "No, love, there's nothing wrong," he said. "Nothing. Wondered if you fancied a bit of an outing, that's all." He grinned to himself, unbuttoning his jacket.

"An outing!"

He shrugged carelessly. "There's a lovely blue sky out there. What do you think? Fancy a bit of a trip?"

She was puzzled. "What, now?"

"Why not?"

She gestured, flustered, at the table and the buckets of greenery standing all around. "But I've got all this to do ..."

"It'll keep. Thought we might go over to Little Darley to the Blue Bowl for a bit of a treat." He looked oddly pleased with himself. "Tea and a cake – or coffee, of course, if you'd prefer it. You and me and Patsy."

"Tea? At the Blue Bowl?" She didn't want to hurt his feelings. "Jim, it would be very nice, it would be lovely, but I haven't got the time. If you've run out of jobs you can give me a hand with my logs."

He looked at the table askance. "Oh, I'm no good at that." He shrugged. "Well, could give it a try this afternoon, if you want me to, but you might regret it." He moved to warm his cold hands by the fire. "I just thought you might like to dress up a bit for once."

"Dress up?" She shook her head in exasperation. "Jim, have you lost your marbles? I *have* got things to do, if you hadn't noticed."

He studied the leaping flames diligently. "You could put your new dress on, couldn't you?"

"New dress?" No time for this at all. She picked up the gold ribbon once again. "For goodness' sake, I haven't got a new dress, Jim, are you crackers? Whatever are you going on about?"

"Haven't you? Funny, that. I thought you had." There was a silly grin on his face as he strode across to the hall. "Just hang on!" There were scuffling sounds from Patsy's bedroom, and the twitter of her voice and the deep rumble of Jim's, and then he emerged bearing a large brown paper parcel and with Patsy, giggling, following on behind. He held out the package with both arms, then frowned, took it back and brushed it. "Sorry. Cobwebs."

Patsy chortled. "It's been under my bed!"

"Hope it's all right!" He held it out again, with a pleased, shy grin. "Happy Anniversary, my love."

She took the parcel from him, bewildered. Patsy waved a folded piece of paper under her nose. "Happy Anniversary, Mummy! See, see, I made you a card!"

She frowned. Anniversary? What were they talking about? The word seemed to have lost its meaning. Her mind was a foggy blank.

They were waiting, their faces beaming.

It made her feel very odd, not being able to remember. What the dickens did 'anniversary' mean?

All at once it came to her, in a rush, as if the floodgates of her memory had opened, and she sighed with relief. That's what it was! The seventeenth of December. Anniversary! Their sixth wedding anniversary. Of course! How could she have forgotten? She had been thinking about it off and on all week. Only yesterday she had been rifling through her cookery book, planning to make a cake.

Quickly she bent and hugged Patsy. "Oh, thank you, poppet! It's beautiful. Let's put it on the mantelpiece."

Jim was grinning fit to burst. He nodded happily at the parcel. "Go on, then. Open it."

She tugged at the string and parted the brown paper with mounting excitement. What was it? She gasped, peering at the uncovered treasure. "Oh, Jim!" She shook the soft fabric out admiringly. "Jim, it's a dress!"

"It *is* new," he said worriedly. "Just a bit creased. Been under Patsy's bed for ages. Nancy made it, but she got it done too quick."

"Of course it's new, I can see that!" With a cry of delight she threw her free arm about his neck. "Oh, Jim, it's lovely! It's beautiful! You clever, clever old thing!"

"Hope it fits." She could see him almost swelling with satisfaction. "I took that old blue dress of yours over so Nancy could see about the size."

"The one that got all caught in the brambles? The one I've had since I was about seventeen?" She giggled. "Oh, Jim!"

He was puzzled. "What?"

"Nothing. It's beautiful, darling." She kissed him again, and then Patsy. "Thank you!"

Patsy tugged at the dress. "See the buttons, Mummy! They're little tortoises, look!"

Mary admired them. "So they are! Oh, aren't they really, really sweet!"

Jim straightened his shoulders proudly. "So, are you

coming to the Blue Bowl for tea or not?"

She clutched the dress to her. "Yes, of course, of course we must go! I want to go somewhere I can put my new dress on! It's a lovely colour." She stroked it; might have to iron it a little bit first.

With a big grin and a sigh of contentment he collapsed into his armchair. "Put the kettle on, though, first, poppet? I could do with a cup of tea."

Jim changed as well afterwards, putting on a clean shirt and trousers and his best jacket, and he insisted on driving them there in the trap in case Mary got oil from her bike on her new dress. At the Blue Bowl Mary and Jim each had tea and a scone with butter and jam, and Patsy had a glass of cream soda and a marzipan potato, though Jim had to finish the cake for her – it was making her teeth hurt, she said.

Fortunately it was nice and warm with a fire in the grate, so Mary was able to take off her coat and Jim was able to admire his present. "It fits perfectly, Jim," she told him, with something of surprise. "Same size now as I was then!"

It was a lovely afternoon, though she had a bit of a head-ache when she got home, which she put down to the cold, but didn't mention because she knew Jim would say it was his fault for enticing her out too soon.

Christmas drew on apace. Mary was up to her arms in the sink one morning when Patsy burst into the kitchen ahead of Jim, clutching a handful of envelopes and dropping half of them on the floor.

"Cards, Mummy! Look, look, we got more Christmas cards! And look – see – I made it for you, didn't I, Daddy?" She proudly held out a small, spiky arrangement of dried helichrysomes and larkspur stuck in a lump of plasticine.

Mary held up her hands, dripping soapsuds back into the sink. "For me? Oh, that's so beautiful, darling! When did you make that?"

"Cathy helped me."

Mary laughed. "I see, a little tea-break with your admirers, Jim?" She dried her hands and held up the gift admiringly. "You are so clever, poppet! Next year you'll be able to help me, won't you, when I do the dried flower arrangements and logs for Christmas?" She put the gift carefully next to the anniver-sary card on the mantelpiece. "We'll put it up here, shall we, so Father Christmas can see!"

Patsy began to jump around in circles. "When's he coming, Mummy?

"Only two more nights."

Slipping off his jacket, Jim filled the kettle and set it on the stove to boil while he got out the crockery for tea. Mary glanced over her shoulder at his domesticity with a grin. "Careful, Jim, I could get used to this."

He chuckled. "As soon as the holiday's over, things'll be getting back to normal, my lady, so enjoy it while it lasts. You needn't pretend you're an invalid any more." He ducked, as she tossed a soapy dishcloth at him. "Oh, we've got a Madeira cake," he suddenly remembered happily, wiping his cheek. "Elsie sent it over. She's glad to hear you're better. Sit down, come on – kettle's almost boiling. You need a bit of a break."

He knew she was glad to do it, because she sat down quickly and with a relieved smile on her face. "Shall we open the cards?"

Patsy scrambled to add the ones she had dropped to the collection in her hands. Busy at the pot, Jim nodded at the table. "There's the usual parcel for Patsy from your Aunty May."

"Another nice brush-and-comb set, I suppose! Is there a card from either of them for us?" she added casually.

Jim frowned as he cut deeply into the cake. "Don't think so." He shrugged. "They wouldn't be able to bring themselves to write *Mr and Mrs James Norris!*" He handed her a teacup.

She rattled the spoon hard, stirring it. "Oh, it makes me angry! And it makes me sad."

He sat on the arm of the chair, putting his arm about her shoulder. "Give Aunty May her due, at least she always remembers Patsy."

Mary relaxed into the crook of his arm, sighing. "You're right, it doesn't matter." She giggled. "Give the old dragon her due!"

On Christmas Eve Jim dropped Mary off at St Michael's to help with the decorations whilst he went off on his round, taking Patsy with him. "Don't go doing too much now! I'll be back for you pretty shortly."

It was icy cold in the church, and it smelled of greenery.

"Morning, Mary!" the voice of the verger's wife boomed, echoing, across the nave. "I jolly well hope you've brought us lots and lots! We're not half running short."

Mary shook her head regretfully. "No, Mrs Poulton, sorry, I haven't. I have brought a few bits and pieces, but it's been so cold, and with so many funerals at this time of the year. Jim's going to have to try to buy some flowers in from the market after Christmas or we'll be completely stuck."

She moved to make room in the aisle as Fred Martin staggered past her under the weight of a huge box. "Good morning, Fred."

"M-Morning, Mrs N-Norris." He was such a nice lad, quite handsome and strapping now, such a pity about the stammer.

Cathy took her head out of the crib. "Give those here, Fred." Catching Mary's eye, she smiled. "Morning, Mrs Norris. Are you feeling better? You had a nasty fall, I believe. Must have been such a shock!"

Mary laughed lightly. "Such a silly thing to do! Oh, yes, I'm fine now, Cathy, thank you." The headache seemed to cling to her all the time at the moment, but it wasn't worth mentioning.

Cathy clicked her tongue. "There's another box some-where, there must be! Go and look for it, Fred. I haven't got the donkey or the shepherds, and there are only two kings."

Fred nodded with alacrity, "Righto, Cath!" and disappeared into the vestry. Was there a romance blooming there, Mary wondered? Cathy wasn't a particularly pretty girl, but with her big blue eyes and her straw-blonde curls and rounded figure, she probably had a few admirers roundabouts.

"Mr Norris not with you, Mrs Norris?" Cathy carefully studied one of the figurines.

Smiling to herself, Mary shook her head. "Oh, no, Cathy – he's up to his eyes, I'm afraid." Cathy looked deflated. "Though he'll be in to pick me up before too long." That made her perk up a bit. It amused and pleased Mary how much the women of the village seemed to idolise Jim.

Fred crouched down at Cathy's side, handing her items from the box. "I wonder, Fred, if I could ask you to fetch the green stuff I've brought and take it into the stillroom?" Mary asked. "It's in the porch."

He went, albeit somewhat reluctantly, not wanting to leave Cathy's side yet again.

Mary shivered suddenly. "And see if I've left the door open, Fred!" she called after him. "There's a terrible draught in here."

There was a snapping sound. "Ooh, Lordy!" Cathy stared in horror at the tiny figure in her hand. "Joseph's little arm's come off, Mrs Norris!"

Mary frowned. "Leave him on the front pew, Cathy. I'll get Jim to have a look at him when he comes in."

She was shivering on a stepladder, arranging ivy along a windowsill and trying to ignore her aching head, when she heard the scurry of little footsteps and turned round. Patsy pattered excitedly down the aisle. "Mummy, Mummy, we got a tree!"

Jim, following behind her, shook his head, grinning. "Don't worry, pet, it's not a big one."

"Morning, Mr Norris!" Cathy leapt to her feet, her eyes widening.

"How are you today, Cath?"

"Me? Oh, I'm fine, thank you, Mr Norris." Mary was tickled to see her blushing.

Hurrying back to the pew, Cathy picked up the broken figurine. "Mr Norris, Mr Norris! Look what I've done to poor Joseph!"

"Joseph?" Jim was more concerned with watching Mary on the steps. "Mary? Think you ought to come down ..."

Fred appeared at Cathy's side. "Told you, I'll m-mend it for you, C-Cath ..."

Cathy ignored him, pushing the broken Joseph underneath Jim's nose. "Joseph, see, Mr Norris? I've snapped his little arm right off!" She gave a big sigh. "I'm so clumsy!"

Taking the little figure, Jim turned it carefully in his big hands. "It's all right, just needs a bit of glue." He slipped it into his pocket. "I'll see to it."

"Shall I cycle over later and get him, Mr Norris?" Cathy suggested eagerly.

"No need. I'll have him back when I do my afternoon round." Catching his eye, Mary rolled her eyes flirtatiously. He grinned and moved towards her. "Mary, come on now, love. You've done enough." She climbed down into his arms. "You're freezing, woman. Why haven't you got your coat done up?" he asked her, frowning.

She stood docilely as he did up the buttons. "So cold in here, Jim," she told him, her teeth chattering.

"Let's be having you, Patsy!" Jim called, anxious to get Mary home.

Cathy smiled indulgently at the little girl engrossed in the crib. "Little ones love their crib, Mr Norris!"

Jim smiled deep into Mary's eyes. "Aye, Cath. Big ones do, too."

J im thought that Mary's circulation could do with a brisk walk, and the cottage needed some greenery to add to its paper chains for Christmas decorations, too, so, taking a hessian sack and wrapping up well, they walked slowly all the way down the lane and across the fields and through Farley's

Wood towards Barrows Farm. It was a long time before they found enough holly with berries on; they had stripped most of the holly from the nearby trees already.

In Big Field Jim showed Patsy where a fox had been playing with a hare. "See, here's where the hare's been, see the skiddy marks where he's turned to get away? Then the fox – he's here, see, I reckon he's stopped suddenly and his tracks go almost straight back. He doesn't turn like the hare. Goes up in the air and turns as he comes down."

"Did the fox kill the hare, Daddy?" Patsy stared down at the tracks anxiously.

He shook his head reassuringly. "I doubt it, Pats. Just playing. Foxes don't often kill hares."

In Farley's Wood, its littered floor dappled with frosty sunlight, he pointed upward, whispering: "See, Patsy? See that bit of grey? That's a grey squirrel's tail, that is. Can you see him squatting on that branch?"

Mary laughed. "He's sun-bathing."

"He is, too!"

On the way back Patsy scampered about collecting fir cones, her eyes bright and her cheeks glowing like red apples above her woolly muffler, while Jim climbed high up in the hedge and cut down long strands of ivy and branches and twigs of holly, which he tossed down for Mary to pile into the sack. She dodged, laughing, as the last piece he tossed almost caught her in the face. "Jim!"

"Sorry!"

She picked it up and brushed herself down. "That's enough, anyway. That's fine."

He slipped while clambering down from the bank and hung on to the branch of a tree to save himself from falling.

"No – not another one!" Mary giggled as he pantomimed relief. "We've had enough of invalids in our house to last a lifetime. Come on down, idiot!"

He jumped down into the lane as Patsy came skipping up, the skirt of her coat laden with fir cones. "Look, Mummy – I got lots and lots!"

Jim dusted his hands in satisfaction. "Right, then – let's get this lot home. I've still got my round to do." He lifted the handles of the barrow and licked his lips greedily. "What's for tea?"

Mary collected up scattered fragments of greenery and tossed them in the barrow as she walked beside him. "What do you want?"

He thought deeply for a moment. "Ham and eggs."

44

"Hah! You'll be lucky! How about some nice cheese on toast?"

He mused, frowning. "Any of that rabbit pie left?"

"Yes, a bit."

He nodded. "That'll do then. With some fried potatoes."

"Pig."

She warmed up the rabbit pie and made the fried potatoes and she got out some of the mince pies she'd made for the church bazaar, which pleased Jim no end. They ate supper listening to the wireless, and afterwards crowded into the armchair by the fire, playing games.

"Me, me, me – guess where I'm hiding!" Patsy jiggled on Jim's knee with excitement. He nudged Mary, who didn't seem to have heard her, and obediently covered his eyes.

"Um ... You're in the henhouse!"

Patsy crowed with satisfaction. "No, no, no, I'm not! That's One!"

Mary gave a heavy sigh. He peeked a look at her. She was rubbing her forehead and frowning as she struggled to think. "You're in the – oh, I don't know. Um ..."

He closed his eyes again, smiling. "Under the table? ... Up one of the apple trees?"

Patsy shrieked gleefully. "No, I'm not! That's Three! That's Three!"

Mary's voice was flat and listless. "Where, then?"

Patsy was triumphant. "I'm in my bedroom and I'm hiding under my bed!"

"Oh." Mary sounded completely uninterested. He opened his eyes in time to see her discarding her paper hat and turning away indifferently.

Patsy bounced excitedly. "Your turn! Your turn, Daddy!"

"Ow, mind my knee!" he joked. "Close your eyes, then." He stroked Mary's hair. "Where am I, then? He brushed his lips against her hair. "I know where I'd like to be," he murmured, smiling.

Mary glanced up at him, frowning, and then looked away quickly.

"Still got a headache?" he asked, frowning.

Her tone was sharp. "Don't fuss."

Before she went to bed Patsy watched, thrilled, as Jim set free her letter to Father Christmas to fly off in flaming fragments up the chimney, and put out a mince pie and a glass of ginger wine, with a carrot for the reindeer, very carefully near the grate. It was gone half-past ten before she had gone to sleep and they could deliver her stocking. Closing her door thankfully behind him, Jim directed the beam of the torch and waited for Mary to climb onto the ladder. He stepped on himself, pressing up closely behind her, murmuring into the back of her neck in mock lasciviousness, "I've got a present for you, lady. Hurry up." She didn't rise immediately to the game.

"Don't rush me."

He roughened his voice playfully, pushing against her. "Go on – giddy up! Get up them stairs!" To his great surprise, she pulled away crossly, wriggling from between his restraining arms.

"Stop it, Jim! Leave me alone, I'm tired!"

He was hurt. He held back, staring up, as she climbed up through the trap. After a moment, her face reappeared. She was grinning. "Great big bully."

His face bore a big, happy smile of anticipation as he climbed.

Chapter 6

An unfamiliar, uncomfortable and frightening black mood had been gripping Mary ever since she had arisen from her bed. She slammed the door as she came back in with the bucket of mush and pellets for the hens' evening feed. Marching across to the kettle to put on some hot water to soften it, she glared about her at the clutter in the kitchen. "You can get that lot put away, Patsy," she told her sharply.

Patsy took no notice. Mary watched with building irritation as she continued with her tuneless hammering, and felt herself suddenly snap. "I said, put those bloody things away! I can't be doing with all this bloody mess!" Launching herself at Patsy, she dragged the xylophone forcefully from her hands. "And stop making that bloody racket!"

There was an agonising pain behind her eyes. She could hardly see. "Stop making my life a bloody misery!" she shouted.

Her head swam; the headache and the clutter all about her were making her feel nauseous. A soft rag doll clown grinned derisively up at her from amongst the clutter. Swooping down upon it, she hurled it into the fire. It burst into flame immediately, the clown's face contorting as it melted, the mouth twisted almost obscenely to one side, and one remaining round, black-lashed eye grinning mockingly. She shivered. Patsy screamed.

Mary grasped her roughly up by the arm. "I don't know what the hell's got into you!" She dragged her across the room, not caring if she bumped her into the furniture. "What in God's name have I done to deserve you?" Opening the back door, she thrust Patsy out into the yard. "Out! Out! Out! Go on. Go and pester your father!"

Jim, coming back into the yard, saw a weeping Patsy landing in a heap in the mud and then the door slam. He was staggered. He stared for a moment, then gathered the little girl up. Throwing open the back door, he carried her inside. "It's too cold for her out there, Mary," he said. "She isn't even wearing a coat."

Mary was tossing toys into the chest. "Go to your room, then," she ordered, curtly.

"I want Rosebud!"

Sighing impatiently, Mary tossed Patsy's china-headed doll back onto the floor. Jim set Patsy down and she darted for the doll, snatching it up and cradling it tightly to her chest. Not looking at Mary, skirting the fireplace warily, she disappeared quickly from the room. He could hear her sobbing in her bedroom.

Jim watched Mary for a moment then, frowning, asked, "What's been going on, Mary?"

Mary shook her head, tight-lipped. He stared at her for a moment, then, sitting down in the armchair, started to pull off his boots. "It's Christmas Day. We shouldn't have any arguing."

She slammed the lid of the toy chest and turned, her expression sour. "You should have taken those off outside – now look what you've done! Mud everywhere!" Jim looked guiltily at the trail of muddy footprints from the door as she crossed quickly to the sink. "As if I hadn't got enough to do!" Furiously rinsing out a floor cloth, she fell onto her hands and knees, scrubbing roughly at the floor. "Filthy!"

He set his muddy boots to rest on the fender. "I'm sorry." A bit sheepishly, he got up and moved over to her side. "Hey ..."

Apparently lost in fury, she rubbed even harder. She hissed at him through gritted teeth. "You just don't think, do you?" Scrambling to her feet, she rinsed out the cloth again angrily. "Filthy! The whole place is filthy." Her voice rose shakily almost to the pitch of a scream. "You just carry on, doing as you please, and expect me to skivvy after you!"

Bemused, he tried to put his arms about her, but she shook him off and flounced over to the table, where she began to clatter the plates. Feeling helpless, Jim ran his fingers through his hair. Not knowing what else to do, he crossed and picked up the kettle. "Come on, love – it's Christmas Day! Shall I make you a cup of tea?"

Tears filled her eyes. Her voice rose shrilly. "I don't want a bloody cup of tea!"

Christmas Day passed frostily. In bed that night she lay on her back with her eyes open. Jim finished putting on his pyjamas and then climbed in, lying, though not too deliberately, with his back to Mary. After a few moments, he felt her stir and turn over to face him. She put her hand tentatively on his shoulder, and her whisper was very soft. "I'm sorry."

He felt a huge wave of relief. After only a momentary hesitation, he rolled over and drew her to him. She clung to him very tight.

Much later, he felt her half sit up and punch her pillow, then settle down again. The room was very dark. With a sigh, he closed his eyes again. The bedside clock ticked steadily, and then he heard Patsy's cry. Mary stirred once more restlessly.

"Mu-mm-eee!"

Sleepily, Jim rolled over and peered at Mary. "Patsy's calling." She murmured bad-temperedly into her pillow, hunching up her shoulders and he shook her gently. "Mary, Patsy's calling." She was silent. "Aren't you going down?"

Her voice was muffled. "You've got legs, haven't you? Why me?"

"It's you she wants." There was no answer.

Patsy called again, even more desperately: "Mummmeee! *MUMMEEE!*" Sighing, he got out of bed and pulled on his dressing gown, lit the candle and made his way to the trap.

The door creaked as he opened it and the candlelight cast his wavering shadow on the wall beside her bed. "What's the matter, Patsy?"

Her bottom lip quivered at the sight of him and her voice rose again in a wail. "I want my *mummy!*"

"Well, you've got me instead." Setting down the candle, he sat awkwardly down on the bed and tried to soothe her, smoothing her forehead. "Hush now, go back to sleep, now. Ssh, hush. Hush now, there's a good girl."

She continued to fret and cry. Sighing, he swung his legs onto the bed. What did Mary sing to her? The only song that would come to him was *Poor Old Joe.*

It was a bit depressing, but, strangely enough, it seemed to settle her.

Trekking up and down the ladder in the middle of the night became a more and more frequent occurrence over the following weeks and he didn't like it: took him ages to get back to sleep. When he clambered back up the ladder and back into the big bed, his side of it felt very cold and it wasn't just a matter of icy sheets. When he tried snuggling closer to Mary for warmth, more often than not she would shrug him off with an irritated murmur. He knew well how it felt to have her cold feet against his warm ones, but still, not like Mary at all. It was all very upsetting. It worried him that she didn't seem that interested in Patsy in the day times either at the moment. He tried hard to make it up to the little girl, but he was a busy man.

All in all, what with broken sleep and a growing ache of hurt and bewilderment, which was deeply unsettling, he was finding himself increasingly depressed and bleary-eyed. Half the time he seemed to be living with a withdrawn and increasingly fractious stranger, and he ached for things to get back as they had been before. They would soon, of course – Elsie had said so.

"I don't know what to do, Elsie," he had told her. Embarrassingly, he could hear his voice breaking and he shook his head as tears began to blur his vision. Fumbling for his handkerchief, he blew his nose hard. "She's not right, Elsie. She's not herself. But I don't know how to help her. I feel so helpless."

Elsie nodded wisely. "Women's problems, Jim, that's what it'll be. Probably doesn't like to say anything. Try to get her to see the doctor, I would. Be a bit patient, anyway. Not pregnant, is she?"

He cast his mind back ruefully. It was hardly likely. "No, I don't think so. No."

He tried very hard to be patient with her, but the new Mary wasn't easy and it wasn't just a matter of bad temper. She had become a bit of a demon for house-cleaning, which, if he was honest, made life a bit uncomfortable. She was forgetful, too. Sometimes she forgot to feed the hens or to make the bed or to put together the flowers and moss he had brought into the kitchen, ready for making into wreaths, so that then they had to work into the early hours to get the things ready for a funeral. She'd never have done that in the old days. It all made extra work. At dinnertime on several occasions, he had even found that she had forgotten to get anything ready to eat. She had just shrugged when he asked about it, though she had set about it eventually. On those days he had noticed that she had been in a particularly pernickety, crabby mood.

When he stood outside the kitchen door at the end of a long day, he found himself listening and sniffing hopefully. If he couldn't hear the clattering of dishes, or detect the enticing smell of anything cooking, he braced himself. It could be a bad mood day.

Things went from bad to worse. One morning there had been none of the usual sandwiches which Mary made whenever she knew he wasn't likely to get back at dinnertime, and placed in a brown paper bag waiting for him on the kitchen table. She had been fast asleep, so he had wrapped himself a chunk of bread instead and taken an apple. It was his long round and he was starving by the time he got home. The kitchen was empty and there were no signs of cooking. His heart sank and his stomach gurgled.

"Hello?" There was no answer so he made his way into the tiny hall and called up again through the trap. "Hello?"

Still no reply, though he could hear movement above, footsteps and a crinkling, rustling sound. He climbed up, the rungs creaking loudly under the weight of his boots. Some of the mud caked on the bottoms rubbed off on the rungs and fell down to the floor of the hall. Should have left them on the doorstep, he remembered all too late.

"Anybody at home?" He peered over the trap. "Oh, there you are, Mary! What are you doing, love?" He peered round, bewildered. "Hey – what's all that lot?"

Mary held up a blue blouse, and twisted about in front of the flyblown mirror, trying to catch her reflection. "I wish I'd bought something in red," she murmured, frowning, dropping it. She reached behind her back to undo her buttons. "Red's always suited me."

He climbed into the attic, gazing around him in astonishment. The bed and the floor were littered with opened bags and hatboxes and clothes. Bewildered, he picked up a pair of high-heeled brown lizard shoes. "Where did these come from, love?" She took no notice. Reaching for a green satin evening thing of some sort, she pulled it over her head.

He picked up one of the shiny paper bags. It said 'Beamish', as did another, and the third of them 'Cardwell & Sons'. He whistled through his teeth. Those were expensive shops. "Have your aunties been lashing out, Mary?" Taking no notice, she twirled in front of the mirror, humming a little song. She was wearing bright red lipstick. Mary never wore lipstick. Didn't look like her. It worried him. A cold feeling settled in the pit of his stomach. "Mary? Where did you get these, love?"

"I bought them, of course," she replied airily.

He watched her as she fastened a string of pearls about her neck. He was taken aback. "But we can't afford them! How did you pay for them, Mary? What with? I mean, where did you get the money?"

She looked disdainful. "Oh, Lord, they're not *paid* for," she scoffed. "Of course they're not *paid* for. One never carries cash." She gestured loftily. "The account will follow."

51

"What do you mean, 'the account will follow'?" He tried to make a joke of it. "For God's sake, Mary, have you gone quite daft?" Grabbing a bundle of silky underclothes from the bed, he tried ineffectively to stuff them in a bag. "They'll have to go back, I'm sorry." She frowned at her reflection in the mirror, pulling down the neckline. "Take it off, love," he pleaded. "You'll spoil it in a minute and then they won't have it back."

She tossed her head. "They're not having it back."

He gritted his teeth. "Oh, yes, they are, love." He moved towards her. "Mary, I'd love to buy you these things, but I can't, don't be silly, love. Come on – give that to me." She turned on him like a wild cat, almost spitting and her voice was almost unrecognizable. "You never want me to have nice things!"

That wasn't true and it threw him back on his heels. "Don't say that! Hell, Mary! I just gave you a new frock, I only wish I could give you more."

"Frock?" She sneered, and it made her face ugly. "That ugly flowered rayon thing, you mean?"

He was desperately hurt. "I thought you liked it."

"Liked it? I wouldn't be seen dead in it. It's only fit to feed the hens." She shrugged again. "Anyway, I've torn it."

"Torn it?"

"Torn it up, torn it *up*. Made it into dusters." She gave a peal of laughter. "Oh, you should see your face!"

Her mood seemed to change again quickly. The laughter stopped abruptly and with an expression of impatience and fury, she fumbled at the fasteners. "Oh, here, then! Here, take it. Take it!" Tearing off the dress, she tossed it at him, and then bundled up all the things on the bed. Face distorted with rage, she began to throw them at him one by one. "Here, take it – and here – and here!" He fielded them ineffectually.

"Mary, for God's sake ...!" Her eyes were all narrowed and bloodshot with frenzy. His heart thudding, he advanced on her, hoping to hold her and calm her, but she struggled against him frantically, fingers clawed. "Get off me! Get off me! I know what your game is and you're not going to get away with it – you're none of you going to get away with it!" Her teeth were bared now as if she would bite him "Let go of me! Let me *go*!"

"Mary, Mary, Mary ..." Frantically, Jim tried to soothe her. "There isn't any game – what are you talking about, lovey?" A thought struck him suddenly, sending an anxious shudder down his spine. He froze, holding her at arm's length. "Mary – where's Patsy?"

He could feel a change in her bodily tension. She widened her eyes in amusement, and gave a whoop of laughter, covering her mouth.

"Mary?"

"You won't believe this, Jim – but I've left her behind!"

He frowned, bewildered. "Left her? Left her where?"

"I left her at Dawson's!"

"Dawson's?"

"Dawson's café in town! I left her eating an ice cream." Amusement overwhelmed her. "Chocolate nut surprise!"

Catching sight of his stunned expression, her eyes hardened again, but defensively. "Well, I had to get my hair done." She shrugged carelessly. "Oh, it's all right, somebody will lend her some money. She can get a later bus."

Jim was utterly appalled. "Christ, Mary!"

She shrugged nonchalantly, throwing him a patronising smile. "Oh, don't get into a stew."

He stumbled towards the trap, his heart racing. "It's gone half past four. What time was this, when you left her?"

She seemed totally disinterested. "Oh, I don't know ... about eleven?"

He hurled himself onto the ladder, pausing only momentarily to stare back at her in disbelief. "Christ, Mary – she's only a baby! How could you do this?" He slid half the way, like a fireman, burning the skin of his hands.

Too slow to drive over in the trap. Mr Harfield's lorry. Racing over the fields to Barrows, he found himself praying over and over. Please let her be all right.

Fortunately he found Mr Harfield straight away in the cowshed, and he was happy to give him the nod. He had to spend what seemed like interminable minutes cranking up the engine, but at last it turned over and he leapt into the cab. Driving frantically towards town, he tried to think. Would she still be waiting in the café? Possible. Would she have tried to get on a bus? She wouldn't have known where to find a bus stop – and would she even know the name of the village where she lived? He supposed that Mary would have taught her that, but he'd never thought to ask her. Who did she know in town?

He had other thoughts, too – frightening thoughts – but he didn't want to entertain them. He just put his foot down on the accelerator, as hard as it would go. Narrowly missing a cyclist as he careered round the bend that led to the crossroads, he gave him a furious blast of his horn. To his surprise, when he glanced back angrily, he saw in his offside mirror that the cyclist had pulled up, and had dismounted and was looking after him, waving urgently. It wasn't a man, but a young woman, and there was a passenger on the back of the bike, a small passenger.

He put on the brakes with a screech. The three-point turn he executed was hardly masterly; for a moment he thought he was going to get stuck in the hedge, and the engine almost cut out, but soon he was racing back.

It *was* Patsy! The relief he felt was enormous. Leaving the door open and the engine running, he jumped down and ran to her, sweeping her off the saddle and up into his arms. "Are you all right?" He hugged her tightly to him. "Oh, Patsy! Oh, thank God!" He swung round to the cyclist. It was Cathy.

She brushed the hair back out of her eyes, grinning proudly. "I thought it was you ..."

"Where did you find her?" he asked, almost tearful with relief. "Cath, thank you ever so much."

She stroked Patsy's leg. "Ah, she was ever so upset! All by her little self she was, wandering about the market. Mum looked everywhere for Mrs Norris, she said, but she couldn't find her, so she brought Patsy home with her."

"Daddy, where's Mummy?" Patsy asked, her bottom lip trembling.

Cathy was quite pink in the face with exertion and curiosity. "Mrs Norris is all right, isn't she, Mr Norris? We couldn't think what had happened, her losing Patsy. Not had an accident or anything like that?"

Jim shook his head. "No, no, no – she's fine." Best not think about that now.

He jiggled Patsy, smiling. "Come on, poppet. Say a big thank you to Cathy, and let's be getting you back home." When she had kissed Cathy obediently, he settled her in the passenger seat and then put his foot on the step. "Look – thank your mum very much for me, eh, Cathy? Tell her I'll drop in and see her soon as I can."

He hitched himself into the driver's seat and wound down the window. "And thank you, too, Cathy. I'm much obliged to you!"

Cathy craned to see in. "She's had her tea, Mr Norris – a nice piece of pork pie and some tomatoes and a little bit of bread and jam. Got a good little appetite, hasn't she? Still had room for my mum's chocolate cake."

She waved, still beaming, as he drove away; then he saw her in his mirror remounting her bicycle and, with weary legs, wobbling back in the direction of home.

His relief was mixed with white-hot anger and with perturbation, and his head spun with anxiety as he drove more carefully home. Whatever was Mary playing at? Something was dreadfully wrong.

He was staggered to find that she was carrying on as if nothing had happened when they got home. The table was laid and she was bustling about the kitchen and even singing sweetly as she worked. He threw off his jacket. There was anger in his voice, and accusation. "Well, I found her – thank God!"

She glanced up. She was dressed in an ordinary old skirt and blouse, but she was still wearing the bright red lipstick, he noticed. He wished she wasn't. It didn't seem like Mary somehow, not at all. It was giving him the shivers, must still be a bit shell-shocked.

"Good!" she answered with a smile. "Well, close that door, it's draughty. Tea's ready. Hurry up and wash your hands."

Patsy ran to her, clinging with her arms about her waist. "Mummy, I lost you!"

Mary patted her. "Yes, yes – yes, yes, I know!" She disentangled Patsy, patting her little rear. "Come on now, coat off, wash hands, your egg on toast is ready. Yours too, Jim."

Frowning, he rinsed his hands at the sink and took his place at the table. He suddenly felt very tired. She hadn't even asked where he'd found Patsy.

"Cathy had her," he said, pretending to concentrate on his egg but watching her carefully as he did so. "Elsie found her at the market. Cathy was bringing her home on her bike."

"Oh, yes?" Mary poured out the tea.

Best not to say too much in front of Patsy, he decided. Mary glanced sharply at the little girl, who was crouching at the toy chest, pulling out her doll. "Come on, Patsy – sit down now."

"I'm not hungry."

Mary's back stiffened. "Sit down now and eat!"

He was surprised she was so sharp. "She's had her tea, Mary. Elsie gave her some."

"She can sit down at the table properly until we've finished then."

Jim glanced across at Patsy. "Come on, Mary, she's had a nasty shock, just let her have a little play."

"I want her at the table." The sharp tone in her voice again. "Sit down, Patsy, *now*."

Patsy reluctantly clambered onto her chair, bringing Rosebud with her. "Where were you, Mummy?" she asked plaintively, pushing her plate away.

Mary pushed the plate back firmly, and frowned sharply. "Hush now. Just get on with your food." She took her own chair and, with her head down, began munching single-mindedly on her toast. Patsy poked reluctantly at her egg.

Maybe he'd better keep her with him? Jim winked at her and reached over, pinching a slice of her toast. "Want to come out to the yard with me after?"

She shook her head. "Want to stay with Mummy."

Jim nodded thoughtfully. "Well, okay, then. Don't expect I'll be that long."

After he had gone Mary sat watching Patsy for a moment through coldly narrowed eyes. Then, rising abruptly, she pulled a chair away from the table and set it in the middle of the room. She dragged Patsy onto the chair, grasping her upper arm. "Sit down."

Patsy clutched her doll in bewilderment as Mary rummaged in a drawer and produced a pair of sewing shears. "In future, *darling,* if I say stay put, I mean stay put."

Patsy's lip quivered. "I did wait, Mummy."

"Well, you didn't wait long enough."

Patsy's voice quavered. "I'm sorry ..."

Mary tightened her lips. "Sorry's not good enough. You've a lesson to learn." Her head felt as if it was about to burst with rage. She snatched away the doll. "What's this dirty old thing?"

Patsy looked up at her, terrified. "It's Rosebud."

Mary smiled thinly. Her heart was all ice. "Well, I think Rosebud's been rather a naughty little girl, don't you? A naughty little girl, just like her mummy." She held up the doll. "Look, her clothes are all dirty." The shears bit into the fabric, slitting the doll's dress. Mary laughed. Patsy let out a wail.

The shears rasped, and shreds of fabric fluttered to the floor. "I think she's been playing with those dirty little children from the village, don't you, Patsy?" Mary murmured, holding the doll up to the light. "I think she's got nits. Nits, Patsy! Nits, hiding in her hair." The shears crunched through a curl.

Tears were dripping from Patsy's chin. "NO, Mummy!"

Mary cocked her head, studying her thoughtfully. "I expect you've got nits in your hair, too, Patsy."

"I haven't! I haven't, Mummy!"

Mary shook her head sorrowfully. "I hope you haven't got nits, Patsy, but I think we'd better make certain, don't you?" Tangling her fingers in Patsy's hair, she dragged her head painfully backwards. The shears bit. "I think we'd better cut off all this contaminated, *filthy* hair." The crisp snipping of the shears punctuated the harsh words.

Patsy howled.

Chapter 7

She was still sobbing in her bedroom when Jim came back in, and Mary was sitting in the armchair, gazing blindly into the fire. She seemed oblivious both to him and to Patsy's wailing.

"What's up with her, Mary?" She took no notice. He stared at her, breathing heavily with distress. This was breaking his heart.

Her head was bent and her lovely dark hair gleamed in the firelight. He reached out and stroked it tentatively. "Mary?" She glanced up at him with almost a snarl, and he withdrew his hand quickly. That wasn't the way to go.

Patsy howled louder. With a sigh, he went in to her and sat down on the bed. "Here, here, here ... what is it, poppet?" he asked, gently. She wriggled away, sobbing. He patted her ineffectually. "Come on, now, lovey. What? What?"

She mumbled something, the words distorted by her tears. He leaned closer, frowning. "You what, lovey?"

She arched herself, bottom up, hands spread helplessly on the pillow. "I w- want m-my H-HAIR!" she sobbed.

He went back into the kitchen and took the hurricane lamp from the centre of the table so that he could see what she was on about. When he saw the poor, spiky little head he could hardly believe his eyes. He could feel his eyes blazing, but Patsy needed comforting first. He held her until she had sobbed herself to sleep, then strode back into the kitchen.

"How could you have done this to her?" he roared.

Mary shrugged indifferently, reaching forward to poke a log further on the fire. "It needed doing."

"Don't be so blooming daft!" He was at his wits' end. This couldn't go on. He slumped down opposite her. "Mary." She didn't stir. He leant forward intently, studying her face, his hands clasped tightly between his knees.

"Talk to me, Mary," he pleaded. "Tell me what's going on."

For a long moment it didn't seem that there was going to be any response, but, then, abruptly, her hands flew to cover her face and she began to cry, great heaving sobs from somewhere deep within her that broke his heart. "I can't, I can't, I can't, I can't!"

He slid onto his knees, putting his arms quickly about her. "What can't you do? Mary?" he asked her gently, his voice trembling. "Can't talk to me? Can't what?" She shook her head. He held her tight, letting her cry for a while, but at last he had to go on.

He drew back, moving her hands from her face and holding on to them. "Come on, Mary, love. We need to sort this out. Are you poorly? Whatever is it?"

He wanted to ask, *it is me? Wishing you hadn't married me?* But he didn't, because he didn't want to hear the answer. She stared at him, the sobs subsiding, though her chest continued to heave, then abruptly, all at once it was as if something inside her head gave a tiny click. She shivered, dragged her hands away from his grasp, pushed herself back in her chair and drew her cardigan about her neck more tightly.

He glanced at the fire. It was getting a bit low. "You're cold?" He reached over for the empty log basket. "I'll go and get some more."

"No!" The vehemence of her reaction startled him. He looked back at her. There was look of pure terror on her face. "Don't. Don't open the door!"

"Why ever not?"

"Don't open the door."

Aching for her, he took hold of her hand. "Hush, hush, I won't then." She clung to his fingers.

They sat holding hands until after midnight. Patsy had sobbed herself to sleep. Jim felt entirely helpless. Nothing broke the silence but the occasional screech of an owl and the steady ticking of the kitchen clock.

He didn't deliver any logs or vegetables the next morning; he couldn't bring himself to leave Patsy with Mary. She wouldn't talk to either of them, anyway, just sat in her dressing gown in the armchair all morning, gazing blindly into the fire.

He got the remains of the chicken that they'd had for Christmas dinner out of the meat safe and he and Patsy ate some of it in some bread. Mary wouldn't have any, and the cup of tea he made her sat on the hearth till it had gone stone cold.

When Patsy had gone off to play in her bedroom, he crouched down by Mary's side. "I think you should come with me and we'll pop over to the surgery, see what Dr Humphreys has to say. You're not yourself, you know that. I don't think you're very well."

She shook her head and drew her gown closer round her body. "I'm all right."

"No, you're not, love ... please?"

But she wouldn't be persuaded, though she let him fetch her a glass of water and a powder from her medicine chest for her headache, and smiled at him wanly after she had taken it; she did seem more herself.

"I ought to get one round done, Mary," he told her, as he put their plates into the sink. "Will you be all right here for a bit on your own? I'll take Patsy."

She waved a hand listlessly. "Yes, go, Jim, I'll be fine." She rose to her feet, a bit wobbly. "I'll just look and see if we need anything from the shops."

While she was doing that he went up to the attic and did his best to package up carefully all the things she had brought home from the shop. The swathes of tissue paper almost defeated him. By the time he had the garments all wrapped up they didn't look nearly as pristine.

Patsy enjoyed the expensive shops, dodging about on the carpeted floors between the racks of frocks and coats and looking at herself in the mirrors, but he felt awkward, shabby and gawky, like a fish out of water – especially in Beamish's department store, which smelled of perfume and was very posh, and where the saleslady with tight grey pincurls, magenta cupid's bow lips and a powder-caked nose proved very snooty. She examined each item carefully, holding them up with her fingertips before grudgingly accepting them. He made something up about the clothes not fitting, and it was a huge relief when at last the bags were all gone.

On the way home he drew up outside the doctor's surgery. Leaving Patsy with a bit of paper and a pencil in the van, he went inside. Dr Humphreys had just finished seeing his afternoon patients, and was bustling out of the door, but when he saw Jim he nodded reluctantly and led him back inside. "I can give you two minutes. Nothing serious, I hope, Jim?"

To Jim's relief, he didn't seem too much worried. "I think it's just all down to tiredness, you know," he said at last, when Jim had stumbled through his description of events.

Jim frowned. "But it's more than that, surely, isn't it, Doctor? I mean, the headaches and losing her temper and –

well, it's just not like Mary"

"She needs a bit of a break, probably. Have you thought, perhaps, of taking her for a bit of a holiday?"

"It's not easy, running a market garden, to take any time away." *Never mind the money.*

Dr Humphreys looked at his watch. "On her own, then? Has she any relatives she could stay with for a few days?"

Jim was doubtful. "Only her great-aunties, you know, the Miss Buckleys, on Broad Street, and I don't think she'd want to stay with them."

Dr Humphrey rose from his desk. "Well, then, the only thing I can think of is perhaps someone to lend a hand? Take some of the weight of things off her shoulders?" He moved across and opened the surgery door. "A bottle of Wincarnis too, perhaps? A glass or two of tonic wine in the evening might just do the very trick."

Still dubious, Jim crossed hesitantly towards him. "What about the headaches, though, Doctor?"

Dr Humphreys frowned. "Well, if they don't get any better in a couple of days, try to get her to come into the surgery."

Jim nodded doubtfully. "Yes, Doctor. I'll try."

Dr Humphreys waited at the front door for Jim to pass. "I'd do that, you know," he told Jim as they walked quickly together down the path. "Get her somebody to help about the house. Let her get her feet up for a while!" He clambered into his car. "Above all, don't worry!" he shouted cheerfully above the engine noise.

There was some kind of thick, weighty curtain dangling inside the back door when he and Patsy got home. "What's this doing here?" he asked Mary, who was dressed now and busy at the table, sewing. He stared at it as he put down the groceries she had asked for on the draining board. "Going to be a bit of a nuisance there, isn't it? Going to get in the way when we go in and out all the time."

She glanced over. "Need to keep out the draught. You took my new clothes back, then, did you?" she added acerbically. "Or did you give them to *her*?"

He sighed. Not again. He felt very weary. "Who's 'her', Mary? There isn't any 'her'. You know that, Mary. I took them back to the shops."

She shrugged. "Doesn't matter. Doesn't matter. She can have them. I don't care."

He took off his jacket. It was very warm in the kitchen. She had the fire blazing. As he stared, a chunk of burning log rolled out and onto the hearth. Moving quickly, he stopped it with his boot before it fell over onto the rug.

Patsy climbed onto a chair and reached over tentatively to peer at the thing that Mary was making. "What are you making, Mummy? Can I do some, please?"

"Mind, Patsy." Mary took a pin out of her mouth. "I'm making sausages."

"Sausages?" Patsy chortled disbelievingly. "Sausages? No, she's not, is she? Is she, Daddy?"

Mary held up a long, thick, sausage-like shape made out of the same material as the door curtain. "Yes, I am. That's what you call these. They're draught excluders. You put them along the bottom of the door to keep the cold air out."

Her expression changed abruptly, suddenly becoming pinched and grey. She shivered and turned her head quickly, peering, frowning. "Did you close that, Jim?"

"The door?" He peered behind the curtain to make sure. "Yes, why?"

She shivered. "Still feel a draught."

He blew out his cheeks. "Surely not! It's suffocating in here! It's roasting!"

Her eyes darted about the room anxiously. "Got to be careful."

He stared at her for a moment. "You worried about Patsy catching a cold?" Moving behind her, he laid his fingers against her forehead. "I wonder if you're running a bit of a temperature."

She brushed away his fingers with an impatient hand and he flinched, feeling hurt again. "Jim – be careful, won't you? Mind the pins!"

Things seemed fairly normal again next morning, and he set about the rest of the day's work with relief. Later, he glanced at Patricia as he emerged from the outhouse and smiled to himself to see her happily playing at mud pies, with a spoon and a number of household utensils in the small patch of earth close by the back door. "What a mess! What are you up to, Patsy?"

Absorbed, she murmured, "Cooking."

Grinning, he disappeared into the orchard as Mary appeared at the back door. Her hair was tightly bound up in a scarf and she wore her floral pinafore and household gloves. Her eyes narrowed with anger as she saw Patsy.

"PATRICIA!" Crossing swiftly, she dragged Patsy away from the patch of soil. "For God's sake, what are you doing?" She looked around, and darted forward, picking up a wooden spoon. "My spoon! My saucepans! You naughty, naughty girl!"

She shook the child, almost incandescent with rage. "How dare you take these things from the kitchen, you thoughtless, wicked girl? Look at you – you're filthy! Get in the house at once!" She hesitated. "No ... no, on second thoughts, I'm not having you like that in my clean house." Dragging the child roughly to the water barrel that stood close to the downspout of the shed, she began to rip at her clothing. "Get these dirty things off at once."

Patsy's arm was stuck in the sleeve. It infuriated Mary further. She tugged at it, her face contorted. "OFF! Off! Get them off! Now!"

Grasping Patsy firmly by the back of the neck, she pushed her head down close to the surface, and began roughly splashing her with icy water. Ignoring the little girl's wails, she scrubbed at her face and arms, panting, teeth bared, eyes wide and staring, almost spitting her words. "Like a gipsy! Like a dirty little village gipsy! *Dirty. Disgusting. Filthy.*" She ducked Patsy suddenly, pushing her under the water and then dragged her up again, shaking her. "Dirty. Filthy. In your *hair* ..."

"Mary! For God's sake!" Alerted by Patsy's screams, Jim burst breathless into the yard, just in time to see her push Patsy's head beneath the surface for a second time. "Let her go! Let her go! You can't –" Dragging Patsy away, he crouched down, cradling her to him, stroking her frail back. She was shaking violently. "It's all right, pet, it's all right ..."

Almost incandescent with fury, he glared at Mary over the child's shoulder. "How could you, Mary, how could you, lovey? How could you? It's only a bit of mud."

Mary stood stock-still, her hands hanging loosely, her jaw and fingers clenched and her chest heaving with the exertion of her rage. Swallowing his anger, Jim tried to coax her. "Only a bit of mud! Come on, love, be sensible. It's not worth making such a fuss about it."

Hoisting up Patsy, he kissed her on the cheek and then carried her over to Mary. "See, she's sorry she made a mess, aren't you, Patsy?" She buried her face in his shoulder. He jiggled her gently. "Come on, say 'sorry' to Mummy and I expect she'll say 'sorry' to you."

Patsy turned warily towards Mary. Jim smiled. "Go on, lovey – give her a kiss." Gingerly, Patsy leant forward.

There was a long pause, and then Mary sneered. "Stupid bastard." Turning abruptly, she stalked back to the kitchen door. At a complete loss, Jim stared after her.

Once he had held her and petted her until her tears had died away and she had stopped shaking – though he hadn't – he took her small hand in his work-roughened one and walked her with him down to the vegetable patch. "Come on. We'll leave Mummy on her own for a little while, shall we?" As much as anything, he needed to calm himself until he could find the words to speak to Mary. He felt too full of disbelief and rage.

"I didn't do anything, Daddy."

He tightened his jaw, squeezing her hand tight. "I know, pet. I know." He glanced down at her tear-stained face and drew to a halt, suddenly becoming aware that her teeth were chattering. "Your clothes are all wet. I'm sorry, love, I didn't think. Let's go up to the house and –"

She dug her heels in with a wail, shaking her face fiercely. The tears were starting again. Crouching, he drew her into his arms, patting her soothingly. "All right, all right. Shh, pet, 's all right." He didn't want to go in much yet either. He wasn't ready. "Look, I've got a jacket in the potting shed. We'll get those wet things off and pop that round you for the time being."

She looked exhausted. Once he had her wet things off, he drew his own pullover down over her upstretched arms and then made her a little nest on some clean dry sacking in the corner, covering her with the old jacket that was kept hanging on a peg. Her eyelids drooped and her eyes closed almost immediately, though she gave a sort of juddering hiccough.

So that he could stay in the potting shed and keep guard, and to help calm his mind and decide what best to do, he began potting-on runner bean seedlings. A repetitive job was what was needed, and there were quite a few.

It was very dark and scary on the road to the village with the tall hedgerows and the trees above them whipping and whispering on either side; she couldn't really see where she was going and it felt as if she was running in treacle, but she kept on running, because she had to get to the village shop. And, at last, there it was in front of her. She hadn't remembered that it was quite so far, nor that it was on a corner, but at least it was there, and there was a light shining inside. It was open, then. Relieved, she pushed open the door. There were no customers in the shop, only old Mrs Bevis, wearing her crocheted shawl and her round wire glasses, peering down at her from behind the jars of boiled sweets. Breathing raggedly, legs shaking, she crossed over to the counter and pulled herself up onto her tiptoes. "Please ..."

Mrs Bevis smiled kindly. "Yes, my dear?" She didn't seem at all surprised that Patsy was out so late and all alone. "Yes, my dearie? What can I do for you?"

Patsy drew in a quavering breath. "Please, have you seen my mummy? I can't find my mummy." She heard her voice give a strange little sob at the end.

Mrs Bevis smiled thoughtfully. "Have I seen your mummy? Well, now, let me see, I might have done ..."

Still smiling, she bent down and took something heavy from underneath the counter, setting it tenderly on top. It was a big sheep's head. It was a big sheep's head with round dull eyes and a lolling tongue and Mrs Bevis delicately turned it round so that its eyes were staring blindly at Patsy, then sighed in satisfaction. "There, now. Is this your mummy?"

Horrorstricken, Patsy could only shake her head.

*Mrs Bevis frowned. "No, dear?" Putting her mittened hands each side of the head, she raised it up carefully. There was another sheep's head inside. She smiled, her eyes twinkling. "Well then, is **this** your mummy?" Patsy numbly shook her head.*

"Not that one? Oh, dear, dear!" Mrs Bevis set it beside the first one on the counter. Underneath was still another. She stroked it gently "This one, then, dearie? Perhaps this one?" Terrified, Patsy began to cry. "Tut-tut ... Not that one? I see ..."

*Mrs Bevis was chuckling now, and she had already lifted that head off and there was still another and then another, making a big row on the counter, each one more tongue-lolling and goggle-eyed than the last. Her voice had a funny sort of ringing sound that was getting louder and louder. "Is **this** your mummy? Is **this** your mummy? Is this your mummy? Is **this**?"*

Patsy began to scream. "No, it isn't. No, it isn't! No, no, no, no, no, NO!"

Waking with a start with her chest still heaving and tears running from her eyes and her nose, she instantly felt her face crumpling. "MUMMEEEEEEE!"

Chapter 8

Cathy was all-abuzz with an early-morning mix of lack of sleep, trepidation and excitement as she pedalled hard between the lush green hedgerows towards the Norris's cottage on her rusty bicycle. She wasn't nervous about what she would have to do about the cottage. It was only small, after all, and she was used to housework and to little ones, after helping Mum. But working for Mr Norris! He was another thing.

She had walked out with Fred for the second time the evening before, and she had really enjoyed it. She was even getting used to his stammer, she hardly noticed it any more. He had made her promise to meet him after church on Sunday, and she had, and it was nice looking forward to that, too. But seeing Mr Norris every day! To be working in his cottage! Everybody knew he was potty about Mrs Norris, but she'd had a crush on him for ages. It was almost the Dream of Dreams! The very thought of it made her face flush pink and turned her bones to jelly in a thrilling and pleasurable way.

She could see it now; well, the chimney of it, and a bit of roof. It was set in a bit of a valley and surrounded by too many trees to get a clear view, but once she'd got round the bend and over the bridge and up the hill and along the lane a bit, she'd be almost there.

To see him every day! It had come as a complete surprise to her.

"She was brought up as a lady, after all, Elsie, not like the likes of us," he'd been saying despondently to her mother, just as Cathy walked into the room. "They brought her up to live in a nice comfy house and not a freezing little cottage without even a bathroom or an inside lav. Doing all the washing, scrubbing floors – she should never have married me."

Seeing her come in, Elsie had turned to Cathy sharply.

"Cath, see where the two little ones have got to and then bring me the washing in." So she'd had to go and hadn't heard the rest of it, but he'd looked a bit happier by the time she came back in. He was sitting in the chair by the fire drinking a cup of tea and Mum had said, "Now, Cath, I've been talking to Mr Norris," (as if she hadn't noticed) "and Mrs Norris could do with a bit of help, like, at the cottage, so I've arranged for you to go there in the mornings."

Her heart raced with excitement, but she tried to sound a little bit concerned. "Will you manage without me?"

Mum had seemed set on it. "Oh, yes, of course I will! I was just being selfish wanting to keep you with me. We must all help each other."

So she had smiled shyly at Jim.

Dismounting now, she opened the gate and leant her bicycle against the hedge. Fumbling in her saddlebag, she drew out the bag containing her apron, then hesitated, scanning the front of the cottage and chewing her bottom lip nervously. She patted her hair, pushing stray locks back into place, smoothed down her coat, then drew in a deep breath and walked round to the back door.

To her relief, Mr Norris was just crossing over the small yard and his face brightened as he saw her. "Oh, good! Good girl, Cath! Nice and early."

He was so handsome, in an older, rugged sort of way. Nice thin cheekbones and darkish mousy tousled hair that glinted when the sun shone. Lovely eyes too, grey and sort of slanty.

Catching sight of an escaping wisp of hair, she tucked it back hastily behind her ear. "Oh, wouldn't have wanted to be late, Mr Norris, not the first day – nor any day, of course! No, I'm a good timekeeper, my mum says I'm like a little clock, if I want to be up at six, say, I just bang my head on the pillow six times." She jerked her head enthusiastically. "Six times, like that, and then at six o'clock I'm wide awake, on the dot, it's not a problem. Or five o'clock, or seven o'clock, I can do any time at all. I could do twenty-four minutes past five if you asked me to."

Mr Norris grinned. "I won't be doing that." He squared his shoulders. "Right then, let's get you started." She caught what might have been a flash of anxiety pass across his eyes as he glanced at the kitchen window, but he opened the kitchen door firmly. "Come on in."

The kitchen was warm and bright with a nice fire flickering. Mrs Norris was just finishing drying the breakfast things at the sink. He propelled Cathy forward, patting her cheerfully on the back. "Here she is, love, bright and early!"

Mrs Norris took time to fold up her tea towel carefully, then turned, leaning back against the sink and surveying Cathy coldly. Cathy was surprised to see that the lovely dark hair that was usually soft and wavy was limp and greasy, and tied back tightly from her face in an unflattering way, although the clip that held the front back had a feather on it. It looked quite odd.

"Morning, Mrs Norris," Cathy murmured, reddening under her peculiar stare.

The corners of Mrs Norris's lips tugged upward briefly, then silently she turned back to the sink. Mr Norris hesitated and Cathy saw another worried look flash into his eyes before he turned and smiled encouragingly at her. "Hang your coat up, Cath," he told her.

She turned obediently to the hook on the back of the door, though she watched surreptitiously over her shoulder as he moved across to stand at Mrs Norris's side. Lowering his voice, he murmured, "It's all right, isn't it, love, Cathy coming? You did say." Mrs Norris just shrugged. "It's too much for you trying to cope with everything on your own." He drew her around to face him, studying her face anxiously, and smiled in a light-hearted fashion, giving her waist a light squeeze. "You weren't brought up to it, were you, quite apart from anything else!"

Mrs Norris smiled thinly. Cathy felt the coldness of her right across the room. It was very strange. She was usually so friendly and nice.

Undaunted, Mr Norris glanced encouragingly over his shoulder at Cathy. "She can come in the mornings, then her mum can have her home in the afternoons to help her with the little ones." Cathy nodded, smiling. Turning back to Mrs Norris, Mr Norris gave her waist another, more hearty, squeeze. "So there we are! Suits everybody!"

There was silence for a moment. Cathy waited, scuffing her toe awkwardly. Suddenly, Mrs Norris's face softened and broke into a smile. Mr Norris's strong shoulders seemed to sag down in relief. Kissing Mrs Norris's forehead quickly, he murmured softly. "That's it, Mary!" He gave her another loving squeeze.

Mrs Norris seemed to uncoil too, though there was still a sort of stiffness about her. She turned to Cathy, the sweet smile still on her face. "Well, Cathy! You'll want to know where everything is," she said politely.

Cathy nodded. "Yes, please, Mrs Norris."

"I'll be off, then." Releasing Mrs Norris, Mr Norris took a few steps towards the back door, then grinned again at Cathy. "Right then, see you at dinnertime!"

He glanced back at Mrs Norris, then hesitated, and crossed back to her, taking her once again in his arms. Cathy sighed. Couldn't let go of her, could he? Wasn't fair! Why wasn't it her? He was so romantic!

"You are pleased, aren't you?" she heard him murmur. "I want you to be pleased."

Mrs Norris smiled brightly. "Of course I'm pleased! I always wanted a maid."

There was something in the way she said it that made Cathy nervous. There was a sort of edge to it. It didn't sound quite right.

"That's what she is, Jim, isn't it?" Mrs Norris went on, twinkling innocently up into his eyes. "Someone to do all the dirty work?"

He seemed to have noticed the oddness of it, too. Cathy saw the muscles of his neck tighten. "Don't work her too hard, love, she's only young." He laughed. "Don't want you both cracking up!"

There was an intense silence. Mr Norris tried to back-pedal hastily. "I mean, you'll feel better now that you're not ... not so tired! I mean, not so strained." He tried another laugh. "You know!"

Mrs Norris remained silent, and after a while he released her with a sigh. "Right, then." He shrugged. "Well, I'll see you later." He smiled at Cathy as he moved to the back door. "Make yourself at home!"

He shut the door a bit hard. The sound of it seemed to echo in the ensuing silence.

The kitchen clock ticked. At last, Mrs Norris stirred. "Yes, come along, Cathy," she murmured silkily, "make yourself at home!" The odd way she was smiling made Cathy feel very nervous.

"We must see if we can find you an apron," Mrs Norris suggested, gaily, with her pretty little giggle. "Don't want you ruining that pretty dress!"

"Oh! I've got one, Mrs Norris!" she told her, flourishing it.

Mrs Norris smiled serenely. "That's all right, then! Now let me see, what shall you do?" She clapped her hands. "I know! You can make Mr Norris's bed! You'd like that, Cathy, wouldn't you?" Taking her by the hand, she hurried her towards the door. "Come on!"

There was something funny about the way she said it.

Uncertainly, Cathy hung back, but Mrs Norris tugged her hand impatiently. "This way, this way!" She was still smiling. "No, no, silly, come on! Don't be shy!"

The steep ladder leading up to the attic made Cathy feel nervous. It was very steep. "You do have to be careful here," Mrs Norris told her over her shoulder in confidential tones as Cathy gingerly pulled herself up behind her. "Hang on tight – you wouldn't want to fall!"

"Well, there you are, then." Mrs Norris gestured extravagantly at the double bed: "It's all yours!" She gave that funny smile again, and a little giggle. "I don't want to watch you, do I?"

She patted a trunk at the foot of the bed. "Clean linen here. We haven't got a copper; I'll go and put the kettle on, you'll have to wash the dirty ones in the tub."

Her eyes suddenly went all pale and cold. Giving a small, odd sort of shiver, she moved to the small window. To Cathy's surprise, for the window was small and overhung, and the attic fairly dark already, she drew the curtains tight closed.

For a little while after Mrs Norris had disappeared downstairs Cathy tried to manage in the semi-gloom, but it wasn't easy. She got the quilt and blankets moved off the bed, but kept bumping into things, and she couldn't see if the entire floor had been boarded over; theirs hadn't, at home. Scared of falling between the joists, she opened the curtains again a little nervously. The place needed airing, actually, even if it was a bit cold; according to Mum, a bedroom window should be opened at least half an hour every day. She pushed, but it took a bit of effort to shift it and as it swung open, folded pieces of soggy newspaper and damp rag tumbled inside into the room.

Better leave it then. She closed the window hastily. Rain blowing in, anyway, with it open. Gathering up the fallen bits and pieces she shoved them back between the window and the sill as best as she was able. They had to be there to serve some useful purpose. Perhaps they felt a bit of a draught? She could feel a flow of icy air, but most of it appeared to come from the unlined underside of the roof.

Peering up at the greyish lath and plaster, with cobwebby patches here and there between the rafters, she shuddered. Must be spiders up there – imagine them letting themselves down slowly in the night onto your nose, or down your nightie!

She sniffed the cold air. It smelled quite nice up here, though, sort of soft and powdery. Violets, or something. Must be Mrs Norris's scent or talcum powder.

Now she could look around and get her bearings. In the bit where she was standing there was the double bed and a couple of old bedside tables – one of which she recognised as an orange box on end – with a white crocheted mat on each, and a half-used candle in a holder. The orange box one had a small, loudly ticking clock on top, too.

At each side of the bed lay a rag rug, one different shades of blue, one grey with a blue middle. There was a dark brown dressing table with a rather fly-speckled mirror under the window, and on it stood a willow pattern vase containing dried blue and white larkspur. Bits of the flowers had crumbled away and lay scattered about the bottom of the vase. There were quite a lot of photographs and Mrs Norris's bits and bobs on the dressing table, too, and a small, needlepoint-covered stool stood in front of it. That was all, apart from the linen chest and, along one wall, a row of clothes on hangers dangling from a length of cord.

Conscious that the floor would probably creak and Mrs Norris down below might guess that she was having a snoop, she tiptoed towards the big crossbeam that cut across the middle, peering into the gloom at the other end. Only half the floor had been boarded over, the bit where she was. To get over there, to poke around in the trunks and boxes she could see resting on the joists, she'd have to sling a leg over the cross beam and then balance carefully as she moved from joist to joist. There could be interesting things in there, but she turned away. Not just now, anyway.

She had a bit of a peep at the stuff on the dressing table whilst she was dusting the top, admiring a pretty silver-backed hairbrush and hand mirror. There was a spray scent bottle with a dark blue silver-meshed bulb. She sniffed it. Parma violets.

One of Patsy's crayon drawings was stuck to the mirror above the dressing table. Somebody – Mrs Norris, probably – had written in capital letters MUMMY, DADDY AND PATSY HAVING BREAKFAST, and it had been copied carefully in a childish scrawl. *Ah, sweet.*

Some of the photo frames were expensive ones, silver. There was a nice little snap of Patsy as a baby, and one of Mrs Norris holding her, and another of Mr and Mrs Norris and a very little Patsy at the seaside. In the middle, in a handmade frame decorated with dried flowers and seashells, Mr and Mrs Norris were standing on the steps of some building. Mrs Norris was wearing a day dress and hat, and the building must have been the Registry Office, because both of them were wearing buttonholes, and Mrs Norris had a posy in her hands. Mr Norris looked very smart in a nice dark suit. Mrs Norris was looking up at him adoringly, and he was beaming out at the camera, as pleased and as proud as punch.

And they'd run away to get married, Mum said ... Cathy sighed. It was *so* romantic! Though if she ever decided to marry Fred, or anyone else, it would have to be a proper wedding, with a church and bridesmaids and a long, white dress. Mrs Norris's outfit did look very plain.

There were photographs of two other people that she didn't know – a man in uniform and a pretty woman – Mrs Norris's parents, perhaps? Poor little girl, she thought, welling up momentarily with sympathy. Can't have been all that much older than our Pauline and our Chrissie when she lost them both. Poor, lonely little girl.

She picked up the wedding photograph again. The man wasn't as nice looking as Mr Norris. *Nobody* was as nice as Mr Norris. She sighed dramatically. Oh, Mr Norris ... Jim ... She blew him a kiss. Why didn't you wait for *me*?

A sound from downstairs made her hurry back to her task. The easiest way to get the dirty bedclothes down from the attic seemed to be to throw them through the trap, so she bundled up the disheveled sheets and pillowcases ready and peered over the edge cautiously before letting go. They fell on the floor with a plop. Poor Mrs. Norris; how far up the ladder had she been? To think; she fell right down there ...

The cold was getting to her. Having remade the bed with teeth chattering, she collected the candles from the bedside tables and set them on the floor by the trap ready to be taken downstairs, then reached under the bed for the jerry, hoping it would be empty. It wasn't. She carried it carefully over to join the candlesticks. She'd need two hands to get *that* safely down the steps.

She ran her eye over the room. *Blow it, forgotten to draw the curtains. Damn.*

The kitchen floor was a disgrace, she noticed when she got back downstairs, with bits of fir and moss and fragments of flower petals and puddles of water all over it; it would have to be done shortly. Mrs Norris was nowhere to be seen, but she had taken down the washing tub and got out the dolly peg, and she'd mixed the blueing too, so it wasn't too long before Cathy was ready to hang everything out.

The washing line was up on a bit of a bump at the back, beyond the first orchard and the henhouses, so it was quite a long way to go with the heavy basket and her arms were aching by the time she got there. She could hear Patsy's voice somewhere down the garden, and the regular clunk of a spade.

Mrs Norris was not in the kitchen when she got back to the house. Cathy, feeling peckish, was peering into a cupboard on the wall when she felt eyes burning into the back of her neck, and swung round. Mrs Norris was standing, quiet as a mouse, tucked into the tight corner between the dresser and the outside wall and her face was all pinched and tight. Cathy put her hand to her heart with a laugh. "Oh, you gave me a start, Mrs Norris! I was just looking –"

Mrs Norris fluttered a hand to silence her and pressed back harder into the corner. Her eyes were almost feverishly bright. "They're listening ..." she hissed. "You left the door open, you stupid girl!"

Puzzled, Cathy gazed around. "Who is, Mrs Norris?"

"Close the door, quick. Draw the curtain."

When Cathy had obediently drawn the heavy door curtain across the closed door, Mrs Norris breathed a sigh of relief. "You need to be more careful."

What was she on about? Cathy frowned. Mrs Norris moved out of the corner. She had got her outdoor coat on and, though it was a nice, red wool one, quite smart, she did look a bit of a mess. She'd been doing something to herself, put a ribbon of Patsy's in her hair, but hadn't brushed it properly so that it was all hitched up and fuzzy and tangled, and she'd put on a bright red lipstick all uneven, so that it was smeared on one side of her upper lip.

Best not to stare at her. Cathy clasped her hands. "What would you like me to do next, Mrs Norris? I thought, maybe the floor?"

"Run out of things to do for him?"

"Eh?" Mum had said Mrs Norris was behaving a little odd, but she was quite peculiar. "I'm here to help *you*, Mrs Norris."

Mrs Norris gave her a strange, cold smile.

C athy kept out of her way as much as possible. She didn't actually see much of Mr Norris. She saw him setting out on his round, taking Patsy with him, and he was late back, arrived as she was leaving and about to close the back door.

"All right?" he asked anxiously as he unloaded the empty sacks and boxes. "Everything go all right, Cath? How's Mary?"

"She's ..." He looked so worried, she didn't want to say Mary had rather frightened her. "She's all right, Mr Norris.

She's in the kitchen setting the table."

He looked relieved. "What's for dinner today, Cath? Aren't you stopping?"

She blushed. That was nice of him. "I think it's faggots today, Mr Norris," she told him shyly. "I just did the potatoes, Mrs Norris did the rest. Oh, and I did some carrots, so there's carrots ..."

He opened the passenger door of the van. "Come on, Patsy." Patsy climbed out reluctantly, carrying a colouring book and a pencil. Cathy smiled, taking the book from her.

"What've you been doing, Pats? Oh, dot-to-dot ... Oh, look – that one's an engine. You've done that neatly."

Patsy reached up excitedly. "And this one ..."

"Oh, yes, a steamboat ... and a teddy ..." She laughed. "Oh, see, you've given him a bright blue nose! Must have a cold!"

"Daddy had a cold."

"Did he?"

"When my mummy fell down the ladder, my daddy had a nasty cold, so he was up in bed."

Mr Norris interrupted, looking a bit upset. "Come on, Patsy. We'll see Cathy again in the morning." He opened the back door. "Oh, blast this blooming curtain!" He smiled at Cathy as he ducked, pushing it aside, but it wasn't a proper smile. He seemed to have gone all sad. "Thanks, Cath."

Chapter 9

Jim woke up that night to find Mary missing, and at first felt a sense of relief. Patsy must have been calling, and for once Mary must have gone down to her. Perhaps she was on the mend after all. Dr Humphreys must have been right; having Cathy around, even for one day, had made a difference.

He found it very hard to drop off to sleep again. Things kept going round in his mind. Was there any way he could manage a bit of a holiday for her as well?

If he'd had the money to make proper provision for her, with a nice house, and somebody like Cathy to help right from the very start, and hadn't needed her to make the wreaths and things on top of everything else, she'd very probably have been as right as rain.

Shouldn't have asked her to marry me.

All my fault.

At last he gave up, threw back the bedclothes and reached for the candle and his dressing gown. A cup of hot tea might settle him.

There was no sound from Patsy's room, and he opened the kitchen door as quietly as he could, not wanting to waken either of them, then came to a halt, startled. Mary was sitting huddled in a dim pool of light spilled by the oil lamp on the kitchen table. She was working feverishly at a wreath, thrusting stems of fir haphazardly into a mossed base. By the side of the table stood several completed crosses and wreaths, all bare of flowers except for a few white hellebores and odd clusters of brown and slimy bits of dead, frosted chrysanths. The tap dripped icily in the empty sink.

As he watched, she shivered violently, glanced nervously behind her towards the door, then, rising swiftly from the table, rearranged the heavy curtain. Crouching and mumbling to herself, she pushed one of the bulky cloth sausages she had made under the bottom of the curtain more firmly, then moved quickly to the window.

"Mary?"

She didn't seem to hear him. Reaching under the curtain she ran her hands about the panes as if searching for something, and then tucked the curtain back tightly once again. Returning to the table, she reached for another piece of fir. She was shaking. "Don't let go for a minute," she murmured, and gave a tiny sob.

"Mary?" She started back in her chair with a cry as he moved towards her. He held out his hands, open palmed. "Mary – Mary, it's only me."

Her face was carved with distress. Her eyes looked strained and bloodshot and her breath was coming in great swooping gasps. He crouched beside her, putting an arm about her shoulders. "It's me, Mary."

"It's all too much."

"I know it is, I know it is, Mary." He put gentle pressure on her arms. "Come on, poppet. You've done enough for now. Come on, lovey. Come on. Come to bed."

H e went down to the post office the next morning and rang the surgery. "You've got to come and see her," he told Dr Humphreys, when at last he came to the phone.

The doctor was pleased to see Cathy in the kitchen with Patsy. "Good man!" he said. "Took my advice. Good man!"

He negotiated the ladder, though, with suspicion. "Can't you put in a proper staircase, Jim?" he asked. "You'll have that daughter of yours up here in no time, and you don't want another accident, do you?" Jim's stomach churned with guilt.

Mary was asleep, with her mouth open. Jim sat on the side of the bed and shook her gently. "Mary ..." She opened her eyes, and for a moment he had the distinct and very unpleasant feeling that she didn't know him, but he pushed the idea to the back of his mind.

"The doctor's here, pet," he told her. "He just wants to have a look at you." He slipped an arm about her. "Here – let me help you sit up."

I 'm giving her some tablets to slow her down a bit, help her to stay a bit calmer," Dr Humphreys told Jim, opening his bag in the kitchen when they were back downstairs. "Her blood pressure is a bit high too, be better if we can stop her getting so over-wrought. Get a rug on her, let her sit out in the open air when it's not raining."

He counted out some pills. "One in the morning and one last thing at night. Let her sleep as much as she can."

Jim nodded. "You still don't think it's anything major, then, Doctor?"

Dr Humphreys shrugged. "I don't think so. Let's just see how it goes."

Whatever the doctor had given her, they weren't very good sleeping tablets. Jim found her downstairs again the next night. She had built up the fire to a blistering roar and had brought in all the wreath frames that he had dismantled that morning and was agitatedly struggling to make them up once again. It took longer this time for him to persuade her to leave them and to go back to bed. It was very dispiriting.

Patsy was frightened. It was dark in her room apart from the pattern made by the paraffin stove on the ceiling, but Mummy had brought in a candle and the flame of it leapt and flickered throwing strange patterns all across the walls as she moved and it was very scary. It made Mummy in her long dressing gown look very much like a witch. She kept talking to herself, and she had tucked Patricia in very tightly, so that she couldn't move her arms or her legs. She had turned up the wick of the stove. Patsy could smell the hot, stuffy fumes from the paraffin and it was making her feel sick.

Mummy was doing something now at the window, pushing something all around the window frame. "Mummy, I'm hot," Patsy whimpered, but Mummy didn't answer. She drew the curtains tightly and then fell onto her knees, crawling along the wall and feeling around with her hands. She was talking to herself again. "Somewhere, it's in here somewhere ..."

Patsy began to cry. "Mummy, I don't like it!" She wriggled, trying to free herself. "Mummy, I've got to – Mummy, I'm too h-hot!!"

"Yes, yes, I've got to ..." Mummy dragged Patsy's stool to the door. Climbing onto it, she stuffed a bundle of clothing into the little air hole above the door through which Patsy sometimes watched for her candlelight coming down in the night. "You have to stop the draught getting in, Patsy," she told her, panting. "It sneaks in when you're not looking and it creeps in and whispers to itself inside your head ..."

It didn't sound like her. Patsy sobbed louder. "Mummy, I'm f-frightened!!"

Mummy climbed down from the stool and took an armful of Patsy's clothes from her chair, rolling them into a bundle. "It can't be helped, Patricia. This is for your own good. You wouldn't like it if they got in, you wouldn't like it at all."

She pushed back the hair from her face and got down on her hands and knees again, pushing the bundle under the door. "They're very clever, you know," she told her as if it was a big secret, speaking over her shoulder, and somehow her face brought back the face of the sheep's head in Mrs Bevis' sweet shop in her dream. It was Mummy's face, but it wasn't. Her eyes were all shiny and glary. It made Patsy whimper with fear. It was horrid.

The sheep-mummy went on feeling round the door. "They try to make you think that it's just a little breeze blowing, a tiny little draught, but they are riding in the wind, once you've got the germs, they know, and they don't rest until they've got inside your head and teased and pulled until all the raw red nerves come squirming out, squirming and wriggling out ..."

"I don't like it! I don't like it!" Patsy wailed. She couldn't even hide her head under the bedclothes.

Mummy stood up again and pulled the bundle away just a little, then turned the handle of the door. She began to back out, pulling the bundle back into position behind her. "Prevention is better than cure," she muttered in that horrible voice. "Don't let them smell your guilt. A good child is a silent child who keeps its own counsel and suffers to be pure again."

Even if Mummy did look like the sheep, she didn't want to be alone. "Mummy, don't go!"

But the door closed and Patsy heard the sound of the key turning in the lock.

H ours later, Jim woke suddenly with a start and stared into the darkness. Mary was still breathing heavily at his side. Everything seemed quiet except for the hooting of a solitary owl.

He turned on his side and was almost asleep again when his ears once more caught a faint cry from below. He groaned and lay with his eyes closed for a few moments but when she cried out again, anxiety prickled him and he couldn't settle. With a heavy sigh, he slid out of bed, felt for his slippers and reached for the candle.

He could usually see the faint light thrown out by the paraffin stove through the air hole above the door, but not tonight. It must have run out; maybe she was cold. To his great surprise, her door seemed to be locked. He could see the keyhole, but there was no key there. Alarmed now, he put his ear to the door. "Patsy?" There was silence.

He hurried into the kitchen, but there was no sign there of the key. "Patsy?" Still silence. Really worried now, he set down the candle on a rung of the ladder and put his shoulder to the door. Powered as he was by adrenalin, the lock gave way fairly easily, but the door still wouldn't open properly. Something was holding it. Warm air laden with strong paraffin fumes seeped out into the hall through the crack and he felt his heart pounding.

"Pats? I'm here. Daddy's coming, Pats!" Feeling around the base of the door, he found something soft but substantial on the other side, and shoved it away, forcing his way inside.

The paraffin heater cast a baleful glow in the tiny, fume-filled room and threw a livid pattern on the shadowy ceiling. Patsy lay loose-limbed across her rumpled bed and for a terrible, terrible moment he was afraid that she was unconscious – or worse. To his relief, though, she whimpered feebly as he swept her up into his arms. She was drenched in sweat, her flannelette nightie soaking. *Bloody hell!*

He carried her into the kitchen. Dragging back the door curtain and kicking away Mary's homemade draught excluder with another curse, he threw open the back door. Fresh night air swirled over them. Patsy's chest fluttered. "Daddy, I'm thirsty ..." she whispered.

Cathy found him in his vest shaving at the kitchen sink when she arrived next morning. Patsy was curled up under a blanket on the armchair by the fireplace with her doll.

"Morning, Mr Norris!" She smiled self-consciously, trying not to stare. He grunted, and she busied herself with her apron.

"Cath?" He glanced over his shoulder. He looked desperately tired and drawn.

"Yes, Mr Norris?"

He turned back to the sink. "Keep a close eye on Patsy, will you?"

She nodded. "Yes, Mr Norris."

"She might be ..." He hesitated. "Well, she's not been too good. I'm going to ring the doctor." He reached for the towel and dried his face roughly. "Mary's in bed. She's had a couple of tablets. Don't think she'll wake up yet."

She was glad to hear it.

He sat down, pulling on his boots. "I'd take Patsy in to the surgery, but I'd rather he came here, he can have another look at Mary at the same time." She felt so sorry for him; his poor face was haggard with distress. "I'll go to the shop to make the phone call, then drop off a few things quickly round the village." He stood up, looking at her anxiously. "Do you think you'll be all right, Cath? Shouldn't be more than an hour."

"Oh, yes!" The way Mrs Norris had gone all weird had scared her to bits, making her wonder during the night if she really wanted to come again, but now that she was there, it didn't seem so bad and she was keen to help him. "Patsy'll be fine with me," she told him confidently. "I'm used to little ones being poorly. What's up with her, exactly? Is she likely to be sick?"

He took down his jacket. "She's – well, she's feeling a bit dizzy, and she's got a headache, so she says. She's been coughing and ..." He shrugged. "Don't know about being sick. She hasn't, so far."

He opened the door. "Do you think you could rustle up a bit of dinner for us today, Cath? Early will do, if you've got to be off, but I don't think Mary's going to be up to it."

She felt pleased as punch. Cooking was one of the things she knew how to do best, and she could really show off. "Of course I'll do that, Mr Norris."

He looked relieved. "I think there's a bit of bacon, and, of course, there are eggs. Flour and a few tins of stuff and such like in the cupboard. Vegetables outside in the store shed; just see what you can find."

"Would you fancy a nice apple pie, Mr Norris?"

He clearly liked the sound of that. "I would! Lovely. There are some nice windfall Bramleys, if you want – not the ones on the shelf, the ones in the basket."

"Righto!" She beamed, delighted to have pleased him.

After he'd gone, she rumpled Patsy's spiky hair. "What is it, lovey? Aren't you feeling too well? Tell me if you feel sick. Our Johnnie's been sickly; he's been backwards and forwards to the lav like a headless chicken for the last two days."

Patsy didn't respond. Cathy shrugged. "Well, you sit tight there, then, while I scrub this floor, don't want you paddling over it while it's wet, do we?"

She did the floor and then, seeing that Patsy seemed to have dropped off to sleep, made her way into the hall. She peered up into the gloom of the attic through the trapdoor a little nervously, but all seemed quiet. She was surprised to find the small window wide open and a pile of clothes on the floor. The bedclothes were in a crumpled heap. It smelled funny.

She tidied it all up as quickly as she could, going through possible dinner recipes in her head. She wanted it to be nice ... What veg might there be? Leeks, probably, Swedes, carrots ... Onions and potatoes, of course ... Cabbage, possibly. Bacon and leeks with a nice sauce made with onion and a bit of top-of-the-milk? Bacon omelette? Onion and bacon soup with dumplings? A bacon and egg pie? She'd have to go through the larder cupboard and the meat safe, before she could make up her mind.

Patsy woke up coughing after about an hour and said her head hurt and she felt a bit dizzy. Cathy shook her head gravely. "You're definitely going down with something, pet."

She fetched her a drink of water, but Patsy threw it all up. "Poor little soldier!" She made her comfy on her knee and after a few minutes Patsy dropped off to sleep again, so Cathy settled her gently in the chair and went back to the pastry she was making. She had used the last of the butter as well as lard in the making, which was extravagant, she knew. This pastry, though, had got to be light and crumbly and utterly delicious. It was for Mr Norris.

The potatoes were on, the cabbage prepared, a bacon-and-egg-and-leek crumble and an apple pie were in the oven, the kitchen floor re-mopped, the table set and Cathy was just working her way through a pile of ironing when she heard Mrs Norris's voice."Still here, I see?" She sounded cold as ice.

Cathy started nervously. "I've not been here that long, Mrs Norris. It's not even half past eleven."

She set the iron back on its stand in the fire to reheat, trying hard not to stare, but Mrs Norris looked extremely strange, even worse than yesterday. She had her dressing gown on still, but with a shawl wrapped tightly about her shoulders and a woolly scarf on top of that. Her hair was all sticking up all on one side, and she'd got her aim wrong with some bright red lipstick once again. Her expression was really weird, sort of blank and penetrating, both at the same time.

Sweeping her out of the way, Mrs Norris turned on the tap and began to rinse her hands furiously. "Hoping he'll be back in soon, I suppose," she murmured, stiff-backed, gazing though the window above the sink. "Her hair is turning quite green, you know, with worrying about it."

What was she going on about? Nervously Cathy bit her lip.

Taking up a cloth, Mrs Norris began to dry her hands. "You can't help it, you know, when your head hurts."

Cathy nodded, trying to smile. "I don't suppose you can, Mrs Norris."

Mrs Norris set down the towel and began to move slowly round Cathy, studying her through narrowed eyes, then moved conspiratorially closer. "You know what's happening, don't you?" she asked, with a cunning gleam in her eye. Cathy shook her head. Mrs Norris's eyes widened, reddening suddenly with rage. Her voice thinned to a hiss. "You come in here with your germs, thinking I won't notice, removing my shoes."

Patsy, in the armchair, shrank. Mummy had that glary-eyed sheep's-head look on her face again. She didn't even sound like Mummy. *It's my bad dream again.* She shuddered, scrunching up her hands tight so that her nails dug into her palms. *Wake up,* she told herself, terrified. *Wake up, wake up, I don't like this, wake up …*

Hearing her whimper, Cathy tried to speak calmly. "Patsy, pet – just go in your bedroom." Mrs Norris had clearly gone potty! She dodged, trying to make for the door, but Mrs Norris was blocking it. "I got to go now, Mrs Norris. Look, look, I got to go!"

Mrs Norris grasped her arm and brought her face right up to Cathy's. Her breath smelled very strange. "He got an axe, you know, and split open my head." She bent her head, parting her hair a little for Cathy to peer at her crown. "You can see them all wriggling away, look, see?" She tugged viciously at her hair. "Tugging at my nerves, attacking their vibratory qualities …"

She was talking double Dutch! Cathy tugged frantically against her grasp, and screamed. Patsy began to sob, too. Mrs Norris's nails were biting into Cathy's arm as she hissed. "You can see them, can't you, dragging them out of my brain …"

Cathy screamed again. "Let me go, Mrs Norris!" Behind her she heard Patsy's voice rise to a terrified wail. "Go back in your bedroom, Pats!" she shouted. "Now! Go on, lovey! Shut the door!" Patsy made a faint move to obey, then shrank back again into the chair, wailing even more frantically.

Cathy was the younger and fitter, but Mrs Norris seemed to have the strength of two women. Dragging Cathy towards the fireplace, she reached down for the iron. "You have to burn them out – scald them out!"

Cathy struggled against her. "Let me *go*!"

There was saliva dribbling down Mrs Norris's chin. "This is the best way, honestly – they can't stand heat and fire." She brought the heavy iron up close to Cathy's head and cocked her head, listening.

Patsy closed her eyes tight and shook her head frantically. "No, no, no, no, no …"

Mrs Norris's eyes were wide and filled with some sort of fearful, righteous fervour. "We have to do this, Cathy. You know what they are saying. It's for your own good. Sh, can't you hear them?"

Cathy could hear the iron sizzling and feel the heat of it on her cheek. She reared back, tears rolling. "Mr NORRIS!"

Chapter 10

Jim was feeling quite sick with fear and worry as he made his way into the village. *Mary, oh Mary, come back, love, whatever's happened to you ... Come back, come back, come back ...* He chanted it in his head like a spell, in rhythm with the clatter of Meg's hooves on the lane. She *will* come back, she *will* come back, she *will* come back ...

He might as well have had his eyes closed, for all he saw on the way.

He got hold of Dr Humphreys on the Post Office telephone straight away this time. "You've got to come now, Doctor," he told him tersely, after explaining what Mary had done. "We can't go on like this." He hated himself for saying it. "She's getting to be a danger."

The doctor said he'd come as soon as he could, probably between one and two, and Jim had to be satisfied with that. To add to his troubles, a lad on a motorbike collided with the side of the trap. He wasn't hurt, but old Meg took a nervous fright, rearing with eyes rolling and tail flattened hard down, and the offside wheel was broken. It took him a while to soothe Meg and then he had to unharness her and lead her round to Bob's livery whilst he got the wheel fixed temporarily, although it had really had it.

Impatient to get home, he glanced at his watch. This was no bloody good. At twenty-four, Meg was too old for this game. A new wheel would be expensive. It was time he got a bloody van.

Meg and the trap got Jim home, but only just. The poor animal was sweating and shaking and collided clumsily with the stable door as he guided her in. He rubbed her down well and put on a rug, and was just getting some bran out of the bin to warm for her when he heard Cathy's yell. Adrenalin rushing, he dropped the lid of the bin.

C athy was quivering. She could feel the red-hot iron now, glowing close to her cheek.

"It's the metal, you see," Mrs Norris explained to her carefully, as if she were a schoolmistress. "They're afraid of metals. They're frightened now; that's good. You can hear them whispering."

Flinching, Cathy screamed again. "Stop it, Mrs Norris! Don't!" She craned despairingly towards the window. "Mr *NORRIS!!!*"

"Ssh!" Mrs Norris shook her head, smiling quite gently as she moved the iron closer. "It's the heat, of course, the heat, that's all. Don't worry now. We'll soon be having them."

Beside herself with terror, Cathy opened her mouth, closed her eyes tight, and shrieked.

As Jim burst into the kitchen he had only a moment to take in the scene: Cathy, hands shielding her face, screaming, rigid with shock and fear, Patsy, wailing in the armchair, and Mary ...

As he watched, Mary's teeth clenched, the iron she was holding fell noisily to the floor and her eyes rolled back in her head. She began to fall. As he reached out his arms to catch her, her slender body began to convulse and jerk.

H e stood with Dr Humphreys at the front gate, watching as the ambulance drove away down the lane. "We couldn't take her to the Cottage Hospital, d'you see?" Dr Humphreys said apologetically. "They are not equipped."

Jim shook his head. He was in shock. His face felt frozen. "I can't bear it."

Dr Humphreys put a hand on his shoulder. "Come on now, man. Brace up."

Jim's tongue felt too thick to move. "But I've had to say I want her put away, in a – in a lunatic asylum!"

"It'll be temporary, only temporary. A Temporary Status Order, that's all it is."

Jim dashed away a tear. "You know what they call it round here, they call it the madhouse, the loony bin. They'll all know about it in the village. She'll never live it down."

"Oh, it'll all be forgotten. They'll sort out the problem ... She'll be back home before you know where you are!"

Jim blew his nose. "I suppose so."

"Good man, good man! Chin up." The doctor squeezed his shoulder once again. "You can go over there tomorrow. Get a good night's sleep!"

Patsy struggled in Cathy's arms and reached for him

imploringly as soon as she saw him. He took her, holding her tight. "You go home, love," he said to Cathy. She nodded, obviously relieved and went to get her coat.

"I don't think I can come in tomorrow, Mr Norris," she said as she came back, pulling on her coat.

He shook his head. Couldn't think straight at all. He was all numb inside. "No, of course not. I'm so sorry, Cath."

Cathy held her coat close to her chin. She was still shivering a bit, and pale as a sheet, poor kid. "What's wrong with her, Mr Norris?" she asked.

He shrugged helplessly. "I don't know, Cath."

She hesitated. "Will you be all right with Patsy? Shall you manage?"

"Daddy!" Patsy buried her face in his neck, clinging even tighter round his neck, digging her heels into his back.

He hugged her even more closely. "It's all right, lovey. Ssh."

Cathy was waiting at the door, looking desperately anxious. "We'll manage, don't you worry," he told her, trying to smile reassuringly. "Things'll have to hang fire for a while, that's all. I shall cope."

Patsy just wouldn't sleep. Having been up and down the ladder like a yo-yo, he sat at the edge of her bed in his crumpled pyjamas, running his fingers distractedly through his hair. She wailed even louder and he heaved a heavy sigh. "Oh, Patsy, we've got to get some sleep. Be a good girl."

Yawning, he swung his legs back into the bed and pulled the blankets over them. "Okay, okay!" Outside, a cockerel crowed. He closed his eyes wearily. "And now it's the bloody dawn chorus."

Patsy hiccupped and snuggled up close to his side, her arm about his chest. After a while, he tried again. He had only managed to get one foot on the floor, though, before she reared up. "Daddy?"

He froze, holding his breath. "Yes, Patsy?"

She gave another tearful hiccup. "Daddy, where's my *proper* mummy gone?"

He took Patsy with him the next morning when he went to see Mary. He had thought to leave her for a while with Elsie, but the distressed child had kicked up such a fuss when he had pulled up the trap outside her door and tried to lift her out of it, that he had given in. He had got Tom Parks to let him leave the trap in his yard and turn Meg into his field, and took Patsy with him on the bus. Maybe Mary would like to see her, he told himself. It might do her good. It might calm her.

It was a mistake. The place they had taken Mary to had frightened Patsy, and they hadn't let him see Mary anyway. He tried to argue with them, but they were adamant that she was best without visitors for the time being.

At last a chap – some sort of security warden, Jim supposed from the heavy serge uniform and the heavy bunch of keys dangling from his belt – showed him firmly to the door, with a very tearful Patsy squirming in his arms.

"Best if you don't bring the little girl again anyway, squire," he told Jim, kindly enough. "Doesn't know what to make of it, do you, pet?" He attempted to chuck her under the chin in jovial fashion, but Patsy shied away, snarling. He grinned, unperturbed, showing blackened stumps of teeth which only served to frighten Patsy more. "Your mum's not feeling well, pet, that's all. You'll be all right. Dad's going to take you home now, give you a nice tea, eh?" He winked conspiratorially at Jim. "A nice iced bun, eh? How about that? A big fat juicy iced bun!" He gestured with his head towards the bottom of the drive before turning back inside. "Tea shop down by the bus stop. They do a very nice jap fancy, by the way!"

When the door had closed, Jim stared at it for a moment then hoisted the snivelling Patsy up onto his shoulders. "Come on, then, love."

It was a long walk back down to the bus stop. Clicking his tongue as if to old Meg, he broke into a jog. "Home, James, and don't spare the horses!" It was difficult to see the drive clearly: tears blurred his eyes. Holding Patsy in place with one hand, he brushed the back of his fingers against them to clear them. The place had frightened him, too.

Jim, you look terrible; grey as a sheet!" Elsie clucked around him in her kitchen like a mother hen when he got back to the village. "Here, sit down here by the fire while I get this little one tucked up for a bit of a nap. She looks absolutely exhausted. Hang on – let me move the washing. There."

He gazed blindly into the flames, then shook his head despairingly when she came back again and sat down opposite him, waiting. "There's no garden, Elsie. Mary ought to have a bit of garden. No garden, nothing. Just tufts of grass and weeds all around, growing in cracks in a sea of concrete."

And a high wall all around, too, with broken glass on top. A great, grim, grey stone building like a prison. Inside, the smell

*of overcooked mince and cabbage overlaid with disinfectant,
and the whole place echoing with footsteps, clanging doors,
echoed shouts and pitiful weeping.*

Jim shuddered.

Elsie clicked her tongue, distracted by the twins banging
open the back door and making excitedly for the staircase.
"Just a moment, Jim." She raised her voice crossly. "No,
Chrissy, Pauline, not upstairs – Patsy's not very well; she's
having a sleep. No, and not in here either. Go back and play
outside." Once they had been shooed out she settled into the
chair opposite him. "To tell you the truth, Jim, I don't suppose
she knows where she is," she told him gently.

His head ached so he felt it might be bursting. "She looked
at me, you know, Elsie. Just for a moment, before they took
her away."

She was puzzled. "Looked at you?"

He shook his head. "I mean, really looked at me. My little
Mary. *'What are you doing to me, Jim?'* That's what her eyes
were saying." His voice broke. "I'm a traitor, Elsie."

She crossed quickly to his side, putting her arms about
him. "Jim, Jim, don't blame yourself – you mustn't feel guilty,
lad."

"Oh, but I do, Elsie." He covered his face with his hands
and she rocked him as he wept. "I do, I do, I do, I do, I do ..."

He was calmer in a short while. Elsie made them some tea,
and put a drop of brandy in it. They drank it gazing quietly
into the fire; then with a sigh Jim set his mug down in the
hearth. "I suppose they will have to know."

"Of course they will." Elsie shook her head. "No getting
around it."

"Can I leave Patsy with you and pick her up after?"

"Of course. She can stay with us for a bit if you like, sleep
with the twins and Cathy."

He shook his head. "No, Elsie, thanks. I think she'll be
needing her dad."

She nodded. "Cath says she'll be coming back in the
morning."

"She doesn't have to."

"She wants to, Jim. She's a sensible girl. She'll get over it."

He was greatly relieved. "Well, tell her I'm very grateful."
He stood up. "I'd better wash my face and have a bit of a tidy
up before bearding the lions in their den."

She nodded. "Well, come on, then – I'll get you a clean
towel."

He hesitated before going out through the back door. "I'm

supposed to ask if anybody in the family has had a mental illness."

Elsie chuckled. "Oh, my word, Jim – they're going to love you for that!"

As soon as he mentioned the asylum, Miss Louise gave a scream, and then fell to gasping for breath. Nancy had to be sent to fetch her smelling salts and hold them under her nose, and then had to tuck her in bed.

In the event, though, he was surprised how well Miss Buckley took it. She was shocked, of course, naturally. She kept him standing, hat in hand, and listened intently as he stumbled through the story, then she rose and stood stiffly at the window, staring out. She was silent for a long time before she turned back, and she suddenly looked older to Jim than when she had turned away, though she still held herself ramrod straight. She had gone as white as paper, and her thin lips had all but disappeared, but she held herself quite together. "Now, kindly tell me again precisely what the superintendent said."

He did his best. "Well, there are lots of things they can try, apparently. One or other of the treatments they've got is bound to do the trick. That's the idea behind this Temporary Status Order, you see. Finding out what's wrong and what's the best thing to do for her needs a bit of time and it'll allow them that."

Despite the argument for it, it still made him feel quite sick. When the superintendent had given him the papers to sign he'd sat in front of them for ages, unable to pick up the pen. He couldn't bear it.

"I should have stuck by her and managed somehow," he'd said despairingly. "She'd have got back to normal before very long. It's probably just depression and I can't blame her. It was too much to ask of someone like Mary. I knew it was. The kind of life I brought her to was just too much for her."

The superintendent had frowned. "Mr Norris, this is not a minor depression, is it? You have your little girl to think of. Dr Humphreys reports that you said it yourself – Mrs Norris was becoming a danger." Jim only wished he could erase those words.

The superintendent fiddled with his pen. "We are very hopeful of a recovery within the six-month period that will be allotted, and indeed after that there is provision to request that it be extended for two further sessions of six months. It's only after that that she would have to be released or certified within twenty eight days."

It came as a bolt form the blue. "Certified! Certified, sir? Certified?" He tried to make sense of the word. There was a great weight sitting on his chest. "I can't do it."

The superintendent frowned. "Look Mr Norris: if I felt that we couldn't do anything for your wife and if authorised colleagues confirmed my opinion, then judicial detention could be ordered now. You understand? A compulsory detention order ..."

Jim felt a rising panic. "No."

"... but I'm not saying that."

"You're saying then, you think you can make her well? That you can do it?"

"There are many things we can try. There is always hope, Mr Norris."

Defeated, Jim had slumped back against his chair. "What do I have to do?"

He waited, too tired to think at all now, as Miss Buckley walked slowly about the room, frowning and reflectively tapping the fingers of one hand against the back of the other. At last she came to a halt in front of the fireplace. "Oh, sit down, man, sit down, before you fall down!"

"Thank you." Relieved, Jim sank down onto a chair.

"I have decided what we will do." She was plainly satisfied with the result of her deliberations. "We shall do two things, Mr Norris. Firstly, we shall pay for Mary to receive her care in a private establishment. Mary is my sister's child. She is not a fit person to be a state-aided patient in a public institution."

Jim opened his mouth to speak, but she held up her hand peremptorily. "Not a word, Mr Norris. Kindly hear me out." Taking off her glasses, she produced a handkerchief and wiped them clean, and Jim, who was studying her closely, could see that her eyes were a little damp. Ignoring this and replacing the glasses on her nose, she carried on stalwartly.

"We are not rich, Mr Norris. We do not have unlimited funds, but for the time being at least we shall all be shielded from the worst excesses of the local gossips and Mary will be well-cared for."

Jim felt as if he might cry. A horrible lump of pressure was building up in his throat. "It's all my fault ..."

She was impatient with him. "Stop feeling sorry for yourself! My goodness gracious ... I don't think that wallowing in guilt and self-pity is going to do Mary any good, any good at all. We must look to the future."

He nodded wretchedly. "Yes, I suppose you are right."

She frowned. "There's no 'suppose' at all, Mr Norris, no 'suppose' at all! Mary's welfare must take priority."

"Thank you." He blew his nose hard. His words were muffled but they were all that he could say.

She moved briskly back to the window. "Now to the second thing. I have not yet discussed this with my sister, but I shall as soon as she has recovered her composure. Obviously, the child must come here."

Jim was puzzled. "The child? Patsy?"

"It will be inconvenient, I know, and she will have to learn to be quiet around the house – my sister cannot take too much noise and excitement these days. Children these days are so boisterous and self-willed, it will do her no harm to have to learn control and self-discipline."

"Oh, but I thought –" He shook his head emphatically. "Oh, no, Miss Buckley! There's Cathy! I mean, she's a good girl, good-hearted, and she's fond of Patsy. She's coming back, says she's got over her shock; she's going to take care of Patsy. It's all arranged. And I am about the place a great deal of the time."

Miss Buckley tossed her head scornfully. "Most unsuitable."

Very agitated now, Jim rose to his feet. "Oh, but you don't know! Patsy – she has nightmares and things! The kid's had a bad time, she needs me, she'll need her daddy about."

Miss Buckley was gracious. "You would be able to visit her, of course, whenever you wished. Nancy might prepare a little tea for you. You could even take her down to your farm with you at weekends occasionally if you wished."

He spoke sharply. "Garden. It's a market garden."

"Garden, then." She crossed to the bell pull. "Bring her belongings down for her in the morning. She will not need a great many. We shall provide for her."

"No." He drew himself up stiffly. "Sorry, Miss Buckley, it's very kind of you but she's my little girl, and she ought to stop with me."

She paused, appearing genuinely startled. "Your attitude surprises me, Mr Norris. The plan is eminently sensible. We can have no idea, from what you say, of when Mary will be able to return home, which leaves you with sole accountability for bringing up the child for an indefinite period. I really cannot imagine that you would prefer that she be cared for by a ..." She hesitated with raised brows. "Well, let us say, to receive her main female influence and example from a young person with little or no education, from a common village background, rather than from Mary's own aunts."

His fingers clenched on his hat. "I have complete faith in Cathy."

She scoffed. "Misguided confidence, I fear."

Though he rarely lost his temper, he could feel it rising now. He tossed the hat aside. "You can't say that, you don't know her."

Her anger matched his. "I don't need to know her, Mr Norris. It's the principle of the thing, especially under present circumstances."

"Under present circumstances, what Patsy needs is me."

She sighed heavily. "What she *needs*, Mr Norris, is a proper home."

"She *has* a home, Miss Buckley, with me, in the cottage."

She rolled her eyes disdainfully. "Please don't remind me of that dreadful place. I prefer not to imagine Mary living there."

He was fighting now. "But it's what Patsy knows, she has all the garden, she's got her toys, she's got a lovely little room ..."

She smiled thinly. "I am glad to say that I have never seen the inside of the cottage. The exterior view is bad enough."

He was hurt now as well as angry, forgetting his own recriminations. "It's been good enough for Mary."

When she spoke, her tone was very dry. "Has it, Mr Norris? Has it really?"

Exhausted suddenly, he shook his head, quite drained. "Of course it hasn't been good enough. That isn't what I meant."

She sighed. "And how are you going to cope, Mr Norris? Do you want the child speaking like a village urchin?" She shrugged dismissively and turned back to the bell pull with resolve. "This is ridiculous; I will have no further argument. The child will stay with me."

Anger and determination drove him from his chair. "She is coming home with me, Miss Buckley." She opened her mouth to speak again, but he forestalled her. "I am the child's father; and what I say, goes."

Chapter 11

He didn't even try to get Patsy to bed; he took her with him as he saw to the essential tasks round the yard and the garden and then, as exhausted as she was, he put her onto the ladder and climbed up behind her to the attic. She curled up close beside him, falling asleep as soon as her head hit the pillow, though he heard her whimper and moan once in a while as the night drew on. She was restless, too, and he began to feel quite bruised from the kicking of hard little feet in his side. Didn't sleep himself, not a wink, maybe drowsed towards morning, and got up feeling hot-eyed and tense with anxiety, and even more tired than when he had gone to bed.

To his surprise and relief Cathy did arrive the next morning, looking a bit pale and under the weather, and a bit guarded, but quite ready to start.

"How – how is Mrs Norris?" she asked, looking round the kitchen warily as if she might be hovering in the corner.

He shook his head. "I don't know, Cath. I'm going to go over there again this afternoon."

"Do you want me to stop with Patsy while you go?" she offered. "Mum doesn't mind. She said to stop if you wanted. She won't be expecting me."

He looked up, relieved. "That'd be great, Cathy. Would you mind? I was wrong to take her yesterday; it's not the place to take a little one. She's still asleep just now. She's up in the attic, by the way. I took her to bed with me." Cathy ducked her head and nodded, looking suddenly a little flushed. "Mrs Norris wouldn't have approved but she doesn't sleep well at the best of times and she was very upset yesterday," he explained. "You will keep an ear open for her, won't you? Hope she doesn't give you any trouble."

"We'll be fine, Mr Norris." She opened the cupboard door.

"Um – what would you like me to do you for dinner?" she asked, staring at the meagre contents of the shelves.

He still felt too numb to eat much. "Don't worry, I'm not hungry."

She put her hands on her hips and shook her head reprovingly in a motherly fashion. It tickled him how like a younger version of her mother she looked. "Oh, Mr Norris! I'm sorry, but you've got to eat, you know!" Closing the cupboard doors, she opened the meat safe, finding that almost bare as well. "You need some shopping doing, Mr Norris. Tell you what: I could make a list and get some things at the village shop later, and bring them in the morning."

"That'd be very kind." He rummaged in his pocket, frowning. "Though I've not got a lot of change ..."

"I'll put it on tick, Mr Norris. I'm sure Mrs Bevis won't mind."

It was good to have someone taking over. Jim nodded. "It's pay day. I'll be collecting some money later when I do my round."

S he called it 'shepherd's pie without the shepherd' when she put his dinner out on his plate after he came in at twelve, and it was very nice, too, sort of leeks and carrots and things instead of any meat, and unexpectedly tasty. He managed quite a bit of it, though Patsy, looking wan with big red circles under her eyes, wouldn't touch it and Cathy had to scrape off some of the potato and mash it with a bit of cheese before she would pick up her spoon. She had woken up crying in the attic, and it had taken Cathy quite a while to calm her and to persuade her into her clothes. She'd left almost all of the porridge that Cathy had made her, and ignored any attempts to chat to her or to involve her in what Cathy was doing. Instead she had spent more or less all that was left of the morning behind the kitchen armchair, fiddling with her little doll. Though she'd seemed pleased to see him, even Mr Norris had had a job with her to get her to the table.

He nodded approvingly as he laid down his knife and fork. "You're a good cook, Cath!"

She blushed. "My mum says that."

"And your mum is quite right!"

Patsy had finished all the cheesy potato, too, she noticed and had started kicking monotonously at her chair leg. It was irritating. Cathy eyed her reflectively. Mum had warned her that in her opinion little Miss Norris was just a bit spoiled.

"Probably comes from being an Only. You'll have to be firm

with her, Cath, or you'll make a rod for your own back. I know she's having a bad time, so you'll need patience, but she'll run rings around you if you let her," Elsie had said.

"Don't do that, pet," Cathy murmured to Patsy.

The kicking continued, if anything more strenuously, but Mr Norris didn't seem to notice. Cathy tried to ignore it, returning to her main consideration. Did she dare yet, she wondered? She eyed him carefully. He was draining his cup.

Do it now: he'll be off again any minute.

She drew in a deep breath. "Um, Mr Norris ..." she murmured, licking the last scrap off her fork and colouring even more deeply. "How long will Mrs Norris be in there? When do you think she might be coming home?"

He sighed, gazing bleakly into space. "I don't know, Cath. There's no telling."

Patsy's kicking became more aggressive. It was very annoying. "If you've finished, you might as well leave the table, pet-lamb," Cathy told her firmly. "You can go and play in your room."

She looked anxiously at Jim after Patsy had flounced through the door. "I hope you don't think I'm being too strict with her, Mr Norris? I know it isn't really my place."

He shook his head reassuringly. "You're doing a grand job, Cath, though I wouldn't be too hard on her. She's just in a state at the moment."

"I know. She must be missing her mum."

He gave a sort of wince as if the mention of Mrs Norris had inflicted a quick stab of pain and trepidation. He pushed back his chair. "I must get on if I'm to get to the – the whatsit, the er, hospital. I'm afraid Patsy might be going to play up a bit. Sure you don't mind stopping on?"

"No, not at all."

He's going. Do it now.

She plucked nervously at the tea cosy. "Um, Mr Norris?"

He hesitated. "Yes, Cath?"

She bolstered up her courage. "Um, Mr Norris, I was wondering – well, I was thinking, that is, I don't suppose –" She ducked her head, certain she was reddening right up to the ears.

He paused on his way to pick up his jacket, looking worried again. "Are you sure you're going to be all right, Cath?"

She looked up again quickly. "Oh, yes, Mr Norris, it's fine, I'm fine, honestly, only I was wondering ... I was thinking, with such a lot to do and Patsy so bad at nights and every-thing, I could – would you like me to – I'm sure my Mum could manage ..." She drew in a deep breath. "Why don't I come in full time for the moment, Mr Norris? Why don't I stop the nights?"

He was astounded. "I've nowhere to put you, Cathy. Where would you sleep? I can't have Patsy upstairs all the time. It'll become a bad habit."

"I could sleep with her downstairs, I'm used to sleeping with my sisters." She got up quickly and began to clear the table with a nervous clatter. "Honestly, I wouldn't mind!"

He looked as if he was tempted, but he shook his head. "No, no, it wouldn't be right. People would gossip, a young woman living in. No." He pulled on his jacket, opening the door. "Thank you, Cath, but no."

She sighed, disappointed, as it closed behind him. Oh, well, it had been worth asking. Dispirited, she began to pile the dishes in the sink.

She was making up the big bed in the attic that she hadn't had time to do before and trying not to think of lots of things her conscience said she shouldn't, when there was a heavy creaking on the ladder and he stuck his head up through the trap. "Besides, I couldn't afford to pay you much more than I'm paying you already," he said, frowning.

Excitement fluttering in her stomach, she shook her head eagerly. "Oh, I wouldn't want any more money for it, Mr Norris! And it wouldn't be for very long, would it?" She glanced at the bed again uneasily. "Mind you, when Mrs Norris comes home, well, then we'll have to see."

He was quick to reassure her. "Oh, she'll be better when she does, she'll be her old self again, Cath, you'll see!"

She held her breath. She could see him thinking.

"Are you sure you wouldn't mind?"

She almost clapped her hands. Would she mind playing house with Mr Norris, even if only for a little while?

"No, no, really! Really, I wouldn't mind at all!"

I k-know he's getting on a bit and that, Cath," Fred said, frowning, as they wandered through the churchyard after morning service, "but I can't say I like the sound of it at all."

"Getting on a bit? He's not 'getting on', Fred Carter, that sounds as if he's old! He isn't old, he's mature, that's what he is." She linked an arm with his. "He's a real gentleman, Fred, you needn't have any worries."

He scoffed. "Oh, come on, Cath! He sells logs and potatoes and he rents a bit of land. He's g-got no money."

"He's a *gentle man*, Fred. He cares about people and he's

nice to them. That's what makes a gentleman, Fred, not money." She shrugged. "Anyway, I like him and Mrs Norris – at least, I liked her before she went all peculiar – and I really want to help."

He wasn't convinced. "And that's all there is to it?"

She dug him sharply in the ribs. "'Course it is, you silly!" Pulling her arm away, she began to run. "Anyway, he's married!" Arriving at the lichgate she paused, panting. "If you're going to keep on like this, Fred Carter, you can walk home on your own."

Mum saying 'no', though, really surprised her. It had been her mum's idea in the first place that she went to the Norris's, not hers, after all was said and done.

"I said you could go there to help, Cath, going every day, not to stay there. Who's going to help me with the little ones? Besides, things have changed a bit, haven't they?"

Cathy pouted. "You said it was time I got a job. I'm grown up now. I can't stop home for ever."

Elsie sighed. "Well, there you are then, that's the problem."

Cathy was exasperated. "*What*'s the problem?"

Elsie wiped her hands on her apron, frowning. "Look, Cath, Jim – Mr Norris – I know he's a lovely man, and he's got terrible difficulties and we all want to help, we do really, but, well, that's just what he is – a man. No, Cath, it doesn't do. You may trust him and I may trust him, but can he trust himself?"

She picked up her rolling pin. "And apart from that," she added, flouring her pastry board with a flourish, "there's your reputation to consider, the two of you alone under one roof. I'm surprised he asked you."

"He didn't, I asked if I could do it myself. I can't take it back, now, can I?"

"And what did Fred say, may I ask?"

Cathy shrugged and scuffed her shoe angrily. "Oh, Fred! What's it got to do with him?"

"You're walking out, aren't you?"

Cathy's scowl deepened. "Yes. Well, not really. Yes. Yes, I suppose."

"There's him to think about then, as well. He has got feelings!"

Cathy tried another tack. "Well, there's Patsy. Patsy needs me."

Elsie paused reflectively, and then began to roll out the pastry. Cathy spotted the weakness and leapt upon it enthusiastically. "Well, Mum, d'you see? Do you see? I've got to help her, haven't I? Poor little Patsy, just till her mum comes home! It's my Christian duty."

Elsie just tightened her lips.

Later the next day, though, she paused as they were pegging out clothes together on the line. "Where would he put you, Cath?"

"Put me?"

"This sheet needs ends-to-middling; there's a big hole worn. People's toes'll keep catching in it, make it worse. You can see to that for me tonight. Fold it so that you've got the top and bottom straight, then cut across the hole and sew the top to the bottom. Trim and hem the raw edges where you've cut to make new ends. If you have to do it for any of Mr Norris's, make sure you get them straight. " Elsie peered under the sheet at Cathy. "I mean, where would he put you to sleep?"

Cathy's hopes reawakened. "I'd sleep with Patsy, downstairs, in her room."

Elsie just nodded. "Hm."

Cathy decided not to say any more. There was something in Mum's face that said she might be weakening, and she could be very stubborn if she was annoyed.

It paid off, because next day, after she'd been for her weekly cup of tea and chinwag with her sister Nancy, she said stiffly, stirring the rabbit casserole she was making, "Well, Cath, I've decided to let you give this living-in lark a bit of a try."

Cathy leapt up and threw her arms about her neck. "It'll only be till Mrs Norris comes back!"

Elsie removed her arms firmly. "You can start on Monday and I'll want you back on Sundays, mark you. He'll have to manage for the one night." She began to bustle round the kitchen. "Nancy seems to think it'll be okay. You'll have to keep your head down, mind, make sure everybody sees that it's respectable."

"It *is* respectable!"

"And make sure it's all right with your Fred."

When she broke the news to him, she was surprised by the deepness of the frown that settled on his face and the harshness of his tone. For once, he didn't even stammer. "Just remember you're my girl, Cath."

His warning made her bristle. "And what's that supposed to mean, Fred Carter?"

He shrugged. "Just remember, that's all. That's all I want to say. We are walking out, aren't we? You said so. That means we'll be married one day."

"I'm much too young to be talking about getting wed!" She flounced away along the riverbank. "And in any case, you haven't asked."

He was the old, shy, boyish Fred once again. "I'll ask you, then, Cathy! L-let me ask you!" Catching up with her, he began to sink down on one knee on the muddy towpath.

Hastily she grabbed his elbow. "For heaven's sake, Fred. No, don't do that!" He looked utterly crestfallen and she felt sorry for him. Reaching up on tiptoes, she gave him a little peck on the cheek. "One day, Fred, I'll let you ask me; but not now. Not for a long time yet, okay?"

"He'd better not start getting any ideas, either," he muttered gruffly.

Cathy withdrew her arms and put her hands on her hips. "Fred! Drop it! Mr Norris won't be looking at me in that way! He's known me since I was a baby and he probably hasn't even realised I've grown up." She hoped he had, though. What was the point of having a crush on someone when there was no hope that he'd at least notice she was pretty? "I'm sure he just thinks of me as Elsie's little girl."

He accepted that grudgingly, and she allowed him to put his arm about her as they strolled on along the path, though she was still thinking about Mr Norris. "Mum said she'd laid her bets on it being Connie Baxter that he'd marry," she told him, "till he went headlong over Mary Buckley and Connie went off with some travelling carpet salesman instead."

His face turned grouchy. "Can we talk about something else?"

She thought she had better; he didn't seem to like the subject of Mr Norris, not at all.

M onday came round very slowly. Her mum lent her a cardboard suitcase for her clothes, and Mr Norris and Patsy picked her up with her case in the trap after his morning round.

"You take care of my girl, now, Jim," Elsie warned as he picked up the reins. Cathy opened her mouth. "Mr Norris knows what I mean, Cath. We don't want people talking. Isn't going to be easy in that cottage keeping things apart."

Embarrassment quite took her tongue away as they drove back to the cottage – his, too, and his face had reddened. Patsy fell asleep cuddled next to her, so it was rather a silent ride.

Cathy held out her hand for her suitcase when they got out of the trap, but he shook his head. "No, no – I'll carry it in for you." He felt the weight of it, grinning. "What have you got in here, Cathy? It weighs a ton!"

She bit her lip. "Is it too much, Mr Norris? I brought some bits and bobs for Patsy, and my recipe book – my clothes, of course, and my washing things. Some outdoor boots – oh, and Mum gave me a tin of cakes."

His eyes brightened as she had hoped they would. "Cakes, eh?"

She hurried to the door. "Well, tell you what, I'll put the kettle on and you can try one of them with a nice hot cup of tea. We've got a few Bath buns, some jam rock-cakes, and I think she said a cherry slice."

She found a china plate for the cakes, and a nice table-cloth; quite fine stuff, white, with a slight sheen, and an embroidered triangle of cornflowers in each corner. Mr Norris seemed surprised when he drew his chair up. "We usually only see that when we have visitors." he said.

She was upset. "Shouldn't I have used it, Mr Norris? I just thought it would look nice."

He hastened to reassure her. "It does, it does look nice. Don't worry. It's only, Mary – well, she likes to keep it for best."

"I'll put it away, then, afterwards. I'm sorry." Red-faced, she hurried from the room. "I'll just go and get Pats."

"There is another thing, Cath," he told her, as she came back. She looked at him anxiously. "It's only a little thing, but Mary wouldn't like Patsy to be called 'Pats'."

Cathy reddened still further. "Oh, I'm sorry ..."

He shook his head, himself apologetic. "No need to be sorry, I've not heard you do it before, anyway, just thought ... You know, for when she comes home; in case it becomes a habit."

V ery nice!" he said, when he got up from the table. "I was thinking, Cath – should I take a piece of that cherry slice in to Mary? If they let me see her, of course."

She removed the lid again. "Yes, of course, Mr Norris. I'll wrap it in some greaseproof so it'll keep nice and soft. When are you going in?"

He stamped to settle his boots, and she noticed that he looked anxious again, as well as drawn and tired. "I've some bits to do in the garden, then I'll load up the van, then I'll come in and change. I'll go over to the – the hospital before I drop the orders off." He pulled on his jacket. "Will you be all right, Cathy? Will you be able to cope?"

She nodded. "I'll be fine, Mr Norris."

He paused on the doorstep. "Tell you something you could do for me, Cathy, whenever you have the time – there are some flower seeds on the bottom shelf in the potting shed; can you get them sown out in trays for Mary? You know how to do it, don't you?"

She nodded. "Yes, I can do that. Patsy might like to help me."

"They're in brown envelopes, all labelled – a few annuals, mostly biennials, Antirrhinum, Sweet Williams and the like – she'll be wanting to get them all pricked out as soon as she gets back."

"Pricked out?"

"You know, put in small pots for growing on."

"Yes, Mr Norris, I know what 'pricking out' means," she said hastily, "It's just – well, it only takes a few weeks, doesn't it ...? Will she be back so soon, then, Mr Norris?"

"Oh, yes, I expect so! With all these treatments and things at their disposal, they're very optimistic."

Stifling a shameful tremor of disappointment, she managed a bright smile. "Oh, good!"

He closed the door, then opened it again on an afterthought, looking somewhat uncomfortable. "If you, you know, want a bath or anything like that in the evenings, just let me know and I'll keep out of the way."

She nodded, blushing, and scurried out into the hall.

He came in an hour or so later, and without a word shaved himself at the sink, then went up into the attic. He seemed agitated. "Do I look all right, Cathy?"

"You look very nice, Mr Norris," she told him reassuringly, though his suit was rather worn and very much out of date. "Very smart."

Patsy pattered in from the hall, dressed in her outdoor coat, as he was cleaning his best shoes. "Daddy, can you fasten my shoes?"

He looked up, startled. "Stay here with Cathy today, poppet, you can't come with me on my round – I'm going to the hospital today."

She stamped her foot. "Yes, I *am* coming, Daddy!"

Clearly harassed, he pulled on his shoes. "Not this time, lovely."

Her face puckered. "Yes, I am! I am!"

Cathy tried to soothe her. "I'll take you up to the village on my bike, Patsy, when I've finished. We need some bits and bobs from the shop."

Patsy scowled. "I don't want you." Crossing over to Jim, she leant back against his knee proprietarily, glowering at Cathy. "I want my daddy."

Deliberately avoiding Patsy's eyes, Cathy upended the washing up bowl and rinsed it. "I might even buy some sherbet lemons," she murmured reflectively, "or some sherbet, maybe, with a liquorice stick. I like those!" She stole a peek at Patsy, who was inching away from Jim just a fraction, but then he rose, and she slid back, clinging to his leg.

Cathy turned back to the window. "Or, I tell you what! I think I'll have some of those chocolate drops with hundreds and thousands on that stick all over your tongue!" She turned round, beaming, and began to unfasten her apron. "Now, if Daddy fastens your shoes for you while I pull on my coat, we could go out and sow some seeds in boxes for your mummy first, then you could come with me and you could have some too."

Jim glanced at the kitchen clock. "Cath, I'll have to go," he muttered, running his fingers through his hair. He tried to disengage Patsy's arms from his leg. "Come on, poppet, you must let go! Stay with Cathy."

Cathy took down her coat, heaving a great big sigh. "Well, it's a pity you don't want to come with me, Patsy, because I'm also going to buy a great big bottle of Dandelion-and-Burdock and I shall have to drink it all by myself." She mused, pretending to consider. "Or shall I have Cream Soda?"

Patsy loosened her grip on Jim's trousers. "Can I have Cherryade?"

The seed operation wasn't entirely successful. When Cathy tried to show Patsy how to tip the seed into her hand and sprinkle it all over the surface, she let it fall in one great cluster every time and it took Cathy a long time to try to rake up the seed with her fingernail and scatter it better, before she could finish each tray. She hadn't got very many done before Patsy got bored with the whole process, and wanted to go to the shop.

It didn't dawn on Cathy till much later, when she was panting back again on her bicycle with a Cherryade-stained Patsy on the seat, that she had forgotten to label anything.

Cathy had hoped that she would have had Patsy settled in bed by the time that Mr Norris came home, but she kept getting up again and trailing back tearfully into the kitchen, whining, "Want my daddy!" In a fit of temper, she snatched up the broom with which Cathy was trying to sweep, and swung it round above her head, knocking the bristles into the bunches of flowers that Mrs Norris had hanging from the beams to dry, and scattering fragments of dusty leaves and blossoms everywhere. Cathy grabbed the broom back from her. "Stop it, Patsy! What's your mum going to say?"

That did it. Patsy collapsed in tears. "Mummy ...!"

Cathy gave up with a heavy sigh; she was very tired. "All right, then," she acceded, "you sit there by the fire and look at a picture book. Daddy'll be home soon, don't worry."

She gazed round the messy kitchen. It was so disappointing; she'd so wanted Mr Norris to come back in and be impressed by a nice, quiet, tidy cottage with Patsy tucked up in bed and with his supper hot on the table. As it was, the kitchen was all messy and higgledy-piggledy and he was being a very long time. She peered into the oven. The rashers of bacon that she had cooked so nicely with a few tomatoes were going dry and hard. She wasn't going to be able to show off with *those*!

She was on her hands and knees with a dustpan and brush sweeping up the bits of broken stalks and tossing the contents of the dustpan into the rubbish bin when she heard the trap pull in. Patsy began to wail even louder as Mr Norris opened the door. She darted tearfully to meet him, scowling at Cathy as if she had been knocking her around. "Daddy!"

Almost absent-mindedly he took her in his arms. "'Lo, poppet." Patsy snuggled her face in his neck. He glanced at Cathy wearily, "Has she been all right?"

She nodded, unwilling to tell him how she had been struggling. "Oh, yes, Mr Norris." She shrugged. "Well, just a bit, you know – !"

Patsy pulled at his sleeve. "Will you read me my story? Cathy wouldn't read me my story."

Cathy looked askance. "You didn't ask!"

Mr Norris was troubled. "I should have said; she always has a story. Mary always reads her a story."

Cathy coloured. "Oh, I didn't know. Ours always look at their picture books all by themselves."

Patsy tugged his jacket and he sighed. "Just a minute, poppet, let me get my bearings! Let me sit down for a sec." Patsy ran off into her bedroom and he dropped wearily into the armchair. "Any chance of a cup of tea, Cath?"

Cathy hurried to the stove. "I've got tea in the pot and some bacon keeping warm. Will you have it in a sandwich, or shall I fry up an egg?"

"I don't want anything to eat, thanks. Not hungry."

That worried her, and she looked at him more closely. He was staring into the fire, his forehead furrowed. He looked terribly tired and drawn, poor thing. She put a cup of tea down by his side. "Did they let you see Mrs Norris this time, Mr Norris?"

He looked at her, almost puzzled, then shook his head before returning to his study of the smouldering coals. "They didn't, Cathy. No." After a while, unexpectedly and in a gesture that shocked Cathy, he buried his head in his hands.

Cathy agonised, twisting her apron. She didn't know whether to go and try to comfort him or what. At last, incongruously and stupidly, she said the only thing she could think of. "You didn't need the cherry slice, then, eh?"

She could have kicked herself. When he didn't respond, she was relieved; perhaps he hadn't heard her. She busied herself quietly about the kitchen, and after a few moments, he dropped his hands and reached for the cup of tea. He seemed to perk up a bit after he'd drunk it. "Better go and sort out Patsy."

She heard the mumble of his voice and then, after a while, the creaking of the ladder, and when he came back into the kitchen he'd changed into his old working clothes. He went out into the yard and came back with the feed bucket. Cathy jumped quickly to her feet. "If you show me what to do, Mr Norris, I can feed the hens."

"Eh?" He still seemed in some sort of daze. He shook his head. "No, Cathy, it's all right. They're Mary's province and – well, I know her routine. I'll show you when I've got the time, but I've got to go out and get the van loaded up ready for tomorrow anyway. You stay here and keep an eye on Patsy. We'll get things sorted out – who's doing what and all that, in a day or two." He looked into her eyes and smiled. "You've done a grand job, today, Cath. You have a rest now. Thank you. I'm very grateful."

S he was in the house at night sitting at the table with Mummy and Mummy was sewing in the light of the oil lamp and she was just as she had always been and everything was happy and Patsy realised with a huge wave of relief that the nasty time had all been one of her bad dreams. Then the lamp in the middle of the table flickered, flared up greeny and then sank again and flickered and the room all started to go dark and the hair on her neck began to prickle and she KNEW somehow what was happening and she was terrified because Brer Wolf was coming and he was BAD. It got darker and darker and the *walls of the house began to tremble and she began to cry and she got up and ran round the table to Mummy and Mummy looked up and smiled. Patsy threw herself into her lap. Mummy asked, "What is it, pet?" but her voice was different and scary and when Patsy peered up into her face she wasn't smiling at all and IT WASN'T MUMMY! It was Brer Wolf **pretending** to be Mummy.*

Closing her eyes, Patsy drew in an enormous breath and screamed.

Cathy, dragged abruptly from a deep sleep at her side, tried hard to soothe her. "It's all right, Patsy, it was just a nightmare, pet." But she wouldn't stop screaming and crying and at last the air light over the door showed the faint flickering of a candle. Mr Norris, in his pyjamas and a pullover, opened the bedroom door.

Highly distressed, Cathy gazed at him miserably. "I'm really sorry, Mr Norris ...!"

Half asleep, he ran his fingers through his hair. "'S all right, she'll get used to it." He hovered uncertainly. Realising why he was waiting, she scrambled hastily out of bed and reached for her woollen dressing gown, left thrown on top of Patsy's chest of drawers. He stared at the floor, embarrassed, until she had pulled it over her thin nightgown and slipped quietly out of the door.

Chapter 12

Jim couldn't sleep. With all the work to do about the place, he went off all right, dog-tired, but then woke every morning at about four-thirty with the dawn chorus. The only person he could talk about it to was Elsie.

"I want her to come home, Elsie."

She patted his hand. "She'll be home soon, Jim – they'll get her better soon."

"I hope so."

"Why won't they let you see her?"

"They've said I can, soon. They seem to think it's best to wait till they've sorted her out a bit. They're trying various things."

Elsie stroked his hand. "Chin up, Jim. They'll be doing their best."

"Aye, yes." He shook himself. "They've got her now on some heavy stuff to sedate her so she sleeps a lot; that's another reason. That's what they say. They still haven't got to the heart of the problem, anyway."

He stared bitterly into the empty fireplace. "It's even worse there than I thought, you know, Elsie. I know now why they say 'It's Bedlam' when there's a rumpus somewhere; it's the noise. Even going up to see the doctor, there's shouting there all the time, there's banging, there's people running, there's keys rattling, there's crying – there's laughing sometimes, and that's worse, because there's nothing funny, it's just mad laughter. There's this woman there that keeps shrieking like some sort of demented bird."

There was a catch in Elsie's voice. "Oh, Jim ..."

"I can't bear it." He shook his head. "I hear the rooks cawing in the tall trees round the cottage, you know, Elsie, and the sounds they make are the cries of that woman, and sometimes – sometimes I think it's Mary calling. I hear the dogs from Barrows Farm barking across the fields and they remind me that there's this other woman in that place who can't do anything but run around barking at everyone just like a dog, for pity's sake – and the other poor people who stare at her with their pale faces and their eyes all dull and their hair chopped off all raggedy, they're terrible lost souls and nobody seems to care. And I think: *Mary's in there. My little Mary.*"

There was little she could say to comfort him.

He made an effort to change the subject. "Your Cathy's doing well."

She smiled, pleased. "Is she? I'm glad. She's a good girl."

"Oh, yes. She's getting the hang of a few jobs in the garden, now, too, so that's a great help. I'm going to show her how to see to the hens so she can take care of them for Mary; she's particularly fond of the broodies – think she's really looking forward to when the chickens hatch. She's a lot to do in the cottage as well, though. I hope it's not too much for her. Patsy – well, she's playing up for her no end, I'm afraid, Elsie."

"She'll cope."

Cathy had the towels warming by the fire and was trying all the songs she knew to get Patsy smiling and out of the tub – *What a Friend we have in Jesus, Jesus Bids Me Shine, Clementine, Molly Malone, When Father Papered the Parlour* – and even *With his Head Tucked Underneath His Arm*, which she didn't think was really very suitable. Her throat was really dry with the effort. "Come on, lovey, I've got lots of jobs to do, and that water must be stone cold!"

Grizzling, Patsy clung obstinately to the sides of the tub. Cathy tried to haul her out and she started to yell, pumping frantically with her knees and dousing Cathy with soapy water.

"Oi, stop it, you little pest!" She dried her face with a corner of one of the towels. Her hair was dangling over her forehead in wet rats' tails. Exasperated, she reached for Patsy. "No, that's enough now, come on – you're too big a girl for this." Grasping her by the upper arms, she pulled her out, dripping, and set her down firmly on the floor. Patsy lashed out, catching her on the side of the head, and before she knew what she was doing, Cathy had smacked her back. Patsy howled.

Almost crying herself, Cathy glanced at the clock. Mr Norris would be back from his round any minute and she really didn't want him to catch them like this. She held out her arms. "Oh, come on, lovey, I'm sorry. Come on, come here ..."

With a roar, Patsy pushed her hard in the chest and before Cathy had recovered her wind, she went scampering out of the back door. Grabbing the towels from the clotheshorse, Cathy hurried after her.

She found her in the henhouse, squatting like a naked hen on one of the nesting shelves and clutching one of the broodies. She had left the gate to their run open, and the other hens were scattered far and wide, foraging happily under the apple trees in the orchard and even, a couple of them, setting off towards the lane. Cathy bit her lip; which came first – the chicken or the Patsy?

Patsy was shivering. Right then – that settled that. She ducked inside, holding up the biggest towel ready to trap her. "Right then, come on. Game's up."

Driving back round the bend towards the cottage, Jim was a bit surprised to find Mary's two favourite hens – the two bronze-gold Sussex pullets she called Henrietta and Sophia – stalking down the centre of the lane with their little heads turning and their beady eyes peering round inquisitively, like a couple of old biddies out with their shopping baskets. Drawing Meg to a standstill, he clambered out of the trap. "Where are you off to, then, you two?" Holding out his arms, he tried to shepherd them back towards the gate but, squawking loudly, they set off up one of the banks, making off through a hole in the hedge. He turned back to the trap empty-handed. "Damn and blast!"

Bill, the postman, came puffing up behind the trap on his bicycle. He held out a letter. "Want to take this from me, Jim?"

Jim took the letter, stuffing it into his pocket. "Thanks, Bill. See any bloody hens on your travels, try to hang on to them, they're mine!"

Leaving Meg still in the trap in the yard, he set off at a trot through the orchard towards the henhouse. He could hear Patsy squealing with laughter somewhere among the trees and Cathy's voice calling angrily, "Come here, you little beast!" Sounded as if she was leading poor Cath a right royal old dance. Poor kid. It must be a bit hard.

It was chaos. Hens seemed to be all over the place. Patsy, wrapped in towels, was sitting up in the corner of the lowest bough of one of the Worcester Permains and as he came out into the clearing, she crowed again with delight and almost fell out from the tree as Cathy, hurtling out from behind a gnarled old James Greave in pursuit of a brown Leghorn, launched herself at it in a rugby tackle. "Got you!"

With a triumphant squawk it flapped its way out of her enfolding arms and made off towards the other end of the orchard. Despite everything, Jim grinned. "Hey, you lot! What's going on?"

S he'll have got the old broody rattled, pity about that. They don't like being disturbed when they're sitting." Jim jiggled Patsy, who was sitting on his knee. "Eh? You hear that? You mustn't disturb Mummy's hens, Patsy. You want us to have lots of baby chicks, don't you?"

Cathy hung her head. "I'm sorry, Mr Norris."

"At least we got them all back, so you mustn't worry." He squeezed Patsy. "And you must be good for Cath."

Cathy folded her hands. She was so anxious that she should please him. "So tell me about the feed for them again, Mr Norris ...?"

He repeated the instructions. "Dry mash all the time, a bit of grain at dinnertime, and wet mash in the morning, Cath. You can throw in a few scraps and put in a drop of milk." He drained his cup. "Well, better get on ..."

The envelope Bill had given him was in his jacket pocket. "Forgot about this ..." After reading the first few lines of the enclosed letter, his heart began to leap. Grasping Cathy by the waist he swung her off her feet "They're moving her! They're moving her! Thank God! Thank God for the Old Dragon! Thank God, Mary, for your Aunty May!"

Cathy crimsoned, beaming. "Oh, Mr Norris, I am so happy for you about that!"

Embarrassed, he set her back down on her feet. "Sorry, Cath," he murmured, grinning, "Probably shouldn't have done that! Listen to this, though! Listen to this! She's to be moved to some private place called Leigh House."

Infected by his happiness, Cathy clapped her hands. "Oh, Mr Norris! That is grand! Oh! When?"

He scanned the letter quickly. "Um – Thursday."

"Ooh, that's not far off, then."

He read the words out to her carefully. "*Suitable arrangements for the transfer have been arranged for Thursday next, at some time closely approaching midday. Godbourne is, of course, much further afield ...*"

Cathy looked askance. "Godbourne!"

" *...but I feel that the advantages far outweigh the disadvantages; I am given to understand that the quality of both care and surroundings is of far superior class to that of her present situation.*" He whistled with excitement. "Do you hear that? It's far superior, Cath!"

"Ooh, well, I say ...!"

He resumed his reading, grinning. *"I understand that visiting takes place on Wednesday and Sunday afternoons. However, please note that the Hospital authorities have requested that no visit be made during the first six weeks. –* Blast it! I still won't be able to see her for a while. Oh, hell." He glanced apologetically at her. "Sorry, Cath."

She shook her head. "Oh, dear, Mr Norris, that's a shame!" She suppressed a little shiver of relief.

Too overwrought to keep still, he walked round and round the table, reading. *"I shall be in direct communication with the authorities there, who will keep me fully informed. In particular, I have asked them to let me know the decision that the Board makes at the end of the six months. It is, of course, my fervent hope that my niece will make a full and satisfactory recovery, and will be released to us then."* He felt like jumping up and down again. *"Yours sincerely, May A. Buckley (Miss)"*

Cathy turned to the washing up reflectively. "Does that mean, Mr Norris, if it's so far away – does it mean you won't be able to visit Mrs Norris often even when they let you go? Not very much?" Catching sight of her bright eyes and flushed cheeks in the windowpane, she ducked her head to the sink.

"Eh?" He shook his head firmly. "Oh, I shall go every week, Cath, twice a week, as far as I can." This had made his mind up; he'd have to see about finding a van. "No stopping me, that's if you don't mind hanging on to Patsy. Hell of a long way, but worth it, though, eh, Cath, if she's more comfortable? They don't even call it an asylum. And I expect they've got much better ways of helping her."

Cathy nodded thoughtfully. "Oh, sure to have, being private, sure to have, oh, yes." Seeing that he was preparing to go out into the yard, she dropped the dish mop and dried her hands quickly on the towel. "Oh, Mr Norris, by the way, I've been thinking ..."

"What's that, Cath?"

"Well, it's for Patsy, Mr Norris, to cheer her up. It'll be her birthday, won't it, in a few weeks' time?"

He frowned. "Will it?"

She nodded, certain of her fact. "Oh, yes, the fifth of May. I know it is, because it's the day after our Tommy, only he's two years older, and our mum always sends Patsy a card."

Mr Norris looked mortified. "The fifth ... So it is! Hell! Good thing you reminded me, Cathy, Mary always looks after things like that." He shook his head worriedly. "What shall I get her? A new dolly, or something? What does she want, do you know?"

"I don't know, I'll try to think of something. I'll find out. But, what I was thinking, though, Mr Norris ... why don't I do a party for her?"

"A party?"

She nodded, carried away by the thought "Yes, you know, make a nice cake with some candles, and some jelly and sandwiches and things? Play some games? I could get our Tommy up and our Chrissie and Pauline, maybe a few other little friends."

Mr Norris looked amazed. "Would you?"

"Of course I would!"

He shook his head. "Oh, you are smashing, Cath."

Y ou are smashing, Cath." It didn't have quite the same ring to it, when Fred said it, though it meant quite a lot. He blushed almost to his eyebrows as he mumbled and Cathy squeezed his hand. He slowed almost to a halt. "Can I–c-can I a-ask you now, Cath?"

"Ask me?"

He reddened even further. "Yes, you know ... what I said before."

She felt a flurry of panic. "No! For goodness' sake, not now, Fred. Not yet!"

He scowled, his eyes hardened, and for a moment she was startled to discover a glimpse of a different Fred. "Well, when, then?"

She shook her heads, flustered. "Oh, I don't know, Fred. Ages, yet. I'm not ready. I've told you – I'm too young!"

"But you do promise?"

Pulling away her hand, she started to run. "Come on, Fred. It's such a nice breezy day – let's go up to the windmill." He hesitated for a moment, still looking dour and tense and then seemed to shrug, his expression softening. He set off after her, and soon overtook her, laughing in boyish triumph as he passed. "Come on, Cath!" he shouted, leaping over the final gate and racing towards the windmill. Drawing himself up towards the platform, he paused, peering down towards her and holding out his hand. "Come on!"

Fred's arm was tight about her waist as they clung together on the narrow platform, the wind in their hair and their faces and the huge revolving sails only just missing their heads. She could see for miles.

"Corey's cottage is up for rent, Cath." Fred shouted.

"Is it?" She turned her head away, the wind carrying away her voice.

"I can afford it. I've a trade, Cath, now my apprenticeship's over, Mr Brown's taken me on."

"Good ... Good, Fred! Congratulations!" she shouted, refusing to pick up his cue. Tightly gripping the steel latticework with both hands, she leant back as far as she could against the guardrail, gazing up at the blue sky and the scurrying clouds. "Come here, Fred!" she ordered, laughing. "Come and do this!" Not wishing to be outdone, he clambered across. "Look up through the sails. The clouds are standing still; I'm moving!"

"So they are!" He leant back even further, so far that she loosened one hand to clutch his sleeve. "See, Cath? We're going round and round ...!"

She screamed with delight. "Round and round and down and down ... I'm flying, Fred!" She paused abruptly, feeling a sudden wave of nausea. "Pull me back, Fred. I don't like it. I think I'm going to be sick."

Mr Norris's present to Patsy was a furry toy fox. Mrs Bevis at the corner shop, whose son-in-law was a traveller for Fox's Umbrellas, had managed to get it for him. It was meant to be an advertising fox, but Patsy wasn't to know that. It had lovely, thick silky fur and a magnificent tail that curled around it as it sat. Cathy glanced across at Patsy, who was struggling with the last bit of wrapping. "Shall I do that for you, pet?"

"I'm doing it on my own." The last shreds of paper fell away.

Mr Norris grinned. "Do you like him, poppet?"

Patsy shrugged.

"He's lovely!" Cathy leant over. "What are you going to call him, Patsy?"

"I don't know." She pushed her chair away from the table. "Can I go now?"

Mr Norris looked a little disappointed, though he whispered, "I think she likes it," to Cathy as the door closed behind the little girl.

She looked disconsolately at the present she had bought for Patsy, now lying neglected on the table. She'd been so pleased with it. It was a tin moneybox shaped like a black man in a little waistcoat, red tasselled cap and trousers. Tommy had chosen it, really, but she had thought it was ever so amusing. You put your money on the palm of his hand and turned a key and he slipped the coin into his mouth. The little man had cost her quite a lot.

She moved him onto the dresser.

M r Norris said the forecast for the day of the party was for the wind to drop and for it to get fine and sunny, which was good, as if it had been rainy Cathy wasn't sure how she would have done; there wasn't room in the kitchen for all the children she had invited. She felt quite excited. Now Mr Norris would see how well she could do things – how nicely she could cope.

She was humming to herself and putting the final touches to the party table, when Jim burst in hastily from the garden early in the afternoon. "A sheet – quick, Cath – give me a sheet or something, quick!"

She turned, startled. "A sheet, Mr Norris? Why ever do you want a sheet?" He was rummaging in her washing basket. She frowned. "That's all waiting to be ironed, Mr Norris."

"Don't need it ironed, I just need – Ahah! This'll do nicely!" Dragging out a clean white double sheet, he gathered it up in his arms and hurried back out of the door.

Curious, Cathy hurried after him. Following the sound of children's squeals and laughter she made her way through the orchard into the sunshine at the far side, where she could see Tommy and the other children tiptoeing in a giggling, whispering gaggle along one of the paths winding between the vegetable and flowerbeds.

She drew in a breath, about to call, "Mr Norris?" then shrieked with surprise and alarm as a huge white flapping object rose from a clump of bushes just in front of her. Seeing it, the children screamed wildly with excited laughter and tore off down the path.

"Whoooooooo ... Whooooooo ...!" The flapping object loomed over her for a moment in ghostly fashion, then pounced, enveloping her in a flapping sheet. "Woooooo-oooo!" it howled, pressing her against its hard chest. Her knees suddenly weak, she struggled, but only feebly, laughing. "Mr Norris!" Almost hysterical with laughter, the children scattered.

The spectral shape, releasing her all too soon, ducked down amongst the beanpoles, and vanished. Tommy, braver than the rest, scurried over and peered through the beanpoles, then ducked inside their arch. He emerged at the far end, calling, "Nope! Not here! He's gone!"

The children set off once more in a tiptoeing, shushing, giggling group. Cathy looked around like the rest of them, but she couldn't spot where Mr Norris was hiding, so, reluctantly she turned back to the house.

Goodness, he was ever so strong, and ever so tall. Ooh, that had been really nice.

He caught up with her in the yard, breathless and grinning, pulling off the sheet, and she pretended to scold him. "Honestly, Mr Norris, enough to give any one of them nightmares, give *me* nightmares, never mind Patsy!"

He went in first, crossing quickly to rinse his hot face at the sink. "Whew, warm work!" He reached for the towel. "Where *is* Patsy?"

As she came in from the yard, Cathy gasped, frozen in the doorway. "Oh, Mr Norris!"

He turned, puzzled. The carefully prepared birthday table had been ruined. The jug of orange juice had been smashed and liquid dripped from the best tablecloth. The jelly was splattered all over the floor. The birthday cake with its candles and its pink and white icing had been totally demolished. The wrapping paper had been torn from the little packages that the children had carefully placed on the sideboard ready to be opened after tea, and the little gifts they had contained had been dropped and trodden underfoot. Bits of food and broken crockery were scattered everywhere.

"Oh, Mr Norris." Cathy could have wept.

She had never seen him look so cross before; he was quite scary. His muscles tightened, his face went quite white and he opened his mouth and roared. "PATSY?! Where is she? Little demon!"

He found her at last, sobbing bitterly, wedged in between the side of her bed and the wall, and despite his anger, the sight of the poor, frantic, tear-stained little scrap made him feel great pity for her. Half angry, half sympathetic, he tried to winkle her out. "Come here. Come here, Patsy! Come on, poppet."

She was quite hysterical. "I don't want *you*. I don't want *Cathy*. I don't want *anybody!*"

Cathy found the sheet mud-stained, but not torn, and, without resentment, put it through the wash again next day. Straightening from his digging, Jim caught sight of her struggling to pin the billowing linen on to the washing line and couldn't help but notice the rounded, youthful figure revealed by the tugging breeze. Directed by a sudden gust of wind, a sheet enveloped her face. Disentangling herself, she caught his eyes. For a brief second, something seemed to hang between them in the air, and then the moment passed. Jim grinned, and turned back to his work.

Chapter 13

Not wanting Cathy to see how nervous he was, Jim grinned as widely as he could and gave a 'thumbs-up' sign as he cycled off out of the yard to get the first of the two buses that would take him for his first visit to Leigh House.

He came back grim-faced and silent, the bunch of daffodils and narcissi that he had picked for Mary now wilted in his hand. He wondered now why he had brought them all the way back; he couldn't have been thinking clearly – they'd only go on the compost heap. Changing quickly out of his best clothes, he took the flowers off into the garden with barely a hello to Cathy. He wasn't in the mood to talk.

At suppertime, as he took his place at the table and reached for the jar of pickle, she asked him carefully, "So how was it, Mr Norris? Is it a much nicer place?"

"Nicer?" He was startled. "Yes, it's nicer there, Cath, I suppose – if you can call a place like a mental hospital a nice place at all."

She coloured. "I don't suppose you can, no, not at all."

Jim prodded with his fork at the food on his plate. Nicer? It had still looked grim and miserable to him. The windows had still been high up and barred; it had still smelled institutional, of cold boiled vegetables, mince and antiseptic, though there had been a vase of tall blue larkspur and gypsophila on the reception desk, which made that area slightly sweeter. The corridors had still echoed, though not as badly because in parts at least they had carpet strips along them. There had still been distant, disturbing cries and shouts and laughter. There had still been locked doors.

In some ways, though, he had to say it was better. There had been grass outside instead of concrete, though not well kept. It needed scarifying and a good dose of fertiliser. There had been curtains at most of the windows. The nursing staff he had passed in the corridor had glanced at him, and some had nodded. There was some sort of a dayroom that he had passed, with carpet and a piano and one or two potted cyclamens and a Mother-in-Law's Tongue, but as far as he could see, everyone in there was slumped in a sort of drugged state in the chairs set closely side-by-side around the walls. The nursing staff still had whistles pinned to their uniform jackets, and the men had what seemed to be small truncheons attached to their belts with chains, but their uniforms had been clean and most had had reasonably kindly faces. The receptionist had called him 'sir' and had sent for an attendant to lead him to up to the Chief Medical Officer's room.

Nicer? Yes, it probably was, fair play.

Cathy leant forward, clearly unable to resist probing further. "So, did they let you see Mrs Norris?" His frown grew deeper. "Oh, Mr Norris. I'm so sorry."

He glanced up, surprised. "No, no, Cath. No. They did."

Her eyes widened. "They did? Oh!" She sat back, looking a bit flustered. "And how was she, then, Mr. Norris? Was she all right? Is her room nice? Is she getting better? Bet she was pleased to see you, wasn't she?"

He hesitated. "Not exactly, no." He had no clear picture of the room she'd been in, because he couldn't get the sight of her out of his head. That unkempt, pale-faced little woman, driven by some incomprehensible fear, hate and horror; she hadn't been his Mary. Two or three minutes, that's all they had granted him, then they'd whisked him away in order to sedate her. The sight of him had seemed to set her off in a tizzy. He was deeply ashamed that as she had lunged him, he had flinched. "I couldn't see her for very long, mind."

She shook her head sympathetically. "Ah, that's a shame. It was probably her medicine, wasn't it? I mean, that made her seem a bit quiet? If she didn't seem very excited to see you?"

He nodded soberly. "Could have been, yes." He tried to summon a smile. "Mm. Probably."

"So ..." She toyed with her plate. "Perhaps she's best left alone? Perhaps you won't be going again for a while? I mean, until she's a bit better – it's an awful long way."

He was shocked by the suggestion. "Oh, no. I shall keep on going."

She coloured, biting her lip. "Of course."

"They're very optimistic, you know, very. I saw the Chief Medical Officer."

"That's good."

He forced an optimistic smile onto his face. "Oh, yes, she'll be right as nine pence by the time her assessment comes. They'll have it all sorted by then, don't you worry."

She rose clearing the dishes with a bit of a clatter. "Will you have some pudding, Mr. Norris? I've got a rice pudding with plenty of nice brown skin."

For once, he didn't care about pudding. He was concentrating on Mary. "Oh, yes, Mary'll be home for Harvest, Cathy, mark my words," he promised her with barely wavering confidence. "My Mary'll be coming home."

Nothing was going to stop Jim going to where Mary was. To his disappointment, however, he couldn't manage the journey to Godbourne more than once a week; the journey by bus took up far too much time, and it wasn't possible to get a connection on a Wednesday or a Sunday. He let it be known about the village that he was looking for a van and it didn't take long for one to materialise. As he popped into the Bear, parched, one Friday evening, for a swift half before cycling back to the cottage after another unsatisfactory and depressing visit, there was a bit of cheering news. Tom Perry, the landlord, nodded at him over the bar.

"Found you a motor, Jim, if you want it. Sol Carter says his cousin Will over at Upper Millbury has got an uncle with a Morris commercial he's looking to get rid of; not in bad nick, he says. Doesn't want much for it, not too good at starting on a cold morning and a tendency to conk out occasionally, need to keep your cranking handle handy, but Bill at the Black Cat Garage says he'll look her over for you, hopefully should do you well enough for the time being."

Jim's face brightened. "Thanks, Tom."

Tom stuck his cigarette behind his ear and returned to polishing glasses. "Could do yourself a good turn, there, actually, Jim."

Heartened, Jim took a deep draft of his ale. "How's that, Tom?"

"Reg Carter – that's young Will's uncle – he's got the fishmonger's and greengrocer's in Middle Millbury ..."

Jim nodded. "I know it. Aye."

"Don't deliver there, do you?"

"No, don't go that far."

"Thought not. Well, Old Reg, he's got a bit of brass, you know, and he's just bought two other shops, one in Chetstock and another in Hinton St Andrew. Supplies might be getting difficult, things going on the way they are with all this talk of war. There's going to be a big demand for veg and stuff, that's what I was thinking. Want to get in there, that's what you want to do." Draping the tea towel round his neck, he laid his hand on the pump. "Taking the other half, Jim?"

Musing, Jim moved back a little to let others crowd in alongside the bar. "'Lo, Sid, Arthur, yes, get in there, Ted." The pub was getting more popular then ever with the increasing prospect of the possibility of another war with Germany. Some of the younger lads were quite excited and there was a lot of bravado about volunteering, and nattering about whether there would be conscription, who'd be exempt, having to get the larders stocked up, on and on it went. Old Charlie Coons and Tich Price were in their element, regaling all and sundry with their tales of the Great War. They were in the far corner rabbiting away as Jim looked over into the snug. Charlie had lost two brothers, one at the Somme and one at Paschendale, and Tich had lost his younger brother, his eldest brother, two cousins, a second cousin and an uncle – and one of his legs, too, somewhere along the line.

Jim waited till Tom had served the lads their pints, then moved back closer. "Hinton, you said? And Chetstock?"

Tom nodded. "Aye. Could do it, if you had a van."

"Think he might do a trade-off, Tom? I mean, my produce for his van?"

Tom shrugged. "He might."

Jim held out his glass. "Thanks, Tom. It's worth a shot."

Cathy put her teacup down with a disgruntled clatter. "She's just a spoilt little cow, Mum, honestly! She's not only rude and horrible to me, but to poor Mr Norris, too, who's only doing his best. Sometimes she just clings to her daddy and at other times she shouts and calls him names and even kicks him! Once, she bit his arm."

Mum drew in her breath. "What did he do?"

"Nothing! He didn't even slap her legs. I would have done – or bitten her back!"

"Dear, dear!"

"She won't let me dress her, and goes about wearing the strangest collection of things, she makes me really ashamed. The other day, I caught her setting off to the village in her mum's old pink caminicks and nothing else but a hat! She refuses to tidy up, and if I get cross with her for refusing, she just gets into a huge tantrum and kicks and throws everything all over the floor. She won't eat properly, no matter what I try to tempt her with. She fights and yells and screams nearly every bedtime, just won't simmer down. Often she's still awake when Mr Norris comes in from doing his last chores – then she wakes up again at least once during the night, and won't let me settle her, and poor Mr Norris has to drag himself down from the attic.

Mum gave her an odd look. "Does he now ...!"

"I've got quite used to slipping out and sitting in the kitchen with a cup of cocoa until she's dropped off and he can go back up to bed."

It was very dispiriting. All in all, she hadn't managed to create the nice, warm, smooth-running little home for Mr Norris that she'd dreamed about – and it was mostly Patsy's fault.

Her mum sighed. "Well, you must remember she's a poor little thing who's had an awful time and doesn't understand what's happened. She's probably a bit disturbed, and no wonder. She had a very nasty experience and she's missing her mum. She's greatly to be pitied, Cath."

Cathy sighed. "I know, I know. I do try to be patient. I'm sorry, Mum. It's just nice to get it off my chest."

Her mum nodded sympathetically. "I know." She rose to put the kettle on again and peered through the window before she came back for the pot. "She seems to be playing quite nicely with the kiddies out there at the moment. The twins won't stand for any nonsense. Will you be having another cup of tea?"

It was good to be sitting having a chinwag like two old friends and Mr Norris shouldn't be back for a little while yet. Cathy beamed contentedly. "Oh, go on, then – why not!"

Mum stirred the pot vigorously. "Let that brew." She pushed the plate of biscuits closer to Cathy. "Have another Shrewsbury biscuit, pet – go on, do. If they go in for rationing like they say they will, Lord knows when you'll get another one. There's half a pound of butter in that batch!"

Cathy shivered. "Don't like to think about it. Don't want us to go to war."

Mum shrugged. "No, we all hope we don't, but you have to stand up to people like that Hitler. They say Mr Chamberlain's going to go over there and sort things out."

Cathy preferred to think about Mr Norris. "He was ever so excited, Mum."

Mum frowned, confused. "Who was?"

"Mr Norris, of course." She nibbled her biscuit. "Going to be seeing Mrs Norris again. They promised."

"Thought you were talking about Mr Chamberlain!" Mum shook her head. "Yes, of course. Poor Jim, he's waited a long time. Been ever so down. I hope it goes well for him." She picked up the teapot. "Here – give us your cup."

Cathy pushed her cup across the table. "Here, Mum, you know how Mrs Norris is the Miss Buckleys' niece ...?"

"Yes ...?"

"Well, how did she come to live with them? How did she meet Mr Norris?"

Mum puffed out her cheeks, filling Cathy's cup. "Ooh, well, let's see ..." She passed it back to her, frowning. "Mary; well, her mum was their youngest sister, Maud. Her father died in France, poor man and then blow me if her mum didn't go as well, a year or two later. A weak heart from having rheumatic fever when she was a child, Nancy said, though the gossip was it was a broken heart."

She picked up her chair. "Let's go and sit outside, Cath – sun's all round the back and it's too nice to waste while it's here."

They found space for their chairs outside the back door. The small, brick-walled yard was littered with the kiddies' toys and the air smelt of the bleached washing which hung like a full set of rigging on the line, but there were geraniums and petunias in old tin cans set along every available ledge and on the ground beneath the cottage wall. "Jim brought me those," her mum said, nodding at them. "Bless him! Aren't they nice!"

She leant back, sighing and closing her eyes against the glare. "What was I saying?"

Cathy rolled down her stockings. "About Mrs Norris and –"

Mum opened one eye. "Eh? Oh, yes." She nodded. "You want to look after those stockings, going to be hard to come by in a while, I hear." She closed her eyes again. "Well, let me see ... Mary's dad was a charming man by all accounts, very good-looking, but according to Nancy, there was no getting away from the fact that he was seen as a bit of a wastrel, a man who threw away money. He was the kind who's full of good ideas that come to nothing, do you know what I mean?" Cathy nodded.

"They put up a huge fight against her marrying him, the Buckleys, and there was nothing wrong with the family he came from; it was because if she married him her financial prospects looked rotten. Nancy says she's often heard Miss Buckley say – and in front of Mary too – that he'd thrown away Maud's money, mortgaged the house, left her to bring up her little girl on next to nothing."

She shook her head. "I suppose you should feel sorry for them; they had the same sort of battle when it came to Mary."

Cathy sprang rapidly to Mr Norris's defence. "But Mr Norris isn't like that – he's a lovely man!"

Her mum clicked her tongue. "Of course he is, of course! Not the same kettle of fish at all, but, like I said, it's history repeating itself in a way. No prospects, no money, and they wanted better things."

Cathy frowned, scratching at an itch on her foot. "Didn't Mr Norris's family once own Barrows?"

Mum nodded. "Oh, yes, indeed they did, they were quite well-to-do, farmed Barrows Farm for years. Very well respected family. The Buckleys mightn't have put up such a fuss if Jim had still had Barrows, but he didn't."

She opened her eyes as a door slammed inside and Chrissie and Patsy tumbled out into the yard squealing with excitement, and she straightened, pointing back at the kitchen door. "Out, Chrissie! I told you to play in the front; we're talking here. We want quiet."

Giggling, Patsy pressed against Cathy's knee. "Can we have a biscuit?"

Cathy looked at her mum.

"Oh, yes, go on then! Just one. Then out!" They watched as the little girls ran back into the house. "Doesn't seem too bad?" Cathy's mum murmured.

Cathy sighed. "Just wish she'd be like this all the time."

Her mum sipped her tea, resuming her train of thought. "He lost his dad in the war, too, you know, Jim did, when he was only a lad. He was older than Mary was, when it happened, of course. Lost the farm, too, though it wasn't for want of trying. Most of the lads who'd worked on the farm had gone, too. Jim was always a hard worker, learnt a great deal from his dad – but well, he was enthusiastic rather than experienced. It wasn't his fault."

Cathy was fascinated. "Poor Mr Norris! So what did he do then?"

"Well, he worked as a general farm labourer at Burrows at first, when old Mr Harfield – that's the father of John Harfield, who's the farmer now – when he bought it, then he got to be the stockman, but he was always more interested in the growing side, was Jim. He persuaded Mr Harfield to rent him a few acres of land and a small cottage, so long as he kept lending him a hand. He still does some work for John Harfield from time to time, as you probably know. Built up his small-holding, started delivering ... things were hard for us all. Jim did very well to keep going."

Cathy wasn't satisfied. "But how did he meet Mrs Norris?"

Mum stretched. "Ooh, now let's see ... well, I remember when she first came; she'd have been about seven or eight. She used to spend most of her time in the kitchen with Nancy, and who could blame her? Losing her mum and getting the Miss Buckleys instead!" She sighed. "They were there for her when she needed them, though. It must have been hard for them too."

"What was she like?"

"Who, Mary?" Mum chuckled again. "Well, you wouldn't have known she was going to turn out a beauty. I can picture her now. Scrawny little scrap – and she always had pink eyes and a pink nose from crying, poor little soul. Like a skinny little rabbit, she was." She chuckled. "Turned out to be a real little daisy, though. All the lads in the village fancied her, but her aunties kept her tucked right away. Used to play the piano a lot, and they let her play the organ and for church socials. I often sat with Nancy in the kitchen listening to her playing in the other room. I think that's where Jim first saw her – there, or at a social. He suddenly got quite keen on delivering and you know what he's usually like!"

Cathy reflectively rubbed one of the petals from a nearby geranium over her lips. "Will Mrs Norris come into money one day? From her aunties?"

"Well, there's nobody else." Mum shook her head. "I'm sure they think that's why Jim married her, but it wouldn't have occurred to him – Jim's not like that. Mind you – it will come in handy. I know he worries about things. Poor Jim."

Draining her cup, she stood up decisively, rubbing her back. "Anyway – cutting a long story short 'cause I don't know the ins and outs of it and in any case I ought to get on ... Jim and Mary started seeing each other on the quiet, and then eventually he went to see the Miss Buckleys, to get their permission to propose, and, of course, they said no. Mary was furious. Fought them tooth and nail, she did, and then as soon as she was old enough, she marched him off to the Registry Office and well, you know the rest."

Cathy breathed out a long sigh. "I call that really romantic."

Jim's deep voice echoed inside the kitchen. "Anyone at home?"

Mum craned her neck to see. "That's Jim now."

Hurriedly, Cathy began to pull up her stockings. "Has that

geranium made my lips go red?"

Mum gave her a quizzical look. "You're not being a little bit silly, are you, now, pet?"

Blushing a little, Cathy shook her head. "Of course not!" Straightening her skirt, she sighed dramatically. "Oh well! Back to the grindstone, eh?"

Reg Carter was pleasingly open to Jim's offer to trade. They agreed that Jim would provide what he could for his shops for as long as it took to pay back the value of the van and then see how it went. Reg said that if he was pleased with the fruit and veg Jim let him have, and if his prices were right, he'd consider making a regular order for delivery, which augured well for the future, though Jim knew he'd be hard pressed to keep up regular deliveries for three shops without buying in from a wholesaler sometimes himself, and then what profit would there be? But he wasn't going to worry about that just yet.

Bill at the Black Cat said it wasn't a bad van, even if it had rather dodgy suspension. It didn't look bad, with cream body-work and a green chassis, but it was more than a bit rattly. Cathy was really quite excited about it, and Patsy clamoured to come with him whenever she heard him starting up the engine. She liked climbing up the big step into the passenger seat.

It grieved him deeply that he couldn't show it to Mary.

Chapter 14

For a few weeks they didn't let him see her, and then at last they said he could pop in. "Now be warned, Mr Norris," the orderly said as he led Jim up the staircase; "she's in a calm state at the moment so we have her in the day room, but she's under very heavy medication."

He clutched the bunch of roses and love-in-a-mist that he had picked for Mary tightly, feeling a mixture of exhilaration and trepidation. "Oh. So what does that mean, then?"

"Just that she might not be very responsive, Mr Norris." He held out an arm to hold Jim back as an aide led a shambling patient past. The patient, an elderly man with a turkey's scrawny neck, a huge Adam's apple and bulging, staring eyes, craned his neck to stare back at Jim over his shoulder as he and the orderly walked on after them. The narrow strip of faded crimson carpet down the centre of the corridor sat incongruously with the locked doors on either side, each with a wired grill or peephole, and each one firmly closed.

At last the orderly reached for the bunch of keys at his belt. He studied Jim's face carefully. "You ready?" Jim nodded, aware that his hands were shaking slightly.

The room he was ushered into was high ceilinged and quite big, with curtained windows set high up in the wall. Upright chairs had been set beneath them all along the walls, several of them occupied by dull-eyed women staring silently into space. It was relatively quiet, but for one woman who was crouched in a corner of the room, sobbing heartbrokenly. For a horrible moment, Jim thought that the woman might be Mary, but then he saw that the woman was grey-haired and old.

A long table had been set up at the far end of the room, and a group of patients and aides was gathered round it. One of those sitting with her back to Jim peered back, her face

127

lighting up with excitement, and rising quickly to her feet, hurried over to Jim, clutching him tightly by the arm.

"Here he is, here he is, I told you!" She reached up, stroking his face. She was thin, middle-aged, gap-toothed and exhausted-looking. "You will tell me, won't you? You're the only one who knows."

"Sit down, Bessie." She struggled against the aide who caught hold of her, not ungently, and gazed at Jim with desperation in her eyes. "Please! Tell me where my baby is, my baby ...!"

Jim wanted to say something, but he felt helpless. "I don't know, I'm sorry."

"Here she is, Mr Norris," the orderly said. "Here she is."

Despite his deep anticipation, it took a long moment or two to register that the woman he was looking at was Mary. Like the other patients, she was wearing a faded and ill-fitting grey dress. Her lovely hair had been cut short and was frizzed up somehow all about her head in a dry, dark sort of halo and she looked pale and thin and grey. In front of her on the table were strands of raffia and a partially started basket frame, but her hands were idle. She didn't register his presence, but sat gazing vacant-eyed and loose-lipped at the basket.

His lips were dry. He took a step closer. "Mary? Mary? It's me. It's Jim." She went on staring at the basket. "It's Jim, Mary."

The aide standing near her leant over her, and tried to rally her in an over-cheerful way. "Well now, Mary, it's your husband, Mary. Come along, come on!"

She didn't flicker an eyelash. It made him want to weep. He tried again. "Mary?"

The aide took hold of her fingers. "Let's show hubby how you do it, Mary. We're making a lovely basket, aren't we?" Moulding her fingers about a strand of raffia, she tried to guide her into weaving. "Come on, Mary you can do it!" Mary didn't make any effort to move or remove her hand.

Giving up, the aide put a hand beneath Mary's chin, tilting her blankly staring face up towards Jim. "Look, See? It's your hubby, Mary. Aren't you going to say hello?"

The thorns of the roses were sticking into Jim's hands but he ignored them. "Leave her," he whispered. "Leave her alone, please. Don't." He turned to the orderly. "She doesn't know me."

"No."

Jim nodded. "It's the medication, I expect, like you said – the medication. Be better if I come again another day." Pain was gnawing at his heart. "Won't it?"

The man shrugged. "It's difficult to say."

Jim turned back to the table. Mary was sitting staring vacantly at the basket. There was a small trickle of dribble running down her chin. His heart clenched. He turned to the orderly. "Can I see her alone?"

The orderly shook his head. "Sorry. But we'll give you a bit of space." He nodded to the aides who began to shepherd the other patients out of their chairs and away from the table. When they had moved away, Jim moved slowly round to Mary and crouched down by her side.

"Hey, Mary." He stroked her limp hand. "Well, here's a fine old do!" He brought the roses closer. "I brought you some flowers, Mary, see, from the garden." Petals fell on her knee. He brushed them off carefully.

Putting down the flowers on the table, he turned her head gently so that she was gazing in his direction. Her skin looked pale and thick, somehow. It had none of its usual translucence. Her hair felt sticky and dry. He stroked her cheek gently with the backs of his fingers, swallowing a huge lump in his throat. There was no recognition. Nothing. It was as if she was a goldfish. He could feel tears stinging the backs of his eyes. "It's Jim, Mary. It's me, Mary. It's Jim."

If he was going to blub, he'd better go. Keeping strict control over himself, he put her hand back carefully on her knee. "I'll come back another day, poppet, when you're feeling better."

Leaning forward to brush his lips against her forehead, he thought he heard her murmur, and drew back quickly, peering at her. For the first time he made out a flicker of something in her eyes. "Mary?" There was a new tension in her body. She was really looking at him now; he could sense the difference. Her pupils, dark and small already, were shrivelling to pinpricks. Almost imperceptibly, her head and her upper body began to rock from side to side, then pressing herself back against her chair, she began to let out a rising, quavering wail.

"What is it, Mary?" he asked in consternation. He heard one of the aides call out and rose, meaning to put his arms about her, but before he could do so, she had drawn back her hand and had lashed out at him, dragging her clawed nails across his cheek. He froze where he was in shock.

"Time to go." The orderly who had led him to the day room was at his elbow. "Time to go, Mr Norris. Sorry. Time to go." Aides had rushed over, two of them holding Mary tightly as a third helped him to stand up. Still shell-shocked, Jim let him lead him to the door.

The rumpus was exciting the other women. Somebody blew

a whistle. Mary struggled, screaming incomprehensibly. He held back, trying to see what was happening, as the orderly unlocked the door. "Wait! Wait ... Will she be all right?"

"Best go, sir. We'll look after her."

"You won't hurt her?"

The orderly shook his head. "No, sir, we won't."

Pounding feet were racing towards the door and a man in a white coat pushed past him, breathless, frowning at the orderly. "Who?"

"Mary Norris, again, sir."

"Right."

The orderly glanced at Jim as he made to lock the door. "Call at reception, sir, they'll get someone to see to that for you."

Jim was bemused. "Er ... What?"

The orderly nodded. "Your face, sir. It's bleeding. You've a nasty scratch."

For the first time Jim realised that his cheek was stinging. He nodded slowly, trying to find his feet. "Thanks, Bill ... er, John. Er ... thanks."

There was no more seeing Mary, although he continued to drive the long miles to the hospital as often as he could, sometimes three or four times a week, hoping against hope. Every week the news was just the same: no change. They were still trying, they assured him profusely of that. He clung to every slender vestige of hope they gave him that she'd be better by harvest time, but it was very hard. To take his mind off it, he worked all the hours he could, putting in extra time at Burrows Farm for John Harfield as well as seeing to his own jobs. It wasn't easy, though it was a great help having young Cathy around. She was very pleasant. It tickled him, the way she seemed to think he was a bit of a hero, looking up at him with those big blue eyes. Mary'd often teased him about that. Remembering that cheered him up a bit and made him smile inside, which nothing much else did at the moment.

She was preparing supper when he entered hastily one early evening. "Just give me a quick bite, Cath," he told her. "Bit of bread and a bit of cheese or something."

"Aren't you hungry?"

"Thunderstorms about. Said I'd go over to Barrows, give them a hand with bringing in what's left of the hay."

He stood at the kitchen door munching his bread and cheese and studying the still blue evening sky. "Think it'll hold off for a few hours. With a bit of luck we should get what's still standing in by ten."

When he had gone, and Patsy was at last fast asleep, Cathy put the kettle and the two biggest pans full of water on the stove to boil and took down the tin bath from the wall, then drew the thin curtains through which the evening sun still filtered. Tiptoeing back into the bedroom, she slipped off her clothes and got into her dressing gown, then, rummaging in the half-light, found her best green blouse. Fred had promised to take her to see Errol Flynn in *Captain Blood* at the pictures in on Saturday night, and she wanted to be able to wear it, but there was a button missing. Mrs Norris had a little lidded bowl of loose buttons on her dressing table and she was hoping that one of them would be close enough to provide a reasonable match.

Tiptoeing into the hall, she closed the door, then climbed up the creaking ladder. Seeing Mrs Norris's things up there always gave her a little bit of a shiver, as if she might suddenly hear her with that creepy voice behind her, asking suspiciously what she was about. Even so, she lingered for a moment, re-smoothing Mr Norris's counterpane and imagining him lying there all lonely. Poor Mr Norris! What if Mrs Norris never got better? What if she never came home?

She was ashamed of the little prickle of excitement that fizzled up her spine. What a dreadful thing. Best not to think about it. Press on.

She scattered the contents of the little china bowl onto the crocheted mat. There were a couple of green buttons, but they were a little too small; it would be necessary to sew up the buttonhole a bit. Three or four plain white, one small, three big ... some of Mr Norris's shirt buttons ... a brass button that looked as if it had come from a uniform ... and five of the ivory tortoise-shaped buttons Mum had given Nancy to sew on Mrs Norris's dress; the ones that should have been hers. If these were the buttons, what had she done with the dress?

Pity there were only five of them. She searched amongst the clutter on the dressing table, but the sixth was nowhere to be seen. She hesitated for only a moment.

If Mrs Norris wasn't wanting them, they would look very pretty on her blouse. For similar reasons, she also helped herself to one of the sweetly scented Yardley's Pink Lilac soaps she knew from previous explorations were in a box in the top right drawer. Waste not, want not, that's what Mum always said.

It was very close and warm. She could feel perspiration trickling down her spine and hear thunder rolling off in the distance as she climbed back down the ladder. Mr Norris had been right about the weather. When she drew back the corner of the curtain at the kitchen window, she could see that the sky in the distance was becoming heavy and overcast, though above the cottage the sky still seemed to be blue.

She filled the tub with steaming water and tuned in the wireless to Music Hall. It was a little crackly, but that didn't bother her. Singing along softly to the music, she folded a hand towel and put it on the rim to provide a head rest, then swished the soap around in the hot water so that the scent of pink lilacs rose into the air. Slipping off her dressing gown, she let herself down into the tub, laying back her head and closing her eyes with a sigh as the water caressed her. Bliss!

Thunder rolled again somewhere, but it didn't trouble her.

Down in the hayfields where Jim and the other men were giving every last vestige of energy to the common task, a jagged flash of lightning threw the moving bodies into stark relief. John Harfield looked anxiously at the darkened sky as thunder rumbled directly overhead and one or two heavy raindrops started to fall. "I think we've had it, lads. Get this lot on the wagon, then we'd best make a run for it."

Before the last load could be completed, though, the heavens opened. The sudden cloudburst drove them to throw their pitchforks up onto the wagon and clamber swiftly aboard.

John Harfield peered down at Jim through the driving rain. "Come along with us, Jim – have a jug or two of ale." Jim shook his head. "No, thanks, John. Best get back. I've an early start tomorrow." He closed the gate behind the wagon, then, head down, set off across the fields at a sprint.

Inside the cottage it was growing darker, but Cathy, daydreaming idly in the cooling water as she listened to the rather scratchy music, still had her eyes closed. When the brown Bakelite wireless crackled fiercely and a heavy roll of thunder simultaneously broke above the cottage roof, it startled her. Her eyes sprang open as a flash of lightning illuminated the curtained window, and she was suddenly frightened. This was too close for comfort. Being in a metal tub of water with a storm breaking directly overhead just wasn't wise; Mum said.

A brilliant lightning flash illuminated the kitchen and its accompanying roll of thunder deafened her with its deep rumble. The water in the tub swished and sloshed over the sides of the tub as she hastily struggled to her feet, letting out a scream as the back door banged suddenly open and cold, wet wind rushed inside. A further flash of blue lightning illuminated both the kitchen and the alarming, looming silhouette of a man throwing himself into the room.

Seeing Cathy standing naked and dripping in the tub, Jim drew up with a jolt. It was as if he had been struck by one of the thunderbolts, but it wasn't just the shock of the unexpected. For a long moment he stood frozen, staring, panting and dripping wet himself, as, for the first time, realisation dawned.

She isn't a child. She isn't a child any longer; she's a fully-grown woman.

Thrown into total confusion and embarrassment, he turned and stumbled back into the yard.

A few minutes later, Cathy, exquisitely embarrassed, her dressing gown held tightly about her, opened the door and called out awkwardly into the pouring rain, "Mr Norris? I'm out now, Mr Norris. I've finished."

That night, she lay awake for a long time looking at the ceiling. Jim did, too.

He was shy with her in the morning, though he tried to pretend it hadn't happened.

"Got a funeral to do tomorrow, Cath. I've put off doing wreaths and things for long enough. That side of things is Mary's province really, and I've kept hoping ..." He shrugged. "But we could really do with the cash. Think you're up to giving me a bit of a hand?"

She watched nervously as he brought in all the paraphernalia. "Spread a bit of newspaper on that table, Cath."

She did so hastily, watching as he set out wreath frames and wires and put a sack of moss and two buckets of flowers and fir down beside the table on the floor. "What do I have to do? I'm not very artistic, Mr Norris."

He shrugged. "I can't do it like Mary does it. She's got the proper knack." He paused for a moment and she saw a painful shadow run across his face, but then he stiffened his backbone and drew up two chairs. "Sit down. I'll show you." She could feel his thigh pressing against hers as he reached over for a wire and snapped off a fragment of fir. "We get the fir in all round first to give the flowers a backing. See? Like that – wrap it round and then twist over the wire."

Cathy attempted it. "Like that?" Her fingers brushed against his.

He nodded. "Almost, tighter, or it'll slip." Rather awkwardly, he moved his chair away from hers a little. Feeling self-conscious, she moved hers away a little too.

He didn't speak again until her first wreath was finished, then he smiled. "That's nice, Cath. You've done a good job there."

Mary didn't come home at harvest time. He'd half expected as much after his last visit, but it still came hard. She would come next time, he promised himself, every inch of him, right down to his fingertips, aching from the need of her. She would, definitely. He'd have to be patient. A bit more time, that was all that they wanted to get her put to rights.

But another six months stretched before him like an eternity.

Autumn began to encroach. Disappointment and loneliness seemed to have penetrated his bones like the chill in the air auguring the coming winter. The longing for her clung to him like the muslin-like autumn mists clinging low over the fields every day as he strode over to Barrows at daybreak to help with the milking before getting back to his own work.

Mrs Harfield was kind. Since the news had got out, he'd heard plenty of muttering round the village, which had stopped as soon as he hove into view, but she was one of those who seemed to have genuine sympathy. She brought the men a flask of hot tea each day when they had finished and she always had a quiet word with Jim. Today she had brought a batch of warm homemade cheese scones as well, wrapped up in a napkin. "Go on, Jim – take two."

Having been up before Cath had the porridge on the go, he took two gratefully. "Very nice, Mrs Harfield. Thanks."

She smiled, puffing as she lowered her plump frame onto a hay bale. "And how's your Patsy getting on at school? Does she like it any better, Jim?"

He frowned, wiping the floury crumbs from around his mouth. "Well, she's settling down a bit ... She does let Cath take her now."

Cathy had set out to take her on the first, all-important day, and as it turned out she had had to come home again to get him; Patsy had apparently kicked and screamed all the way there and all the way back, kept making them fall off the bike. In the end, the only way they had been able to get her to go for the first few weeks was if he took her in the van in the mornings as soon as he got back from Barrows, and if Cathy could think of something nice for her to look forward to when she collected her after the bell for home-time went – a picnic, or a treasure hunt for bits of crockery in the stream, or a few pennies to spend in the shop. It had become really quite expensive.

Mrs Harfield nodded. "And is she sleeping any better? Still getting those nasty nightmares, poor little thing?"

"If anything, they seem to be getting worse."

She shook her head compassionately. "That doesn't help."

"No, it doesn't." It meant she was always tired in the mornings and not in any mood to be coaxed out of her bed and dressed. Once or twice, Cathy had had to go with him in the van and get the child into her pinafore and socks and things while he was driving.

Mrs Harfield struggled to her feet. "Well, I'm off to make some corn dollies. We shall miss Mary at the Harvest Festival when it comes to decorating the church; she used to do it so beautifully." She patted his shoulder. "Next year, though, Jim, eh? She'll be with us all next year."

He smiled bravely. "Aye, Mrs Harfield. Aye. No doubt."

Jim, Patsy and Cathy went together to the service. The nave and altar looked quite good, if not quite up to Mary's standard. Vases of wheat, oats and barley had been set out on the window ledges, the pillars encircled with swathes of hops and Old Man's Beard, and the white asters which Jim had donated had been made into a pretty arrangement on the altar steps. Whilst the congregation sang *Come Ye Thankful People, Come* the children trooped up to place their offerings beneath them – golden, freshly baked loaves of bread, jars of jam, glistening tomatoes, polished brown onions, rosy-cheeked apples, purple beetroot, crisp bunches of carrots, bloated marrows, all soon piled up.

When it came to the point, though, Patsy wouldn't carry up the trug basket that Cathy had lined with yellow crêpe paper and filled for her with great care. Jim had a little sympathy with her; nothing wrong with the fruit or the vegetables, but he hadn't had the heart to enter the garden produce exhibition in the village hall afterwards as he usually did, either. Cathy, though, was exasperated and a little bit hurt.

"Will you let our Tommy take it up, then?" she hissed. Patsy shrugged. When Cathy beckoned, he willingly clomped over with a gap-toothed grin and carted it, two-handedly, up to the front.

"That looks blooming heavy. What did you put in there, Cath?" Jim murmured under cover of the singing, wondering if he was going to be short on his orders in the morning.

She blinked, trying to recall. "Potatoes, onions, baby parsnips ..." she whispered.

He rolled his eyes. "No wonder, then."

" ... a jar of redcurrant jelly and some pickled peaches ... half a dozen Worcester Permains and a couple of nice big Bramleys ... two jars of mint and apple jelly ... some Conference pears, a few little jars of chutney ..."

"Bloody hell, Cath!" Remembering he was in church, he glanced guiltily at the Vicar.

She finished her recital proudly: "... and I made a rhubarb pie."

Chapter 15

With Patsy at school much of the day, Cathy had more time these days to help Mr Norris a bit more and it suited them both very well. She had taken to most of the tasks he set her like a duck to water. Although she was very good with Patsy, he got the distinct impression overall that she was happier doing things outside for him than she was with Patsy in the house, especially when they worked together side by side, like when they were digging up potatoes, or pulling up veg and she could chatter. It was nice having her working at his side. He grinned to himself. She was a pleasant, gregarious little thing, was Cath.

Christmas was very difficult. On Christmas Eve he drove over to Leigh House, and was pleased to see they had a big tree up in the hall, though it was a bit sparse on baubles. They didn't let him see Mary, which was becoming par for the course, but still, he was able to leave her some cards and some Christmas presents: a pale blue lacy wool bedjacket that Nancy had knitted and a pair of slightly holey bedsocks made, one each, with pride by Chrissie and Pauline. He also had a big tin of homemade treacle toffees from Elsie, and an iced cake with a tiny fir tree on from Mrs Harfield, which she said she thought Mary would be able to share with the other patients but which, with the treacle toffee, he gave to be shared out by the staff. His own presents to her were a new tin of Pink Lilac, three white Hyacinth bulbs in a woven willow pot, which were, thanks to his judicial forcing, just beginning to flower and release their heavy fragrance, and a tiny brooch.

He was very proud of the brooch. He had found a little curl of Patsy's fair baby hair in a brown envelope in Mary's dressing table drawer so he'd had the brooch made up especially at the jewellers in town, with a delicate silver frame and the tiny curl of Patsy's hair inside on a blue velvet backing. It had cost him dearly. It was disappointing, though. They gave it back to him for safekeeping.

It was the pin, of course. He should have thought; she could have hurt herself, or others.

They went over to Elsie's for their Christmas dinner. It was a grand meal, goose and a big plum duff, and Patsy seemed to enjoy it, playing with the other kids with hardly any sulking or being rude or quarrelling for once, and Cathy was in her element, fussing non-stop around him, but Jim found it very difficult. He couldn't help thinking about the Christmas when the first signs had started, when things had begun going wrong.

Cathy was looking very pretty that day, in a new print dress with a little belt, a closely fitted bodice, a skirt smooth over her hips and a loose sort of floppy, collary thing about the neck, he did notice that. It gave her a lovely little womanly figure. He told her so, on the way home. "You look really nice in that dress, Cath, it suits you. It's got a nice – well, a very nice shape." She blushed quite pink. She was ever so pleased.

It snowed quite a bit overnight and he awoke in the attic room to a quilted silence. As always, his first thoughts were of Mary. *I wish you were here, my love.*

Snuggled down in bed in curled brown loneliness, the eiderdown wrapped and tucked around himself so that he wouldn't be too aware of how empty the big bed was, he was very comfortable, but was soon dragged out of his nest by a racket downstairs, Patsy yelling and Cathy ineffectually trying to soothe her. Overtired and over-excited, Patsy was in a terrible mood that day, and his attempts to build a snowman out of the thin layer of snow didn't cheer her, so instead, when necessary chores were over, he took them both out for a Boxing Day walk.

The icy fields were exhilarating. A pale lavender sun peering low over the hedgerows lit up the fields with a rosy glow, setting the ice crystals glittering. Cathy ran ahead, pulling Patsy by the hand. "It's so pretty, Mr Norris – it's like walking on pink diamonds!"

Grinning, he watched the two of them, wrapped up in their scarves and gloves and wearing woolly hats. Patsy looked a bit peaky still, but Cath looked grand. Her cheeks were as rosy as the snow, buttery blonde curls peeped out from beneath her red knitted bonnet, and her clear blue eyes shone with the cold.

There was no doubt; she was a really pretty girl now. He corrected himself. No, not a pretty girl: a really nice-looking young woman.

A lucky lad, that Fred. She'll make that Fred a very happy man. The thought made him feel strangely jealous; the flash of jealousy made him feel ashamed. *Don't be so bloody daft.*

Cathy was turning round again, gesturing. "Mr Norris? Shall we go through the woods?"

The snow hadn't penetrated inside the wood where the thick black mud was thickly carpeted with dissolving fallen leaves and the spiked shells of chestnuts, and beech trunks gleamed like ebony church pillars in the distant depths. Patsy and Cathy both seemed to find it enjoyably scary once amongst the trees; they clung closely to him, one on each arm.

"Whoo! – what's that, Mr Norris? Cathy jumped, throwing her arms about him as a branch somewhere cracked with a sharp snap like a witch's knuckles. She smelled of fresh air and something sweet and powdery and her rounded body felt like a warm soft cushion against his body.

He grinned. "It's just the weight of the snow."

She shivered pleasurably. "Ooer ...!" Peering up at him from under her woolly bonnet, she widened her eyes admiringly. "I wouldn't want to be in here without you, Mr Norris!"

It made him feel quite the man.

*H*e had a trug of sweet peas on his arm, which was strange, because he didn't grow sweet peas. Miss Buckley's voice was sharp. "Is that man at the door, Nancy? I wish to speak to him."

He sighed, hovering on the doorstep. Bloody hell, not again; what would it be this time? The carrots last week weren't straight enough or clean enough? One of the Bramley cookers had a wormhole?

"Nancy, for goodness sake, woman, it's draughty with that door open. Tell the fellow he may step inside."

"Yes, ma'am." Hastily, Nancy beckoned to him. "You're to come in, Jim."

Quickly, he stamped the clinging soil from his heavy boots, winked at Nancy and ducked his head in order to enter what was a strangely vast and very gloomy kitchen. Nancy closed the door behind him quickly.

"Yes, ma'am! What can I do for you?" Was that a piano playing somewhere in the house? He cocked his head to listen.

The narrow nose beneath the glittering wire glasses wrinkled disdainfully. "It is not acceptable, Mr Norris."

It was a piano. It was a piano. She was at home, then.

Miss Buckley rapped on the stone floor with her cane. "Are you listening to me, Mr Norris?"

He stiffened, almost clicking his heels. "Yes, ma'am. Yes, ma'am, the carrots." The piano had stopped and his heart beat faster. She might come in in a minute. He struggled to keep a smile from creeping over his face. "If they weren't satisfactory for you ma'am, I'll not charge you for them. I'll replace them for you, of course."

Miss Buckley sighed with exaggerated exasperation. "Mr Norris, did you not hear me, are you not listening, man? Did you not hear a single word I said?"

Behind him somewhere, Nancy murmured under her breath. "The beetroot, Jim, the beetroot."

Miss Buckley rapped with her stick again. "Yes, man, the beetroot, the beetroot! What have you got to say about them?"

He opened his mouth, but he had nothing to say on the subject of beetroot or on anything else for that matter, because Mary had walked into the room.

Her hair was like a dark, soft cloud; her skin was white and smooth, her smiling mouth pink and firm, her cheeks rosy. Her grey eyes were filled with love.

As a huge irresistible eruption of relief began to force its way upward through his body, he opened his arms wide with a sob. There were tears running unchecked down his cheeks now. "Mary. Mary!" With a cry of delight, she threw her body into his embrace.

She felt rounder, more substantial, than usual, but it didn't matter, nor, strangely, was he at all perturbed when at last he lifted his lips from Mary's sweet mouth and saw that the hair in which he was twining his fingers was fair, not dark. The eyes gazing up lovingly at him were round and blue...

He got up in a very edgy mood and felt very awkward with Cathy for days after that, trying to avoid being near her as much as he was able. He found himself looking at her a great deal when she wasn't looking, though; he couldn't help it.

It helped that he was needed a great deal at Barrows farm that summer. Old Mr Harfield had a heart attack in the June, and then another, and finally, in the July, he passed away.

"John's taking over the farm," he told Cathy, watching her bottling up strawberry jam. A voluminous floral pinny disguised her rounded figure, and he was glad of that. There was a smear of strawberry on her cheek and she wore a slight frown as she concentrated on the task of filling up a line of jars. "Lord, it's hot!" Setting down the heavy pan and tossing back her head, she raised her arms and ran cooling fingers through her hair. Dishevelled now, it seemed to have got even blonder in the sun. He looked away quickly. "But he says if there is a war, he wants to sign up. He's younger than I am; if it's over quickly, I'm not likely to be called, especially working on the land. Asked if I'd take over the running for him if he did."

She sounded doubtful. "How would you cope with both?"

He dabbed his finger at the scrape of jam in the saucer of cold water she'd used for testing and licked it. Noticing, she dipped a teaspoon into a small pot of jam set aside, and held it up to his lips. "Here, try that! It's warm, but not hot."

He sucked it from the spoon greedily. "Hey, that's very good!"

She smiled, pleased, and jerked her head at the bread bin. "Get a bit of bread and have some on it. This is a little pot I've set aside for now."

He spread a thick chunk of bread with butter and the still warm, half-set jam, musing on the future. "I'll take this bit back in with the farmlands, maybe cut out the home deliveries ... Might have to happen anyway."

"Uh-huh ..." He allowed himself a glance at her. She was absorbed in the task again, her movement supple and her plump little fingers moving deftly as she popped on paper covers and snapped on elastic bands.

Drawing out his chair, he settled at the table munching, permitting himself a moment's pleasure, as well as a rest. It was comfortable, homey, in the kitchen, the air a sweet, syrupy fug. The kitchen shelves were already bright with an array of labelled jars filled with preserved fruits, tomatoes, beans, chutneys and jams. Bunches of thyme, mint and other herbs hung from the beams, as well as larkspur, helichrysomes and statice drying for later arrangements as he'd taught her. They'd be all right this winter.

Nice, watching her work. She was a good housewife.

Helping at Barrows helped, too, with the waiting for harvest time again and the final decision about Mary. They let him see her twice, which raised his hopes up, but she didn't look any better and she never looked at him with any recognition again, which lowered them. His emotions, coming and going from the Leigh House, were on a seesaw.

They did say that if the decision went against her being released, she might be better off at some big mental hospital, like Patterson Park, near Alfrestead, which, though it wasn't private, could offer a bigger range of treatments and had more facilities for Occupational Therapy and so forth. They assured him it wasn't like the first place she'd been sent to.

It was also a little closer than Leigh House, which meant he could get there more easily.

Miss Buckley said she'd have to think.

Apart from the happiness of being near Jim, the high spot of that summer for Cathy was listening to the Coronation of King George and Queen Elizabeth on the wireless. She'd always felt a special affection for the Duchess of York, who seemed a lovely woman and nothing like that hard-faced American woman who had stolen the Prince of Wales. Looking at herself in pictures, she'd always felt that if she put a dark-haired wig on to cover her blonde hair, and had some lovely clothes, she could be taken for the Duchess. They were quite short and a little bit, well, nicely padded, and both rather pretty. They were very similar, as far as she could tell.

It was thoughts of Jim, though, that most consumed her as she worked through her numerous tasks. Anything could set her imagination racing. On Patsy's good days – the ones where she was cooperative and slightly more amenable – the hours she spent crouching with her by the stream hunting for treasures of broken glass, pretending they were rubies and emeralds, or those spent waiting patiently against the dusty hedgerow on the road into the village whilst the little girl experimentally prodded sticky pools of tar with sticks after the sun had melted it, or wandering with her through fields redolent with meadowsweet, or the summer woods with the smells of leaf mould and wild garlic in her nostrils, all gave her time to dream. Teaching Patsy to nibble grass stalks sweet as sugar cane, or to gather the red-brown seeds of dock to make sugar for a doll's tea party or to put a furry seed head up her sleeve and wait for it to make its way from top to bottom, she found herself daydreaming about Jim, and it got worse as they approached the Harvest and decision-making time. Anything could trigger her off.

What might happen if Mrs Norris didn't come back?

Anything could do it. It was a surprise she managed to do any work.

The cinema projector broke down twice whilst she and Fred were watching the usual Saturday evening film. The first time, he joined in with the jeering, and the second time he tried to kiss her, but she turned her face away. He drew back, staring at her through the smoky gloom. "What's the matter, Cath?"

She shrugged. "Nothing."

He tightened the arm he had about her shoulders, trying to draw her towards him. "Give us a kiss, then. Come on."

The idea was suddenly repulsive. "I don't want to, Fred."

His eyes hardened. "Come on!" He tightened his grip, searching insistently for her mouth and his persistence irritated her.

She pushed him away crossly. "I said no!" He drew back, puzzled. She knew he was hurt, but there was an empty coldness deep inside and she couldn't help it.

"Why not? What's the matter, then?"

She drew in a deep breath. "I need to talk to you, Fred."

"What about?"

She stared at the back of the head in front of her, tightening her hands in her lap and drew in another deep breath. "I don't want to walk out with you any more, Fred."

He seemed flabbergasted. "Why n-not?"

She was silent, not knowing what to say. He stared at her for what seemed a long time, then he turned back to gaze at the blank screen with his jaw set tightly. "I see."

Poor Fred. Tears suddenly stung the backs of her eyes. "I don't mean to upset you. I'm sorry."

His voice was tight and he seemed to have lost his stammer. "It's that Jim Norris, isn't it? You're in love with him. I knew you were."

She felt her stomach tighten. "No, I'm not!"

"Don't lie to me, Cath. Have you and him – ?"

She was defensive. "What?"

Heat rushed to her face as he rounded on her, his voice rising. "You know what! You have, haven't you?" Heads turned to see where the commotion lay. "You're a little tart, that's what you are, Cathy Glassbrook."

She jerked upright, shocked. "I am not!"

He scoffed. "What do you call it, then? You're sleeping with him, aren't you, you little tart, you're sleeping with him, that dirty old man!"

She tried to keep her voice down, shaking her head vehemently as heads turned all about them, finding the argument an entertaining way to pass the time till the film was rolling again. One or two even stood up to see better. "No, I am not! I'm not! And I've told you, he's not old!"

He gave a harsh laugh and rose, banging up his seat. "Well, he can keep you anyway. I don't want you now. I'm off."

Tears began to roll down her cheeks as she watched him

push his way out along the row, treading uncaringly on toes. "Fred. Fred! Come back, Fred, let's talk!"

She hadn't realised that she was on her feet, too, but to the accompaniment of a grudging cheer from the audience, the projector suddenly whirred back into life. A voice rose from behind her. "Sit down or go after him, love – make up your bloomin' mind!"

She felt quite sick as she cycled home on her bike and had to stop to wipe the tears from her eyes so she could see the road. That was so embarrassing! Well! There *was* another side to Fred. Calling her a name like that! She was better off without him. And when Mr Norris had always been the complete gentleman, poor man.

The dreadful thing was that a part of her kept wishing, wickedly, that he had not.

Jim was clearly very excited and nervous as the afternoon of his big appointment to see Mrs Norris drew near. She waited at the window of the van as he fiddled with his tie. "Do I look all right?"

She nodded, smiling. "Fine, Mr Norris. You look smashing."

He brushed a hand anxiously over the back of his head. "Do I need a hair cut?"

She shook her head. "No. No, honestly, you look fine." He put out his hand to adjust the wing mirror. The poor man was all keyed up in a frazzle of anticipation and dread. She smiled, trying to boost his confidence. "It'll go all right, you'll see."

She felt queasy herself. If the Board's final decision was to let Mrs Norris come home, then her days of playing happy families with Mr Norris were over. He wouldn't be hers any more. On impulse, she stood on tiptoes and leant into the cab, aiming to place a kiss on his cheek, but striking the side of his nose instead as he turned towards her. "Good luck, Mr Norris."

He looked startled, but he smiled. "Thank you, Cathy." For a moment, she thought he was going to kiss her back, but instead he revved up the engine. "Better be off."

She clung onto the window, unwilling to let go. "Mr Norris, if things have – well, if they've been going well – will they be letting Mrs Norris come home with you tonight?"

He was distracted now, running his fingers through his hair again as he turned his head, ready to reverse. "Might do. I haven't said anything to Patsy, just in case. Don't want her to be –"

"Disappointed. No." She finished the sentence for him, letting go of the window. She smiled bravely. "Oh, well, let's hope!"

Not meeting her eyes, he revved up once more, inching the van back. "Got to go."

She stood back, waving one hand and twisting her apron in her other. "Good luck then. Bye, Mr Norris." She watched wistfully as the van disappeared out into the lane.

The atmosphere in the room hinted at disappointment, but he wouldn't let himself be sunk before they'd uttered the words. Knowing he was sitting there like a lemon, twisting his hat in his hands, he gazed at their faces, hoping to see a smile break.

A large, highly-polished desk separated Jim on his isolated chair from Dr Humphreys, the psychiatrist in charge of Mary's case, another colleague who was introduced to him as Dr Porter, and the Chief Psychiatric Nurse. The men were grouped around the desk, on which were spread out what he assumed were Mary's case notes. They muttered amongst themselves and their expressions were very grave.

Dr Humphreys cleared his throat and looked over at him at last. "Ah, Jim. Bad news, I'm afraid, Jim."

He found himself unable to respond.

The psychiatrist, whose name Jim had forgotten already, steepled his hands on the desk. "Mr Norris, I don't like failure, but there it is. We have tried everything at our disposal, and Mrs Norris ... Her condition remains totally resistant "

Jim summoned his inner resources and managed a whisper. "So ... What happens now?"

The psychiatrist shrugged.

"You're not permitted to apply for any more extensions?"

"We've had the maximum time allowed."

Dr Humphreys shook his head. "That's it, then, you see, Jim. That's it, man, I suppose."

"Pity." The psychiatrist looked at his colleague for confirmation. "Certification then."

Jim's chest felt too tight to speak. "It's final?"

Dr Porter nodded. "Certification, I'm afraid so, yes."

Certification. Neither the word nor the world made any sense to Jim. Mary. *Certification.* The doctors were talking to him, but he didn't take in a word that they said.

Forever. Certification. Mary forever gone.

Dr Humphreys moved slowly over to him. He was vaguely aware that the others were leaving the room, and that they were talking softly amongst themselves.

"Pity."

"Great pity."

"Still ..."

"Still, he's going to take it very hard. Nice fellow."

"Salt of the earth type. Yes, it is a shame."

Dr Humphreys put his hand on his shoulder. "Jim?"

Now that the others had left, there was deep silence. As if he was listening to the wireless, Jim heard sharp footsteps echo somewhere and a door slamming loudly, then silence fell again.

Dr Humphreys squeezed his shoulder, trying to hearten him. "Brace up. Brace up, Jim. I'm really sorry, man."

It wasn't real. Not Mary. It hadn't happened. Didn't believe it now.

"Come on, I'll find you a cup of tea."

Chapter 16

Cathy peered through the window with some trepidation as she heard the van drawing in to the yard and felt a wave of relief. He was alone.

She dropped the curtain, her hand quivering and stood still for a moment, pulling herself together. She was a bad girl, she was. Heaven help her, Mum would be so ashamed, but she was just so *glad*!

The kitchen looked nice. She had laid the table ready for supper with bread and butter and cheese, some tomatoes from the greenhouse, nice fresh lettuce and some hard-boiled eggs. Tormenting herself as she did so, she had set out plates and cutlery for three people and her first instinct was to get rid of one set of them, but she hesitated at the last moment, and put them all back.

She peered out once or twice more, but each time he was just sitting in the van staring blankly into space. It seemed ages till he came into the kitchen. When he did, the blind misery apparent in his posture and on his face made her even more deeply ashamed. She didn't dare speak.

He didn't speak either, just shook his head, and there was such bleak and inextensible misery in his eyes that it brought tears flooding into her own. She gulped, trying to dissolve the huge lump that had appeared in her throat. "Oh, Mr Norris."

He didn't seem to know what to do. She saw him take in the three places laid at the table and a small muscle flickering along his taut jaw line. Turning away, he murmured gruffly, "Is Patsy all right?"

She nodded. "Sound asleep. She went like a little treasure today, tired out; been playing out most of the afternoon. I've hardly seen her."

"That's good." Moving over to the dresser, he stood studying the shelves. He picked up and put down again one of the small jugs and then another. "I'll go and have a look at her in a minute." He was so tense that he was like a board.

She filled the teapot quickly. "Supper's ready, Mr Norris."

He nodded, keeping his back turned to her. "I'll go up and change."

He stood at Mary's dressing table beneath the window in their tiny attic room and pulled out one of the drawers. The contents smelled of her scent even after all this time. Gloves. Some scarves. Buttons. A posy of felt flowers meant to be put on a hat. Some lace oddments, also for trimming. A clothes brush. Not much else. He closed the drawer again.

A few of her dark hairs still clung to the bristles of her silver-backed hairbrush. She was keeping those; probably intended to make a plaited brooch for Patsy like her mum had done for her. Taking up her comb he fished out the loose hairs carefully, then opened the cross-stitched bag that hung on the mirror post and pushed them gently inside.

Her small red leather jewellery box. He opened the box carefully. There were so few things inside there, too; so very little he'd given her. Her mother's brooch; a gold locket. He tried to open it but his fingers were clumsy and the catch was far too small. Some wooden beads, a glittery brooch with shiny blue enamel wings, and a pair of earrings; the glittery diamante necklace he had given her their first Christmas. Nothing else. He ran the diamante necklace through his work-roughened fingers. Pretty, but it had only been cheap; he'd said one day he meant to buy some real diamonds, and she'd laughed and said "If you do, you do, and if you don't, you don't, but always, Jim; forever. These will always be the best."

Dropping the necklace abruptly, he snapped shut the box.

Cathy looked up anxiously as he strode through the kitchen, but he didn't say a word.

Grasping a spade that came to hand in the darkened shed, he strode on blindly through the orchard and threw off his jacket, letting it fall on the ground. Amongst the late potatoes and the still growing leeks and kale, not caring where he was digging, he thrust the spade into the ground. Blindly and furiously digging, heaving great clods of earth back somewhere over his shoulder, he tried to fight stoically through the pain. The effort he expended in the first hour was tremendous and all at once with exhaustion came a breaking of a great wave of grief. An agonising, rippling cry of stark, bleak loss and despair escaped him. Dropping the spade, he sank onto his knees amongst the furrows. Blotting out the moonlight with his earth-stained hands, he began to weep.

Cathy, moving quietly through the shadowy orchard, heard him and began to run The ground was uneven and she struggled for balance as she made her way across the open ground to his side. The sight of him so broken stabbed at her heart.

Sinking down, she put her arms about him, rocking him. "There, there! Hush, hush. Oh, don't."

He turned suddenly in her arms, burying his face in her neck and clutching her so tightly that it hurt, but she didn't care. His whole body was heaving in an agony of grief. Balancing herself more securely on the rutted ground, she cradled him in her arms with his face buried deep in her breast. Brushing her lips against his forehead over and over again, she could feel the heat of his breath and the wetness of his tears through her thin blouse and she stroked his head as he wept with trembling fingers. "Hush, love, don't cry, don't cry."

With a groan, he reared up suddenly, heaving himself above her and searching for her mouth. Sinking back against the bare earth, she tightened her arms about his neck as his salty lips sought for and found her own.

It wasn't the most comfortable experience in the world. It hurt rather, actually, and sharp bits of stone pressed painfully into her back, but it didn't matter. The rich, frantic excitement in her blood swept away the discomfort. It was happening! He was making love to her! Jim was!

When it was over and he lay heavily upon her, his breathing ragged and his heart pounding so that she could feel it through his chest, she clung to him, delighting in his weight upon her, cradling him, tangling her fingers in his hair. The smell of damp earth and the perfume of the sweet peas on their supports at the far end of the vegetable plot clung to her nostrils. The dark shape of a bat swooped silently across above her head and she smiled up into the night sky. It had happened. Fred had the right of it now, but she didn't care. She stroked his hair gently. Oh, Jim.

She could have lain there forever, but after a few moments, she felt a different tension grow in him. Drawing away a little, he stared down as if trying to distinguish her features, then he reared back abruptly, leaving her arms empty and his eyes wide with panic and shock. "I'm sorry. I'm sorry, what am I doing, I'm ever so sorry, Cath!"

She shook her head, which was difficult, flat on her back. "It's all right."

He sat up, his elbows on his knees, and covered his face with his hands. "I didn't mean to do that." His voice was all shaky.

She raised herself on one elbow. "It's all right. Really. I didn't mind."

He shook his head. "Cath ..." He was shocked by what he had done, she could see that, even in the darkness, and a wave of embarrassment and misery washed over her. He'd been thinking she was Mary, that was all.

She swallowed, and her voice was dull. "You didn't really want me, then." Disappointment tasted bitter. "It's all right if you didn't."

He sounded strangely angry. "Of course I wanted you, Cath." He was on his feet, now. Clouds had come over the moon and he was just a tall dark silhouette; she couldn't see his face, though she saw him shake his head as if he was lost for words. "Of course I did!"

He did! It was all right, then. Relief splintering the disappointment, she sat up, and he crouched down, taking her hands, closing his fingers around hers tightly. He sounded distraught. "Never think I didn't want you; but it's not on, Cath. It's just not on! You know that, don't you?"

She held her tongue silent. *He doesn't know what wants,* she comforted herself. *He's just too full of misery tonight to think properly.*

He was waiting, so she nodded silently and he seemed relieved.

"You go on back to the house, then." Helping her to her feet, he dusted the earth carefully from her skirt. "I didn't hurt you, did I? Sure you're all right?"

She nodded. "Yes, I'm sure." She shivered a little, and hoped he might give her a cuddle, but instead he stepped back quickly, thrusting his hands in his pockets.

She hesitated. "Are you coming in?"

He turned away at once. "Thought I heard a fox about last night. I'm going to have a recce. Might be a while. Don't worry about me. You go on to bed." The word hung between them in the night air with an awkward resonance.

She could feel the blood still pounding in her throat. Her voice was a whisper as she nodded meekly. "Okay."

S he lay awake for what felt like hours, listening, far too overwrought to sleep, experiencing the breathless moments in his arms over and over again in what seemed like glorious Technicolor. She had herself so worked up that when at last she heard the hall door open and saw the flickering of his candle flame through the trap, she held her breath, believing that he was coming to her door.

Beside her, Patsy sighed in her sleep and turned over. Don't be so daft, she told herself crossly; he's not going to come in here. But her body cried out to him and long after her ears had picked up the creaking of the ladder and the flickering had faded from sight, she found herself throwing back the eiderdown. She was halfway out of bed on her way to the ladder before she managed to restrain herself. It was a very long night.

It was a long night for Jim, too, though he got up very early whilst the house was still and quiet. He strode off to the bottom of the garden and climbed aimlessly over the fence leading to Middle Field, then clambered down through Bottom Field, and across Smedley's Piece and past Harfields and back up through the copse, startling rabbits and stumbling over potholes and tussocks in the dark, trying to sort it out in his mind, but it was hopeless. And how could he have done that, anyway? Bloody state he was in. Poor Cath.

He shouldn't have said he'd wanted her; it wasn't fair to lead her on when he wasn't going to let anything happen again. He'd wanted her all right, of course he'd wanted her. More and more, whenever a bare arm slipped into his mind, as it did, or the sweet curve of a cheek, or the tiny pulse at the base of a soft white throat, or the tempting shadow barely disguised by the thin fabric of a summer frock, the face they belonged to was more and more Cathy's.

Sitting across the table from her and watching the way her eyes closed when she slipped her spoon into her mouth, the twitch of her throat as she swallowed, her eyes opening again as if after lovemaking – it got worse every day. It was all he could do to eat, even when he was hungry, and for him that was saying something, when she was such a good cook. When he needed release it had been more and more often Cathy's face he had imagined on the pillow now, which had shamed him deeply. He was ashamed and at the same time angry with her for making him feel like that when he wished he didn't, and on top of that he felt a huge disloyalty to Mary because he bloody well did! The whole thing frightened him and made him breathless. Might be better if she went back to live with her mum.

But he would miss her if she went. She was a good girl, was Cathy. When she smiled, and there was that dimple peeping, he temporarily forgot the heartache and the longing for Mary, and her presence was salve to his wounded soul. She was good for him, and for Patsy. Patsy needed her. Yes, he decided, pausing with his candle at the bottom of the ladder and staring at the closed bedroom door. Don't make any hasty decisions. For Patsy's sake, be wise to think a little bit more.

When she got up in the morning, later than usual after her poor night's sleep, Cathy took care to brush her teeth and hair and pat on some Pond's Cold Cream and a little hint of 'Evening in Paris' behind her ears before he came back into the kitchen, but he kept his distance. He spoke to her very politely, but that was as far as it went.

She studied him every time his back was turned, drinking him all in, his tall, lanky frame, his strong back, his broad, hard shoulders, his sun-browned forearms with the small hairs on them glinting when they caught the sun. She'd been in his arms! He'd kissed her! The silvery dart pierced painfully through her. He'd said he wanted her! He had!

Just wait.

"I'll take Patsy with me on my round today," he told her without meeting her eyes as he harnessed up Meg. "Want me to drop you off for a bit at Elsie's?"

She nodded. "Please."

It was a silent ride. Neither of them said a dickey-bird. When they got there, he sat for a minute, staring out at the road ahead, before getting out and moving round in the silence to give her a hand down. She found herself breathing shallowly, and held herself in awkwardly as she stepped down close to him.

His arm did brush her chest, though, just a little, and he almost jumped. "Sorry."

She had forgotten about her fear of seeing Mum after the incident in the picture house, but she didn't seem to have heard any gossip about it, and didn't mention Fred, which was a huge relief. Studying Cath carefully, she gave an approving nod. "You've got some roses and your eyes have got a bit of a shine."

"Have they?" Glancing at herself in the mirror on the kitchen wall, Cathy brushed a fingertip softly over her lips.

Mum clattered the dishes in the sink. "Oh, in case I forget! Miss Buckley is asking to see Patsy. Nancy says you're to take her in for her tea on Wednesday – and make sure you're prompt, mind – three o'clock."

Cathy looked askance. "I don't know if Jim'll like that, Mum ..."

"So it's 'Jim', now, eh? I see!" Mum gave her a quizzical look, which Cathy pretended not to notice.

"Well, you know he had a quarrel with them. He and Mrs Norris."

"Hmph. So you're not calling her 'Mary'?"

"Mum!" She gave a disdainful laugh, reddening. "We see each other every day, that's all. Silly to go on calling him 'Mr Norris'."

Her mum sniffed. "It's usual, though, with your employer."

Cathy tossed her head. "Anyway, I don't think he'll like it if I take Patsy there."

"You won't, you mean!"

To Cathy's surprise, when he and Patsy got back from his round, he agreed with Elsie that she should take Patsy. "Ought to do it for Mary's sake, I suppose, probably owe it to Miss Buckley."

"They won't keep you long, Cath," he told her encouragingly, though she noted that he still didn't catch her eye. "They won't know what to do with her when she gets restless. They'll be calling you to take her home before you know where you are." He paused, frowning. "Only thing is – next Wednesday's the day I've arranged to go over again to Leigh House and I'm to see the superintendent at five. Don't want anything to interfere with that."

"She could go on the bus, Jim," Elsie suggested, bustling with the dirty cups and saucers to the sink. "How would you like that, Patsy, eh, a nice ride on a bus? And maybe – just maybe – if you're a good girl and nice and polite for your aunties, Cathy'll take you to the village shop before you walk back up the lane. In fact, here ..." She took down a toffee tin from the mantelpiece. "Wait a minute. See, here's a whole sixpence! If Cathy thinks you've been good, you can buy a quarter of dolly-mixtures or something else nice." She winked at Patsy as she handed her the coin. "Eh? How about it? Treat yourself to a bit of something tasty before they bring in this rationing. Here, pet lamb, I'll let Cathy look after it. You see what you can get with that."

On the way home, they both seemed to find it easier with Patsy sitting between them. They played 'I Packed My Trunk' and 'The Parson's Cat' with her, which was quite amusing. At one point, Cathy slipped up and called him 'Jim'. He didn't seem to mind.

It was all right him saying it wasn't going to happen again, but now that it had, it had made her longing for him even worse. She daydreamed him into her tasks all day, and lay awake at night imagining herself in his arms, almost sick with yearning, but it was plain that he meant to stick to his guns.

She made every effort she could to look especially nice,

wrapping her hair into pin curls when she went to bed, and putting cold cream, a dab of rouge and a little mascara on every morning even before going out to see to the hens. Whenever he was out and she could find the time, she studied assiduously the beauty section of the copy of *Enquire Within about Everything,* which Aunty Nancy had given her for her birthday, and gave herself homemade face packs made with various mixtures of things like lemon juice and egg white and honey like it said, and rinsed her blonde hair with chamomile water to make it gleam – she even took to steaming her face with chamomile water, though that made her go red as a beetroot and she had to do it early in case he popped in later in the day.

He didn't do that very much, actually. He seemed to stay out much more than usual, and when he was in he seemed a bit withdrawn, and definitely rather crabby. He was obviously feeling dreadful about the whole thing, which made her very miserable. All in all, it was as if it had never happened, except that they weren't as easy with each other as they had been before, so everything felt actually very much worse.

He did feel something, though; she could see that. Once he put his hand on her shoulder, and she looked up at him eagerly, but he reddened and took it away immediately as if her shoulder was red-hot. Whenever her hand brushed his, passing him the marmalade, or her knee touched his under the table, he jumped like a scalded cat. He wouldn't meet her eyes for more than a second or two. But he was adamant. Nothing seemed to bring back the old Mr Norris, not even when she pulled out all the stops and dressed up in her nicest clothes and made him something extra special like steak and kidney pudding for his dinner. If anything, he ate less than usual on those occasions, and then, muttering something about having to do something-or-other, went off on some errand as soon as he was done. It was so depressing. She seemed to do a lot of washing up with tears dripping into the washing-up bowl.

Naturally, Patsy played up no end when the time had come for her to get ready for the bus ride to see the Great-Aunts on the Wednesday, but eventually the bribe of a shiny sixpence to spend in Woolworths afterwards got her into her clean skirt and cardigan. She clung tightly to Aunty Nancy's hand as she led her into the morning room, but Aunty Nancy was smiling when she came back to Cathy in the kitchen.

"She'll be all right for a bit, I think – Miss Buckley told me to get out the Stereoscope and some games and the leather box with her granny's bits and pieces and Patsy's spell-bound at the moment with the glass eye she's found."

Cathy shuddered. "Glass eye? Ugh – what?"

Aunty Nancy chuckled. "Miss Mary used to be fascinated with it, too, when she was little. It's a blue one – looks just like a marble. Belonged to Miss Mary's gran."

Rain pattered on the windowpane. "Turning nasty." Aunty Nancy glanced at it as she put on the kettle. "She's ordered their afternoon tea for half past three, so I'll just get the things ready, then we'll have a good old chat. I've made some little gingerbread men, thought Patsy might like those, and there's some nice jam tarts and egg-and-cress sandwiches."

Cathy felt her tummy rumble. "Sounds very nice."

Aunty Nancy chuckled. "Don't worry – there's plenty for us two as well!"

By the time the sandwiches were ready and the tea was brewed, it was so dark in the kitchen that Aunty Nancy had to put on the lights. Cathy jumped to her feet as she lifted up the heavily laden tray. "Can I give you a hand?" She was dying to have a peep round the big house.

"You can bring the pot – pop on the cosy – and the hot-water jug, if you will." The bell on the wall rang imperiously and Aunty Nancy frowned. "They're getting impatient." She carried the tray over to the door and stood waiting for Cathy to open it. "If you're right?"

The hallway seemed vast to Cathy, and echoing, rather like the church hall. Her shoes clattered noisily on the shiny tiles. Embarrassed, she raised herself onto tiptoe. There were some dark oil paintings of people and one of a great big stag, several lamps on side tables with coloured glass and beads dangling, and the curtains at each of the wide, heavy doors leading off the hall were dark green and heavy and musty.

Cathy suddenly felt very nervous as she followed Aunty Nancy into the room. She had seen the Misses Buckley about town from time to time, but had never spoken to them, and they had such a fearsome reputation that for a moment she wished she hadn't offered to help.

It was too late, though. The first thing she was aware of was the strong smell of medicine. She kept her eyes on her hands, which were shaking, until she had set down the pot and the jug.

"So this is the girl." Miss Buckley had a very haughty, bossy sort of voice, just as Cathy had expected.

Aunty Nancy nodded. "Yes, ma'am, this is my sister's girl, Cathy."

Cathy bobbed nervously. "Good afternoon, Miss."

"Hm." Miss Buckley's washed-out blue eyes raked her from her toes to the top of her head, then flicked away again dismissively. She was seated, her back ramrod-straight, with Patsy at a Snakes and Ladders board set out on a small, round, high table. Seeing Cathy, Patsy looked up and made as if to rise. "Sit still, child. We haven't finished."

She subsided reluctantly, looking scared. Cathy caught her eye, and winked, then glanced surreptitiously about the room. The other Miss Buckley, pink-faced and semi-balding, was fast asleep and snoring faintly with her mouth inelegantly open, propped up with pillows on a bed in the far corner.

"Now then." Miss Buckley drew Cathy's attention, and she stiffened. "I was going to convey my message via Nancy, but as you are here ... The weather has become most inclement, and the forecast is dreadful, so I have decided that Patricia will stay."

Cathy was startled. "She'll stay?"

Miss Buckley tapped her foot. "Stay, girl, stay! It is far too wet for her to hang around at a bus stop or to walk along a country lane. If the weather has improved in the morning, then you may come back again and take her home. If it has not, then, obviously, for the time being she will continue to stay." Patsy looked up, shocked.

"But she can't!"

Miss Buckley drew herself up still further. "I beg your pardon?"

Cathy was flustered. "I'm sorry, ma'am, but – well, Ji ... Mr Norris – I don't think he'd like it if I did."

"You are his spokesperson?"

"No, ma'am ..."

"Do you consider Mr Norris to be an intelligent man?"

"Yes, ma'am ..."

"Does he care at all for his child?"

"Well, yes, of course, of course he does, ma'am, he loves Patsy ..."

"Well, then. The matter is closed."

Cathy was tongue-tied, bereft of argument. "But ... but ..."

Miss Buckley nodded at Nancy. "You may give this young person her tea in the kitchen, Nancy, before she goes. You may lend her an umbrella and some galoshes." She glanced narrowly at Cathy. "Mind now, I shall expect to get them back."

All she could think of all the way home was: *We're going to be on our own.*

Chapter 17

There would have been opportunities, even with Patsy around, if he'd wanted them, but this was the first time in the evening that the little girl hadn't actually been somewhere in the house. It was now or never. She felt ever so strange, really wound up and buzzy, almost feverish, as she went about her evening chores and then got down the bathtub. She avoided using Mrs Norris's Pink Lilac in case it reminded him of his wife, and had to resort to lavender flowers tossed into the bathwater, realising too late that she should have put them in a bag. It took her ages to clear out the tub.

She was dressing as she heard him drive into the yard, and her heart was beating rapidly as she hurried into the kitchen, patting down her hair. "How was it, Mr Norris?" she asked.

He shrugged. "Oh, just the same. No change."

"Ahh."

"Patsy okay?" He sat down wearily at the table and she hurriedly got out the boiled ham she'd prepared to serve with tomatoes and pickles for his supper.

She nodded, taking her chair. She picked up a ripe tomato, sniffing its rich earthy scent. "Mm, lovely."

"Get to sleep all right, did she?"

To delay answering, she bit hard into the tomato, closing her eyes in appreciation of the sweetly scented taste. "'Mm, these are ever so good." He was staring at her. A trickle of juice had escaped her lips, and she licked it away quickly. A slight frown flickered across his face.

What would he say? Swallowing the sweet flesh quickly, she pushed the bowl towards him. "Here, have one."

"No – um, no thanks." Dropping his gaze, he pushed away his plate. "I'm sorry, Cath, not hungry. Sorry you've had the trouble."

She was too distracted to be disappointed. "No trouble."

She drew in a deep breath. "Um, actually, Patsy's not here."

He looked up again anxiously. "What's happened? Is she all right?"

She hurried to reassure him. "Oh, yes, she's fine! Fine. Um ..." she drew in another breath. "Um, Jim ..." She bit her tongue, hearing herself calling him that aloud, but he threw her a faint, tired grin.

"'S all right, you can call me Jim if you want."

She blushed, staring down at her knife and fork. "It's just – well, Miss Buckley, she said as it was raining so hard, she'd got to stay the night. I'm to go and get her in the morning, if it's stopped. I couldn't help it. Miss Buckley wouldn't take any notice of me. I did say you wouldn't like it. I'm sorry."

He was silent. She glanced up at him from under her lashes. He was staring at her, but it was difficult to read his expression. She could feel her heart beating. The kitchen clock ticked loudly in the silence. After a moment, he cleared his throat and looked away. He picked up his cup. "I see. Patsy all right about it, was she?"

She found herself gabbling. "Well, she was a bit surprised, not that happy about it, but Miss Buckley had her playing Snakes and Ladders, and she'd found a glass eye that she liked – it used to belong to –" She bit her lip. Best not to mention Mrs Norris, even in connection with her gran's glass eye. She shrugged. "To somebody ... I forget."

She took another peek at him and felt a shiver of excitement as she realised his gaze was on her breasts. Her heart started pounding as he rose from his seat. He was weakening. It was going to happen. At last, he was giving in.

She waited, holding her breath as he moved slowly around the table until he was standing over her. Taking hold of one of the little buttons on her blouse, he ran his thumb over its shape. She shivered, feeling his knuckles against her breast. He drew in a breath and his tone was chilly. "Where did you get these from?"

She was startled. "Pardon?"

He tweaked the button. "These buttons on your blouse. Where did you get them from?"

Oh, heck, Mrs Norris's pretty tortoise buttons! She was wearing the green blouse. She grimaced, flustered. "I don't know, I found them somewhere."

"I put them in Mary's drawer."

She coloured, feeling guilty. "Oh. Oh, yes, I remember now."

A small nerve was throbbing at the side of his jaw and

his tone was full of restrained anger. "I won't have you going through my wife's things."

Bitter disappointment flooded in and mingled with her guilt, and sudden anger rushed in on top of that. Bloody Mary! She felt hot tears rising. "They were just sitting there, going to waste. And any way, they were meant for me, Mum said. Mary doesn't want them, not where she is! What use will they ever be to her in that place? She's never coming back, and I –"

She broke off in a little cry as he grasped her arm roughly, pulling her from her chair. His voice was low and harsh and measured, and the fury in his eyes made her knees tremble. "Don't say that! We don't know that. Do you hear me? You will never say that again – never!"

The silence that followed rang loudly in her ears. His fingers were pinching her arm. Staring up at him, feeling all hot and cold and shocked and shaky and disappointed and out of control, her knees sagged suddenly and she found herself helplessly beginning to cry. "Oh, dear, I'm in such a muddle!"

"Hey, hey ..." Taken aback, he let go of her arm. Sobbing bitterly, she bolted for the door.

Why ever had he spoken to her like that? They were only bloody buttons. Jim could have kicked himself.

After searching all the outhouses and the greenhouse and the hen house and the orchard, he found her at last curled up behind the Red Hot Pokers at the edge of the lawn, still sobbing as though her heart would break. Feeling wretched, he crouched down, rocking her, cradling her to his chest. "Cath ... Cathy, I'm sorry, come on now, hey, don't cry!"

The warm, wonderful, safe feeling as he held her let it all came out in a rush, and it was true, all true. "Oh, Mr Norris, I know you love Mary – Mrs Norris – and I know I shouldn't have taken the buttons and I know that I can't take her place, but ..." Tailing off in a squeak, she drew in another shuddering breath. "I do love you, Mr Norris! I do love you, and I don't know ... I can't bear it! I do want ... but you said ... and I can't ... you don't want ... I can't just be here, Mr Norris. Not any more." She drew in a quavering breath. "I think I'd better go away."

She wanted so much for him to jump in with an immediate "No!" but instead, he sighed. "Come on, stand up." Drawing her to her feet, he took out his handkerchief, and gently but ineffectually tried to wipe away her tears, frowning as he did so. "I understand," he said.

She swallowed a sob. That was it then, was it? He was going to let her go. It was all over. She'd have to go back and live with her mum.

"My fault, the whole thing. I shouldn't have done that, in the garden. I shouldn't have done that. I know I've hurt you." Keeping his eyes from meeting hers, he cleared his throat. "Mind you ... mind you, if you wanted to stay, you could trust me, you'd be quite safe, I'd never do it again."

Cathy blinked. She pushed away his hand. "But I want you to! I want you to, I do! Don't you understand?"

He met her eyes then, looking flabbergasted. "You want me to?"

"I do!"

He seemed shell-shocked. "But what about ..."

She stamped, losing control again and flailing her arms in the air. "I don't care! I don't care about anything! I just want to be with you, and if I can't be – if you don't want me – if you can't, because of loving Mrs Norris – well then, I'll have to find another job. I can't stand it." She dissolved once again in tears.

He ran his fingers through his tangled hair. "Cath, Cath, you're very young. Your mum trusts me."

"Bit late to worry about that, Mr Norris!" Seeing his expression, she was sorry. She softened her tone. "All I want is that you want me."

He sounded angry. "I want you to stay."

She felt a touch of exultation, but suppressed it, needing to be sure. "I might stay. But it'll only be because you want us to be together, not just want me to lend a hand. When we – when we were in the garden, you said that you wanted me. Do you?"

There was a long silence as he stared at her, then he sighed. "Oh, Cath. You know I do." It felt as if the sun had come out inside her. He stared at her for a long moment, his eyes filled with a sort of agonised desperation, then with a kind of a shudder, opened his arms to her helplessly. "Oh, Cath. Oh, Cath, come here."

She was coming home. Feeling his lips on hers was utter magic.

"Just one thing, Cath," he murmured, breaking off for a moment with a frown. "If we're going to – well, be together –" For a moment she was worried, but when she opened her eyes to look at him anxiously, he was grinning. "You'll have to stop calling me 'Mr Norris'. I've said you can call me Jim."

Unlike Cathy, Patsy was very unhappy when she woke up the next morning. She had woken in the night as she always did, but she had been afraid to call. She had just hidden right under the bedclothes listening to the wind howling and the pattering rain until the morning came and Aunty Nancy had arrived and had taken her to have a wash.

It was icy cold in the bathroom. Her teeth chattered as she stood in her nightie, barefoot on the linoleum floor. Aunty Nancy had been going to help her, but Aunty May had come into the bathroom and had sent her back downstairs. "I shall supervise the child myself, Nancy. You may go and see to the kippers."

Aunty May started by telling her that she wasn't brushing her teeth thoroughly enough, and then she handed her two flannels, both white, but each marked with a differently coloured cross embroidered in one corner.

"This red one, Patricia, is for when you wash *down there*. It is very important, Patricia, for a young lady to wash *down there*. It is very important to wash *down there* every day, Patricia. From the front to the back, always."

Embarrassed, she nodded, but Aunty May was running water into the basin and had her back turned, so she didn't see. She glanced round sharply. "Answer me, child! If I say something to you, I expect you to answer – and always use a person's name when you are talking to them. When I tell you something, Patricia, you should always answer."

Patsy's lip trembled. She felt like crying. "Yes, Aunty May."

The soap Aunty May gave her to use was hard and green and smelled of medicine. She showed her a glass jar with some sort of greenish-white jelly stuff in the bottom. "This is for the last bit of your soap," she told her briskly. "It is waste-not, want-not, in this household, Patricia. Never let me see you throwing anything away." The green soap was hard and didn't make many suds, but she had to scrub herself for ages underneath Aunty May's eagle eye, especially her ears and knees and the back of her neck. To her horror, Aunty May even wanted to watch her wash '*down there*', to make certain that she did it properly.

Aunty May was very rough when it came to doing her hair. She wielded the hairbrush very heavily. When Patsy winced, Aunty May said, "Pish-posh, child! Stop that nonsense!" so she had to keep biting at her bottom lip instead.

There was one nice thing, though – Aunty May tutted a bit as she fastened the buttons on Patsy's grey pinafore skirt. "Growing out of it. And no hem to let out! What a bother." She stood looking down at Patsy with her hands clasped and the wire-framed glasses on her thin nose glittering and her head cocked to one side a little, and she was almost, but not quite, smiling. "We shall have to get you a new dress. What colour do you like, Patricia?"

Patsy whispered back hopefully, "Pink?"

It was just as cold in the morning room as it was everywhere else. There was a fire in the small grate, but it was barely alight, and the other aunty, Aunty Lou, had the chair nearest to it so Patsy had to sit at the opposite side. It was very quiet, too. Nobody talked. The only sounds she could hear were the wheezy ticking of the big grandfather clock in the corner, the occasional tinkle of cutlery or clink of china, and a funny clicking noise whenever Aunty Lou was chewing her bread. It fascinated her, but Aunty May caught her looking. "Patricia! It is impolite to stare!"

The things they called kippers were cold and very whiskery and the bones kept getting stuck between Patsy's teeth. She didn't like them at all, but didn't know how to say. It made her want to cry again. She tried to hold back the tears, but Aunty Lou got very flustered. Her fat pink cheeks got very wobbly. "May, does the child have a cold? I do hope she hasn't a cold. I catch cold so very easily."

Aunty May frowned. "Patricia, do you have a cold?"

Patsy shook her head. "No, Aunty May," she whispered.

"Then why are you sniffing? Did you not bring down a handkerchief?"

Aunty Lou waved a hand distractedly. "Tell the child to leave the table, May. She is making me feel quite unwell!"

Aunty May gestured to Patsy. "Come here, child." With her white napkin still clutched in her fingers, Patsy scraped back her chair. Aunty May scanned her face carefully for a moment, and then said, quite gently, "Would you like to go upstairs to play?"

Patsy nodded.

"Then put away your napkin."

Still sniffing, Patsy carefully folded the starched napkin, but her eyes were too blurry to fit it into its tortoiseshell ring. There was a huge sob in her throat that was struggling to come out, and she was losing the battle to hold it back. Quite gently, Aunty May took the napkin away from her. "Leave it, child, leave it!" she murmured.

Turning back to the table, she began to insert the napkin efficiently into its holder. "You may go now," she said briskly. "Go along, Patricia. You may run along."

She couldn't play when she got up to the cold, unfamiliar room. Instead, she did what she did at home when she was feeling miserable; she climbed over the bed and squashed herself down into the gap between the bed and the wall, and pulled the eiderdown over her, then let the tears come trickling out.

Mummy ...!

Chapter 18

J im, have I got a big nose?" Standing on tiptoes, Cathy peered into the small mirror over the sink and folded her blonde hair into a heavy roll over her forehead.

"What?" Jim tore open the envelope that Ted the postman had handed to him just as he was coming in. Looked like Miss Buckley's writing. What did she want, then?

"Only it says in my magazine that if you've got a big nose, you should wear your hair in a bolster fringe. Would it suit me?"

"What the dickens is a bolster fringe?"

She turned to face him, holding the roll in place. "Like this, see. Look, Jim. What d'you think? Does it suit me or not?"

He glanced across at her, distracted. "Eh? Oh, um – oh, not sure about that."

She turned back to the mirror. "Perhaps I haven't got a big nose, then. Would you say my face is round, or long, or heart shaped?"

He unfolded the single page that was inside the envelope. "No, you haven't."

She was puzzled. "Haven't what?"

He blinked. "Haven't got a big nose." He scanned the letter.

Dear Mr Norris,

I am disappointed that poor Mary has made no further progress over the years since her move to Patterson Park, despite all the recommendations. However, since you appear to be satisfied that she is being kindly treated and that they are doing everything there to help her that they can, and since my money is no longer required for her support, I feel that I should direct what dwindling resources are left towards her daughter's education instead. As you are aware, I am not happy with the current arrangements and I have no doubt that

*she will be much better served by a few years spent at a good
boarding school ...*

He didn't absorb the rest; he was too stunned.

"Patsy was crying again when I left her at school today.
Seems to hate it again these days, don't know why," Cathy
told him, experimentally twisting the fringe into a row of
kiss-curls. "Oh, and you know what you were saying, Jim,
about how those scrap metal men have carted off all the iron
hurdles from the Barrows' hayricks? Well, they were in the
school this morning, taking off the iron gates! I suppose every
little helps."

She chuckled gleefully, waving the hairbrush for emphasis. "Oh, and here's a good bit – do you know what else I
heard? Those Miss Buckleys, they've had to have evacuees!
Listen to this! Well! They both had cooties, didn't they and
you can imagine what the Miss Buckleys thought about that,
and Nancy said – are you listening, Jim, it's ever so shocking!
Nancy told my mum that the little lad ... he's only six, or was
it seven? – well, anyway, he messed up his pants – they were
his dad's trousers cut down short, poor kiddy, that's what
they both were wearing – and he didn't know what to do with
them, his dirty pants, 'cos he'd forgotten there was an indoor
lav, you see, and he couldn't open the back door, so he hid
them in the piano stool in the parlour and *Miss Buckley* found
them! Can you imagine!"

"No, I can't." Jim was still staring at the letter. The bloody
idea ...! What a bloody cheek, interfering old battle-axe.

But what would Mary have said? Would it have pleased
Mary?

Crumpling it up, he stuffed it in his pocket. "Well, yes,
actually, I can. Poor kid."

"Yes, poor little things. Anyway, after a great big rumpus,
she made Nancy go out and buy some new clothes for them, so
that was nice." She frowned into the mirror, musing. "Maybe
I ought to have a perm."

Patsy was still desperately upset when Cathy went to meet
her in the afternoon. "Oh, it was so sad, Jim!" she told
him, folding up the freshly dried sheets. "I know sometimes
she annoys me and she's a big girl now, but she was really
crying, she'd got all – you know, a runny nose. I told her
teacher."

He spoke through gritted teeth. "Little blighters."

"No wonder she's been getting upset. Still teasing her

about her mum! You'd think they'd have found something else to amuse themselves with after all this time. Children can be so cruel!"

He came to a decision. "Ah, she'll be better off out of it," he said roughly, pulling on his jacket and opening the back door abruptly.

"What do you mean?" Tight-lipped, he shook his head and she watched, bewildered, as he strode away across the yard.

He didn't quite get round to telling her that evening, nor at bedtime, but he put a restraining arm about her as she reached over for her dressing gown in the morning. "Cath –"

The candle flickered as she fumbled for the sleeves of her dressing gown. "I'll have to go down, Jim. Patsy might wake. It'll be light soon."

He pulled her back towards him. "Hang on a minute. Wait."

She giggled, dropping the dressing gown and sliding back close to his side. "One minute, then. Just one." Ducking her head beneath the quilt, she pressed her lips against his chest. He threw back the edge of the quilt, making the candle flame flutter even more brightly. "No, Cath, just listen. No."

She giggled again, manoeuvring herself down the bed. "Don't want to listen." Her voice was muffled.

He arched his body. "But I need to tell you ... Mary's Aunty May –"

She reached up blindly, pressing her fingers against his lips. "Ssh ..."

As she disappeared still further beneath the bedclothes, Jim groaned and gave up the struggle. "Okay. You win."

He tried to break his news again a little later as she was preparing the bucket for the hens. "What I was saying earlier, Cath, about Mary's Aunty May. She sent me a letter." He watched her carefully; she could take this the wrong way. "Like I said, I got a letter, and the thing is ... the thing is, Cath, she wants to pay for Patsy to go to boarding school."

She was staggered. "Boarding school! But why?"

He glanced at the hall door. Didn't want Patsy hearing about this yet. "Ssh!"

She put her hands on her hips. "Why, Jim? I'm not good enough, I suppose?"

"No, no, it's not that!" he assured her hastily, if not entirely truthfully.

"Anyway, she's too young, Jim! And she'll be going up to the Central School next term. It's a good school, our Frankie's doing ever so well."

"Not the same though, is it?"

Her voice rose again. "I never put you down as a snob, Jim Norris!"

He was insulted. "I'm not, I'm not, but think about it, Cath! Nobody'll know about Mary. All the advantages she'll have! Be honest, if Patsy was your daughter, would you turn down the opportunity?"

She slammed her hands on the tabletop. "Yes, I would, I would! I wouldn't want my daughter growing up looking down on me – that's what'll happen, Jim, she'll start looking down on you!"

His voice rose angrily, too. "She won't, she won't!"

He wasn't a hundred percent sure that she wouldn't but his fists clenched and his mouth set in a stubborn line. "Anyway, I've decided."

They loaded up the van for the morning delivery in silence. Jim cranked up the engine and jumped in, avoiding meeting Cathy's eyes.

"I won't be in at dinner, and I'll be late back this afternoon. Going over to see Mary when I'm done."

'Seeing Mary' wasn't something that actually happened, of course, she knew that. It just meant that he'd drive the winding miles over to the Mental Institution, sit around for a bit, have a few words with a nurse, or with a doctor if he was lucky, and then turn round and drive all the way back. He'd been doing it for years. All it meant was that he'd be even more depressed when he got back, as if he wasn't crabby enough at the moment already.

Still miffed, she stalked back into the house and into Patsy's bedroom. "Hurry up, Patsy, you're going to be late for school."

Patsy hunched more deeply into the bedcovers. "I don't want to go."

"Too bad. Get up and don't be daft." As soon as she had said it, she was sorry. She sat down quickly on the bed. "Come on, Pats – it'll be all right now. I've told your teacher."

Patsy shrugged her off roughly. "Leave me alone. I'm not going."

"You are, lovey, you have to. The king says; it's the law – all children have to go to school. Come on." Cathy tried to winkle her out by tickling. "Let's be having you!"

Patsy lashed out with her feet beneath the bedclothes, catching Cathy painfully in the stomach. "I'm not *going!*"

Cathy saw red. Pulling off the eiderdown, she grasped Patsy's arm and tried to manhandle her out of the bed. "Oh, yes, you are, my lady! Come on, out of there!"

Patsy's shrieks were ear piercing. "I'M NOT BLOODY GOING!!!!"

"Okay, you stay there then, see if I care." Cathy marched crossly to the door. "You can stay there all day, and don't expect me to bring you any breakfast. You can do without till dinnertime."

S he had the wireless on, tuned into *Workers' Playtime* and was laying the table for supper when she felt his arms slip about her waist.

"Sorry."

She turned into his arms. "I'm only worried about you. And Patsy."

"I know, I know. I'm sorry."

She clicked her tongue, shaking her head ruefully, though she couldn't suppress a grin. "I forgive you; thousands wouldn't."

He chuckled. "It's been a horrible day. Oh, I've missed you ..." Fired by the relief of reconciliation they were lost for the moment in each other, but their passionate embrace was terminated abruptly by a sudden sound from the hall. Pink-cheeked, Cathy moved quickly to the stove and a frustrated Jim sat hastily at the table before Patsy could stomp sulkily into the kitchen. She moved straight to the table without looking at either of them and once there, sat with her elbows on the table and her head buried in a book.

Cathy carried over two plates of food, setting one before Jim, and then nudged Patsy, waiting to set down the other. "Come on, lovey! Did you wash your hands?" There was silence.

Jim glanced across. "Cathy's talking to you, Patsy."

Sour faced, Patsy made room for the plate. Smiling, Cathy whisked away her book. "We don't want this at the table, do we?" Putting it on the dresser, she carried her own plate over to the table and began to tuck in eagerly.

"Mm, quite tasty, don't you think so, Jim? It's called a Lord Woolton Pie. It's only veg like carrots and swedes and cauli and things all chopped up with some oatmeal and parsley and vegetable extract and then you cover it with potato, but it doesn't half sound posh! I got the recipe from Gert and Daisy on the wireless. They had some nice recipes today. I thought Patsy and I might try to make a carrot tart later, what d'you you think, Pats?"

Patsy shrugged, scowling. Cathy tried again to involve her

and lighten the mood, chuckling, "Here, what about this, Pats? I heard it this morning.

Those who have the will to win
Cook potatoes in their skin
For they know the sight of peelings
Deeply hurts Lord Woolton's feelings!"

She collapsed with giggles. "Don't you think that's funny?" Patsy continued to scowl into her plate. "Well, it made me laugh!"

Jim suddenly realised. "What are you doing at home, Pats? Why aren't you at school?"

"I hate school."

"Yes, but you have to go."

"I told her that, but she wouldn't have it." Cathy shook her head. "You'll have to go in tomorrow. We'll say you've been a bit poorly."

Scraping back her chair noisily, Patsy rose abruptly and stamped out of the room.

Cathy shook her head as the back door slammed behind her. "She is in a state."

"Ought to have some manners." Jim put down his knife and fork and pushed back his own chair.

"When are you going to tell her? About the boarding school, I mean?" She hesitated, but just couldn't leave it. "Jim? D'you really want her to go? You are certain?"

His lips set tightly and she held up her palms placatingly. "All right. All right. You know best."

Patsy didn't raise much objection when he broke the news. She seemed quite intrigued. "Will it be like the Chalet School?"

"I don't know, pet. Where's that?"

"Switzerland."

He grinned. "Then probably not. Not much skiing and cuckoo clocks and stuff, as far as I'm aware."

"Probably more like the Manor House School, then."

He was equally ignorant of that. "Maybe."

If she was worried or excited, she didn't show it. She seemed to accept it as a fact of life, continuing to slink about the place withdrawn and sulky, but to Jim's surprise, Cathy grew quite excited as the months passed and preparations went on apace. The idea of not having Patsy around was growing on her. It would be very nice to have the cottage all to themselves, with no need to slip back to share Patsy's bed before dawn, or skulk around in corners.

Her only disappointment was that Miss Buckley insisted on ordering Patsy's new requirements herself and having them sent over to the house. It was fair enough – after all, she was paying – but Cathy was still miffed. It was her place. Who had been looking after Patsy all these years? Besides, she'd come to fancy the idea of drifting round some posh shops.

She disguised her frustration with a general moaning about how much more sensible it would have been to have asked Nancy to make her a lot of the things, or to find out if there was a second-hand uniform shop at the school, instead of spending such a great deal of money. She also threw in her own bit of weight by handing over slightly wrong measurements, to make sure that the sizes Miss Buckley ordered would not be outgrown for a good long time. In view of the war effort and all, she reported to Elsie. She was quite proud of herself for thinking of it. It was only sensible.

At last, with only a few days to go, the collection of the items on the long list was completed. Beaming, Cathy entered from the hall with an unwilling and glowering Patsy dawdling behind. "Come on Patsy – come on, lovey. Show your dad!"

He stared at Patsy. She looked so small, lost and gawky in the brand new and over-sized gymslip, shirt and blazer that he didn't quite know what to say. "Aye! Aye, lovely! Smashing."

Patsy sighed heavily. "Can I go now?"

Cathy nodded happily. "Yes, go and take it off, lovey. We want to keep it nice and clean."

Jim waited till she had left the room, then he murmured awkwardly, "Isn't it – ? I mean, I don't know anything about these things, Cath, but isn't it just a bit, well, big?"

Cathy shook her head confidently. "She'll grow into it."

He was still uncertain and a little anxious. "Don't want her to get teased there as well, you know. Just looks a bit ..." Lost for the right words, he shrugged.

Cathy bustled about confidently. "She's still a growing lass, Jim! They'll all be the same, the growing ones, you'll see! They'll all have uniforms that'll last a year or two. Any sensible mum will have done like me." Seeing his face and realising her slip, she blushed.

With a struggle, he managed to surmount the moment. "You're just doing the best you can for her, I know."

Patsy was a little bit tearful when the time came for her departure, though Jim was even more upset, having decided during the night that it was wrong to send her; she might not like it, and anyway, they ought to keep her at home, not miles away with a war on. Reporting their farewells at the train station to Cathy, he struggled to reassure himself.

"She was a bit nervous when she saw the other girls, but she was all right once I'd handed her over to the teacher who's going to be in charge on the journey. Seemed like a nice woman: very smart. Quite exciting, for Patsy, going for a long journey on a train! She'll have some fun once she's settled down – and she'll still be in the countryside, won't she, be safe there as much as she is here."

"Of course she will!" Carefully beginning to pin back the collar of Jim's second-best shirt ready to sew it on the other way round, Cathy shook her head. "Fancy, Miss Buckley suggesting hiring a car to take her there and to bring her home again for the holidays!"

She sniffed. "If you ask me, she probably didn't want to start her off on the wrong note, seeing her rolling up in your old van with everyone else in their dads' posh whatsits, Jaguars and things."

"We've probably none of us got the petrol." Though there could be a grain of truth in it, he admitted to himself; he had felt a bit out of place at the station in his shabby suit and ancient trilby compared to the other parents in their smart suits and coats and flashy hats. There hadn't been many other fathers, mostly mums.

She concentrated her gaze on the tiny stitches. "I could have come with you, Jim."

"Aye, Cath, I know that."

She scuffed her toe. "Ashamed of me or something, Jim?"

He hastened to reassure her, putting his arms about her. "Of course not, love; not for a moment." He kissed her firmly on her round pink cheek. "Never."

He was too ashamed to admit, even to himself, that, deep down, a tiny part of him actually was.

Hemlines have gone up, then, Cathy?" Sadie Pickering threw her a measuring gaze.

She shrugged, concentrating on her flashing knitting needles. "I believe so, Mrs Pickering, though I'm usually in trousers now."

Mrs Pickering nodded. "Hm." Glancing up briefly, Cathy saw her surreptitiously exchange a knowing look with her neighbour, Renée Tingle.

Setting aside her knitting to wipe a dewdrop from her nose

with a fine white cambric handkerchief – one of the perks of the haberdashery business on Queen Street she now ran with her daughter – Mrs Tingle eyed Cathy beadily. "So what are you doing now, Cathy, now that Patsy's gone off to school? Don't suppose you'll be staying on without her at the cottage. No doubt you'll be coming back home?"

Cathy reddened. *So it's starting; I knew I shouldn't have come.* The last meeting of the ladies' knitting circle in her mum's kitchen, at which socks, balaclavas and gloves for the forces were fabricated for despatch to the WI, had ended in a right ding-dong between her and her mum after everyone had gone, from which she hadn't really recovered.

"You can't stay there on your own with Jim, now, it's not right, Cath!" her mum had said. "It's not proper! You know how people will talk."

Failing to find any argument to put forward short of telling her the truth, eventually Cath had lost her temper. "Well, I'm going to, Mum, and that's that. You can't stop me." The sound of the back door slamming had echoed in her ears all the way home.

Despite that, to her great surprise, as the women round the table awaited her response in bright-eyed, prurient interest, Elsie rallied to her cause. Her thickening fingers still darting skilfully as she fabricated a thick grey sock made by unravelling the wool from three old pairs of Tommy's outgrown school ones, she shot Mrs Tingle a calm, cool look. "Oh, I think she's still got her work cut out, Renée, don't you, with Jim Norris spending a lot of his time at the farm? And Patsy'll be home, of course, anyway, quite a bit of the time; they have long holidays at these boarding schools. I hope there isn't going to be any silly gossip." Her eyes carried a flicker of warning as she glanced around the group and smiled.

Cathy felt a rush of gratitude mixed with a raw flicker of chary suspicion. Did Mum know?

J im was waiting for her, leaning on the bridge as she got off the bus at the top of the lane. His bike was leaning against the overgrown hedge. "Thought I'd hang about and walk up with you."

"That's nice."

She waited till she was sure they were out of sight of the main road and then drew up and turned, flinging her arms about his neck. "Give us a great big kiss."

He did so and it was lovely. Setting off again, she linked her arm through his. Walking slowly up the lane between hedges laden with blackberries and garlanded with bryony, she felt a sudden wave of melancholy. Be so nice not to have to worry about stupid tongues wagging; so nice if this was all above board.

She smiled up at him cheerily, though. "How did the gardening talk go?"

He shrugged. "Oh, you know ... it was fine. I just gave them the gist of it really, how to get the ground ready for vegetables and stuff, what sort of things you can grow. There was a bit of a debate, whether or nor to grow flowers."

"Can't see you not growing any!" *If only to have some to take to Mary,* she added spitefully to herself, immediately regretting it. "Anyway, people are going to need the seeds in the future, aren't they; people like us have got to keep them going. Besides, lovely bright flowers – they cheer everybody up."

"Got a leaflet today from the RSPCA, telling us to feed chickens on weed seeds and berries and nuts," he told her, as they drew near the cottage gate. "Have to know which are poisonous and which are not, which can be dangerous."

Dropping his bike, he reached up into the hedge, plucking out a juicy blackberry and then clambered back down. Slipping an arm closely about her, he drew her to him, holding the rich purple berry temptingly above her lips. "This one, for example," he told her. "It can make you very sleepy; best only to eat it when you're sure you're about to lie down."

He was very late going off to Barrows for the evening's milking and Cathy saw to the hens and chopped up some logs in the dark with just her petti on under her coat.

There were distinct advantages to being on their own.

Chapter 19

Patsy had been allocated the fourth bed along in a row all down one side of the long dormitory, so it hadn't been possible at school to make herself a hidey-hole down the side of her bed like she did at home. After a few weeks she found a place behind the equipment shed near the netball court where nobody went and when things got too bad she took herself off there and wept. It wasn't a bit like the Chalet School, or like Mallory Towers. She hated this place, and she hated meal times and she hated the teachers and most of all she hated the other girls – and after the first few weeks, she didn't care if they knew.

"Please, Daddy, please, please!" The girls were allowed one telephone call a week, and at first she tried and tried to get Daddy and Cathy to take her back home, but neither would listen. As far as they were both concerned, she was stuck with it; Daddy had been upset when she cried, but just said she'd get used to it as time went on and 'chin up, it'll get better, pet,' and Cathy, well, she tried to sound sympathetic, but Patsy knew very well that she just wanted her out of the way. Cathy was kind enough, but she wasn't really interested in Patsy. All she really wanted was Dad.

Cathy, in fact, she was beginning to see now, was a little bit embarrassing. "Was that your mother?" some snooty big girl in an older class had asked the first time with a snigger, after Daddy and Cathy had gone, Daddy, almost painfully proper in his best suit and starched collar, and Cathy, dressed in her best with too much lipstick, teetering in scuffed white high-heels and with a stupid little purple hat anchored firmly with a hairpin into her over-curled blonde hair. The little gang had cornered Patsy in the corner of the netball court. Snorting superciliously, the big girl had rolled her eyes at the others. "Did you see Norris's mother?"

Patsy was quick to contradict her. "Who, Cathy? Oh, she's not my mum."

"Who was she, then?"

"She–she's just our housekeeper." It sounded posh and it was true, wasn't it? The girl hadn't given up. "So where's your mother, then? Why didn't *she* come to school?"

The aching sickness in her tummy; the thick black swimmy feeling in her head. Not telling them that. "Oh. She's dead."

Emerging with Ted the postman and Bill Shiplady from a special parade in the makeshift guard post and armoury in the village hall in a bit of a hurry, Jim paused at the bottom of the steps to slip on his bicycle clips ready to cycle quickly over to Barrow's. Ted slapped him on the back. "Cheerio, Jim. See you at the exercise tonight."

"Eh?" He grinned. "Oh, right. Cheerio, Ted!"

The doors of the hall swung open to release a gale of laughter and another group of men clattered down the steps. Sam Pearson paused on the bottom step, lighting a cigarette, grinning knowingly. "In a hurry, Jim?"

Jim swung his leg over the crossbar of his bike and paused. "What's that?"

Sam nudged Arthur Meeks who was hovering like a grinning acolyte at his side. "Don't blame him, eh, Arthur?"

Arthur sniggered slyly. "Ah, he's got it made! Nice little cuddly sparrow, nice little cosy nest."

Jim tensed as Sam licked his lips lasciviously. "No rationing for you, eh, mate? Get rid of one woman, get another one in!"

Jim swung his leg back off the bike, his face clouding threateningly.

"What's she like, eh, Jim? Bet she's a goer, bet she's a right little cracker, often fancied her myself." Arthur sniggered.

Jim dropped his bike, fists clenched, but Bill Shiplady grasped his arm with a restraining hand. "Not worth it, Jim, mate. He's a mucky lad. You take no bloody notice."

He had been conscious for a long time that whispers were going round. When she'd first moved into the cottage, it was really just good-natured quipping that he'd heard, just the blokes at the farm and then from the Home Guard having a bit of a laugh; a bit envious, maybe, nothing serious, like they might be of any man sharing a house with a pretty young girl, no harm meant by it, and that was the way it had gone on. Since Patsy'd gone off to school, though, the tone of the whole thing had got very much worse, especially with a few of them like Arthur and Sam, and he'd really had enough of it. It was making him feel very bad.

He didn't make it home for dinner. He snatched a bite to eat with the other workers at Barrows, and then cycled back after a long afternoon's hedging to take part in the exercise, which involved holding the church against a platoon from the next village. When he did get home, quite late that evening, Cathy was all changed ready for bed and when she kissed him, he knew that he pulled away too fast. There was a tight, dark, unpleasant knot in his stomach.

Avoiding her eyes, he ate his supper silently and then went across to the dresser and lit his candle. "Bit tired, pet." It wasn't a lie. "Think I'll go up to bed."

"Oh." She was waiting for him to ask if she was coming up but he didn't.

"I'll see you tomorrow." He knew she was hurt, but he felt cold and unyielding and couldn't undo the knot.

After Evensong Cathy walked close by Jim's side, wishing she could slip her arm through his. At the corner, he swung onto his bike, then hesitated. "Cath, there's something I want to say to you. Wait up for me, eh? Meeting'll be finished by about nine. I shouldn't be too late back."

There was something in his eyes that said this was important and he held her gaze for a long time as if there was something significant he wanted to tell her. Her heart fluttered, wondering, as she watched him stride away.

Now that Patsy was going off to school, could he? Would he?

Riding off, he turned at the corner and raised a hand and she waved back, feeling a rising tide of excitement. She was sure of it now. Jim was going to propose.

She washed her hair and dried it in front of the stove and changed into the blue dress which was Jim's favourite, then started to work her way through the ever-growing pile of darning and make-do-and-mend, but she was too nervous and excited to get on very fast. When she heard Jim opening the shed door to put his bike away, she darted quickly to the mirror to check her hair for the umpteenth time, then composed herself quickly again with a sock and the darning mushroom.

She had just pricked her finger painfully with the darning needle when he opened the door. She smiled warmly. "Patrol go all right tonight? No problems?"

"No." He sat down wearily at the table.

"Aren't you going to take off your jacket? It's a warm night." She rose eagerly. "Here, pet, give it to me!"

He shook his head. "Cath, sit down."

She did so, feeling even more flustered. As always when discomforted, she chattered. "I saw the new land girl at Barrows today. She's feeling a bit hard done-by, I think. Seems a bit of a townie; not taking very well to country life!"

He shrugged. "The girls are okay, but even with old Ernie the cowman as well in the afternoons, the farm's too big to handle." He fell into silence.

Cathy jumped to her feet. "I'll put the kettle on."

He frowned heavily. "Cath, I said sit down!" he told her roughly.

Shock at his abrasive tone drove her to sit meekly. When she had settled, he drew in a deep breath. "Look, Cath, have you thought about it yet?"

"About Patsy going off to school?"

He shook his head. "No, Cath, about you. Now that she's gone, we'll have to think about you. For one thing, now you're not looking after Patsy, you'll have to register."

"I can register as a land girl," she suggested eagerly. "I can be another land girl for you. You can share me between here and there. Like I said, you need a new girl."

Jim's face darkened. "No! For Christ's sake, Cathy! No, you can't." There was desperation in his face and in his voice. "Look, Cath, people are talking already, even with Patsy here, and now she's gone – no, no, it isn't right for you to stop here any more. I'm sorry."

A deep silence followed. Rigid with disappointment, Cathy rose stiffly. "I'll make you a cup of tea."

Jim slammed his fist on the table. "I don't want a bloody cup of tea! Look, Cath –"

A huge surge of hurt and anger welled up in her and burst. "No, you look, Jim! I don't care what people think, you ought to know that by now, so why should you? Do you think I haven't heard the gossip? I've even had to fight my mum! Do you think I'd still be here if it wasn't where I wanted to be more than anywhere else in the world? I *want* to be here, Jim!"

He answered harshly. "Well, I don't want you here, not any longer."

His words seemed to drop into a deep, dark, endless well. There was a buzzing in her head. Stunned, she turned away and busied herself with the kettle.

Already wishing he could take it back, Jim rose and put a

tentative hand on her shoulder. "Cath? Cath, I didn't mean it like that."

She didn't respond. Pouring out the kettle with a shaking hand, she scalded herself and winced, cradling her hand.

"Hell, Cath! No, no –" He forced her to turn. "Let me see ..."

She shook her head. "It's nothing."

That made Jim angry. "Yes, it bloody well is!" His own hands were shaking and he held tight, desperate to convey his remorse. "I didn't mean to hurt you, Cathy. You've been the making of me, of me and Patsy. It's just that I –" He shook his head. "I can't *marry* you, Cath."

Staring down into her eyes, he willed her to understand. "I can't marry you. I can't. Never. And it's not right, it's not fair! Knowing what they're all saying ... it's nearly finishing me." He could see the pain and incomprehension in her round blue eyes, but he had to go on.

"But I'm all mixed up. I see you, and I watch you ..." He was losing the battle with himself. "Oh, Cathy!" With a ferocity that was almost cruel, he pulled her into his arms.

After only a moment's hesitation, Cathy clung to him.

In bed that night as they lay at last exhausted, Jim gazed up at the ceiling, frowning. "What have I done to you, Cathy?"

She pressed her lips against his chest. "Made a loose woman of me! And I'm glad."

"I can't marry you, Cath."

"Jim, hush. Stop talking. Hush."

Next morning, he caught hold of her skirt as she was dressing. "Cath, what I said last night –"

She spoke quietly. "I heard you."

He rose on one arm. "If you move out to your mum's, we'll do as you said. Get yourself posted to Barrow's as a land girl. That way we can be together sometimes."

There was silence as she finished fastening her buttons. When at last she spoke, she did so calmly and evenly. "It's not that you can't marry me, Jim. You don't want to."

He was outraged. "I do want to! I want you every day!"

"But you don't want to *marry* me."

Why couldn't she understand?! "I *can't!*"

There was silence as Cathy brushed her hair carefully, watching him through the mirror, then she said, "You're not still in love with Mary, are you? Not like she is. Not after all this time."

Now it was Jim's turn to be silent.

Putting down the brush, she sat beside him on the bed.

"You know they'd let you divorce her, don't you, if you wanted to?" she said gently. "If somebody's incurably insane, you can."

Jim shook his head stubbornly. "We don't know it's incurable, not forever, do we? Suppose she got better. I can't just abandon her. Mary is my wife!"

She took his hand. "Don't go kidding yourself, Jim. They've given up. She's not going to get any better. When was the last time they told you there was any hope?"

She touched his cheek wistfully. "I do *want* to marry you, you know. One day, I want to have your baby."

S o you're doing all right, then, pet?" Jim turned away from the chattering throng in the Post Office and put one finger in his ear so that he could hear her better.

"Yes, I'm fine."

Patsy's voice sounded a little flat and thin, but nevertheless he was reassured. It was probably the phone line. "That's good! Everything's all right this end. Cathy sends her love." Nodding at Molly Cartwright and Sam Digby who were waiting in line for the phone, he mouthed at them, "Won't be a minute."

"I'd better go, Pats. Keep up the good work, eh? Keep smiling!"

Her voice was even fainter this time. "Yes."

"Right, then. I'll ring you again next week. Bye-bye, poppet."

There was a slight pause during which he could hear a strident bell ringing. "Sounds as if you need to be off, too. Is that for your lessons?"

"Yes."

"You'd better hurry along, then. Right. Bye-bye, then lovey. Bye."

He smiled to himself as he set down the receiver. It was good to think that she was happy at the school now. He had had his doubts when she'd seemed so miserable, but it looked as if she had settled.

W hen she had put the receiver down, Patsy dragged herself miserably along the corridor towards her form room. St Winifred's was horrible. Nobody liked her and nobody wanted her to be with them at all. The days seemed to drag on and on forever. She hated the work. This afternoon was particularly grim – History test today before they were let out for Games, and she hadn't even attempted to swot up. History was so *boring*. All those stupid names and dates and things were just impossible.

Miss Mills was waiting, her whiskery chins wobbling as she supervised the line of girls assembled outside the classroom door. "No talking, girls!" Patsy followed the silent file into the chalk-smelling classroom with its tall, narrow windows high-set in the walls and climbed onto her chair like the others in the familiar stupid routine. If you got the answer wrong, Miss Mills screwed up her sour face and called you a stupid girl and you had to stay on your chair and then stay and make long lists of dates and things instead of going to Games. It also meant at least one House Demerit, which meant braving the House prefects' anger and, if they felt like encouraging it, the revenge of the other girls.

The thought sent her into panic. She could try it again; it usually worked with the other teachers. Quickly, she put her hand up before Miss Mills could get round to her. "I've got an awful headache," she told her when Miss Mills raised an untamed eyebrow and lifted her chin enquiringly. "Can I go to the San, please, Miss?"

Miss Mills clicked her tongue. "*Another* headache? Really, Patricia, there must be something wrong with you. That's the third time you have complained of one this week."

Patsy put a shaking hand to her head and forced a tear to trickle. She was getting good at that. "Oh, Miss, it's aching again dreadfully, my head."

"Have you ever had your eyes tested? Can you see the blackboard all right?"

She pretended to squint. "It's bit blurry, Miss." She covered her forehead with her hands. "Ooh! Ow, it does hurt!"

Miss Mills sighed heavily. "All right, then, sit down. Wait till the bell rings. Put your head on your arms."

Patsy sat down carefully, enjoying the envy she could read on the other girls' faces; served them all right. Whilst lowering her head obediently, she stuck her tongue out at the girl next to her and smiled in triumph into the darkness of her woolly cardigan sleeves.

Jim finished his deliveries, then went home and got the beetroot lifted and stored on their bed of brushwood and straw in the far corner of the garden, whistling as he worked. Cath ought to make it soon. For once, he felt quite full of the joys of spring. He paused, grinning, as he caught sight of her ducking towards him through the apple trees. "Hello, love!"

She was out of breath, and very muddy. "Keep away from me – I've been mucking out the pigs!" Standing on tiptoes, she pressed a quick kiss onto his mouth.

He wrinkled his nose. "You do smell a bit."

"What do you expect?" She teased him, putting her hands on her hips and thrusting out her chest. "Shall I go back to Barrows?"

He grinned, admiring her breasts. "How long have you got?"

"Carol's covering for me. About twenty minutes, give or take ..."

"Okay, then." Grinning, he relinquished his spade.

She headed back for the orchard. "Give me a couple of minutes – I must have a bit of a wash!"

They didn't bother climbing up the ladder. They hardly ever did. It was all too urgent. He just locked the back door.

"This is ridiculous, Jim," she told him afterwards, fastening up her trousers. "The girls all know and I'm sure everybody guesses. Why can't I stay?"

He set his mouth stubbornly. "You know why."

"It's ridiculous." She glanced at the clock. "Crikey, is that the time? I'd better run. You've some sausages in the larder cupboard for supper. Mr Martin let me have a couple as a special treat."

He fried up the sausages later with a bit of fried bread, then poked around in the larder for something else to eat, but it all seemed to need cooking. Eventually, he cut himself another doorstep, spread it with a bit of marg and had that with a cup of tea, and then went to bed in Patsy's room to save climbing up the ladder – cosier, somehow, on his own. He felt very unsettled. He might have missed Patsy, but just as much, or even more, he missed Cathy.

It wasn't that he was missing out on sex; he was rather enjoying their urgent, passionate sessions, especially when they were too far from the cottage to seek its shelter. Taking her under the sky on the hard ground – or, sometimes, as a touch of luxury and when he remembered to take one along, on a rug – under the branches of the Big Field copse or on the bracken on the leeward side of White's Hill or on the mossy banks of the trout pool down by the old mill did have a certain thrill, even though autumn was drawing in, and it was sometimes bloody cold. It wasn't that.

He was bloody lonely.

Mary was lonely, too, though she didn't know it. Mary didn't know anything much. She didn't fight *Them* any more, not often, anyway; she had given in. *They* just were. Some of them shouted a lot and pushed her, pinched her sometimes, but she didn't mind or care. She always knew *They* would win. She never thought to ask who *They* were any more. It didn't matter.

Her eyes were very heavy to lift, so most of the time she didn't bother. Her limbs didn't want to move much, either, so she didn't make them, except sometimes when *They* made her walk round and round in a ring with other grey women *They'd* captured. She quite liked that, though there was nothing to see, only high grey walls, and it didn't last long, but there was a feeling and a faint scent in the fresh air that touched her cheeks which faintly stirred her foggy memory and made her long for something, something that was so sweet it made the tears flow, though she didn't know what it was.

This time *They* were dragging her and pushing her somewhere, lying flat on her back. *They* were always leading her or dragging her somewhere or other, poking and prodding her, forcing her to drink nasty little poison pills, or to swallow some potion. She tried not to swallow them, because often they made her very sick, but *They* had their ways and though she got angry and restless sometimes, for the most part she had given up fighting them.

She could see lights passing above her when she opened her heavy lids just a little. *They* had stuck pins into her earlier. *They* were wicked, cruel. She was used to that, too. They did it a lot when she was restless and she had been restless a lot recently. This morning, she'd heard *Them* whispering together, conspiring, and the next thing, *They* had her here like this. She dragged up her lids a little once again to see. Some big double doors looming, two coloured lights above, one red, one green. Red for stop, green for go. She still knew colours.

A banging of doors. A jolting of whatever she was lying on. A mixture of smells in her nostrils. Something sharp and at the same time cloying. Something else she didn't recognise, but feared. She struggled, trying to call out, trying to sit up, but her body was too heavy. Besides, there were firm hands on her shoulders.

"Now, now, Mary, lie down quietly, there's a good girl."

Some things being passed very tightly about her arms and her thighs. Couldn't even wriggle. They were holding her down. She gasped as firm hands took her head and forced it backwards. They stopped her closing her mouth again by pushing a hard nasty-tasting rubbery block of a thing between her teeth so that she had to bite on it. She gurgled.

"Steady now." One of *Them* was looming above her. He had

a white mask over his mouth and nose. She was afraid to look at him so she closed her eyes quickly and kept them shut. She was very, very sleepy now.

"Good girl."

Cathy was full of questions when he got home from visiting. "So, come on – tell me! How did she get on with this, this electro-whatsit? EC what-d'you-call-it?

He brushed down his best trilby hat and put it carefully on its shelf. "ECT."

"That's it. Is it doing any good?"

"Not yet. They wouldn't expect it to. Only the first one. Got to finish a whole course."

She grimaced as she set a bubbling dish upon the table. Some sort of stew. He wasn't very hungry. "Rather her than me. I mean, that's dangerous, isn't it? Having electricity running right through you? Is it like that electric chair in that American film? Fancy, having electricity going right through you! Doesn't it burn you up? Oh, the poor thing. Poor old Mary!"

He sat down at the table, "It's only mild electricity that passes through her brain, as I understand it. Just part of her brain; it sort of jars her. They said it sometimes has very good results."

"Well then, we'll hope." She served out the stew, then nodded at his plate. "D'you want bread with it?"

"No, thanks."

She eyed him understandingly. "You don't like thinking about it, do you?"

They'd said she would sleep for hours afterwards and had let him in to sit with her for a bit; said it'd be quite safe. She'd looked so small, so lost, so hopeless, lying there fast asleep with her mouth open, dribbling a bit and snoring. He'd sat with her for an hour before they told him to go, but she hadn't moved.

"No, I do not."

Chapter 20

I'd like to decorate Patsy's room for her," Jim told Cath as they were dressing hastily one afternoon. "For when she comes home for the summer holiday. Freshen it up, make it a bit more ladylike. What d'you think?"

"Ooh, I say!" Absence had been making the heart grow fonder. Cathy had tried very hard to be a mother to Patsy, and she did love her, sort of, but, as she admitted silently to herself and occasionally to Elsie more and more frequently, if truth were told, she didn't like her. Although she hadn't approved of Patsy going off to boarding school, she had been ever so impressed by the place and had enjoyed showing off about it a bit in the village. Jim was a bit disappointed that Patsy wasn't actually getting very much of a glowing report from her teachers and that she still seemed somewhat withdrawn, but apart from that, there was the one very positive result of Patsy's absence from home. Cathy had had Jim all to herself.

It would be too much to say that she was looking forward to the holiday, therefore, but all in all it did mean that she felt much more generously and kindly towards Patsy. She nodded, beaming. "Oh, she'd like that! I could help you."

"Can't afford any wallpaper, mind, it'd have to be distemper." She was already in Patsy's room and he followed her, gauging how much he'd need to buy. "But we'll pick a nice colour. Do you think she'd like green?"

She was already in nest-building mode. "I could make some nice curtains – I'll see if my mum's got an old sheet I could dye. We could stipple the walls. I saw it in a magazine. Or ..." She waved her arm, describing an arc. "We could put a nice zig-zag pattern, or a border of flowers, cornflowers or something all round under the picture rail."

He frowned. "Here, hang on, I'm not that much of an artist

with a brush!"

It was quite exhausting, trying to get the room ready on top of all the other things they had to do, but at least it gave them an excuse to be together. It did something else for Cathy, too. It made her more determined.

He had kissed her goodbye one afternoon behind the hedge leading to Bottom Field and was eating his usual solitary meal later that evening when she came in out of the blue. Puffing, she set down a pile of bags with a decisive flourish. He stared at them, puzzled. "What's all that, love?"

"I'm not hiding and sneaking any longer."

He ran a hand uncertainly through his hair. "Nothing's changed."

She set her jaw determinedly, taking off her coat. "Yes, it has. I'm moving back in."

"No, Cath." He watched her hanging her coat on the peg behind the door. It looked right there. "We've been through all this."

She tossed her head. "I really don't bloody well care."

He knew he was going to let her. He couldn't help it. He wanted her back too. "What about your mum?"

"She's not stupid. She's guessed what's been going on."

Thinking about Elsie troubled him. "Does she know you've come?"

"I told her. She just carried on with her ironing." She bent down and fished out a crumpled brown paper bag from one of her bags. Setting a greaseproof package on the table, she grinned. "Then she just said to give you this cake."

Later, as they were sharing it for supper on a tray in bed, Cathy waved her slice in the air with a flourish. "And I'll tell you another thing: there's a dance on tomorrow night at the village hall. And we're going."

It was the one and only time she ever saw Jim hit anybody. She hadn't thought he'd had it in him. It was a bit of a wild swing, but it got Arthur Meeks smack, right on the chin. He went down like a stunned ox.

Up to that point, he'd managed to ignore the whisperings and sideways glances, most noticeable when they walked in as she had insisted, chins up and arm in arm. They were playing 'String of Pearls' when they got there, and it was her favourite, so she made Jim dance with her straight away, though he wasn't much good at it. Heads turned and curious eyes followed them as they half-galloped, half shuffled bravely about the dance floor under the fluttering bunting.

It had been going quite well. Lots of people had talked to them and nobody said anything to their faces, but it was at the half-time break, when Jim had gone over to the trestle tables that constituted the bar, that Arthur, Sam Pearson and a lad she didn't know, in NCO uniform, presumably on home leave, cornered her as she came back into the hall from the makeshift Ladies, trying to block her way and manoeuvre her back outside.

Fortunately, Jim spotted them. She could see him elbowing his way across the jitterbugging dance floor as she tried to force herself past their close-ranked barricade.

"Well, Cathy Mayberry, nice to see you, love," Arthur murmured, leering down at her lasciviously. "Been telling my cousin here all about you. In business tonight, are you? Got time for the three of us if we nip out around the back? My cousin's only got a twenty-four hour pass, so he'd better go first. Give us a kiss, though, to be going on with ..."

He had grabbed her by the waist and was trying to plant a slobbery, beery kiss on her tightened mouth just as Jim reached them, wrenching him away with a hand upon his shoulder. Arthur staggered, but recovered, grinning, though there was resentment in his bloodshot eyes. "Don't be mean, Jim, share and share alike, eh? Tarts like a bit of variety. Don't keep her to yourself."

That was when Jim hit him. He would have gone after him again, and Sam and the NCO would have had a crack at Jim, but she clung tightly to his arm, and Ted Samuels, Bill Turnbuckle and young John Harfield, also home on leave, had followed him across from the bar and got between them, keeping Jim, Sam and the NCO at bay. "Leave it, Jim." Eyes narrowed, panting, he let them hold him back.

"No more, okay?" That was all he said to Arthur as he staggered to his feet, holding his jaw, but in a tone that held such an icily unequivocal warning that it made even Cathy shiver.

Arthur made to push past him, but Jim held out a restraining arm. "No more, lad," he told him coldly, once again. "Have you got that?"

Arthur, shamefaced, nodded. "Aye."

Cathy was most impressed.

As the last waltz drew to a close, she linked her arms about his neck and kissed him, not caring who was watching. "My hero. Can't wait to get you into bed."

He grinned. "You little demon."

Back at the table they were sharing with Bill Turnbuckle and his wife, she picked up her bag and linking her arm firmly with his, held her head up with pride. She spoke deliberately loudly. "Well, we'd best go, we've to be up early in the morning."

As the door of the village hall closed behind them, Jim breathed a sigh of relief. "You're a brave girl, Cath."

Smiling, she squeezed his arm. "'S all right, Jim. One day you'll marry me."

Taking Patsy by the hand, Cathy dragged her proudly into her bedroom. "Well, what d'you think, pet? Do you like the colour? Your dad's worked ever so hard, he has, been getting ever so crabby with the matching up! I did the stencilling. They're supposed to be roses, see, but I'm not sure they've quite worked." She gazed complacently around the walls. "What d'you think then, lovey, eh?"

Patsy stared round at the walls disparagingly and then turned up her nose. "I think it's ghastly."

Cathy gasped. 'Ghastly'! Where had she got that from? "Do you, indeed? Well, don't you dare tell your dad."

Jim looked up eagerly as she went back into the kitchen and her heart bled for him, so she smiled brightly. "She just needs a bit of a chance to get used to it."

As his happily expectant expression slipped from his face, she hastened to reassure him. "It's lovely, Jim. It's just –" She's a little madam, that's what it is. "Well, she just – she doesn't know what she wants right now."

"Oh."

Cathy nodded. "She's a bit mixed up. I did warn you." Poor thing, but she had warned him. She crossed over quickly to the kettle. Better make him a cup of tea.

Despite the bad start, from Cathy's point of view, the holiday passed fairly peacefully. Jim was extremely busy, so she made a considerable effort at first to involve and amuse Patsy, like suggesting that they should make some cakes together or that she should find names for the new bantams or come into town on the bus for a look around the shops, but Patsy didn't really want to know. She even seemed to prefer being at Miss Buckley's, though she moaned about her aunty's obsession with correct posture and all the horrible exercises involving rulers down the back of her jumper and balancing books on her head she made her do!

In fact, though Cathy had been half expecting it, the way she turned her nose up at her was very hurtful, the snooty young madam! Hadn't taken her very long to learn to be a snob.

She seemed to want to be alone, so eventually Cathy let her. Despite her description of its new décor as 'ghastly', she actually spent much more time in her room than she had previously done. Jim brought down from the attic an old wind-up gramophone of Mary's and some records in a dusty box and though she had been a bit disparaging about it and the records were all out of date, she spent ages playing them over and over again and reading and scribbling in what she called her 'diary' behind her closed door. Cathy got really sick of hearing 'Begin the Beguine' over and over again, and as for the particularly crackly version of 'Everything Stops for Tea' ...! It drove her crackers.

Patsy hadn't anything much at all to say to Cathy. She was only their housekeeper, after all.

At the end of the holiday, Dad drove her back to the station, where she clung to him. "I don't want to go back, Daddy!"

He was quite surprised; she hadn't seemed to have enjoyed being at home very much at all.

It wrenched at his heart. She was actually crying. "Do I have to go back? Can't I stay here, please, please, Daddy?"

After his inner doubts and searchings, his impulse was to say, 'Of course you can stay here, pet,' but he had also been giving a lot of thought to Patsy's future. She was very lucky; if she packed it in now, she'd be throwing a great deal away. Besides, though she had seemed a bit down on occasion, this was probably just first-day-of-term nerves. "Do you really not want to go back, Pats?"

She hesitated and he saw it. "You'd have to go to the County School, you know. You'd have to cycle in."

The smoke from the approaching train was emerging from the distant tunnel. "There's a lot to be said for it, you know, there is really. You're a lucky girl. It'll teach you a lot, give you a lot better chance." He brushed back her hair from her forehead. "Don't you think you could give it another try, eh? Be a brave girl and give it another try?"

She was silent for a moment, and then she dropped her arms resignedly. "All right."

There were quite a number of girls on the train also going back to school, but nobody spoke to Patsy – nobody ever did, apart from the teachers and a few unpopular girls like Specky Wilson or Poppy Blakemore who was so fat and who had a lazy eye, or Diane Sutton, who was as stupid as a tadpole and not quite right in the head; let the other girls make her drink ink and things like that. There was nobody else. Nobody liked her.

She knew that they all found her odd and a terrible sulk, but she couldn't help it. Wasn't her fault; it was just the way she was.

But she wished she wasn't.

She sat scrunched up in a corner of the carriage, staring miserably out of the window. Wouldn't really have wanted to stay home, anyway. It wasn't just that the new decoration of her room was *hideous,* nor that Dad, though he had been delighted to see her and had made a big fuss at first, had been too tied up with delivering to the shops and growing vegetables as well as his Home Guard duties and Cathy to have very much time for her.

She scowled at the passing landscape. They were sleeping together, now, too. Who did they think they were kidding, pretending that she didn't know?

And it wasn't because there was always something about her bedroom that made her feel scared inside and made her have dreadful nightmares; she was used to that and though the decoration was horrible it did seem a bit less creepy now that it looked a bit different.

But she had realised now that the girls at school also all thought she was *common,* and, listening now to them chattering happily, describing their exciting and glamorous hols, and worrying about what she could say if anybody should speak to her and ask her what she had been doing, it was that which brought hot tears prickling to her eyes and forced her to dash them away with her sleeve before anybody could see. She hadn't ever dared even to tell Poppy or Specky Wilson what her home was like, but this time she had hated being there at the cottage; really *despised* it, it was *horrible.* No wonder nobody ever invited her to join in. Why couldn't she have the kind of homes and families that the other girls probably all had? Poppy's father was a Colonel and Maud bragged that she lived in a castle, and Daisy Partington's brother was an Honourable and her sister had *two* houses, one in a place called Marlow, on the river, and one in Italy, as well as what she called a 'pied-a-terre' in London. Even Diane's father was a Dentist.

Cathy really was common, her dad hadn't got the kind of job that you could brag about, and the home she came from wasn't the kind you talked about, not at St Winifred's. If it had been, things would have been all right. And they were kind enough, but they hadn't brought her up *right,* Dad and Cathy. Everybody could tell what kind of a girl she really was. It was plain to everybody that she wasn't quite *normal.* She would never be one of *them.*

The next year ticked on by. It was difficult to look as if she didn't mind not being talked to; meal times were much the worst. It was much easier when she was away from the others and could relax a bit. Familiar though she now was with the buildings and the grounds, it was still very difficult to find places where she could actually *be* on her own. The bathroom was pretty good, especially on bath nights, but if only she could have locked the bathroom door it would have made another perfect hiding place without the fear of intrusion, somewhere she could just lie and think and imagine and pretend she was anywhere else but here – except home, of course. On a yacht, perhaps, in a silky white dress, surrounded by her glamorous friends and sipping a cocktail from a tall, frosted glass like the ladies in the magazines she'd stolen from the polish-scented Visitors' room. Taking a curtain-call, with the audience clapping and cheering, or a film star with people pushing to get her autograph. Somewhere everyone adored her.

Anywhere but here.

Bath nights were on Tuesdays and Fridays and she had opted for Tuesdays because there were more people vying for the baths on a Friday, especially when there was an exeat and they were going home. Tuesday was a day she looked forward to. She was glad when it came around again and she could hurry down in the evening with her washbag.

The water would be almost cold by now; she was always the last in the line. There was an advantage in that, though. The girls were not allowed to hang around, so as they had all taken their baths except her, they would all have gone off down to the hall to have their evening milk and biscuits, and so there was no fear of anyone trying to come in or needing to use the bathroom after her. If she did without the snack herself, she might even have a whole half an hour of peace and quiet lolling in the water before the bell rang for bedtime.

Slipping a hand into her pocket, Patsy brought out the jar of bath salts that she'd taken from Vanessa Morton's locker, and ran the tap, watching as they dissolved, turning the water a rather unnatural blue. It promised on the label that the salts would produce a lot of bubbles, but they didn't really, even though she swished her hands round and round in the water for quite a lengthy time. The smell was nice, though, generally flowery, nothing really specific, but better than the general odour of sweaty bodies, wet towels and carbolic. The first time she'd taken something from anybody's locker to make her bath times more exciting, its fragrance had turned out to be Pink Lilac, and she had been sick into the bath water. For some reason the smell of Pink Lilac always made her sick. She always looked very carefully first now.

She hid the empty bottle up in the lavatory cistern.

The water wasn't as cold as she had feared; in fact it was still quite hot. She ran in quite a bit more than the regulation five inches, letting the bright blue scented tide rise well over the painted plimsoll line before turning off the tap and climbing in.

Lying back, she let the blue water trickle through her fingers. "H-ow ... N-ow ... Br-own ... C-ow ..." she enunciated slowly, trying to round the diphthong just as Miss Tingle, the elocution teacher, had instructed her. "Howw ... Noww ... Browwn ... Coww ..."

What else was there? "Faather's Caar is a Jaguaar and Paa drives Raather Faast ... AH-h-h-h-OW!" Practising gave way to an anguished shriek as someone behind the bathtub grasped her roughly by the hair. Sitting up abruptly with a great whooshing of bathwater, she tried in vain to disengage the hands. "Let go! You're hurting me! OW! Let me go!" She could hear muffled giggles and conspiratorial whisperings. There were several of them, then. To her enormous shock, her head was suddenly and roughly forced down underneath the water and she shrieked, swallowing bathwater.

As she came up again, choking, whoever it was still had her by the hair and somebody else got her by the shoulders and between them they shoved her back under again, holding her there for longer this time. She struggled frantically, trying to get up for air as her head swam with a grey, bloodshot mist, but every time they let her up, as she opened her mouth to scream they pushed her back under the water. *Mummy, Mummy, Mummy! ...*

A terrifying, oozing blackness swam over her, filling her whole being. She tried and tried to draw in air but only swallowed water, and when they let her go at last, slamming the door and scurrying off laughing down the corridor to the peremptory sound of the ringing of the bedtime bell, they didn't hear her scream out loud at last as she came up choking from the water.

She couldn't stop screaming even when Matron came along and hauled her out and wrapped her in a towel. She was still screaming when Matron tried to give her a cup of cocoa in her room. Matron was both touched and puzzled when she called her 'Mummy'.

"No, Mummy, no, Mummy – No Mummy, no, no, no, NO!"

Chapter 21

School life began to get better only when she was almost sixteen, and even then it all started very badly.

She had changed into her pyjamas one evening and was hiding the half-dozen pink, blue and mauve Sobranie cigarettes that she had just pinched from Veronica Barry's shoe bag under the mattress when the door opened and Serena Gore-Hamilton, Isabel Carrington-White, Vanessa Perry and Marina Worthington strolled in, clad in their dressing gowns and swinging their wash bags nonchalantly. They were the most admired, feared and envied set of girls in the form and she wished so much that she was one of them. Feeling her heart thudding, Patsy dropped the mattress and ducked her head, scowling.

Marina smiled sweetly, closed the door and leant back against it, still smiling. Serena's face broke into a sweet smile. "Ah, Norris." She wasn't usually so friendly. Patsy straightened warily.

Serena sank with practised boredom onto the window seat and, smiling too, Isabel and Vanessa moved to her side, like some kind of personal bodyguards. Marina leant back against the door, and giggled. Serena nodded. "Come here, Norris." As Patsy hesitated, she sighed impatiently. "Oh, come here!"

Steeling herself, Patsy moved towards her warily. Gracefully inclining her head, Serena hospitably patted the seat beside her. "Sit down."

Marina giggled again as Patsy sat gingerly, but Serena silenced her with a look, before turning again to Patsy. "We've decided something."

Patsy shrugged uncomfortably. "What?" she muttered sulkily.

Serena shook her head. "Nothing to worry about – on the contrary! We're going to let you join our set."

Patsy stared at her. Serena's green eyes were wide and innocently earnest, and, looking round, she could see only friendly smiles on the faces of the others. Allowing her guard to drop a little, she found herself stumbling excitedly. "Really? I mean – why? Why me?"

Serena shrugged. "You want to, don't you?"

Patsy nodded. Of course she wanted to.

Serena clapped her hands. "Well, there we are, then! Now, when someone is inaugurated, we always have something special. A *Set* Special." She threw a glance at Marina, who opened the door and peeped out, then closed it again, nodding. She turned back to Patsy. "So, if you do want to join us ... are you ready?"

Patsy shrugged, trying to subdue a flutter of apprehension. She swallowed hard and tried to smile. "Yes, all right, then. Yes."

Serena smiled in satisfaction. "Good. Then watch and follow." She gestured imperiously with her head. "Isabel, Marina ..."

It was plainly a ritual the girls had practised before. Moving swiftly in unison, Isabel and Marina threw open the side windows of the bay with a flourish and then fell back to the sides, and Serena stepped forward in turn, facing the open window on the left. Slowly, gracefully, she let her dressing gown fall. She was naked underneath. Patsy stifled a gasp, hoping she wasn't blushing, then watched spellbound as Serena tossed her long, fair hair back over her shoulder and stepped up onto the windowsill. Isabel, Vanessa and Marina began a low but excited chant. "Out. Out. Out. Out ..."

Open-mouthed, Patsy watched Serena step out carefully onto the narrow ledge. The chant continued as, facing inward, she began to inch her way across the central pane. As she reached the right hand window, it altered. "In. In. In. In. *IN!*" To the girls' cheers, Serena slipped in through the window. She bowed deeply. "Next – Isabel!"

She robed herself again as Isabel took off her dressing gown, and moved in turn out onto the windowsill. Patsy stared, worrying desperately about taking off her pyjamas, but Serena slipped a friendly arm about her waist, urging her lightly, "Come on, Norris, join in!"

The others smiled and nodded in approbation as she raised her voice obediently. "Out. Out. Out. Out ... In. In. In. In ... *IN!*"

Vanessa was out and in almost before Patsy had realised she had started and Marina went last, more nervously than the other three. Halfway around, a gasp went up as she missed her footing and almost fell, reminding Patsy that the window must be about forty feet above the ground. It felt as if a hand had closed about her throat.

I can't!

Recovering, Marina climbed back in, breathless, and wrapped herself up quickly in her dressing gown. She nodded at Patsy. "Now her!"

Serena squeezed Patsy's waist. "Now you, Norris." She smiled sweetly. "Go on, you have to do this; it's easy. You mustn't be afraid."

If it means being one of them, I've got to do it.

Slipping off her pyjamas and trying not to think about being naked, she climbed carefully up onto the sill. The ground seemed a very long way away. As the girls begin their chant of "Out! Out! Out!" she began to inch very cautiously along the narrow window ledge. She could see them all grinning out at her as they chanted, and tried to smile back.

Suddenly, as she reached the central pane, Marina pounced, slamming shut the 'out' window. Patsy glanced quickly towards the other window, but as she did so, someone slammed that shut, too. The girls' faces appeared on the other side of the central pane, screaming gleefully in unison, "*OUT!! OUT!! OUT!! OUT!*" After a few moments, their faces disappeared and their cruel laughter faded. Somewhere inside, a door slammed, then there was silence.

Clinging to the window. Patsy risked a queasy look down. The far-off ground swam a little. She was dizzy. Leaves blew across the driveway far below. The wind was getting up. Shivering, she clung, an isolated little figure, a long, long, long way up.

It was a long time before she was spotted by Mr Gates the janitor on his evening round, and it had started to rain. By that time, she was chilled to the bone, so cold she could hardly speak. Matron made her take a hot bath with mustard powder in it, and questioned her for ages; so did Nancy Stitch, her housemistress, so-called because she also taught needlework and had lips as tight as if they had been hemstitched together. This time, they were practically invisible.

They let her sleep in the sickbay and then, the next morning, they brought her breakfast on a tray and let her miss lessons, and the Headmistress, Miss Wainwright, demanded to see her – which showed how worried they all were. She had refused to tell them who had done it to her, though, not even Miss Wainwright, who was tall and beady-eyed and wore a monocle; she wasn't sure if it was because she was scared of retribution, or was being noble.

Anyway, she hadn't split. It was partly because of that that she dared to brave the dining room at lunchtime; it was the best way to show them all that she didn't care.

They cast her sly looks and whispered with their heads together as she made her way to the class table, seating herself as far away from them as possible. When Miss Blackburn rang her little bell to say they could leave, she sat tight, letting the rest of the girls go out before her.

Feeling the hair at the back of her neck prickle, Patsy recognised that Serena had paused casually beside her and she gazed stony-faced at her plate.

"Well done," Serena murmured.

Patsy was made daring by her own bravery. "You're a cow. You're all cows."

Serena laughed. "Silly goose! Well done for not splitting on us. I tell you what: come to my house party."

Patsy gave a disbelieving sneer. "I'm not that stupid."

Serena laughed again. "I mean it, next exeat. Come to my house party. Go on." She moved on, waving a hand lethargically. "It'll be a hoot."

Talk about Father's Car being a Jaguar! There were three cars outside and all with gleaming bodywork and glittering chrome. Expecting an unpleasant surprise any moment and overwhelmed by her surroundings as well as by her companions, Patsy kept to the back, following warily as Serena led the party upstairs. The house was just beautiful – and so big! Even bigger than she had imagined. It was HUGE!

They were all obviously very much at home. Feeling like a fish out of water, Patsy perched awkwardly on the bottom of the bed. Serena's bedroom alone was bigger than the whole ground floor of their cottage. She had a huge bed with a pink satin bedspread, onto which Marina and Vanessa flung themselves immediately as Serena wound up a gramophone. Isabel sank onto the padded stool in front of the dressing table and began rummaging amongst the items on the top before yanking open the top drawer. Picking up a lipstick, she applied it carefully and then examined her reflection in the mirror. "Yuk! This looks absolutely bloody ghastly! What *is* this? 'Tangerine Glow'! What did you buy this for, darling?" Serena laughed, and crossed to fling open a wardrobe which seemed full to bursting.

Any minute now they were going to make a fool of her. Her

dress was ridiculous; she would look like somebody's grand-mother. For goodness sake, why had she ever come?

They hadn't taken any more notice of her than usual in the run-up to the weekend, but neither had they tormented her, and though she had heard no more about the weekend, on Friday morning Serena had paused by her bed. "The car's coming at five-thirty. Bring something for the evenings. Don't be late." Smiling vaguely, she had drifted out of the dorm.

It had taken Patsy all morning to decide whether or not to go, but by lunchtime she had done so and spent the afternoon break going through clothes to find some suitable things to wear, both in her own locker and in others in the dorm. Couldn't touch the Set's things for this, of course. They'd recognise them instantly.

The only items of possible use were an embroidered filmy scarf which she found in Jennifer Bailey's locker and a nice cream silk petticoat in Susan Conway's, both of which she nicked and stuffed into the bottom of her suitcase, together with a Crème Puff in 'Cameo', a packet of rouge papers and a pair of stockings gathered from various drawers.

At last, in desperation, she packed the calf-length blue-grey flowery-sprigged Viyella dress with the lacy collar that Aunty May had given to her at Christmas. Totally old-fash-ioned and childish as it was, it would have to do.

Dad was always early collecting her, and in order to avoid his grotty old van from being spotted, she always dragged along her bag and waylaid him a little way down the road. It was no different this time, though she left her suitcase in the bushes up by the car park and ran down empty handed.

He was doubtful and a bit aggrieved when she broke the news. "Cath'll be disappointed. She's made a cake and a trifle and she's got a nice cheese rarebit ready for your tea. Pity you don't let us know, love."

She felt a burst of impatience. "I didn't know till today. It would help if you had a bloody telephone. I couldn't have got a message to you in time."

"Don't swear." He frowned. "No, I suppose not. Who's coming for you all, pet? Her dad?" He straightened, taking hold of the driving wheel. "Should I go in and have a word with him?"

She shook her head quickly. "No! No. It won't be her da – her father. It'll be the chauffeur, I expect."

He whistled, impressed. "Chauffeur, eh? That's posh!" He slipped a hand into his pocket and riffled though his change. "Best give you some spending money then." He counted it out carefully. "Here's ten bob now, don't lose it: two half-crowns, two florins and a shilling – and a penny in case you need a stop on the way. Is it far?"

She dropped it quickly into her pocket without looking. "I've no idea. Thanks, Dad."

He leant out of the window, watching as she ran back up the road. A chauffeur! Mary'd be pleased. Good to think she had some nice friends. "Have a nice time then!" he called after her. "Remember your P's and Q's!"

The girls changed out of their school uniforms, chattering happily, while Patsy watched them with envy. They had all brought such lovely clothes; 'Utility' obviously no longer had any place here. Vanessa's bluebell-blue bias-cut moss crêpe dress had a skirt which clung closely to her thighs and then swirled out at the ankle and looked terribly sophisticated and smart. Without any bashfulness, Marina casually stripped off in front of them all and slipped, bra-less, into a narrow, emerald green silk dress with a deeply draped front. Patsy was almost shocked: she looked really grown-up – at least twenty-one. Isabel had a real short fur wrap and had brought two dresses to choose from, one softly draped in ruby red which she tried on with jet beads and elbow-length black gloves, and the other a delicious creamy coffee colour with a satin-edged peplum at the waist and a huge sequined gold flower on the bodice. She settled for the latter. It was very sophisticated and she looked stunning, though she pronounced herself bored with all her wardrobe. "I am definitely going New Look! You know – *Mr Dior!* So's Mummy."

Serena also took time to make her mind up, pulling one dress after another from the big wardrobe and dropping the discarded ones on the floor. They seemed to have forgotten Patsy, who sat abandoned on the bed, feet together, watching them all, goggle-eyed. When she thought of what was waiting in her suitcase, she hoped they *would* forget her. *So* embarrassing!

Hair and make-up took another hour. Serena, finally dressed to perfection in sapphire silk faille, as she described it, with plunging neckline and a matching silk flower holding up her hair, beckoned to Patsy at last. "Come here, Patsy. Show me what you've brought."

Unhappily, Patsy opened the cardboard suitcase she had been trying to hide with her feet, and unveiled the Viyella concoction.

Serena wrinkled her nose. "Ugh! You can't go down to

dinner wearing that rag, Norris. Mummy'd have a fit." Patsy felt herself crimson.

Rummaging reflectively in a huge, polished wood wardrobe, Serena held up a long, navy blue silk and crêpe mix dress with a fitted bodice, puffed sleeves and a panelled skirt. A row of tiny covered buttons led up to a prim collar. "Try this. Navy's In. It's a bit out of date and the colour looks a bit dull to me, but I think it might suit you."

It looked a bit disappointing. Patsy reluctantly undid her dress. What a good thing she had found the nice cream petticoat; the underwear the others were wearing all looked sparkling new and was, quite frankly, gorgeous. The others clustered round to watch as Serena helped her to dress, then parted to let her look in the mirror, collectively studying her reflection over her shoulder. They nodded approvingly, displaying some surprise. "Oh, yes!"

Patsy gasped. The dress transformed her. She looked so grown-up, a little bit mysterious, understated and elegant.

Serena tilted her head critically. "Stand up properly. Turn round. Hm, not bad ..."

"Not everybody can wear something as plain as that, but you can, Norris. You could be a model." Isabel frowned. "Can we do something about her hair?" Swooping to the dressing table, she gathered up Serena's silver-backed brush and a handful of slides and bobby pins. "Sit down."

"Not bad at all," Serena drawled, grudgingly, when it was coiled up and tweaked into waves to her satisfaction. "Needs some decent shoes." She hesitated over a triple row of shoe-boxes, all labelled, then opened one and tossed a pair of navy shoes towards Patsy. "Here you are. See if they'll fit."

She hadn't worn proper high heels before. They were a bit tight, but she got them on and stood up, testing them, with the aid of a hand on Vanessa's shoulder.

Serena frowned. "Don't wobble. Straighten your knees. Lean back. Keep your tummy in. That's right."

A gong sounded somewhere down below and Patsy's tummy started to flutter. What were Serena's parents going to be like?

Serena tripped over to the door. "Okay? Everybody ready?" As they all fell in behind her, a tall, slightly overweight, fair-haired and glossy-cheeked young man appeared in the doorway to a gushing chorus of greeting from the girls. "Hello, Hugh!"

Serena rolled her eyes sardonically. "God, my bloody brother! This is Hugh, Norris, my elder brother. He's horrible."

He stared at Patsy, giving a little whistle. "By Jove! I say – is this the one, Serena?" He grinned, kissing Patsy's hand and making a light bow, then threw open his arms invitingly. "Your lucky day, ladies! I'm going to spread myself around."

The dining table glittered with polished silver and sparkling glassware, and the party was waited on by a very old butler and a little parlour maid. Thanks to Etiquette lessons from Miss Allyson she knew which knife and fork to use, so that was all right, but making conversation was very difficult, even with the fragile flush of newfound confidence imparted to her from her glamorous outfit. Serena, the other girls and Hugh all talked a lot, though, so it didn't really matter that she hardly said a word.

To her fear and consternation she was seated next to Serena's father, introduced to her as Henry, who was sleek and plump and rather handsome in a red-faced and slightly raddled way. Her mother, Barbara, was incredibly thin, silvery blonde and rather vague and vapid. Her older sister Marigold, who looked very much like Serena, ignored all of the girls completely. Her companion, Gregory, dark-moustached, sullen and rather mysterious looking, was a new beau, some sort of ex-RAF war hero, it seemed, with whom she was obviously smitten.

The other guest was a middle-aged man with a bit of a speech impediment and a receding chin. Patsy didn't quite catch his name, but she gathered that he was over from South Africa and was the Honourable Something-or-other and, presumably, a family member since he kept calling Serena's mother 'Couthin Babwa'.

"So what does your daddy do, pigeon?" Serena's father, who had kept staring at her through the first two courses, filled up her glass for the fifth time as the dessert dishes were placed in front of them by the silent, uniformed maid. She smiled back at him. This was really rather splendid. Her head felt decidedly swimmy, but she had a lovely warm glow inside. He had his hand on her knee. It felt warm and damp and heavy.

She thought quickly. "Um – land. Yes. Yes, that's right. Um – Daddy's in land."

Henry nodded knowledgeably. He squeezed her knee. "Takes a lot of caring for, does land."

Barbara leant forward at the far end of the table. "And tell me about your mummy, darling – is she an old stop-at-home like me?" She had a rather silly, tinkling laugh.

A sickening quiver. Patsy took another hefty gulp of wine and shook her head casually. "Um – she's away a lot."

Barbara raised a finely pencilled eyebrow. "Oh, yes, doing what?"

She glanced at the other girls, because of course they thought her mother was dead, but they all seemed to be engrossed in some complicated story Hugh was telling. "She's – she's an archaeologist."

Henry held out a silver cigarette case and she took one, impressed. Just imagine her dad doing that! He held out a lighter and she bent her head to light the cigarette. Senior Service, too! Stronger than she was used to. The acrid smoke caught the back of her throat, and she took another drink of wine quickly to stifle a coughing fit.

Barbara was waiting. Patsy's wine glass was almost empty again. She drained the last drop. "She's in Egypt at the moment, actually." She was starting rather to believe this story. "Then next month she's off on a very important dig in ... in Mesopotamia."

She watched, fascinated, as once again Henry refilled her glass. His hot knee was pressed firmly next to hers. Her glass, his face and Barbara's were beginning to swim alarmingly, but nevertheless she took a hefty swig.

"Mesopotamia! Well I never!" Barbara tipped her head, frowning. "I wonder if she knows old Badger, Henry?"

Henry raised his rather bushy brows. "Jove, yes! Old Badger Barclay! Dry as dust." He squeezed her knee again. "Know him at all? Great authority on – what is it, Barb? Phoenician artefacts?"

Barbara waved the long cigarette holder held delicately in her elegant fingers. "Goodness knows, darling, haven't the foggiest!" She tinkled self-deprecatingly with laughter. "Nothing as glamorous and fun as Patricia's mummy, I'm quite sure!"

The nearest image Patsy could come to as a mother-figure apart from faint memories of dark hair and a gentle singing voice and tortoise-shaped buttons before things changed forever, was Cathy. She had a flash image of her the last time she'd seen her. Red-faced and perspiring, wearing an old pair of Jim's trousers, hair tied up in a headscarf, her apron bloody, she had been trying to trap a chicken. They had scattered, squawking and fluttering.

"Bloody hell! Hells Bells! Come here, you little demon!" She had pounced victoriously. "Got you!" Tucking it firmly under her arm, she made ready to wring its scrawny neck. "Now!!"

Patsy had her first sexual experience late that night with Hugh on the games room billiard table. He went off early the next day, back to London, but before he set off, she saw him whispering secretively with Serena in a corner of the courtyard. Serena glanced in her direction, giggling. Patsy distinctly heard her say to him, laughing, as she turned back, "Glad you enjoyed it, darling! Happy Birthday!"

The others knew about it too, she could tell. She told herself it didn't matter so long as she was still *IN*. It would be worth anything to be tolerated as a member of the Set.

Chapter 22

Gazing up at the imposing, mellowed ivy-covered buildings, Cathy gasped as she did on each of her annual visits to Parents' Day. "Ooh, I say! Ooh, I say! Ooer!"

Jim glanced across at the grounds. "They've got it back to flowerbeds, then. Looks a bit different from when it was dug over and laid to cabbages and broccoli. They must have worked their socks off to get it looking like this. I reckon some of that turf's been laid, not seeded. Bit bloody pricey to cover an area like that. No wonder the fees cost such a fortune."

He'd have liked to have strolled around, have a word with their gardener. It was unusual for him these days to have the opportunity of driving right the way up to the school. As a general rule, Patsy would be waiting on the roadside some distance beyond the gates when he came to meet her, so he hadn't turned in through the iron gates except when dropping off her trunk or picking it up again at the end of term. He was always touched to see how eager she was to jump into the van.

The sides of the drive, and, as far as he could see, the forecourt, were lined with parked cars, but he just managed to find a space big enough for the van between a Morgan and an MG TF. Cathy kept letting out little squeaks of anxiety. "Jim – you're going to hit his bumper – do take care!"

It annoyed him. "Crikey, Cath – for God's sake, there's plenty of room ...!"

The Bedford, a recent acquisition and only a couple of years old, was his pride and joy, but he had to admit to himself, if not to Cath, that it did sit a bit incongruously amongst the expensive vehicles. There would have been no getting away from its obviously commercial purpose even without its green lettering along the sides. He stared enviously at the Morgan: beautiful car, that. Imagine having one of those purring along the country roads. Not much use, though, for deliveries.

Cathy, very nervous, tucked a stray wisp of blonde hair back under her feathered sugar pink cloche. "I hope I look all right ..."

Jim straightened his tie. "Of course you do, love," he assured her loyally. "You look lovely." She did, actually. He wasn't sure about the hat, or, indeed, the colour, but the full-skirted coat with its narrow waist, recently purchased from C&A, gave her a lovely, plump little figure – what did they call it? 'Hour glass'.

She retouched her lipstick, a vibrant Yardley pink which she had tracked down triumphantly in Boots, and licked and pressed her lips to set it. "Seems a pity her Aunty May couldn't have come along. She might have liked to see where her money's gone now Patsy's nearly at the end, you know, Jim."

He rolled his eyes. "Oh, yes, I can just see her sitting in the back."

She took him seriously. "Don't be silly, Jim, she'd have got a chauffeur."

He shrugged, and put a hand on the door handle. "Anyway, she's not well enough, so there you are. Not been herself since Aunty Lou died, really; misses having somebody to boss about. And to look after," he added as an afterthought, telling himself, be fair.

He glanced across her. "You ready now?"

She climbed out carefully, smoothing down her skirt, and clung tightly to his arm, tottering slightly in her new, very high-heeled shoes as they walked towards the main entrance. He could have wished she hadn't insisted on greeting everyone they passed like an old friend. "*Good* afternoon! *Lovely* day for it!" You could tell from the blank looks and the vague belated smiles that they thought it quite odd. And her normal voice was much nicer; no need to be struggling to sound so posh.

He stifled his irritation. She was only trying.

Letting out a squeak, she released her arm from his as they climbed the wide granite steps, and hesitated, fumbling in her handbag. "Hang on, Jim – wait a minute!" Slipping a plain gold band surreptitiously onto her fourth finger, she closed the bag and took his arm again, smiling. "That's better!"

Members of the teaching staff, impressively arrayed in mortarboards and silk-lined hooded gowns, were already taking their places on the stage as they made their way into the hall. The seats allocated to parents at the back of the hall were almost full, but they found two in the middle of the last but one row and sank down, staring round at their surroundings.

Richly coloured glass at the high windows and ornately carved wooden panels gave the feel of an ancient high church.

Everything smelled of lilies and floor polish, though at the back of the heavy scent, Jim thought he could detect a tantalising hint of mince and boiled cabbage. He was very hungry. Cath had been too busy titivating to get him a proper dinner. There would be tea, though after, in the marquee, that was something to look forward to. Last year there had been several kinds of cake as well as sandwiches. His tummy rumbled at the thought of it and Cathy glanced at him sharply. He grinned apologetically, mouthing, "Sorry!"

He put down the programme and turned his attention back to the stage, upon which was set a gleaming oak table bearing an array of shining silver cups and piles of books ready for the presentations. Cathy fanned herself. It was very hot. Craning to study the teachers, she nudged Jim, "Ooh, look at that pale blue hood, Jim, that's so pretty! Which university is that? And that one's got fur! D'you think Patsy might go up to university?"

He grinned. "That'd be something to write home about!"

She giggled. "Ooh, I say!"

Suddenly, with a thump of hands on the piano keys, some invisible body down near the front of the stage brought the gathering to attention and when the chatting and whispering had stopped, launched enthusiastically into a spirited rendering of *Immortal, Invisible*. Two by two and form by form the pupils trooped in, the older girls leading them, silently and mostly meekly into the vacant seats in the front half of the hall. Cathy saw some of them scanning the rows of parents, though, grinning and waving when they identified familiar faces.

"Ah, don't they look lovely, Jim? Talk about spit-and-polish!" Half rising excitedly, she tried to pick out Patsy. "Can you see her, love?"

He squinted down the hall. "Is that her? Side of the third row?"

Cathy shook her head. "No, no, that one's hair's too dark."

Isabel, sitting next to Patsy, turned and caught sight of the animated Cathy in her bright pink-feathered hat and coat bobbing up and down at the back of the hall, and grinning, nudged Patsy, who turned ready to share the joke.

Spotting her, Cathy's plump face broke into a beam. "There she is, Jim, look!" Mouthing excitedly, "Hello!" she waved a gloved hand animatedly. Tentatively lifting his own hand, Jim grinned proudly.

Patsy's face tightened. She turned away quickly. *Bloody hell.*

The marquee set out on the side lawn was emptying, but Jim, Cathy, Patsy and Isabel, together with Isabel's parents, were still taking afternoon tea. Jim and Cathy had been a bit late getting there, because Patsy hadn't turned up for ages to escort them as she was supposed to. They'd hovered for a full twenty minutes on the front step, with Jim, hungrier now than ever, getting very restless as he saw other people making their way happily across the lawns towards the their afternoon tea. "Do we need to wait for her?" he asked Cathy, frowning, as the entrance hall emptied. "She'll find us there, won't she? Couldn't we just slope in? If we leave it any longer, there won't be anywhere to sit."

Taking pity on him, Cathy had just been about to agree and had taken his arm, when she spotted Patsy. "Ooh, she's got somebody with her, Jim, one of her friends, she looks nice, isn't that lovely! Hello, Patsy, thought you were never coming!" Cathy half opened her arms welcomingly, ready to embrace her, but Patsy didn't seem to notice. The friend she was with, a slender, dark-haired girl, stepped forward brightly instead, offering a polite hand.

"How do you do, you must be Cathy, I think, and you must be Mr Norris. I'm Isabel." She glanced over her shoulder. "My parents are just coming, they're talking to Miss Wainwright. I thought it would be nice if we had tea together."

Her eyes danced wickedly, and though she bit her bottom lip, she failed to stifle a giggle. She lurched slightly, and for a horrified moment, Cathy thought that Patsy had pinched her or something, but the next minute she was smiling calmly and openly at them again, so she must have been mistaken. Patsy, though, looked decidedly sulky. Cathy shrugged; well, they were used to that.

Patsy, indeed, was mortified and could hardly bring herself to say a word, never mind eat a morsel, during the excruciatingly embarrassing tea. Cathy, on the contrary, was very pleased with herself. Ever so far back, Isabel's dad went. She had trouble understanding what he said sometimes, but was satisfied that she'd put up a pretty good show, which was as well, because, like Patsy, Jim hardly said a dickie bird. She was especially proud of having remembered to hold out her little finger stiffly when she drank from her delicate china cup.

Isabel's mum was a bit terrifying. Spanish, apparently, dark-haired and sleek with very black round eyes, and was ever so elegantly dressed, so that Cathy was glad she had taken the plunge and lashed out on her new pink outfit. Her dad had a neat moustache and wore a navy pinstriped suit and, whereas her mum barely said a word but merely smiled rather distantly – probably didn't speak the language very well, Cath decided – he went on at long length about things like it being a great shame that they'd done away with morning dress for these occasions.

How peculiar, Cathy thought, delicately nudging back into her mouth a sliver of cucumber that had escaped her sandwich. Why ever did they call it 'morning dress'?

Whatever did he wear for mornings? Just fancy if she'd turned up in the old trousers of Jim's, tied up with a leather belt that she wore for seeing to the pullets, or in her quilted floral shortie dressing gown with her hair in curlers. It was a different world.

Patsy, bored, sulky and embarrassed to the depths of her soul, was longing for Speech Day to be over, but worse was still to come. Cathy turned excitedly to face her. "I nearly forgot to tell you! Or did you tell her, Jim?"

She waited expectantly until he shook his head, then leant across the table, beaming. "Your dad's getting a greengrocer's shop!"

Patsy cringed. Isabel stifled a giggle. Cathy turned to her parents. "We have a market garden, you see. Well, Patsy will have told you."

Jim had come a bit to life at the turn in conversation. Now he was on familiar ground. "Been running it in conjunction with the farm next door. Ran the place for him for the duration, and now he's got used to having the extra land, doesn't want to renew my lease."

Oblivious to Patsy's reddening face, Cathy prattled happily. "It's time we had a bit of a change. We'll be renting ever such a lovely little house – in Palmer Street, Patsy, we'll be ever so cosy! Nice little kitchen, and a bathroom ..."

She leaned closer, her voice rising for emphasis. "And an indoor lav!"

Later, as they set off for home, Cathy relaxed, but murmured with a frown: "I shouldn't have said all that, Jim, should I? All that about the shop. I get carried away. I didn't know what else to talk to them about."

He set his face. "It's nothing to be ashamed of. She's no reason to be ashamed about us."

"No, suppose not." She stared down at the imitation wedding ring. With a sigh, she pulled it off, and slipped it into her handbag. Jim couldn't help but notice.

Cradled cosily in Jim's arms that night in the attic room, she stared into the darkness wistfully. "You know, Jim, in all these years, you've never said you loved me."

He was startled. "Haven't I?"

"Be nice if you occasionally said so."

An owl hooted outside somewhere amongst the trees. She thought he wasn't going to answer, but he did. "I will, then."

After that, though, he lapsed into silence. She waited, but he was quiet, so after a moment, she gave up and turned over. If he couldn't, he couldn't. It would have been ever so nice, though ...

After a moment, she heard him murmur very quietly. "I do love you, Cath."

Next day, he went to the church in town and sat in an empty pew for a very long time. The vicar wasn't around, for which he was grateful. He wouldn't have known the man, and the vicar wouldn't have known Jim from Adam, either. Anyway, he wasn't in the mood for talking. He just wanted to think things out.

It didn't help, really.

A couple of days later, still feeling very uncertain, he went to see Dr Humphreys. "What's your opinion, then, Doctor?"

Dr Humphreys was a bit impatient. "Do it, man, do it! See a solicitor, get things rolling. It's very sad, but there it is. Mary won't be back. You've a lot of life ahead of you yet, don't waste it. For your own sake, don't be a bloody fool!"

On the next Sunday, he drove over to Patterson Park. He hadn't been expecting to see Mary, but she was asleep, drugged heavily, and they let him sit in with her for a bit, though only with one of the male orderlies sitting in a chair outside the door. She was in a room by herself now. It had a locked door. Her hair on the pillow seemed even thinner than when he'd seen it last time. There was quite a bit more grey. She was heavily asleep, though her eyes were just a little bit open. Her lips were dry and flaking and her jaw was slack, her heavy, rattling breathing occasionally breaking into a loud snore. He picked up her hand, and it felt heavy and lifeless. The skin felt dry when he brushed it gently with his thumb. He murmured to her gently, trying to get inside her mind.

"Eh, Mary? Would it hurt you, darling? Would you mind? She's a nice girl, been very good to Patsy. I ought to do the right thing by her ... and I am quite fond ..." To his surprise, a wet droplet landed with a splash on the back of her hand. He hadn't known that he was crying. There was a cloggy frog in his throat. "I do miss you, though, Mary. I do wish you could come home."

Chapter 23

The psychiatrist in charge of Mary's case agreed with Dr Humphries. After that, there was her aunty. He drove there on his way home, debating with himself all the way whether or not to tell her what he was thinking of doing. He owed it to her, probably; Mary was her only relative, apart from Pats.

Parked outside, he made up his mind. Tell her, mind; he wasn't going to ask her opinion.

Nancy came to the back door in a state of great agitation. "She's not well, not well at all, Jim! She's had another little stroke. I've had the doctor, and he says she should go into the Cottage Hospital, but she won't let me get her dressed."

"Does that matter? They'll take her in her nightie, won't they?"

A tear trickled down Nancy's lined cheek. "Yes, but she doesn't want to go. You know she's always been an independent, private person. I tried to tell her it was for the best, but she started to cry. I've never seen Miss Buckley cry before. It made me feel so dreadful."

Jim scratched his head. He had no idea of what her resources were. "What about a private nurse?"

Nancy considered, looking hopeful. "I wonder ..."

"Patsy's not got that long to go at school now. I suppose she could afford it." Nancy looked exhausted. He drew in a deep breath. "Do you want me to put it to her?"

She was relieved. "Oh, Jim, I wish you would."

She was in the downstairs bed in the morning room now, the one that had been set up for Aunty Louise. She did look frail, and her mouth had been pulled down slightly in one corner by the second stroke, but there was the same line of determination in the set of her chin. "Nancy will care for me. There is no need for anyone else."

He was going to have to be tough with her. "Nancy can't cope. It needs someone who knows what they're doing, someone with medical experience."

Her fingers plucked fretfully at the coverlet. "I won't have it."

He sat down on the side of the bed, surprising himself with his own temerity. "Look, Aunty May ..." It sounded strange, coming from his lips, but he felt strangely affectionate towards her. "You're going to need somebody to be here at nights, in case you need anything. Nancy's the same age as you, you know. You can't expect her to be up and down and then to keep going in the daytime. It's heavy work, caring for an invalid. And it'll worry her. She won't know what to do if you ..." He was going to say 'have another stroke', but he changed it to: "... if you have a poorly do. What about if you just had a nurse in for the nights?"

She pursed her lips. "I don't know about that."

"She could come in at say, eight o'clock, give you a bed bath, that sort of thing, keep an eye on you during the night, make you comfortable, maybe bring you a hot drink if you fancied one, check you're having the right medication, sort your bed out, all those things, and go off again in the morning."

"Hm." Judging by her expression, it was looking hopeful

Jim pressed his advantage. "I'll have a word with the doctor, shall I, see if he has someone he can recommend?"

She sniffed. "I could go that far, I suppose. Mind you, if I don't care for her, I shall say so."

He nodded. "Well, then, we'll find you someone else."

It was stuffy in the morning room; it could do with the windows opening for a bit. He wondered if he dared suggest it and decided against it. "Do you want me to prop you up a bit? There're some more pillows on that chair. You don't look very comfy."

"Thank you." She felt very stiff and frail. Having cleared the pillows from the chair, he drew it up to the bedside.

"I've been to see Mary."

She seemed very far away. "Yes?"

"They let me sit with her. Looks very ..." He wasn't sure how to describe her. "Very frail."

She frowned. "How many years is it now?"

"A long time."

"It seems like yesterday. Time flies. *Tempus fugit.*"

"Yes, it does. Yes, yes, indeed."

She glanced at him, her eyes suddenly sharp and beady. "So no change, at all?"

He looked away. "'Fraid not."

"No. Patricia ... does she remember Mary?"

He hesitated. "I'm not sure. I talk about her sometimes, but she never mentions her. Worries me sometimes that she doesn't."

"It must have all been terribly painful. The human brain is sometimes useful; it blocks things we had best forget." He was conscious that she was still staring at him. "I'm glad you called," she said eventually. "I intend to make over a small sum to Patricia as soon as she finishes school. She will, of course, inherit this house and whatever money is left when I am gone, but I thought, a small sum now, for her continued education ..."

He shook his head. "You don't need to do that."

There was flicker of her old sternness. "Do not gainsay me, Mr Norris. She has had a good education, even though she may not always have made the best of it. Did you know that I have had to put some pressure on St Winifred's latterly to keep her on from time to time?"

He was shocked. "I didn't, no. Why?"

"Miss Jarman, the Headmistress, you know, is an old colleague of mine; she keeps me informed." He could have sworn she looked tickled. "They have considered expelling her twice."

Now he was horrified. "They haven't! No! Why?"

There was a definite glimmer of amusement in her sore old eyes, but she only shrugged. "Various incidents. Schoolgirl nonsense. Fortunately, I have some influence; there would have been little you could have done."

"I could have gone to see them." He was prickled, angry now; she always made him angry. The earlier feelings of affection faded away and he felt his body stiffen. "I'm her father. I had a right to know. You should have told me!"

She took no notice of his remonstrations. "I had been considering a finishing school, but funds are running a little low, especially if I am now to be forced to employ a busybody."

"A finishing school? Etiquette and flower arranging? Cordon whatsit cooking? She doesn't need any of that."

"Perhaps not. I do have my doubts. But a good typing course, perhaps, or a course in librarianship – though I doubt she has the temperament for that." She shrugged. "Something, anyway, along those lines. I shall consult acquaintances about it."

He drew in a deep breath. "I'm sure she'd be very grateful, but I'll make any decision about what my own daughter does."

"We'll see." She closed her eyes, dismissing him. "I'm tired, now. Tell Nancy I shall have a cup of Bovril and a little bread to soak in it in about an hour's time." She looked as if she had fallen straight to sleep, but she spoke again drowsily as he was about to leave the room. "Did you want my blessing, Mr Norris?"

He paused, startled. How the hell did the old woman know? She must be a mind-reader.

Her eyes were still closed.

"I did, rather."

She nodded. "Then you have it. You're a good man, Mr Norris." She sighed. "One day, I may call you Jim."

He had one more call to make, to the solicitor in town, and then, that night, in the attic bedroom, he studied Cathy's face as she was drifting peacefully to sleep, and drew her to him, tenderly stroking her hair. "Do you still want that baby, Cath?" Puzzled, she opened her eyes.

"Because you can have one. Well, not just yet, maybe in a year or two. Soon." Teasing, he deepened his embrace. "We'd better get in some practice."

She blinked. "You mean –"

His face broke into a beam. "Going to marry you, Cath! I've been to see them. Got it all in hand."

No way was Patsy going to become a secretary or a librarian! She was horrified at the suggestion. A secretarial course was found and booked, though, by Aunty May, and presented as a *fait accompli*, as was a gentlewomen's hostel. Her dismay was such that it dawned on Patsy only very slowly that it would be a good way of getting to London.

She lied, of course, to the girls; she had to. They had been driving her deeply into misery with all their talk of all the exciting things they were going to do next – Coming Out, a University, a Finishing School, even, in Isabel's case, a year in Florence. On Friday nights they all nipped out over the wall when they could to sneak into the Riverside Inn, and on that last Friday before the end of term, when the boys from Borley were celebrating too and the drinks were flowing extra freely and she should have been feeling especially cheerful, they were all on about nothing else again and instead she was feeling utterly miserable, unwanted and left-out.

It was something she had often fantasised about, but when she found herself taking a deep breath and coming out with it, she surprised herself too. They were all quite knocked out and for once, she really was the centre of genuinely admiring attention. It was a glorious moment. She waved a hand expansively, trying to make it sound she and Cathy and Dad travelled up and down to London all the time. As if. "Yes, we had just popped down to London for a couple of days when it happened."

"You lucky, lucky thing!"

"And he just picked you out of the crowd?"

"That's fantastic!"

She was in full stride. It came easily. She had had this fantasy so often that it was like a real world. "'Excuse me, miss,' he said, "do forgive me and I hope you don't mind my stopping you, but I was studying you as you walked along, and I work for a major modelling agency. If you are interested, I am sure we could find you a great deal of work.'"

They were all taken in.

"Oh, wow!!"

"What was he like?"

"How did you know he was genuine?"

"I didn't, but he gave me a card with his phone number, and it looked all right, you know, very professionally done."

"What did he say? What else did he say?"

"Oh, I can't really remember!" She was blustering now. "He was very gentlemanly. Very complimentary. Said I was just the type they were looking for. I could have a really successful career."

"I always said you'd make a model, didn't I?" Isabel looked as green as grass. It made Patsy glow inside; she was enjoying this.

Vanessa squealed. "You were actually spotted, just like Marilyn Monroe! You're going to be a film star!"

"Well, probably not a film star." She tried to sound modest, conscious that she was smirking. "It is a fashion agency, not film."

"Well, you never know!"

She waved a laid-back hand. "Anyway, I went along and his agency liked the photographs they took, and they've said that they will take me on their books. They have some huge contacts; a lot of well-known designers, big magazines like *Vogue*."

Vanessa squealed again and clapped her hands. "*Vogue*! Oh, wow!"

"Can we see the photographs?" Serena demanded, holding out her hand. "Have you got them?"

She had to think quickly. "No, I haven't got copies yet; I will be getting some, of course, for my portfolio."

"For your portfolio! Oh, wow!"

Over the last few weeks of term, the idea firmed up in her head. Fantasy, she determined, was going to be reality. She had no idea how this was to be achieved. The only thing she did know was that secretarial school was definitely not for her. She would move into the hostel and she'd have to put in some attendance on the course for a week or two while she got her bearings before forging a letter making some sort of excuse that wouldn't have the school ringing Aunty May, like having been taken too seriously ill that it would be impossible to carry on for the time being, or something. Then she would be free to forge her real career. It was lucky that Aunty May was giving her a separate allowance, enough to live on, just about; great shame that she couldn't get at the fees as well.

She was still the centre of attention. "And your father doesn't know?"

"Why is it a secret? Wouldn't he approve?"

She laughed, tossing back her hair. "Ooh, no! He only just about agreed to a secretarial course. He didn't like the sound of my going off to London even if I would be staying in a hostel."

"What did he say?"

She pulled a disapproving expression. "Drugs and swing and skiffle and all that rock 'n' roll!"

Isabel continued, mimicking Patsy's father's accent derisively. "London? Where's that?"

Marina rolled her eyes in glee. "What a hoot!"

"My great-aunt persuaded him it would be a good idea, and she suggested this place because they have a sort of hostel where the girls all stay, and she had them send us all the details, and I said yes please, and she's booked me in. Mind you," Patsy waved a hand airily, "would anybody have any idea who I could ask to be a post box for me? I have no intention of staying in the hostel, of course. I'll rent a room somewhere. I shall get myself a flat."

They shrieked with laughter. "You dreadful liar! What a giggle!"

"What fun!" Serena subsided behind the table as the laughter faded. "Well, good for you, you've got guts, Norris, I'll say that for you. I always said you could make a model! I'll tell Hugh; he's just off Sloane Square. He might let you use his flat for your post. He'll think it's a scream. You could say he's me, if they'd be worried about it being a man you're staying with." She winked slyly. "No doubt you can find some way of showing your gratitude?"

Marina rolled her eyes in dramatic woefulness. "And I'm just doing all these boring things like going to dreary balls and sailing and things for the Season!"

Patsy knew she didn't really mean it, of course, but it was wonderful to be the centre of attention and to have something more adventurous than any of them to boast about for once.

"I'll just write from time to time and tell her how brilliantly I'm doing on the secretarial course," she told them, "and then, after a while, when I'm really established, I'll tell them I've been offered a brilliant job or something and so I'm leaving."

"And what if they find out? Could your father make you come home again? What if he says you can't *be* a model?"

Patsy's face grew cold. "I'll be one, anyway."

C athy was in seventh heaven: with all there was to celebrate there must be a special meal. One of the chickens must be sacrificed. She penned one in very easily now and had no qualms about wringing its neck. The plucking of a chicken was something she had down to a fine art too. Normally, she carried out this operation in the yard, but the skies opened as she pulled out the last feather, and she had to complete the singeing of the skin and the drawing of the gizzard and the entrails in the kitchen. By the time Patsy and Jim arrived back from a duty visit to Aunty May, the small space stank and her hands and apron and the newspaper she had spread on the kitchen table was still spattered with blood. Covering her nose and mouth, Patsy drew back on the threshold. "God in heaven, I'm not coming in there, what's that smell?"

"Come in, come in!" Cathy waved her bloodied hands excitedly in greeting and gabbled animatedly. "I'm just making us a nice roast chicken dinner so that we can celebrate! We've got such a lot to celebrate, you finishing school, your dad and me getting married and moving into the new house! I thought I'd pull out all the stops, because it's going to be all stations go packing and everything before we know where we are. And you'll be off on this course. Imagine! London! What an adventure, Patsy! You're a very lucky girl. What's it called, this secretarial college? How are you going to find out where it is? It's a huge place, London. I still think your dad ought to come down with you, you know. Is the hostel place you're staying in very close? Will you be able to walk it, or will you have to catch a bus?"

Patsy glared at the kitchen table, where the chicken was

now nestled, glistening with oil, in a roasting pan. "I'm not going to eat that. It's disgusting."

Cathy shook her head. "Don't be silly, love. You like roast chicken. I made a chocolate cake and a trifle for after. We're going to have a bit of a feast!"

Patsy wrinkled her nose and rolled her eyes disparagingly. "I don't eat things like that. I'm on a diet."

"Don't be a silly girl."

True to her word, Patsy pushed the chicken and the roast potatoes to the sides of her plate, merely picking at a bit of broccoli and a few pieces of carrot.

"You need more than that, lovey!" Cathy remonstrated, disappointed. "You're a growing girl!"

She sneered. "For God's sake, Cathy, I'm eighteen, I'm grown up."

"And don't swear."

"You do. And Dad."

Cathy was flustered. "That's got nothing to do with it!"

Jim, who had been mostly silent so far during the meal, his energies devoted both to trying to digest the thought of his little Patsy wandering round a huge city and to making substantial inroads into his chicken, tried to make a joke of it. "Do as I say, not as I do."

Cathy felt hot and bothered and crabby now. The meal had taken a lot of making and it was hurtful that it wasn't appreciated. "It's not ladylike. I thought they'd have taught you different."

Patsy rolled her eyes scornfully. "*Differently*, for God's sake, not 'different'."

Seeing Cathy's distress, Jim spoke sharply. "Don't correct your mother!"

Patsy drew herself up sharply. "She is not my mother!"

Jim opened his mouth, but Cathy fluttered a hand to silence him. "No, I'm not," she replied quietly. "But I have tried."

There was a horrible silence, and then Patsy pushed back her chair. "I'm not staying here. I'm going out."

"Don't say anything, Jim."

After she'd gone, Jim pushed his food around his plate, distressed. "I just don't like it, Cath. When her Aunty May suggested a secretarial course, I didn't think she meant in London."

Cathy was getting impatient. "You were all for it when she wanted to pay for her to go to boarding school."

He pushed away his plate, disgruntled. "That's a different

thing. It's a dangerous world out there. London's a long way, Cath. I'd really rather she stopped round here."

"You'd have liked it if she'd have wanted to go to university!" Cathy gathered up the dirty plates crossly. "Well, you can't stop her, Jim, her Aunty May's paid for it, and she's given her some money. A secretarial college sounds like a really good thing; plenty of demand for a good secretary, I should imagine. She should find herself a nice little job after that. Anyway, if she stayed, what's she going to do round here?"

"She could get a job at the Westminster Bank or somewhere. I don't know, there must be something." Disgruntled, he moved over to the armchair, pulling on his boots. Cathy, scraping the wasted food into the scrap bucket, glanced over at him. He was frowning down at his feet, his lips tight and a tiny pulse throbbing at the corner of his jaw.

She sighed wearily, turning on the tap. "It'll be all right, love. She'll be all right. You're not to worry."

Chapter 24

Patsy had never been into the village pub before. It was low-ceilinged, dark and smelly, stinking of old beer and cigarette smoke and working clothes and nothing like the nice riverside place they had frequented on illicit outings from school, where the brasses shone and the glasses glittered. The customers there had been different too – sometimes pupils from the Sixth Form at Borley, the nearby boys' school, though mostly local gentry or people from boats moored up at the bank, and occasionally travelling representatives, but they were all fun to talk to, appreciated a pretty girl, and weren't shy of putting their hands in their pockets for the odd cocktail or a gin and tonic. Here, they all seemed to be dull, ugly local men, some still in their working clothes, and a lot of them old, her father's age at least. There were no women. Seeing her enter, they fell silent, and despite her bravado, she felt a little awkward as she walked up to the bar. "A gin-and-tonic, please."

The bartender, a grizzle-haired man with a pock-marked nose and watery red eyes eyed her suspiciously, then turned and poured out the drink. "Take it over to that table," he told her, pushing it across the bar.

Patsy pulled herself up onto a splintery barstool. "No, thanks, I'll be all right here." She thought he was about to argue, but instead, he shrugged and turned away, picked up a tea towel and started to polish glasses. She was aware of him studying her, though, as she sipped the gin.

Taking out the inlaid tortoiseshell cigarette case that she had taken from Paulette St Michel's handbag as a souvenir, she lit a Gauloise. The low rumble of male voices began to rise again round the room and she relaxed a little, feeling the gin beginning to fizzle in her blood stream. This would do for now, but the sooner she was in London having some fun and out of

219

this Godforsaken boring backwater, the better.

She pushed the empty glass across the bar. "Can I have another one, please?"

"Take it easy."

She pushed the glass firmly towards him. "I think I'll have a Bloody Mary this time."

"Is that wise?"

She was stung. "Just get me the drink, please."

Someone rested his elbows on the bar beside her. "Ah, just get the young lady her drink, Bill. It won't hurt her." She glanced up. He looked around twenty-ish at a guess, with sideburns and dark wavy hair, and wearing a sharp but cheap-looking navy suit. The smell of beer and cheap after-shave hung around him, mingling with that of Brylcreem. He seemed familiar with the barman.

"Go on, Bill. Put it on my tab." He winked at her and sniffed. "French cigarette, is that?"

Under normal circumstances, she would have given a boy like him short shrift, but she was bored. He had very blue eyes and a snaggled tooth at one side of his mouth, which gave him a slightly piratical air that she found surprisingly attractive. She held out the case. "Do you want one?"

He accepted, scrutinising and savouring it through narrowed eyes. "Nice change from a Woodbine." Running an appreciative eye over her, he grinned. "So, tell me, what's a nice girl like you doing in a place like this?"

She sighed. *Oh, Lord, not that old line.*

"I know who she is!" The barman moved towards her with her Bloody Mary. "I've got it now. I know who you are. You're Jim Norris's lass. That's right, isn't it?"

Patsy sipped the drink, then wrinkled her nose and pushed it back again across the counter. "Could I have some ice, please, and a slice of lemon?"

"No ice, love; no lemon either. No call for it. Sorry." He scrutinised her closely. "Does your dad know you're here?"

Ignoring him, she stood up from the stool, glancing at the young man at her side. "Shall we go and sit at a table?"

He straightened, a smug grin on his sallow face. "My pleasure."

She glanced back as they made their way across to the table and saw the barman, his eyes upon her, muttering to the group of men at the far end of the bar. They turned to stare as well. She sat down quickly.

The young man in the sharp suit pulled out a plastic comb and ran it though his greasy hair, then pulled his chair close to the table so that his knee touched hers. "So what's your name, then? I'm Gordon. "

She smiled. "Belinda."

He raised his pint glass. "Cheers, then, Belinda. Drink up, and I'll get you another one."

If Gordon thought he was going to have her to himself, he was mistaken. The rare presence of an attractive young blonde had the very few single men in the pub swarming like bees to a honey pot. The first to join them was a double-chinned, stocky lad who had been given such a short back and sides it looked as if he was almost bald. His skin was crimsoned with angry acne.

"Hello, Spike!" he roared, eyeing Patsy and breathing out a fog of beery fumes as he slapped Gordon cheerily on the back. "You off soon, yeah? They'll have those curly locks off you in no time, mate!"

Gordon – or Spike – looked disconcerted, but grinned. "Hello, Brendan. Thought you were in the army?"

"Just been demobbed, not before bloody time." Pulling up a chair between them, he took a deep draught of his pint. "When you off, then?"

Gordon/Spike looked a bit anxious. "Start basic training next week. What's it like, then?"

Brendan wiped the froth from his mouth with the back of his hand. Lighting a cigarette, he blew out a smoke ring and held out the packet to Patsy. "Want one, love? Go on, might as well, army issue."

He lit it for her, then turned back to Gordon.

"What, National service? Total waste of bloody time, mate. Spent two years in Germany twiddling me thumbs and running round Sennerlager. If you're any good at sports, you've got it made, special rations, otherwise it's a dog's life. Only good thing's the beer – and some of the women aren't bad either."

He eyed Patsy lasciviously. "Your glass is empty, love. What you havin'?"

As soon as he went off to get another a round, a broad-shouldered, blond lad with a weathered complexion, wearing muddy trousers and a torn blue-chequered shirt slid into his empty seat and put his pint on the table. Gordon/Spike frowned. "Clear off, Den. Go and play with your tractor."

Den grinned, and drew his chair up closer to Patsy. "Did I hear Bill say you're Jim Norris's girl, love?"

She blew out a careful smoke ring. Her head was swimming already. "Who's Jim Norris?"

"Must have been mistaken." He studied her, head on one side. "Strange, though, you do have a look of Jim."

Den was a chatterer. By the time Brendan came back and slammed down overflowing glasses on the table, then noisily drew up another chair, Gordon/Spike's mouth had turned down rather sulkily. "Shall we move on, love?" he whispered into Patsy's ear. "D'you fancy somewhere a bit quieter? A bit of a walk? Or I know a nice pub down the road."

Actually, Patsy decided, she was having rather a nice time where she was. They were only yokels, and though her tongue was already getting quite tied up when she tried to speak, she was feeling deliciously swimmy and all the attention was quite pleasing.

"Oh, I don't know ... Let's see after we've had another drink. I'm buying. Gin and orange, I think, this time."

The drinks kept flowing. At some point, the interfering barman came over and tried to persuade her to go home, but she dug in her heels, and Gordon/Spike or Brendan or someone, Den, perhaps, she couldn't work out which one, said that he was not to worry, mate, he'd see her home. She thought he'd said she was his sister, but she could have been hearing things.

She was at home in the morning, though she had no recollection of getting there. She had the impression of having ridden home on a scooter or a motorbike with the wind blowing her hair into her eyes, though whose it was, she couldn't say. She had obviously been sick; the rag rug at the side of her bed and the edge of the eiderdown were disgusting. She must have climbed in at her window, because the lamp was still lit in the kitchen and her dad, who'd obviously been waiting up for her, was fast asleep in the armchair when she made her way out into the kitchen to get a drink of water and something with which to clean up the mess.

Her head was throbbing. She tiptoed back to bed again quickly. Good thing he hadn't seen her – and a good thing the girls hadn't seen her with those louts, but it had been a good night. Weird, fragmented bits of scenes from it kept floating in and out of her head as she tried to get back to sleep; she'd been screaming with laughter at some point, she remembered that, and there had been a raucous chorus of songs to which the bartender had tried unsuccessfully to put a stop. She also had some recollection of dashing across the back yard of the pub tugging somebody by the hand and being very wet (had it been raining?). There was the pain of banging her head on some beam, a lot of hay, giving her a sneezing fit, which she had found very funny, and the smell of old sacking. Then there were voices.

"That's it, Belinda, love. Make yourself comfy."

Her voice. "Have you got something, then? A rubber Johnny, a French Letter?"

Then the bit that made her eyes snap open in the cold early morning light. How many of them had there been? A different voice. "Here, I have. Got some in the NAAFI before I left Dortmund."

There wasn't going to be a honeymoon. Jim had wanted to book a couple of nice days for the two of them in Bournemouth but what with sorting out and packing up the cottage and selling off the equipment from the market garden ready for moving into Palmer Street, as well as sorting out supplies for the new shop, Cathy had told him he shouldn't bother; they could do with the money anyway.

She was so excited at the prospect of the move that she could hardly sleep. Everyone had rallied round really kindly with bits of furniture, because of course they were going to need a lot more in the new house than they had in the tiny cottage. Mrs Percival from the ironmongers had given them a whole three-piece suite, still in very good condition and green, too, so it would match the carpet in the sitting room at Palmer Street which was very nearly fitted and was really rather nice with green and orange swirls which Cathy thought very tasteful. The lino and the other rugs and carpets there weren't too bad and they'd have the rag rugs too from Patsy's room and the attic. It was just as well, because they couldn't afford to replace them, not just yet. She and her mum had chosen some nice pieces of curtaining from the Remnant Shop in Chetstock and Nancy was running them up. They had bought new mattresses for the beds.

Cathy was disappointed but put a brave face on it. "It'll be like a honeymoon, Jim, anyway, being in the new house. You'll be able to have your dinner in a separate room from the kitchenette, just think!"

She bustled about the little cottage excitedly, sorting and packing. "I've packed our clothes but I shall want any other suitcases or trunks you can find me this morning, Jim. Can you get them down from the attic?"

Fetching his biggest torch, he climbed the ladder obediently. The air felt close and stuffy and there were dust motes twisting and turning sleepily in the narrow ray of sunshine at the window. She had been sweeping. On the bedroom side of the crossbeam it was tidy, the big bed stripped and the drawers emptied, all their outer clothing gone from the hanging line. "Hope you've left me a clean shirt!" he called down, but she didn't answer.

The cases she had packed were standing ready by the trap-door to be carted down. He took them down first, manoeuvring them through the trap with difficulty, then, climbing up once again and propping up the torch on the beam so that its light could illuminate the gloom on the other side, he began to shift the boxes and other things still there. Many of them hadn't been opened for years.

Cathy was waiting in the hallway with a flimsy grey cardigan in her hands when he brought the last one down. She had an old battered suitcase open. "You're not taking these, are you, Jim?"

"Eh? What?"

"These old things of Mary's. You don't want to take them, too?"

He scratched his head. It felt itchy after being up in the dusty attic. "I don't know ..."

"Well, there's no point, is there? No point in keeping them any longer and I could do with the case."

He felt a sharp pang of distress. "They are Mary's things."

She sighed wearily. "I know they are. I just said that."

"She might want them."

Weariness made her exasperated. "When? When would she want them?"

He was at a loss. "I don't know. One day."

She clicked her tongue in weary irritation. "Oh, Jim, you're just being daft. Anyway, they've all got moths."

He was fretful now. "They haven't, have they?"

She held out the front of the cardigan. "Look here! And here!"

He remembered that lacy cardigan; she used to wear it with the forget-me-not blue dress that Nancy had used for measurement. She had looked so pretty. He had liked her in it. "Have they all got them?"

She bent over the suitcase impatiently, unfolding more clothes. "Yes! Here ... And here ..."

"That's her good jacket! Should have put mothballs in."

"Well, that's it then." She began to bundle the items out of the case. "No point in keeping them. If there are any things still good, I'll give them to the Jumble Sale. The rest'll do for rags."

Half his life – another life – a life with Mary – vanishing

with the cottage. "I'll sort them."

She hesitated, glanced at his remote expression, and then nodded. "Well, don't take too long, will you? We've a lot still to do."

When she had vanished into the kitchen, he took the things from the suitcase out slowly one by one. The old blue dress was there, tucked right at the bottom, crumpled into a roll next to Mary's jewellery box and her hairbrush and things. The sight of it brought him up, and it took him a long moment to reach for it. When he did, he held the soft, creased fabric beneath his nose for a moment, closing his eyes and breathing in deeply. No Pink Lilac any longer. No lingering trace of her clinging to it. Been too long a time.

Somehow its absence hit him worse than its presence might have done; it made his stomach ache.

He left the jewellery box and the silver-backed hairbrush and mirror in the suitcase. She would want Patsy to have them. Patsy might like them one day. Folding it tenderly, he placed the blue dress next to them. It looked so very lost and lonely all on its own at the bottom of the suitcase that his eyes blurred. Getting to his feet again and staring down at it, he blew his nose hard.

No trace of moth holes, at least. For that, he felt strangely relieved.

Patsy was on pins, itching to get away, not least in case the pustule-faced Army lout or the village idiot, Den, should turn up on the doorstep.

Had she? Had they? Couldn't remember. *Must have been utterly mad.*

One of them had to know where she lived, if he'd brought her home on a bike. Gordon/Spike would probably have been off somewhere safely square-bashing, so she didn't need to worry about him. She'd been lucky that Dad had been too busy to go down for a pint at the pub, and, if he'd bumped into him, the nosy barman who had recognised her must have kept his mouth shut. If Cathy'd heard anything in the village, she had kept quiet. She could be all right, sometimes, Cathy, even if she was as boring and common as a cowpat in a twenty-acre field. Everyone in this village was common and boring; the sooner she could get down to London, the better: even secretarial school while she got things sorted was beginning to look good. She tried every excuse she could think of to get there quickly, but Cathy baulked at any suggestion that might mean missing the wedding.

"Your dad would be dreadfully upset, Patsy; you can't do that. He'd be ever so disappointed. You don't need to be there before the fourteenth, anyway, you said."

The best she would agree to was that Patsy would catch the six o'clock train to London after the ceremony and the so-called 'Wedding Breakfast', a tea party at the Mulberry Room at the St George's Hotel, near the Registry Office. "You wouldn't want to miss that, Patsy. It's going to be ever so posh!" Posed for the photographer on the steps of the Registry Office, Jim kissed Cathy's cheek and she beamed up at him, "You look absolutely lovely. A real treat, doesn't she, Pats?"

Patsy smiled sweetly. Personally, she thought that the sprigged net veil that looped down from the crown of her hat made Cathy look like a beekeeper with a bee stuck up her nose. One of the sprigs of embroidered forget-me-nots – or whatever they were – was most unfortunately positioned. The corsage of artificial orchids pinned to her lapel looked ridiculous; it was far too ostentatious. Her posy was sweet, though, and at least the flowers were real. Dad had been up half the night making it, twining together white rosebuds and bits of blue delphinium and frothy gypsophila so that they'd match her dress.

If only she hadn't been so short and dumpy, and if the pale blue rayon peplum-skirted coat dress she had chosen because you 'couldn't tell it from silk', ha ha, had only looked faintly as if she might have bought it somewhere other than a market stall or C&A, and if it had only fastened properly without the buttons straining, she would have looked okay. Her own navy dress with its stiffened swing skirt and its tiny waist and wide, loose reversed collar lined with white, that she had bought for herself at Beamish's with some of Aunty May's money, was much nicer.

Jim held out his arm to Patsy, feeling a deep glow of happiness. "My little family! We want you in this one, Pats! Come on and join us, pet."

She didn't look that happy as she moved to stand beside them. He put his arm about her as she moved close to his side and gave her an encouraging squeeze, though he didn't feel much like it; the thought of her going off to the big unfriendly city still had him worried to death. But she was probably depressed at leaving them. "You'll be all right, you know, pet! You can always come home again if you don't like it."

Come home again? Fat chance. She shrugged, trying not to snap. "I'll be fine, Dad, don't be silly."

The photograph taken, he kept his arm about her. She

wriggled, glancing at her watch. "Dad, it's twenty-five past, we really ought to go."

"Don't worry, I'll get you there, we'll be off shortly."

Cathy leant round Jim, beaming. "Your dad's never late. And you look lovely, too, doesn't she, Jim? Gorgeous! You could be a model, Pats!" She rolled her eyes, giggling. "You'll have to watch it in London, eh, or they'll be snapping you up!"

At the station, Jim purchased a platform ticket, then carried Patsy's suitcases onto the platform just as the train pulled in. He insisted on finding her a carriage with only a lady in it, which took up time, and then, with the bags stowed safely, had to jump out again quickly as the whistle blew and the porters started slamming doors.

He stood waiting as she wound down the window and the heavy engine gathered steam. She looked excited now. "Well ..." Anxiety flared up again. She might look grown-up in her dress and gloves and hat, but she was a baby really. "Take care, won't you? Let us know if you have any problems."

The guard blew the final whistle. Leaning out, she kissed him on the cheek. "Bye, Dad."

There was a judder and a hiss of steam and the wheels began to shift. She was still leaning out. "Ring us, now. I'll be in the Red Lion on a Friday night, or you can arrange something with Nancy and I'll be there for you to ring."

"Okay."

"Don't forget to write to your Aunty May."

The guard's flag fell. "I won't." She began to withdraw as the wheels gathered speed.

He had to jog to keep up. "Write to us, too."

"Okay." She started to wind up the window as white steam billowed past.

He lifted his voice. "Good luck on the course."

"Yes. Thanks."

"If you need any money or anything ..."

She fluttered her hand. "Bye, Daddy."

He stood alone, waving, as the train pulled out.

She did feel a momentary pang as his tall figure receded along the platform, but as the station was left behind, Patsy sank down into her seat with a sigh of mingled relief and excitement. The well-dressed middle-aged woman in the far corner of the compartment was reading; she looked up and smiled vaguely, before returning to her page and Patsy was relieved; lots to think about. Didn't want a boring chat.

The compartment smelled of stale smoke and though there were linen antimacassars to lie your head back against, the maroon moquette on the seats was worn in places and shabby. There was a picture of children playing on golden sand with their buckets and spades above the seat she was facing. *Come to beautiful Weymouth!* it said underneath in big letters.

"No chance at all!" she informed the children smugly. "I'm going to be a famous model, you see. I'm London-bound. Bye-bye!"

Chapter 25

J im was rather worried about Patsy on the few occasions that she did ring him. He consulted Cathy. "She doesn't sound very happy; don't think she likes the course. Maybe she's lonely. Ought I to go down to London, do you think? Make sure she's all right?"

Spotting the chance of a thrilling first visit to the big city, Cathy jumped at it at once. "We could both go, Jim! It would make a nice little break. See Buckingham Palace and things ... We might even see some of the royal family. We could call it a belated honeymoon! We'll have one after all!"

He was very dubious. "Got to have somebody here to man the shop. Can't just close when we've not long opened."

The small, green-and-cream painted shop with JAMES NORRIS (Prop) PURVEYOR OF FINE FRUIT AND VEGETABLES above the door and its pervasive smell of onions and oranges and with the tempting trays of produce in neat array outside was already doing fairly good business. He had taken great pains to make it look nice, with freshly-painted shelving on the walls inside and a new counter as well as racks for the various kinds of potatoes and root veg and, after a great deal of deliberation about the expense and about which kind, had purchased two sets of shiny new scales, one heavy one for the potatoes, and a lighter set for fruit and things. With a fair amount of persuasion from Cathy, who had insisted that it would be essential for taking orders, a telephone was installed at last. It sat in quiet splendour in the little partitioned off area at the back, next to the invoice pad.

"I suppose not, no." *Shame* ... She recovered quickly, attempting one more try. "Do you want *me* to go?" She could just see herself wandering down Oxford Street ... What would she wear for the trip? Perhaps Mum would help her make a coat, or maybe she could persuade Jim to let her buy one –

and she would definitely have to buy a new hat.

He mused, frowning. "I could suggest it."

Cathy was very excited, but Patsy turned the suggestion down flat. "No need, honestly. Tell her not to bother. I'm fine, really. I'm just very busy."

He was both relieved and sympathetic. "Give you lots of homework, do they? Practising your shorthand and stuff?"

She gave a short laugh. "Practising and things. Mm. Yes."

When the call was over, she replaced the receiver with relief greater than her father's. What a laugh! 'Practising'! As if!

What she was really doing was avoiding secretarial college as much as possible and prowling about the streets and squares of London, trying to look as much like a potential top-range fashion model as she could, hoping every day as she set out that today the fantasy would become reality and he – the man with the magic touch, the agency spotter in her story – would tap her on the shoulder. It hadn't happened so far.

It had been an adventure finding her way to the hostel and college – Dad had painstakingly gone through the route with her over and over again with the help of a map borrowed from the library, but the Underground had been bewildering – and so exciting! She had felt very daring. But as far as thrilling went for either the college or the hostel, that was as far as it had gone. London was fabulous, but the school had proved to be as awful as she had feared – dreary and boring, with ever so many rules – and the hostel had been just as bad. Her room was miniscule, with a hard, narrow bed and a tiny wardrobe and no decent mirror or light with which to do her hair or put on her make-up. The shared bathroom at the end of the corridor had an erratic and very noisy water heater, nowhere to set out her things, and seemed permanently occupied. There was a sparsely furnished sitting room, but no male visitors were allowed; the front door was locked at ten o'clock by an old witch of a manageress with weird wiry hair who kept a very watchful eye, and there were even bars on the ground floor windows. The old nosey-parker pretended it was to keep out burglars and intruders, but Patsy guessed it was really to keep the girls in, though she couldn't imagine any of them sneaking out at night or clambering back in – they all seemed too dull and stupid to be any real fun.

Once she had found her way a bit round London, she had found Sloane Square and the King's Road and had started haunting them in particular, but so far she had never caught a glimpse of Hugh and she had heard nothing from him either.

As far as she had been able to establish, modelling schools charged a ridiculous figure unless *they* approached *you* with an offer, so she had lashed out some of Aunty May's money on a photographic session in a dank and dusty third-floor studio with an odd little elderly man with a yellow paisley cravat and an ill-fitting bright brown toupée. He had a cigarette permanently clasped between very bad teeth and peered at her through only one eye in order to protect his sight from its smoke whether he was looking into the camera lens or not. She had sent out the resulting disappointing photographs to a few agencies, but she hadn't heard back from any of them at all. She had looked really horrible; she hadn't been much surprised.

She was studying the latest fashions on the streets and keeping up-to-date with as many magazines as she could run to, adapting her wardrobe as best as she was able since her limited allowance wasn't going to take her far in terms of buying new things. She found some books on fashion and how to be a model in the local library and went to as many free fashion shows during her dinner hour and at the weekends as she could find in the department stores, and every evening not spent slinking hopefully about the streets she spent in experimentation with her hair and make-up and practising glides and turns, sits and rises – and even the posture exercises she had so resented when imposed by her Aunty May during holiday visits. Though Patsy had resented it at the time, all those hours spent parading up and down with a book on her head were lodged in her mind and now she practised it assiduously using her Pitman book and *Typing for Beginners*.

Though she had always made sure to put on full make-up and walk and dress as strikingly as she could, so far the dream had shown no signs of coming true. She had attracted some attention, some of it welcome and some very much not, but not the hoped-for kind. It was easy enough to pick up a few dates and quite a lot of drinks, she had found, so long as you weren't too fussy. She hadn't met anybody she really fancied, or even anybody really nice. By the end of the first year, disillusionment was beginning to set in.

As the course moved on into its second year and she was still stuck with it, her depression and loneliness grew much worse. It was beginning to look as if she was going to have to either give in and go home or really set about getting a job as a rotten secretary – not that she would be any good at it.

Then one evening, out of the blue, quite by chance and

just as remarkable as the incident she had made up out of fantasy – just as she was wandering disconsolately around Leicester Square, uncomfortable in a new waspie and with toes pinching badly in narrowly-pointed white stilettos, she finally bumped into Hugh.

He looked sleek and well-fed and full of himself and prosperous. "So what are you doing these days?" he asked when they had got through the 'Well, I never's!" and the 'What are you doing here's?' and the 'Fancy bumping into you's!" Serena had never given him the message as she had promised, obviously – maybe she hadn't believed her or had forgotten – more likely, though, it had been just a little matter of very sour grapes. Patsy was miffed. All that time hoping that he'd be in touch! She had been wasting her time hoping for him to contact her.

He was doing something in the city, now. A family firm, he said. Desperately boring. His uncle. Of course she stuck to the same old story. Oh, modelling. Yes, she was modelling now.

"Modelling, eh?" He threw a lascivious leer at her bosom. "Glamour modelling, eh? I say!"

"*Fashion* modelling, Hugh, not glamour!"

"Ah!" She caught him eyeing her outfit doubtfully and was chagrined. She was wearing her third best one in the 'being spotted' stakes – one of three boring white blouses which had been obtained for secretarial school by Cathy from the small town department store, this one titivated by having the sleeves cut to bracelet length and turned back to form a wide cuff and worn with a wide belt and a very full claret red skirt bought at C&A, puffed up with as many stiff net petticoats as she could manage, and the whole finished off with a small black pillbox hat and short white gloves. She thought she looked quite smart, but the outfit clearly wasn't *couture.* At least she had put her new false eyelashes on and had only just freshened up her claret red lipstick.

He smiled sleekly. "Apologies, my dear, fashion modelling, of course. And how is it going? Successfully, I hope?"

She batted her heavy black eyelashes, trying to look modest, "Oh, quite successful, I have been fairly successful, yes. Though you probably haven't ever picked up the kind of magazines I've appeared in," she hastened to add. "You know, women's magazines, high fashion. Very boring to busy men like you!"

She tried to drop a few famous names; thanks to her avid reading, she knew those of lots of designers now. A few, she made up.

"Well done." It seemed to convince him. If it didn't he kept it to himself. "My sister's engaged now, by the way, did you know?"

She was amazed. "Serena? Really? She is very young."

"Probably up the duff!" He chortled, then shrugged. "Nice chap, though, chap she's going to marry. Friend of mine. In metals. Loads of money. Argentinean. Met him at a Polo match." He grinned. "Did try to warn him off."

She saw him secretively assessing her figure again. "And what are you doing at this moment, darling? Are you busy?"

When she admitted she wasn't, to her great delight, he insisted on whisking her off to a restaurant table which he had booked and where he had arranged to meet friends. He wouldn't even allow her to go home to change, which was a mixed blessing, because whilst she was dying to change her shoes and put on something more suitable – though she didn't really have a proper evening frock – above all, she didn't want him to see where she lived.

She was very nervous. The restaurant was very posh, and the friends – two girls and three men, the men all extremely confident and smart and already, judging by their drawls, the worse for a drink or two, and the girls really almost too glamorous and very chatty – made her feel like a tongue-tied ugly duckling at first. But they didn't seem at all surprised that he had dragged her along with him, and at least, thanks to those old etiquette lessons at St Winifred's, she wasn't too much at sea. Although the menu was all in French, Hugh didn't even ask what she wanted, but ordered for her *Fillet of Sole Meuniere,* which was some kind of fishy soup, and a huge Peach Melba for after, which sounded utterly delicious.

Dinner seemed a very leisurely affair. There was a man in evening dress casually riffing through soothing melodies at a white piano, and nobody seemed to be in a hurry. Before the food arrived she had already been introduced to several kinds of cocktails – 'Tom Collins', 'Gimlet' and 'Martini'. They were all quite delicious. Hugh promised to introduce her to more of them and even to teach her how to make some. "Oh, but you must learn how! All the difference in the world between a glass of gin with an olive in it and a proper Martini, darling! Style, Patsy – one simply must have style."

Style, yes. Her toes curled in excitement under the table as she struggled to maintain some focus in her eyes. Crystal sparkling, music playing, handsome men and women, drinks simply flowing ... And they don't mind I'm here!

Oh, glory, this is the life!

By the time the unknown soup eventually arrived, she was already quite woozy; it was difficult to make out where to aim the spoon. With every sip of the champagne that followed and of the wine that accompanied the food, her state of intoxication grew deeper and deeper. There was a great deal of laughter and inebriated chatter and when they rose suddenly at last to leave the table, she did grasp that they were going on to a jazz club; Hugh grasped her hand with his hot, sticky one and told her masterfully that she was coming, too. 'Ronnies' it was called, on Gerrard Street. She had read of 'Ronnies' and so she was excited by the opportunity to see it, but, if they did go, how they got there or what it was like remained a mystery; the experience passed her completely by. The first time she struggled vaguely to the surface of a foggy alcoholic sea, she was in a tiny, dim and faintly-scented lift leading up to Hugh's apartment and being penned enthusiastically by him into a corner. Though she didn't care much for his sloppy, wet kisses she didn't offer any resistance, indeed, eagerly kissed him back and even, once they were in his apartment and locked in each others' arms on an enormous fur-covered white sofa, helped him to undress her.

She was, above all, very lonely. She was also depressed, damaged, mixed up, ambitious and desperate to be liked. He was passable-looking, quite amusing, might have contacts, could offer a good time and as for the primary requirement, it seemed he fitted the bill. His was a friendly face.

Chapter 26

There was only one Garibaldi left. When that one had gone too, Cathy brushed the crumbs from the front of the blue waterproof cape covering her clothes and hooked her shopping bag closer to her with her foot, then rummaged inside it, taking out an orange. The baby in her tum had to be a boy; it took after Jim. It was always starving.

It was very hot under the dryer and the smell of peroxide was making her feel queasy. Ducking out from under the big metal hood, but carefully, so as not to displace the rollers, she squinted at the dial. Still twenty minutes to go, for goodness' sake! Carefully resetting it to a cooler setting, she reached for another magazine and settled herself back inside the hood. The orange peel had to go inside her bag; there was nowhere else to put it.

She had only turned half a dozen pages when she saw the picture and frowned, peering more closely. "Well, I never! Well, I'm blowed!" There was no mistaking that snooty look on her face. Eyes sleekly outlined in black kohl, one hand on her hip, the young woman gazed out haughtily from under a Chinese-looking straw hat with a wide turned down brim, rather like a lampshade. "Well, my goodness gracious! Well, I never!"

She scanned the description printed beneath the photograph: *Marie Fitzgerald full dirndl skirt in black silk linen, with white silk linen jacket, nipped in flatteringly at the waist ...*

Her heart felt all fluttery. "Well, for goodness' sake, I don't believe it. Oh, my goodness gracious! It's our *Pat!*"

Hanging out with Hugh and his friends became a regular thing for Patsy. As time went on, she found that, if she showed sufficient 'gratitude' as Serena had put it, he and his male friends and acquaintances would pay for her to eat – and

235

eat well – and to have a good time. They even lashed out for some quite nice clothes and jewellery and 'loaned' her money for her rent if she flattered them enough. Thanks to them she learned to find her way about town and had tried out a lot of things she'd never tried before. High on music, pills and alcohol, and on being young in London, she forgot her inner unhappiness and began to have a very good time. This must have reflected in her appearance, because when one of Hugh's girl friends, who – to Patsy's enormous envy – was an established model herself, had offered vaguely in a drunken haze to give her an introduction to her agency, Patsy had harassed her into actually doing so, and even lending Patsy some of her clothes, to her huge amazement.

After that things started happening very quickly. They actually took her on! Her first assignment turned out to be demonstrating a refrigerator, but the photo shoot was for an advertising campaign and the photo went into a number of newspapers and magazines. Over the remainder of the year she was given work modelling in the lunchtime and afternoon fashion shows at Debenham & Freebody's, Dickens and Jones and at Harvey Nichols, and did several independent showings for up-and-coming or hopeful designers – though nobody really top-range, which would have been the real break-through.

After that she did a series for Cutex, and then, with several more quite big advertising campaigns in the pipeline, tossed her shorthand instruction books and pads and pencils into the waste paper bin. She had only at that point broken the news of her change of career to her dad and to Cathy, who up till then had been under the impression that she was going to make a nice little career for herself with a furniture importer in Bow. Why she had told them her future employer was a 'furniture importer', she didn't know – or why 'Bow'; she didn't even know where it was. It was just the first place name that had come into her mind. Didn't matter; they wouldn't know either.

Though he had many reservations, her dad had grudgingly accepted the switch, and Cathy had in fact been over the moon about it. "Your mum would have been very proud!" Over the intervening years more work had followed and she had finally found herself able to rent her very own, quite comfortable, flat. The latest shoot had been the biggest one yet.

Despite the impressive assignment for *Vogue*, what Cathy didn't know – because Patsy kept Jim and Cathy very much at the vague periphery of her life – was that because of her racy, boozy way of life, she was in danger of seeing it all go as swiftly as it came.

People in the business were just beginning to talk.

Manoeuvring herself out from under the hairdryer, Cathy fumbled with the cubicle door. Mr David seemed to be in with the client in the cubicle next door; she could hear him chatting animatedly in his nasal Liverpool accent. Knocking at the three-quarter door, she thrust it open excitedly. A strong smell of perm solution pervaded the small space. "Mr David, Mr David, have you got a moment? I want to show you this."

He rolled his eyes, holding his gloved hands in ill-disguised irritation. "What is it, Mrs Norris? You won't be cooked yet, dear. Pop back under your dryer, there's a good lady. I'll be with you in a minute, dear."

Cathy held the open magazine beneath his nose. "But it's Patsy! Patsy! Look here, see, that's our Patsy in *Vogue!*"

He squinted at the photograph. "Who, dear?"

"My daughter – my stepdaughter – Patsy. Doesn't she look lovely!" She displayed the photograph proudly in front of Mr David's client. "See there – *Marie Fitzgerald dress.* That's my daughter wearing it. Stepdaughter. That's our Patsy!"

"Oh, very nice, dear! Love the hat."

After another quick glance Mr David returned to dousing his client's hair with perm lotion, and Cathy whisked the magazine away quickly in case it got splashed. "I thought your stepdaughter was a secretary, Mrs N?"

Cathy was engrossed again in the photograph. "Eh? Oh, yes, she did go off to do that, but that was a long time ago. I thought I told you, she's a model now. A fashion model." She glanced back at him, frowning. "I did tell you, Mr David, don't you remember? I remember telling you! I was telling you she was doing fashion parades at teatime in that posh shop, whatsit – Harvey Nichols. I was saying about how I was going to go down on the train and see her doing it, but she said I shouldn't bother, because she wouldn't be able to talk and she'd have to dash off afterwards."

"Yes, yes, dear, vaguely. I do remember. You said what a busy life she leads!"

It was so hot! Cathy fanned herself. "Oh yes, she's ever so busy! In ever so much demand, hardly ever gets home, much as she'd like to. She's all over the place – does lots of cat walking and things, that's what she usually does, some magazines, of course, but this is the first time she's ever been in *Vogue.* "

"Well, our own homegrown pin-up girl! Tell you what, Mrs Norris, dear, tell her to pop into the Salon when she's at home next, I'll do a free shampoo and set. Don't want them thinking we can't do a nice hair-do outside London, do we!"

"That's a good idea!" Cathy beamed. "We could put a picture in the *Weekly News.*" She fluttered the magazine proudly. "Can I take this home with me, Mr David? I must show it to her dad!"

Jim's feelings, when she showed him the photograph, were rather mixed. "Much rather she'd have stuck with the secretarial course," he told her, as she donned her green nylon overalls in the shop to help him box up the orders ready for delivery. "Seven pounds of King Edwards, by the way, for Mrs Overton," he added, "She wasn't very happy with the Wiljas I sent the other day."

"Do you know what I mean, though?" he added, weighing out a pound and a half of sprouts. "I mean – a model. It sounds a bit disreputable, I think."

Cathy waved a hand dismissively. "Oh, it's perfectly all right, these days. Don't be silly, Jim. All the girls want to be models – that or airline hostesses. She's very lucky. And her photo in *Vogue,* now, too! That's a step up for her. It's only the really nice looking girls who get to be successful photographic models, you know. Our own homegrown pin-up girl, that's what Mr David said! I'm going to cut it out and put it up there on the shelf over the scales, so everyone can see it. You ought to be very proud."

He shook his head. "Oh, I am, I am! But you know what I mean."

"You're too old fashioned."

"I suppose so." He grinned. "Shall I give her a ring? Congratulate her, like?"

"Do that, Jim. Yes, that would be very nice."

It was to be hoped she was in for once, of course, she thought, helping herself to another orange. She tried to explain to him each time what a busy life Patsy must lead, here, there and everywhere, but he was always disappointed when he got no reply.

He was lucky this time, anyway. She could hear his voice rumbling on. Finishing Mrs Overton's order, she put up the 'CLOSED' sign, then followed him into the stockroom. He had a big smile on his face as he spoke into the receiver. "Aye ... well, bye, then – and well done, eh? Tickled pink, Cath is! Bye, love!"

She picked up the sweeping brush as he replaced the receiver. "I've done Mrs Overton, and I'm going to clear up now. We'll leave the other orders till the morning."

Jim stared wistfully out of the small, cobwebby back window. "I wonder if she'll ever come back here to live?"

Cathy sniffed. "I doubt it."

He shrugged. "Mary'd love to have seen that photograph." He followed her as she hurried back into the shop. "I was thinking I might go and pay her a little visit if it's as big a thing as you say, Cath, for Patsy – she is still her little girl!"

Cathy's spirits fell. "Oh, I don't like it when you go there, Jim! It upsets you far too much, seeing how she is, and it upsets me. You come home with that black dog on your shoulder and you're not worth living with for days!"

He thought of Mary as he had seen her the last time he had visited, sitting drowsily on an upright chair in a corner of the Day Room. They let him sit by her quite often now when she was being docile. Docile, he knew, meant 'drugged'. She had been crying, though, that day, tears trickling unchecked down her hollowed cheeks and dribbling from her chin. It had upset him badly. She had been rocking lightly and mumbling rhythmically to herself in a broken stream of incoherent words. He had tried to take her hand. She wouldn't have it. He had had to leave.

He shook his head now. "I can't help it."

She bustled about crossly, sweeping bits of cabbage and lettuce leaf and fallen fragments of flower petals and soil from the root vegetables into a pile in the corner. "She won't know what the dickens you're talking about! She won't have the foggiest, she never does! She doesn't even know you!"

Jim's chin set stubbornly. "She's my responsibility."

"*Patsy's* her next of kin," she said determinedly, shovelling up the rubbish and dropping it into a sack. "She's quite old enough to take on the visiting, and you should let her do it as the general run of things."

He frowned, his mouth turning down at the corners. "Oh, but, Cath –"

Her back was aching. "No, Jim. For once, you listen!"

They were both silent for a moment or two. Then, resting a hand in the hollow of her back, she eyed the shelves reflectively. "Shall we have a tin of mandarin oranges for our tea?"

It took a fair bit more nagging from Cathy to get him up to it, and when Jim unwillingly put it to her, Patsy's reaction startled him more than he had expected. It wasn't fair to ask her really. He'd expected her not to be very keen, but she was patently horrified.

In fact, she felt sick. "What, me? But I don't even remember her, Dad and she won't know me."

"She doesn't know me either."

"Then what's the point in visiting?" She felt dizzy at the very thought of it.

He was mystified that she couldn't see it. "One of us has to visit her, love."

"Why?" She sounded very tearful and he could have sworn she was stamping her foot like a child. "Why? I'm not going."

"Pats, she's your mother, love."

She hadn't thought of her mother very much for years. It took Patsy aback how abundantly the frightened tears flowed.

The baby was a boy, and they called him Stephen. After all the oranges she'd eaten, Cathy half expected him to have ginger hair, but the fluffy down on his scalp suggested he was going to be fairish brown, like his dad. She gazed in adoration at the little bundle wrapped up in the white woollen lace shawl. "He's got your eyes too, Jim, look."

Jim had a huge lump in his throat. "My son, Stephen." He gently touched one of the baby's hands with his forefinger and the baby grasped it immediately. "He's got good hands. He'll make a gardener."

"Well, he's soon going to get bored with the bit we've got now, Jim. Mind you, you have got it lovely!" she added hastily, peering out through the net curtain. It was only a small front garden guarded by a low privet hedge, but he had put a lot of effort into it. Edged by salvias, verbena, geraniums and lobelia and small shrubs, a narrow gravel path wound around a central circular bed containing lavender and an Iceberg Rose, lovingly coaxed by Jim into a standard. A Lombardy Poplar in one corner perfumed the air in season – you could smell it, coming down the road. She was very proud of it. Their garden was much neater and prettier than anybody else's on the road.

He gazed out of the window with her. "I was wondering about taking out the buddlea, it's cutting out a bit of light."

She rested her head on his shoulder affectionately; he was always doing something in the garden. Whereas she herself took her greatest delight in the little house with its living room, proper separate sitting room for best, its walls decorated in a lovely, heavy relief pattern of whorls in plastic paint and then painted pale green, and its built-on kitchenette with a real gas stove – and, of course, the bathroom and the separate lav upstairs – Jim pined more than a bit for the open air and his big garden. The back garden here wasn't very much bigger than the front, and in it dahlias, honeysuckle and clematis, geraniums, nasturtiums and other annuals grown on the kitchenette windowsill and eventually set out in pots had to fight for space with the tiny pocket-sized lawn, Cathy's washing line, Jim's potting shed, and the small patch devoted to herbs and salad vegetables.

"Have to get an allotment. We could do with one anyway now, now we've got three mouths to feed." He lifted a corner of the white shawl and stroked the baby's cheek gently. "Eh, young man?"

She smiled. "What did Patsy say when you rang her?"

He grinned. "Oh, she's very pleased, of course! Delighted."

"Was she? What did she think of the name?"

He shrugged. "Didn't say. Didn't have long to talk to her, but she's promised to come and see him. She was in a bit of a rush."

"That's unusual." She meant it sardonically, but he didn't seem to notice. "Has she been to see Mary?"

"She didn't say she had."

She clicked her tongue. "But she will go? She does accept that it's really down to her now? Your first duty is – well, it's to me, now, isn't it, me and the baby?"

He sighed. "She does, she said she would – stop worrying." He released her waist. "Now then, as to your tea ... I brought some nice mushrooms home, we could have those if you like, on toast."

She smiled. "That would be lovely."

He hesitated at the door, frowning. "How do you do it when you sort of cream them?"

She sighed. "Let me change the baby and then if he'll go down I'll come and do it."

He looked relieved. "Well, if you're sure ... I got a couple of custard tarts from Pinnington's, so don't you be thinking of trying to make any cake for after."

She rolled her eyes. "Don't worry, lad. I wasn't going to."

M usic blared outside. A car engine was racing. Someone pressed heavily on the horn. Patsy groaned and fumbled for the clock. Her head felt as if it was splitting.

Ten past one.

The sunlight beaming through the roughly drawn curtains was agonising. It made her feel sick. Dropping the clock, she closed her eyes again quickly, burrowing under the blankets. Something horrible was happening today. She could feel it looming.

Outside, the driver hooted his horn again impatiently, and

then again. A car door slammed, and then her doorbell rang demandingly. After a few moments, something rattled at the windowpane. A man's voice called her name. "Pats! Patsy, blast it, get yourself in gear!"

She opened one eye. It sounded like Marcus. Realisation dawned slowly. He was giving her a lift, her car being in the garage. It was Wednesday. Promised to be there four o'clock Wednesday.

Going to see her mother today.

The nauseous feeling overwhelmed her once again. Oh, bloody hell.

Forcing herself out of her nice, safe bed, she pushed open the window, squinting painfully out. "Shut up, Marcus. I'm coming."

He gazed up at her, hands on his hips. "You look gorgeous. Love the hair do."

She winced. "Oh, shut up."

He laughed. "Get your skates on, darling, for God's sake! Could have had another couple of pints."

Leaving him to saunter back to his low-slung, white TR2, she staggered into the bathroom and peered at herself blearily in the mirror. Fuzzy hair still standing in a confused beehive; bloodshot, piggy eyes with dark circles below them, reddened nostrils, and a deep crease down her cheek where she had slept on it too heavily. Bloody good thing she wasn't working. She peered at her tongue, and put it away again quickly. Yuk.

She was still wearing last night's clothes. The stiffened net petticoats under her swing skirt were now crumpled into scratchy, improbable shapes. She'd been to The Flamingo, and then on to the Scene Club, as far as she could remember, but she had no idea who with. Life was so non-stop at the moment, and the alcohol and the blizzard of drugs that swirled about her – not just dope now, but downers at night so she could sleep and the wonderful little purple pills to pick her up again, occasionally even cocaine – meant that a lot of the time she could hardly remember who she was, or where she was meant to be. Days and nights were passing in a blur. She was late for jobs now, quite often, and her skin was not as good. She'd even missed one whole show, which was very bad, especially since there were fewer demands for her these days. Too many attractive young girls coming up. She was getting too old already.

It scared her. She knew how it felt to be young and hungry for the limelight. She had been one of them once.

The thought sidled into her head again.

Going to see her mother.

She pushed it away, staring at herself in the mirror. *Tomorrow, I am going to stop.* She had said it before, but somehow the drugs and the alcohol managed to dissolve away the hard knot that was a permanent fixture in her middle – temporarily, at least. Without them, it came back; sometimes she still had nightmares.

Going to see her mother ... the faintest smell of Pink Lilac ...

Saliva filled her mouth suddenly and her image swam in the mirror. She was going to be sick. She lurched for the lavatory quickly.

Bloody hell.

M arcus wasn't in his car when she finally emerged, pausing to pull on a shoe. He'd left the music blaring, though, so he hadn't gone far. Knowing immediately where he would be, she made for the Rose and Crown across the road. "You can bloody well wait for me to finish this now," he told her when she found him at the long bar. "Want one?"

She glanced at her watch and nodded, sinking onto a barstool. "Give me a vodka then, darling, and light this bloody cigarette."

She was happy to avoid moving on. An hour had passed before they poured themselves out of the pub. Marcus took off with a roar before she was settled, so that she fell into her seat with a jolt. "Damn it!" She battled against the wind to tie on her headscarf. "How long do you reckon?"

"Near Corminstone, you said – this place, Patterson Park?"

Her headache tightened. "Yes, Corminstone. No, nearer Alfrestead."

He laughed. "You're going to be hell of a late, my pet." He glanced at her. She looked very uptight. "So when did you last see her?"

Taking out the lipstick case from her handbag, she tipped out one of her precious pills and popped it into her mouth, then passed one to Marcus. Her throat was dry. "I don't know. Years ago."

"Do you remember her?"

She shrugged, staring out the speeding countryside. There was a dense black cloud at the back of her brain. "Not really. Sometimes I think I do. Most of the time there's a sort of – a sort of mother-shaped hole."

He was very curious. "And what's wrong with her? When did she go loopy?"

She didn't want to talk about it. "They say she had a fall."

She was feeling sick again. She needed to change the subject. "Coming to Bernie's tonight?"

"Might do, later." Marcus shrugged. "Seeing Tony."

Her stomach was in a tight knot. "Pepsy wants me to go to Silverstone with him tomorrow."

He raised a brow. "Going?"

Patsy shrugged in turn. "Might do. Pierre Lapotaire's doing the last race, and there's a big party after. Collie's going to be there, taking photographs."

"Bagsie me. Yum yum."

"He's not queer."

"Really? How very sad."

They found it without too much difficulty and he slowed down as they neared the entrance. "Pity the pubs'll be shut now – we passed one a minute or two ago. I could have hung out there."

She peered at her watch. "I won't be long anyway, darling, it's past visiting time already." Opening her bag she took out the lipstick case, tidied her hair as best she could and popped yet another pill quickly.

He frowned. "Sure you're all right? I could come in with you."

She slammed the low door and pulled on gloves; full camouflage for courage. "No need. It's not as if she's going to know who I am. Anyway, my father says that very often you don't actually get to see her at all, depends how she is. It may be that I just get to see the sister or the doctor."

She could hope.

"Okay." He held out a silver flask. "Want a slug of this then, touch of Dutch courage?"

With her back to the entrance doors, she took a quick gulp. "Thanks, darling. Keep me some for after." Handing it back, she planted a quick kiss on Marcus's balding crown. "Ten minutes, promise, then we'll get straight back to town."

It took a lot longer than ten minutes, because this proved to be one of the rare days when the staff judged Mary calm enough to have a visitor. Patsy felt sick with horror when the staff nurse said so. For a moment, she nearly turned back to the door.

Instead, feeling numb inside, she followed him, click-clacking incongruously in her high heels along the corridors. It was horrible, with a nasty, institutional sort of smell about the place, and jarring noises in the background – doors slamming, a bell ringing, somebody cackling with laughter. They passed other people on the way, some of them very weird looking, and she was conscious of them all staring, even those who were not quite so weird-looking and were presumably staff. In her white, three-quarter length clutch coat, full-skirted black dress, gloves, pearl earrings and choker, she felt like a creature from another world. She forced her eyes downwards, fixing them on the scuffed heels of the staff nurse as he went before her.

"Nearly there," he said, as they climbed a second flight of stairs. Half way up somebody somewhere up above started screaming. Patsy's hand tightened on the bannister and she froze. Panic began to rise inside her. She slowed to a halt. "Is there a bathroom somewhere?"

The staff nurse peered down at her. "Are you all right?"

"I feel a bit sick."

He looked worried. "Visitors' is on the ground floor, near the entrance."

"Oh." She shook her head and started climbing again. Her knees were wobbly. "Never mind, then. I'll be all right." She nodded when he asked if she was sure, but she wasn't. She needed a drink. Opening her handbag, she surreptitiously popped another pill. She was beginning to feel quite buzzy and blurry; perhaps that was just as well.

He paused outside a door on the next landing reaching for the keys dangling from his belt. "Here we are, then." He went in ahead of her, holding it open. Her feet were glued to the floor. He lifted his voice. "Visitor for you, Mary. Here's your daughter."

It was a young female this time; they usually sent a male. They had caught her by surprise. She usually pretended to be asleep, of course, when He came; it was safest that way. These Special Agents looked deeply into your eyes, she had discovered that. One of their little tricks, of course, trying to see into her brain, preparing to pounce; their fingers were all clawed, ready, their fingernails especially long. He always did it. Sometimes he tried to hold her hand. He was very clever. If she hadn't been pretending to sleep, she would have scratched him and bitten his hand. Or worse. She did sometimes. As it was, she had had to let him hold it.

It wasn't too bad.

Don't *you* try holding my hand, she warned the female silently.

She dropped her gaze quickly to the floor, letting her eyes glaze and her eyelids droop half shut and her jaw sag loosely as if in a trance. Though she couldn't see the Special Agent woman now she could sense the threatening, crackling atmosphere that surrounded her. This was a dangerous one. She mentally sent her the warning.

Don't *you* try holding my hand.

Bored, Marcus pushed himself away from the car door on which he had been leaning for the last twenty-five minutes and began to mooch about the forecourt, kicking up the gravel. Bored with that, too, he flung himself back into the driver's seat, opened the hip flask and drained the last drops from it before lighting a cigarette. Blowing out the smoke in a long stream, he willed her to get a move on. Come on, come on, come on, come on …

Laying his finger on the horn, he pressed it hard. *Come on!*

He had finished a further cigarette, his hip flask was empty, and he was almost asleep when she startled him, jolting him awake abruptly as she flung herself into the car. Sitting up, he gunned up the throttle immediately, swinging the car round towards the gates. "'Bout bloody time …"

He glanced at her as he straightened out onto the main road. Her cheeks were all streaked with mascara; she'd obviously been blubbing. He felt a pang of sympathy. "Bad, was it?"

She shook her head stiffly. Reaching across, he fondled her thigh. She was tense as iron, though he could see her shivering. "Worse than you thought, eh? Never mind."

His kindness, or maybe his kindness coupled with the alcohol and too many of her little helpers, triggered something. It was the sheep's head all over again. Like magma in a volcano that had been blocked for centuries, an agonising pain that had been buried somewhere very deep within her forced itself remorselessly to the surface. Curling up slowly and painfully in the seat like a tiny child, she let it come screaming out. "Is this your mummy, is *this* your mummy is *this* your mummy is *this* your mummy is *this* your mummy …?"

"*No, no, no, no, no,* NO … NO!"

Chapter 27

1967

"It's Friday. It's five to five. And it's ... CRACKERJACK!!" Excited cheering mingled with the theme music blared from television in the back room and Jim winced, mentally tuning out the din. He was getting quite good at that these days. It helped, too, that, although he wouldn't admit it to Cathy, he was getting just a little deaf.

Placing the salmon pink pelargonium he was carrying onto the sideboard tenderly, he rearranged the pots already crowded on the windowsill, then fitted the new pot into the space he had created and stood back. Didn't look quite right ... The scarlet begonia looked somewhat out of place now that the orangey pink was there. Picking up the begonia, he pushed along the pots to equalise the spaces in between and stood back again.

"Turn that down a bit, pet! Stephen! Turn that telly down!" Cathy's voice from the kitchenette, shrill with irritation, managed to penetrate his imaginary ear mufflers. The sound level from the television remained the same. Her voice rose even louder. "Tell him, Jim!"

He nodded to himself. Better without the begonia. Find it another home somewhere. Still staring at the pleasing array on the windowsill, he raised his voice firmly but amiably. "Stephen, if I can hear your mother, you can. Turn it down."

The telephone rang in the hall. After a moment, Cathy answered it, sounding a little harassed and out of breath. "Hello, 2552?" He picked up the begonia, cocking one ear. "Oh, hello, love, how are you?" There was a faint note of forced enthusiasm in her tone. She raised her voice. "Jim? Jim, it's Patsy!"

He made his way eagerly into the hall, cradling the begonia. "Pat? Is it Patsy?"

She handed him the receiver and he took it, his face alight with pleasure. "Patsy!"

Grimacing, Cathy whispered to him hoarsely. "Jim, it's all ready ... I've cooked you a nice piece of gammon – don't let it all go cold!"

Patsy obviously heard her. "Dad? Sorry, were you just going to have your dinner? Didn't realise it was so late."

"Dinner?" Having had mince and mash followed by golden syrup pudding at least four hours ago, he was puzzled for a minute, but then he understood. "Oh! Oh, our tea, love. No, no, it's all right – it'll keep!" Catching his words, Cathy reappeared at the door to the kitchenette, wiping her hands on a tea towel. She pulled an irate face.

He could hear music playing in the background. "Have you got friends in?"

It was her turn to be puzzled. "Friends? No ..." Her voice sounded a little odd. "Hang on a moment, Dad ..." He waited patiently. When her voice came again, she sounded normal. "Sorry, just putting on my lipstick."

"Are you coming down to see us?"

"No, I can't. No, not this week, sorry." His spirits fell again a little. "I'm going up to Scotland, actually. Gorgeous house, right on the banks of a loch."

Swallowing the pang of disappointment, he made an effort to sound cheery and knowledgeable. "Lovely. Loch Ness, is it?"

He heard her sigh heavily. "No, not Loch Ness, Dad. There are other ones." He heard a faint clink and a metallic rolling. "Damn! Hang on again, Dad, will you; dropped an earring."

The begonia needed deadheading. Balancing it carefully on the tallboy, he pulled off the browning flowers and dropped them into the tray of the umbrella stand. *You need a bit of a feed, don't you? Give you some after a little while. After I've had my tea.*

Patsy was back again. "Hello? Dad – you still there?" She sounded a mite out of breath and crabby.

"Yes, I'm still here!" He straightened. "It seems ages since we saw you, pet."

"I was thinking, actually, I might pop down next week."

He brightened again immediately. "When?"

"I could probably manage the Sunday afternoon."

He beamed. "Okay! Okay, Sunday!" Raising his voice, he

called excitedly into the kitchenette. "Sunday? Next Sunday, Cath? That's all right, isn't it?"

Cathy called back, "Tell her to come at five o'clock and have a spot of tea!"

"'Scuse me, Dad ..." He made way as his daughter, nine-year-old Michelle, clattered down the stairs and pushed past him en route to the kitchenette. Patsy was saying something. He closed his eyes, pressing his ear to the receiver. "What, love? What? She's got to have what? A what?" His frown deepened. "What the dickens is that? Is that serious?"

He turned his face to the wall to blot out distraction as Cathy emerged from the kitchenette with plates of bread and butter and Madeira cake and carried them into the back room, calling over her shoulder. "Michelle, get the H.P. Sauce on your way in, please."

"Is it for the headaches? I know her sight's been bad ..."

"Bib-bib, out of the way, Daddy." He flattened himself still further as Michelle, her mother's abundant fair curls escaping from plastic slides that looked like yellow-and-white daisies, followed Cathy, bearing the teapot and a sauce bottle. "Bib-bib."

"No, for the epilepsy, I think, Dad, like I said. It's some new treatment." He heard her doorbell ring in the distance and could sense her impatience. "Um ... don't know much about it, but I wouldn't worry. Look, that was my doorbell. Sorry, I've got to run."

He was worried, though, he couldn't help it. "Oh, dearie me! Oh, dear. Oh, poor old Mary!"

She was impatient with him. "Look, it's not serious, I don't think so, just a sort of exploration, something they want to try." Her doorbell rang again more urgently and she raised her voice irritably, "Coming, for God's sake!" then sighed crossly. "Look, Dad, don't worry, I'll be seeing them when I come back and I'll know a bit more about it then. Don't *worry*, for God's sake! I wish I hadn't told you now!"

Cathy hurried back to the kitchenette as he replaced the receiver. "Let's hope she comes this time! What was all that about?"

He followed her to the door, frowning. "Mary's got to have an air – something or other, some sort of investigation. Apparently she's been having more fits now, and being sick."

Cathy spooned hot oil over the four glistening fried eggs in the frying pan. She made a sympathetic face. "Ah, poor thing!"

He stared gloomily at the gammon, though it looked tasty. "Patsy says it's nothing to worry about."

"She'll be fine, Jim. They know what they're doing. This

place she's at now, they're much more up-to-the-minute with their – you know, their methods. Patsy said so when they moved Mary." Levering out the eggs, she slid them onto plates already laden with gammon, tomatoes, processed peas and a large mushroom apiece. "And how was Patsy?"

He shrugged. "Still dashing about."

Cathy clicked her tongue disapprovingly. "She ought to have settled down, you know, by now. I keep saying it. Should be married by now, have a nice little family, have a baby. She'll be past it before she knows where she is. And what's she doing with the rest of the money she got for Aunty May's house?"

"I didn't ask."

She sniffed and stabbed at a round of fried bread, dividing it. "Still wasting it, no doubt. It's time she found another job, or a husband. Still messing around with this fast lot, even though she isn't doing any modelling. She wants to keep the money for a rainy day."

"She bought the flat and her little car."

She rolled her eyes dismissively. "The flat!"

He was defensive. "You haven't seen it, love. It's very nice, you know. Fitted carpets. Built in wardrobes. Got a washing machine and a dryer, you know – and central heating." He paused reflectively. "Of course, it hasn't got a garden."

"And it's miles from the shops, up seven flights of stairs and hardly any room to swing a cat!"

He didn't want to concede that he had thought it was horrible on his brief visit. "There is a lift."

"But where would you keep a push chair? Where would the kiddies play?" She shrugged. This wasn't going to cheer him up. She picked up two plates and smiled brightly. "Come on, go and sit down, it's ready."

He made his way ahead of her into the back room, where the table was laid and Stephen and Michelle were glued to the television in the corner. The slight spark of irritation that he was already feeling flared into an angry glow. "Isn't there a news programme on, Stephen? I can't be doing with all that racket when I'm having my tea."

Afternoon light forced itself between the blinds. Patsy peered groggily at the sleeping body sprawling beside her and groaned. "Oh, not you." Picking up the clock, she focused on it with difficulty, then slumped back onto the pillow with a moan. Promised to drive down to Chetstock today. She felt terrible, but she was going to have to get up.

She elbowed Hugh's snoring form lethargically. "Hugh? Get

up." He stopped snoring for a moment, spluttered, half choked and then began again. She stared at the ceiling, willing herself to rise. Her eyes felt dry and gritty. *Come on, get up, get up.*

Throwing aside the bedclothes at last, she pulled on her ruffled, shortie dressing gown and shuffled into the sitting room. In the reeking, desolate wasteland that was the aftermath of last night's party she searched for her cigarettes, found them under a cushion on the sofa and, switching off the table lamps en route, wove her way back to the bedroom door. "Hugh? Bloody well get up!"

He wasn't going to move; she'd have to leave him there. Yawning, she shuffled into the tiny fitted kitchen. There wasn't any food apart from half a wilting prawn cocktail left over from her last dinner party a week ago and probably lethal by now, some mouldy cheddar and half a grapefruit, drying out. God, she needed to get herself together and get herself a job. Good thing she was going out to tea. The idea of something nice layered with chocolate fudge icing or a bowl of Cathy's raspberry trifle had a certain appeal. Must still have a touch of the munchies.

Taking out a half empty bottle of milk, she drained it thirstily, then took out the grapefruit. There was a third of a bottle of gin amongst the empty bottles left on the worktop above the cutlery drawer. She contemplated it for a moment, then put down the grapefruit and reached for the gin instead.

It was a horrible day, with a blustering wind and rainwater gurgling in the gutters. Emerging from her flat eventually, she stood disorientated for a moment, then fumbled for her car keys, dropping her bag into a puddle in the process. Hugh's motorbike was jammed in between her little car and the blue Ford parked close behind. She glared at it crossly.

The key didn't seem to want to fit in the car door lock. She got it in eventually, but she had to swear at it. Kicking off her high heels, she started the engine, revving it rhythmically whilst she searched for music on the radio. The Rolling Stones; they'd do.

Reversing, she heard a telltale thud and glanced into the mirror. Hugh's bike was half over, she must have bumped it. No time to go back and look. Pulling out of her space, she accelerated away with a roar.

Sleeping with Herpes Hugh again: she must be mad. Serve him right if she'd dented his wretched bike, anyway.

In Palmer Street it was blustery, too, but the skies were still quite blue. Stephen, wishing he could go off to Highfield

251

Park to play footie with the other lads, was riding idly up and down on his bike and practising wheelies. In the greenhouse, Jim was fiddling happily with his plants and seedlings.

After tea, if she's got time, I'll take her down to the allotment; get her some broad beans and a few shallots and carrots to take home. Don't like the peaky way she's looking these days. A few fresh veg will do her good.

Have to show her my Dahlias. She'll like the Claire de Lune best, probably; the ladies do, more delicate. They're coming on a treat.

Inside the steamy kitchenette, Cathy was singing along to the radio as she sieved icing sugar over the top of a lemon sponge. Bored like Stephen, and getting hungry, Michelle wandered in from the hall. "When's she coming, Mum? Are we going to have fish fingers?"

"Tra-la-la-la-lah ..." Cathy dusted off her hands. "Not today, lovely. We're having salmon sandwiches – red, not pink, for a bit of a treat – and I'm going to do some fish paste and egg-and-cress as well."

Michelle wrinkled her nose. "Yuck, just sandwiches?"

"You won't go hungry. I've made some cheese straws and some nice jam tarts as well as this lemon curd sponge." She reached for the tea towel. "Do me a favour, lovey – go and tidy and plump up the cushions a bit in the sitting room, make sure it's looking ship-shape. I did give it a nice polish and things earlier, but I think your dad's been sitting in there with his paper and you know what a mess he makes. Oh, and take those little bowls of crisps and peanuts with you and pop them on the coffee table."

She sighed, once Michelle had gone. *All this fuss ... I sometimes wonder why I bother. It's not as if we were even sure that she was going to turn up.*

Still ... It meant a lot to Jim, and she cared very much about that.

When it got to half past four Jim went upstairs and had a wash and brush up, and put on his best jacket and a nicely ironed shirt. Cathy got changed as well, using the opportunity to give the turquoise blue Orlon sweater dress (recently bought from her Great Universal catalogue) an airing. She made Stephen come in off his bike and have a wash, and Michelle come into the bedroom so she could brush her hair.

Stephen resented it. "Why do we all have to get dressed up, Mum? It's only Patsy."

Cathy pulled some of Michelle's fair hairs out of the brush. "Because we don't see her very often. Because it pleases your dad." She applied the hairbrush once again to Michelle's head, frowning. "You've got a lot of knots in here, lovey. How would you fancy having a nice elfin cut? I've got a picture in *Woman's Own* I could show you."

Michelle pulled away. "No! I like my hair! Don't want to cut my hair!"

The memory of little Patsy's distress after her mum had cut her hair off had made a very strong impression on Cathy. She waved the hairbrush in surrender. "Okay, I was just thinking! I'll not make you cut your hair if you don't want to." She studied her own reflection in the dressing table mirror. "I might just go in for one myself, actually. I think this French pleat is a little bit ageing."

"I'm going to pop into the front garden, keep an eye open," Jim said, once he was ready. "She'll be here any time now." Cathy nodded. Watching him go out eagerly onto the landing, all clean and polished in his clean white shirt and Sunday best tie, her heart felt full of love for him – and it ached.

Over an hour later, as she had half-expected, he was still pottering out at the front, and it was beginning to rain. To distract them from their hunger pangs, Cathy let Stephen and Michelle switch on the television and went to the sitting room window yet again. Munching a handful of peanuts that she'd snatched up from the bowl on the coffee table, she pulled aside the curtain and frowned disapprovingly. "Come on, come in," she mouthed.

He wouldn't, though, so she fetched his old raincoat and took it to the front door. "For goodness' sake ... here, put this on." The next time she looked he was wearing it, and had got himself a bucket and trowel and begun weeding. "Weeding in the rain! I ask you! It'll be me he comes to when he's got himself pneumonia. Silly man!"

Ignoring Michele's' efforts with the cushions, she plumped herself crossly down in a chair. By half past six, she had finished her *Woman's Weekly* and there were hardly any peanuts left, but he was still out there, wet hair plastered to his head, peering hopefully up and down the road.

Stephen came in, scowling. "Mum, when's she coming? Can't I go round and see Pete?"

She glanced up sharply. "No, you can't." Rapidly coming to a decision, she pushed the *Woman's Weekly* into the magazine stand. "Go and get your dad. I'm not waiting any longer. We're going to have our tea."

253

S lowly, slowly, the sitting room clock inched its way up to half past ten. Lips pursed, Cathy sat knitting on the sofa. Fortunately, the complicated pattern of little llamas did provide a bit of a distraction, otherwise, she knew, she would have blown her top. Jim sprawled, grim-faced with disappointment, in his armchair. "Why does she do this kind of thing?"

Not trusting herself to speak, Cathy knitted more furiously. He stared at the gas fire gloomily. "You'd think she'd have rung."

She held her silence. The clock ticked on the mantelpiece.

"That car of hers might have broken down." Heaving himself out of the armchair, he pushed back the curtain and peered out through the rain-lashed pane. "D'you think I ought to get ours out and go and look for her?"

She stabbed herself with her knitting needle. "No! No, Jim, no, don't be so silly; you wouldn't know where to look. Something better will have come up, that's all – or she'll have forgotten all about the arrangement – be out somewhere having a good time with her fancy friends. Forget about it, Jim." Angrily, she fastened off her wool. "Mind you, I shall be having a few words to say when I do see her!"

He dropped the curtain miserably. "You don't think she'll come now, then?"

"Of course she won't! It's too late, now." She got up decisively, setting aside the knitting. "Come on, it's time we went up to bed."

"I think I'll stay up just a bit longer."

H e'd known what they had come to say before they'd asked him if he was Mr James Norris, father of Miss Patricia Norris of 76A Princes Buildings, Brewer Street, SW18. He'd known as soon as he heard the doorbell ringing at six o'clock in the morning. He'd known as soon as he'd seen the two of them on the doorstep with the police car parked behind them on the road.

It wouldn't have been Mary. If it had been Mary, the hospital would have rung – or Patsy would have. They'd have called her first.

"Some lads on their way home from a gig, sir, that's who found her. They'd parked up for a minute and gone into the woods so they could have a pee."

The constable had coughed and corrected himself as Cathy, white-faced, came into the sitting room clutching her dressing gown. She clung tightly to Jim's arm.

"Relieve themselves, sir, behind a tree, you know ... And

that's when they found it. Her car. She'd run off the road, somehow, and smashed into a tree. The front of the car ..." He grimaced. "Well, sir, it was quite a mess."

Jim blotted out the picture. "How ..." He cleared his throat. "How did it ...?"

The other policeman spoke. "We don't know yet, sir, how it came to happen. We'll be running some tests ..."

Jim shook his head blindly. Glancing up at him, Cathy stepped in quickly. "Can you leave us alone, now, please? He's very upset."

There was something he had to ask. Jim struggled to speak. "Where is she? How can I ... Where can we ...?"

"Yes, sir, we shall need you to identify the body, sir, if that's all right."

Later, when he got back from the mortuary, he went and sat by himself in the front room. The clock ticked. Heavy rain spattered at the window. A car passed in a burst of pop music, its tyres hissing on the wet roads. Another car passed. Running feet passed by. Nearer the house, a small child called, "Mummy!"

After a pause, it called again, more urgently. "Mummeeee! MUMMEEE!"

Jim wept.

Chapter 28

Chewing a Murray mint, Cathy stared through the windscreen at the recently built rectangular red brick buildings and at the neatly landscaped grounds. "It's a nice place, Jim; better than the other one."

Still concerned, she glanced at him. "It could have waited, you know. They'll be looking after her. You're pushing yourself too much. You've barely got the funeral over. It takes time to get over ... I mean, losing a child, it's all wrong. It's a shock to the system."

"I need to tell them. I'll feel better when it's over." He sighed as he tossed away his cigarette stub. Reaching in first for the bunch of freesias lying on the back seat of the Mini, he shut the door and straightened his tie, staring over nervously towards the building.

Cathy wound down the window. "Give us a kiss, then."

He did so.

She patted his cheek. "If I'm not here when you get back, I'll have gone for a bit of a walk."

He nodded. "I'll try not to be very long."

He had got finding his way around in the last place down to a fine art; across through the echoing entrance hall, up the stairs to the right, along the corridor, turn right again, along the corridor, up another flight, along to the left, up another flight and the staff room for Mary's ward was third door on the left. If he'd had to see the psychiatrist in charge, that would be across the entrance hall, up the stairs to the right, along the corridor to the left, and his door was the one at the end. This new hospital was a strange land to him, though, and wondering where to go was adding an extra dimension to his anxiety.

He studied the signboard outside the main doors, then went in and found his way towards the reception desk. The receptionist, a tired-looking middle-aged woman with mousy hair in a wispy pleat, looked up enquiringly – almost as if he was rather a nuisance.

He tried to smile. "Good afternoon. Could you tell me where I ought to go to ask about Mrs Mary Norris, please?"

She picked up a chart, following the lines down with a bitten fingernail, then looked up, frowning. "It's not Mr Norris, is it? Mr James Norris?"

He was surprised. "It is, yes, that's me. Jim Norris. I'm Mrs Norris's – well, I was her husband."

She looked back at the chart. "Right, well, I seem to have got a note here ... Could you hang on a moment, please?" She twiddled with her switchboard. "I'll just let Dr Kenning know you're here."

He shook his head. "Oh, no, nobody's expecting me, I haven't got an appointment or anything. My daughter, she usually comes, but, well ..." He swallowed hard. "Something's happened and I ought to report it. I just wanted to have a word with the Staff Nurse or whoever's in charge of Mrs Norris's ward."

She spoke into her mouthpiece. "I have a Mr James Norris at reception, Sandra, come to see Mary Norris, and there's a note in the diary that if anybody should come in or ring about her, Dr Kenning wants to see them. Is he in his office now? Shall I send Mr Norris up?"

The Sandra person must have said that she should, because when she'd finished with the call, she leant across the desk and pointed to a lift in the corner of the hall. "You can take the lift up, Mr Norris. Second floor, his secretary's room is the second one on the right. It's clearly labelled, so you can't go wrong."

He was bemused. "What for, do you know? This Dr Kenning – who is he?"

"He's the psychiatrist in charge of Mrs Norris's case."

"I see. And what does he want? I mean, have you any idea what he wants me for?"

"I'm afraid not, no." She busied herself once more with some paperwork.

He stared at the lift. "Right ... Second floor?"

"And second door on the right. You can't miss it." She had all but forgotten about him already.

He made his way into the lift. It smelled just a bit of urine and antiseptic; a crumpled crisp packet and sweet wrappers and a few cigarette stubs were scattered across the floor. *Somebody ought to clean this up a bit,* he thought. *Wasn't like this at the old place. At least they had kept it clean.*

He stared at the floor indicator flicking over. At least, too, seeing this Dr Kenning meant he would be telling the man at the top about Patsy. In his experience, nurses and orderlies were always rushed off their feet, and it wouldn't have been unexpected if whoever he spoke to on the ward forgot to record the information, then they'd not have known with whom they would have to get in touch in the future.

In the event, Dr Kenning wasn't ready for him after all. It was much nicer in Dr Kenning's secretary's room than it had been in reception, with a clean beige carpet and filing cabinets all round. There was even a small armchair. He had been sitting in it for twenty-five minutes nursing the freesias and distracting himself by worrying about the yellowing leaves of the little azalea she had on a cabinet underneath the window, and which looked to him as if it had been potted up in ordinary compost and not ericaceous, when the phone on her desk rang at last. Sandra, or whatever her name was, answered it in her deep brown voice and then smiled across at Jim. She was a very attractive woman with light blonde hair done up in some sort of complicated knots, though he could have done without the pale whitey-pink lipstick she was wearing that seemed to be all the rage. "Dr Kenning is ready to see you now, Mr Norris." He felt a nervous ripple in his stomach. "If you'll follow me, please?"

He ran his fingers quickly through his hair and, straightening his pocket flaps, walked after her. At least the wait had given him time to mentally rehearse what he needed to say so that he wouldn't get emotional and let himself down. As she knocked at an adjacent door and pushed it open, he drew in a deep breath.

Here goes, then. It'll soon be over.

Dr Kenning turned out to be a well-padded man of middle age in an expensive-looking dark grey suit and a magenta silk tie with a small gold tiepin. A matching handkerchief was tucked into his breast pocket, and when he stretched out his short, fat legs from behind his polished walnut wood desk, Jim was surprised to see that he was wearing toning magenta socks.

Even in the stress of the moment, it occurred to him that it was odd to see a man who took so much trouble with his clothes.

He had a funny way of talking, too, as if he had something delicious in his mouth that was making saliva flow and he said 'om ...' rather a lot, which struck Jim as a bit unusual. He seemed nice enough, though. He listened attentively, leaning his elbows on the desk and resting his chin on clasped hands as Jim talked. When he had finished, he leant back, shaking his head with a sigh. "Terrible! Terrible thing, Mr Norris. Really. That explains why we haven't seen anything of Miss Norris. My commiserations, indeed, commiserations, yes."

"Yes." Jim straightened his back. "Anyway – how about Mary? Has she recovered from this Air-whatever-it-was Patsy told me about?"

Dr Kenning hesitated, then riffled through some papers on his desk. "Om – oh, yes! Yes, indeed. The Air Encephalograph was most revealing."

There was a rap at the door, and the secretary entered once again, this time with a tray. Dr Kenning seemed relieved by the interruption, and leant back, rubbing his hands. "Ah, yes, coffee! Good, good, good!" The secretary set down the tray and smiled at Jim, and left the room. Beaming, Dr Kenning popped a biscuit into his mouth, added a generous helping of sugar to his coffee and stirred the cup vigorously. Jim shuffled in his seat, eyeing the refreshments, wondering if there was a place here where visitors could get a cup of tea. He'd had too many peppermints in the car; he was very thirsty.

"And have you found out what was giving her the head-aches?" He was suddenly afraid. "It's not bad news, is it?"

Dr Kenning shook his head vehemently, and took another deep gulp of his coffee. "Oh, no, Mr Norris, oh, no, no! Om ... it's fair to say that Mary has improved considerably, in fact."

Jim was greatly relieved. "Oh, that's good! That's good!"

"In fact ..." Looking self-satisfied, Dr Kenning pelicanned another biscuit. "In fact, I think we can say that the decision to investigate was well-justified."

Jim nodded. "So have you been able to take her off some of her medication? Have these fit things stopped? They'd got worse, I hear. What was causing them? I didn't like to think about her being like that."

Puffing a little with professional pride, Dr Kenning set aside his cup. "What the AECG revealed, Mr Norris, was a splinter of glass embedded in the frontal lobe."

Jim was puzzled. "Really?"

"Such a foreign body, sitting there for a long time, walled off, disturbs the local environment, d'you see?"

Jim struggled to understand. "For a long time ...? You mean it was from the accident she had, when she fell down a ladder? She was carrying things on a tray. There was broken glass at the time." He could still hear the crash and tinkle. It made him dig his fingernails into his knees.

"Bacteria set in ... build up of inflammation ... raised inter-cranial pressure ..." Dr Kenning glanced over his spectacles at Jim. "Do you get my drift?"

Frowning, Jim leant forward, resting his forearm on the desk. "Sorry, sorry ... are you saying this – this bit of old glass, it was ... that was making her sick?"

Dr Kenning nodded. "Sick, yes, severe headache ... blurred vision ... minor fits ... We were lucky it hadn't led to an abscess. Very lucky."

"And you took it out, this – this bit of glass?"

"Oh, indeed we did."

Jim sat back, startled but relieved. "Well, that's good! And she's feeling better? And can I see her, then? I've felt very guilty, you know, about leaving all the visiting to Patsy, but my wife felt – I mean, Mary hasn't even recognised either of us for years."

"Yes, yes, you can see her." Frowning, Dr Kenning started capping and recapping his pen. It was a very nice one, expensive-looking, shiny black, with a gold clip. "But Mr Norris, let me just say ... let me just warn you that you might find the interview somewhat, om, distressing."

"Well, to tell you the truth," Jim found himself admitting sheepishly, "I have never looked forward very much to coming to see Mary. I've always found it a bit, well, you know, upsetting."

Frowning deeply, Dr Kenning started capping and recapping his pen once again. "Om, Mr Norris, as you are obviously aware, Mrs Norris suffered amongst other things from what is known as temporal lobe epilepsy."

"Her fits, yes, that's right."

"The most likely cause was thought to be the closed head injury she sustained in, in, om ..." He leafed through the file of papers.

"1935. She fell off a ladder. Like I said."

"Yes, yes." Dr Kenning closed the file and picked up his pen again. "Over the years various treatments have been tried with what one would have to call very limited success. The same has to be said of her general psychological condition."

A bolt of sharp pain shot through Jim's heart. "I know."

"To cut a long story short, Mr Norris; nowadays there are a number of om ... neurosurgical techniques which have been shown in many cases to bring considerable relief."

"From the fi –" He corrected himself. "From the epilepsy, you mean?"

"Indeed. But also, there were a number of similarities

between Mrs Norris's case and others quoted in the literature – patients who had previously been of sound behaviour who had developed certain forms of epilepsy as a result of closed head injuries ..."

"Like her fall."

Dr Kenning nodded. "That's right – and who had begun to display certain, om ... well, for example in certain cases, severe or pathological aggressiveness, psychosis schizophreniform in others, occasionally manic depression, depending on the site of the lesion and so on and so on, are you with me?"

Jim was struggling. "You're losing me a bit, but I think I get the gist of it."

"The abnormal behaviour is not linked to or due to the epilepsy, but merely concomitant with it, both having been triggered by the same trauma. But where improvement following on from, for example, surgical removal of temporal lobe foci can be quite helpful as far as treatment of the seizures is concerned, the surgical procedure has also in some cases been followed by some quite remarkable changes in psychological condition and behaviour. For this reason as well, we decided that undertaking the procedure would be worthwhile in Mrs Norris's case. It was."

"Are you telling me ..." Jim spoke slowly, trying to grasp the enormity of what he seemed to be saying. "Are you trying to tell me that Mary's herself again?"

Dr Kenning frowned, pursing his lips. "Well, om, perhaps not quite that, Mr Norris; we can't expect that, not entirely herself. Mrs Norris has been institutionalised for many years. She has been under multiple regimes of medication for a very long time. This can have an accumulative effect, we don't expect miracles but, by and large and overall, I would have to say, there is a vast improvement, yes."

He cleared his throat, frowning. "There is another complication, Mr Norris and I must mention it since you wish to see her. Mary is at present very much confused. She doesn't remember where she has put things, she doesn't recognise members of staff." He grimaced slightly. "However, Mr Norris, I know that *you* she is anxious to see, though she may be – om ... puzzled, shall we say – by your appearance."

Jim was embarrassed. He glanced down at himself. He'd thought he was looking all right. Perhaps it was the tweed jacket, rather than a suit. "I've not had to go to work today. I thought ..."

Dr Kenning sighed heavily once again and enunciated slowly and clearly. "Mary is suffering from extensive amnesia,

Mr Norris."

Jim shook his head. "But that's something she's had right from the beginning."

Dr Kenning steepled his hands. "Mr Norris, there is currently a gap in Mary's memory of what? Om ... Some thirty years?"

Jim stared at him in silence.

"It may not last, of course." Dr Kenning unfolded his hands and rested them on the desk. "But do you understand me, Mr Norris? You do see what I mean? She is currently expecting to see a young man, a man in his what – his mid, late thirties? A man who is just recovering from a nasty bout of flu. A young man, Mr Norris, with a young daughter – a daughter who may have suffered recently a severe scald from, as I understand it – om, boiling soup? She is anxious to see you, Mr Norris. She is anxious to know how the child is."

Jim's voice was barely a whisper. "Oh, bloody hell."

S till chewing her Murray mints, Cathy wandered away from the car park and across the grounds, following a narrow gravelled path amongst the flowerbeds. Passing a nurse sitting on a bench with a rather odd looking woman who looked as if she might be a patient, she greeted her cheerfully. "Hello! Lovely day, isn't it, especially after all that rain!"

The woman picked nervously at the loosely knitted hand-made purple jumper she was wearing over a thin floral frock, shook her head violently and cowered against the nurse's side. "I've got to go in now, I've got to go in now, I've got to go in ..."

Cathy was disconcerted. "Sorry, sorry ..." She glanced apologetically at the nurse. "I didn't mean to startle her." She hurried on quickly. It was a bit frightening; you wouldn't have thought there was anything much wrong with the woman at first glance. It just showed.

The path she was following led her towards the perimeter of the grounds, where a high wall topped with bits of broken glass barred her progress any further. She'd got the wind up a bit now; it was a bit scary. You didn't quite know who you might bump into or who might be lurking in the bushes. Not that they'd let them wander out here all on their own, of course, she reminded herself, only with a nurse for escort, like that woman. Couldn't afford to let them escape. They'd be keeping good tabs on them, the staff would, and that was for sure. Still, don't want to get right out of sight.

Turning back hastily, she followed another path and made her way back up towards a grassy bank within distant sight of the car park, There should be a bit of a view from there; with a bit of luck, she'd be able to see over the fields on the far side of the wall.

She could. The fields stretched gold and beige and green into the hazy distance towards some distant low hills. Plonking herself down on the grass, she rummaged for another mint, then rested back on her hands, turning her face to catch the last rays of the late afternoon sun. What a lovely spot. Nice for them, being out here in the country. Bit inconvenient for visitors, but still ...

Failing to restrain a small sigh of pleasure, she felt guilty. Poor Jim. Of course, she'd been desperately shocked and sad herself about Patsy, but it had been a hundred times worse for poor Jim. Losing a child at whatever age must be the worst thing in the world, but it was bound to have got him thinking again about Mary. She could see it in his eyes and sense it in his long silences. It didn't bother her, it was only natural; all his earliest memories of Patsy would be tied up with her mother in his mind.

She sat up, shading her eyes and gazing over towards the car park. Didn't seem to be much movement. Visiting time couldn't be over just yet. Shouldn't be too long now, though. She brushed off an ant that was climbing, tickling annoyingly, up her leg.

Hope this grass isn't damp. She lifted herself, passing an exploratory hand over her rear, but her skirt felt dry. *Good. Don't want to be giving myself piles. Next time I come I'll bring a rug.*

Of course, this was going to mean Jim taking on the visiting once again. Now that she'd seen what a nice place it was, she might come with him each time; he might like that; might make it easier for him. They could make it a day out; have a proper picnic in the grounds, in the summertime, anyway. She might even go in and see Mary herself sometimes, when they were allowed. The thought made her shudder slightly. Never been in a mental hospital. The loony bin, we used to call it.

Poor Jim.

She lay back, gazing up at the blue sky, wondering what Mary looked like these days. She'd been such a pretty little woman before she went doolally. Bound to have aged. The treatments were bound to have told. She had asked Jim several times, but he had only shrugged. "Oh, you know ..."

She reached over to open up her bag. All the mints had gone. She considered for a moment pinching one or two of the Love Hearts she had bought for Michelle, or nibbling one of the brightly coloured sherbet flying saucers Stephen had asked for, but she resisted the temptation. There were sandwiches in the car.

There was a long silence in the consulting room and then Jim murmured in hushed tones, "What have you done to her? What have you done?"

Dr Kenning shook his head hastily. "We have made every effort to explain the situation to her, but so far at least, she hasn't been able to grasp it. We don't expect it to last. The amnesia may only be temporary."

"But – but think of her pain, man! Think of her pain!" Trembling, he rose to his feet, white-faced and appalled. "I've remarried! I've been married for years. I've got kids! There's Stephen. There's Michelle, she's nine, and Stephen, he's nearly twelve ..." He rummaged in his wallet, producing their photographs. "Here – see, and here ..."

Dr Kenning brushed them aside. "Mr Norris ..."

His hands were shaking now. He couldn't fit the photographs back in his wallet. He let them and the wallet fall. "Mary's daughter – her little Patsy, the one she thinks is five years old – she's not just grown up without her, she's dead. She's dead, Doctor. How is she going to take *that?*"

A raging fire of fierce anger suddenly consumed him and he slammed a shaking hand down on the doctor's desk. Dr Kenning jumped. "Why? Why did they tell me to leave her, to divorce her, if there was a chance of something like this happening?" he shouted. "I'd have waited. I'd not have left her. I didn't want to believe them, but they kept on saying it. *'Do it, man, do it! For your own sake, man, don't be a bloody fool!'* They kept on saying it, that there wasn't any hope, that she'd lost all memory of me, of Patsy ... I was a young man, and Cathy ..." He shook his head helplessly. "Cathy was a nice lass. She *is* a nice lass, She's a good mother. She's been a good wife to me."

Dr Kenning smiled smoothly. "I have no doubt they were offering you the best advice available at the time."

Jim rounded on him again. "You don't know, do you, any of you? You don't know any better than the rest of us. You make out you do, but you don't."

Dr Kenning frowned, disconcerted. "We learn as we go along. New developments ... We have to try whatever we can. We have a duty –"

"A duty? A duty to tell people there's hope when there is none and that they should give up when there might be hope if only they'd wait long enough? How am I supposed to face Mary now?"

Dr Kenning spread his hands pleadingly. "Mr Norris, I do understand ..."

White-faced, Jim stood over him, shaking from head to foot. "Do you? Well, I don't! I bloody don't. I don't understand at all!"

Chapter 29

D r Kenning shook his head. "We are not putting the onus on you, Mr Norris. She's in good hands. It was merely that we felt you ought to know."

Jim felt as if he was drowning. "I don't know what I'm going to do."

There was silence. Dr Kenning picked up his phone. "Om ... Sandra, would you bring a cup of tea, please, for Mr Norris?"

Jim shook his head vehemently. "I don't want a cup of tea! I need – I want ..." Saliva filled his mouth. He was going to be sick. He moved towards the door. "I'm sorry, excuse me, I don't feel ... I need to ..."

Dr Kenning spoke quickly into the phone. "Sandra, come and show Mr Norris where the lavatories are."

Jim shook his head. "I'll find them myself." He only just got there in time, though. They weren't where he expected them to be, off the entrance hall, like they had been at the last place.

Crossing to a washbasin afterwards he splashed water on his face. A trolley rattled noisily past the door and with it the sudden loud clatter and thud of Mary's fall mingled with the wails of Patsy and the sound of breaking glass filled his head once again.

Drawing in a painful breath between his teeth, he clenched his eyes tight as he felt his old self's terror. *"Mary. Mary – what've you done?"*

Opening his eyes, he stared into the mirror. In the harsh light of the overhead neon tube his skin, which he knew to be lightly tanned and weathered from all the time he spent outdoors, looked as grey as his hair. Grey and yellow. His face looked thin and drawn. Cast shadows lurked beneath his eyes. Deep lines ran down from the sides of his chin on either side of his mouth. Lines creased around his eyes from squinting against the sun and fine tram tracks ran across his forehead.

Beneath his eyes a fine network of crow's feet had spread. His shoulders stooped a little. Apart from his belly, rounded a little thanks to Cathy's cooking, his tall, wiry frame seemed to have shrunk a little, collapsing in on itself.

Oh, Mary, I am old now. Would you still know it was me?

He was disorientated when he came out, wondering which way to go. It felt as if the activity of the hospital ought to have stopped in view of the enormity of the situation, but everything was carrying on as normal. The usual sounds of laughter, shouts and clanging doors echoed in the distance. A porter walked along the corridor whistling cheerfully, *Daisy, Daisy, give me your answer, do ...*

Not knowing where he was going, and not sure where he wanted to go, Jim followed him blindly down the stairs.

Upstairs in a twin-bedded room off Springfield ward, Mary stood at the curtained, barred window plucking fretfully at her cardigan, a pale, faded blue on which the wool had bobbled. It wasn't one of hers but there wasn't anything else for her to wear. The short, thin sprigged cotton nightgown she wore beneath it wasn't familiar either; it was obviously hospital issue.

Cars were moving in and out of the car park far below. There were an awful lot of them. They all looked very posh, very streamlined. She strained and blinked, hoping to see Jim somewhere amongst them, wiping away the mist that kept forming, irritatingly, on the glass from her breathing on it and peering out again.

There were hills in the distance. Standfield Mental hospital, they'd said it was. She'd never heard of it, and it worried her, a mental hospital. A *mental* hospital? She'd only bruised herself and cut her head. They must have moved her from the Cottage Hospital while she was asleep. She kept asking them, the people who seemed to be looking after her, but they kept on talking rubbish, such rubbish that it had occurred to her to wonder if by any chance they were all patients who had escaped the staff and were wandering round the place pretending to be them. The idea was quite frightening. You never knew what a mad person would do.

Hearing a noise at the door, she caught her breath and turned, clutching at the curtain. He was here now, one of them, the balding young man in a white jacket who seemed to be here most frequently. He said he was a Staff Nurse, but that couldn't be right and rather supported her theory. Nurses were women – you wouldn't have a man.

He dusted his hands. "Right, love. You might be going to have a visitor. Let's get you all pretty and ready to go to the day room."

"Oh!" Forgetting her fear, Mary hurried to her bedside locker, pulling out the contents and scattering them onto the floor, then darted to the locker beside the other bed in the room and began to search that, too.

He put down the bundle he was carrying onto her bed. "Hell's bells, Mary, what are you up to? What're you looking for, love?"

She crouched down, feeling around the locker. "My handbag, my handbag ... It must be here somewhere!"

"Don't think you've got one, love, have you?"

She was getting frantic. "Of course I have. I never go out without my handbag. I've got to get ready. I've got to get everything ready!"

Crossing over to her, he lifted her to her feet firmly but gently and then began to stuff the discarded items back in the locker. "And this isn't yours, you know, love. This is Mollie's locker. You shouldn't mess with other people's things."

She was puzzled. "Who's Mollie?"

He sighed. "Mollie. Mollie!" He gestured towards a fat, white haired woman asleep in the bed with her toothless mouth open. She was snoring faintly. He was getting cross with her now. "Come on, now, love! Don't give me a hard time!"

He led her back to the other bed. "I've brought you a nice dress to wear, and here's a petti. Let's get you some bloomers." He riffled through her drawer, fishing out a pair of pink interlock knickers. "Right, these will do."

She was so excited. "It's Jim, you see. It'll be Jim. D'you think he'll be bringing Patsy? I don't think he'll bring Patsy, she's only little, you see. No, he's probably left her with Elsie for the afternoon, especially if she hasn't been well. She's very good, is Elsie. She's very fond of Jim."

"That's nice, love." He crouched down, stretching out the elastic waistband of the knickers. "Come on, here we are, oops-a-daisy."

Blushing, she snatched them out of his hands. "For goodness' sake, I can do it myself."

He sat back on his heels. "Okay, go on, then."

She clutched them to her chest. "Turn away, close your eyes, please."

He sat down on the bed pretending to shut them, though she was sure he was peeking, and she turned her back, pulling them on as quickly as she could. They weren't hers either, ugly things, most unflattering, and she was glad when they were on and out of sight. Why were they giving her somebody else's things? She frowned, fingering the fabric of the dress that was lying on the bed. It was flowered cotton, thin and worn. "Whose is this? It isn't mine."

"Never mind, eh?" He jumped up from the bed. "Let's just get it on. Let's have your nightie." Before she knew it, he had whisked the nightie off over her head leaving her standing in the pink bloomers. Mortified, she crossed her arms over her bosom as he held out the dress. "Here we are, love, put your petti on, arms up ..."

"No ...!" She shivered, backing away.

He clicked his tongue and advanced on her, shaking the dress. "Arms up, come on, Mary."

She had backed herself into a corner. Better to cover herself up. Crimson with shame, she held up her arms and he dropped the petticoat and then the dress over her head. Better to do as she was told. He might be violent.

He was pleased with her. "That's it. Good girl. Stand still, let me fasten it up."

While he was doing so, she glanced around the room. "If my handbag isn't here, where do you think they'll have put it? I need my comb and my – my what-d'you-call it – the stuff you put on your hands. I haven't been looking after my hands. I haven't been drying them properly. They're getting all chapped and rough and he'll be ever so cross, here, feel ..."

He took the hands she proffered, running his thumbs over the backs of them gently. "Mary, look. Look at your hands, love. Come on – look at them."

"I don't want to." She tried to wrench her hands away, but he had them firmly.

He shook his head firmly. "You've got to. You've got to, love. Look, I've shown you before. They're not chapped, Mary, they're not chapped at all; they're lovely and soft." He chuckled. "You're a lady of leisure, you are!" He was serious again, holding up her hands. "They're just, well, just the way hands go when you get older. See, the skin changes. See? Look at mine."

Now that he had turned his so that she could see the backs of them, she managed to wrench hers away. Terrified, she clutched them to her chest. "I don't know what you're talking about. I don't know what you're talking about. I just want some stuff." The word came to her. "Some hand cream. Yes, cream! I want some cream." She was shaking.

He backed away, holding up his hands. "All right, love,

all right! I'll get you some lanolin in a minute." He glanced around. "Look, you sit down and have a bit of a rest." Taking her by the shoulders gently but firmly, he manoeuvred her to a small armchair. "Sit down there, see, in your chair." He studied her, looking relieved. "There, that's better!"

Frightened to get up again, she craned to see the window. "No, it isn't, I can't see out. I want to watch for him coming, I must be ready for him when he comes." A thought struck her. "I must wash my hair! I want to wash my hair, it's all greasy. I can't let him arrive and see me like this!"

He seemed exasperated. "They washed your hair for you last night, Mary. It looks very nice."

She shook her head vehemently, panicking, running her fingers through her tangled hair. "No it doesn't, it doesn't, I can tell, I can feel. It's awful, it's a mess ..."

He stared at her thoughtfully, then he said, quite softly, "Would you like me to fetch you a mirror, love?"

A sharp stabbing pain through her stomach transfixed her and she drew back into her chair, trembling. "No, no, I don't want a mirror."

He moved over, crouching down by her side, cajoling softly. "Why not, love? Why not, Mary? Why don't you want a mirror?"

"I don't want one, that's all."

"Come on, love, be brave."

She shrank in on herself still further. "I don't know what you mean."

He sighed and strengthened his voice, speaking more firmly. "Yes, you do, Mary, yes, you do. You know what we've been telling you. You know what the doctor said. Come on, have a little peep into the mirror ..."

She began to cry, trembling all over like a trapped animal. "I can't, I can't, I can't, I can't, I can't!"

Perturbed now, he tried to quieten her. "Ssh ... Okay, love. Hush, hush. Okay ..."

She shook her head frantically, eyes blinded with tears. "I can't ..."

"Okay. Okay." When she had subsided into hiccupping sobs, he patted her knee and then rose to his feet, hands on his hips. "I'll just get you some cream, then, shall I? "

Exhausted, she wiped her eyes. "Yes, please, I just want some cream."

He hesitated, and then crossed over to the door. "You stay there, then. I'll just go to the stock room. Won't be long."

271

Jim found himself standing on the steps outside the main door. Lighting a cigarette with trembling fingers, he moved slowly down the steps. Finding a wooden bench hidden round a corner of a winding path, he sat down. His mind was going haywire, mixing up today and long ago.

Two young nurses hurried by, laughing; a very small Patsy running laughing through the orchard, chasing a hen.

The clatter of crockery somewhere in the building; Mary, coming towards him, carrying a cup of tea and putting her free arm round his neck.

The smell of rain-soaked grass; the smell of her in his nostrils. warm chicken mash, the open air, soap and Pink Lilac.

The voices of visitors hurrying towards their cars, laughing, calling to one another; Mary calling, "I love you ..." Laughing up at him. "Just thought I'd tell you." Hurrying back towards the cottage, calling back, dodging happily through the trees. "Just thought I'd tell you!"

The birds in the distant trees; the birds singing a dawn chorus outside the attic window. The faint smell of roses; the warm, dusty, perfumed smell that was always up there.

Muffled footsteps on the path; Mary walking up and down singing softly to her baby, gently pulling back the shawl and smiling, radiant with happiness. "Isn't she lovely, Jim? Isn't she lovely?"

Oh, Mary, how can I tell you? What am I going to do?

With a sob, Jim buried his head in his hands.

Mary got up again as soon as the man had gone and hurried back to the window, drumming her fingertips impatiently on the pane. "Jim, hurry, please ... Oh, come on, come on, Jim."

The man was back before long, though. She didn't like the way he was smiling and stumbled back to the chair quickly. He was carrying a jar. "Here, love, cream for your hands."

Snatching it from him, she turned away, rubbing the lanolin furtively into her hands. It didn't smell very nice – greasy, like untreated sheepskins – but it was better than nothing. He held something up triumphantly. "Found you a lipstick, too, love. Thought you might like to get yourself a bit dolled up." He put it down carefully on the bedside table beside her and set something else too by its side.

She turned her eyes from it, touched her hair. "A comb. I'll need a comb."

He put his hand in his breast pocket. "You can use mine if you like." He set it down next to the lipstick. "There you are!

Soon be a glamour girl." He crossed over to the other bed and busied himself with straightening the bedclothes. The Mollie woman gave a guttural and rattling snore.

Mary reached for the lipstick and then drew her hand back, shivering, staring at the small, shining mirror he'd put down, as if it was a snake. She shook her head. "I don't use lipstick. I don't want that." She pushed the lipstick and the mirror away roughly. "I don't want these. I just want a comb."

He crossed back to her and picked up the mirror. "I fetched them specially for you, darling. Go on, try the lipstick. See how you look." He brought the small mirror up. She turned her face away, screwing up her eyes.

"I told you, I don't want it."

"Yes, you do, yes, you do, love ... hang on, let me comb your hair." She kept her eyes firmly closed whilst he ran the comb through it. "There, now." She felt him put a hand on her shoulder, giving her an encouraging squeeze, then his hand, cupping her cheek. "Come on, see if I've done it the way you like it. Open your eyes now, that's the girl, come on, have a little look."

Keeping her eyes firmly closed, she flailed, lashing out wildly. "No! I won't!" He swore under his breath, and she heard the mirror splintering on the floor.

Cathy sat up; she had distinctly felt a drop or two of rain. For some time now, the late afternoon sun had been weakening, sinking, the shadows growing longer and the sunshine growing weaker. A chilly breeze was getting up and from the west clouds were beginning to build, spreading rapidly across the sky. She scrambled to her feet. Better get back to the car, just in case; Jim could be there already, anyway.

She was quite surprised to find that he wasn't; they must have let him see her. Feeling her spirits sink a little, she crossed to the car, unlocking it and slipping into the passenger seat with a sigh.

Let's hope he didn't try to tell her about Patsy. Did warn him not to; waste of time and it'll just get him upset. He'll be in a gloomy mood all the way home anyway if they've let him see her, always is.

Feeling her tummy gurgle, she remembered: sandwiches! Reaching into the back for her shopping bag, she pulled out the greaseproof paper package inside it and opened it carefully on her knee, deliberating – fish paste, egg-and-cress, or cheese and tomato?

Egg-and-cress. Taking a big bite, she chewed it pleasurably, settling down to ruminate with a sigh. Not wanting to be mercenary, but if the money Patsy had from her Aunty May should come over to Jim, they ought to think what they were going to do with it. Of course, she might have spent it all, you could never tell with Patsy. Anyway, she might have needed it. Pity she gave up modelling; it was lovely seeing her photos in the mags. Wonder what happened? Who knows.

Fish paste, this time. Cathy licked her fingers, frowning, before diving again into the greaseproof package. Wish I'd brought a vacuum flask. Could do with a nice drop of tea.

She stared up through the windscreen towards the hospital. There was no sign of Jim's familiar form striding down towards the car park. Even after all these years, the sight of him coming towards her gave her a happy shiver. The rain was beginning to pitter-patter on the glass now, trickling down in slow, tiny rivulets. "Oh. Come on, Jim, let's be having you," she murmured crossly. "Time we got home and got the kettle on. I'm parched." Sighing again, she closed up the package of sandwiches, laid her head back and closed eyes.

Three bedrooms would be nice, though, obviously, four would be much better. Somewhere with a bigger garden, for Jim.

Of course, if there is any money, he'll want to put it into the business, but we shall see about that. He ought to retire now; get a manager in to run it. Time Jim gave up work.

There were some very nice houses in Westfield Crescent – semis, but quite big ... or maybe it would be better further along, nearer to the park, the kids could go off on their bikes and play on the swings and things. Somewhere like Beech Grove, quite fancy – a cul-de-sac, or even ... even, if there's enough money, one of those lovely houses on Thornbury Avenue. Always wanted one of those ... have to see how much they're going for.

Imagining it, she sighed wistfully. The white one would be lovely; the white one with green paint.

O*nly a bit of broken glass, but we can't be too careful ... Can't be too careful. They've given up. She's not going to get any better ... Not going to get any better. Mary won't be back ... Mary won't be back. You've a lot of life ahead of you yet, don't waste it ... Don't waste it. Only a bit of broken glass ...*

Jim's head was aching.

Stop it. Stop it. Come on, get up. You've got to go and see her! No, I can't ...

Mary's waiting.

She won't know me.

Come on, you can't keep her waiting and waiting. You said so. It'd be too cruel. Mary is waiting. You can't let her sit there day after day waiting for you, can you?

How can I do it? How can I tell her about Patsy? About Stephen and Michelle? About Cathy?

Mary is waiting.

The two nurses came past again, this time running the other way. Still giggling, they were sharing an umbrella. Their pattering feet made wet splashing noises as they ran. He stared up at the lowering sky and blinked as heavy raindrops fell into his eyes. It was raining. He hadn't noticed.

Mary is waiting.

How can I tell her everything? It'll break her heart.

Chapter 30

He shivered; been sitting still too long. Feeling as if he was ploughing through treacle, he rose at last and walked slowly round to the front of the building where the main entrance and the car park were. The light was poor, the rain was quite heavy now and the windows were beginning to steam up, but when he moved closer to the car he could make out Cathy with her head back against the seat, apparently dozing.

Dear God, poor Cath. How is she going to take this? Only a bit of broken bloody glass ... Your whole life shatters.

Visiting time was long over. Life within the grey building looming over him against the darkening, murky sky was getting back to normal, though a few stragglers were hurrying down the front steps, putting up umbrellas and pulling collars up to their ears and making a dash for the car park. Window by window, lights were springing on in the building, reflected in the puddles forming on the tarmac down below. Here and there figures appeared, silhouetted, at the upper storeys and curtains were firmly drawn.

He stared up at them. *Somewhere up there, Mary is waiting. She'll be on pins, poor love, tearing her hair out. She'll be worried about us, Patsy and me. She'll know it's not like me. She'll be wondering where on earth I could have got to. She'll be desperate to see Patsy. She won't understand.*

He looked back at Cathy. She looked so comfortable, so contented, cocooned there in the fuggy car. *I can't tell either of them.*

Tossing away his cigarette stub, he crossed over quickly and pulled open the car door.

She stirred and made way as he climbed into the driving seat. "Oh, there you are! I thought you'd got lost!"

Wordlessly he started the engine and manoeuvred the car

carefully from its parking space, joining the last cars leaving the car park, the tyres hissing on the wet ground. The car slowly gathered speed as he turned into the drive and headed towards the exit.

She stared at him, disapprovingly. "You're all wet. You were a long time; I take it they said that you could see her. Oh!" Brightening, she unwrapped the greaseproof package, and held it open for him. "Do you want a sandwich? I've got fish paste."

He shook his head. She closed the package up and reached over the seat, putting it back carefully in her bag. They'd do all right for supper with a slice of ginger cake. Resettling herself, she glanced at him. "Well, was it all right, then? What did they say? How was she?"

Jim didn't reply and she sighed. The black dog was back with him; he must have gone in to see Mary. She rolled her eyes. "Yes, thank you, I had quite a nice walk," she told him, tartly.

At the main gate, unusually for Jim, who was a very careful driver, he made a dangerous manoeuvre, almost colliding with a motorcycle. She squawked, alarmed, and clutched his arm. "Jim! For heaven's sake!"

As he drove on, she studied him as best she could in the poor light, frowning. "What's up, pet? What is it?" Stony-faced, he shook his head.

She sighed heavily. "You tried to tell her, didn't you? And now you're all upset." She grimaced wearily. "Oh, pet!" She shook her head exasperated. "I knew it wasn't a good idea. You wouldn't listen."

She caught her breath, perturbed, the reprimand dying in her throat, as she noticed suddenly a rolling pearl of moisture on his cheek, catching the light of the streetlamps.

"Oh, lovey ...?"

Jim was crying.

Someone – not the man, but a woman she had seen before, squat and officious and waddling in a starched apron and cap – had put on the lights and drawn the curtains now, so that she couldn't see out. Miserably, Mary sat on the bed, hugging and rocking herself and murmuring in rhythm with her movements. *"Jim. Jim. Jim. Jim. Jim."*

At last, when she was certain that the fat woman wasn't going to return, she pushed herself up from the bed. Must look out, must see! He must be coming now ...

Staggering a little because the fat woman had made her

swallow some tablets that seemed to be making her drowsy, she crossed to the window and, straining, managed to partially draw back first one curtain, then another, It was dark outside and the light in the room behind her was bright. Shading her eyes, face close to the glass, she peered out into the dark. "Please, Jim ..."

It was impossible to see anything. Maybe he couldn't leave Patsy. Maybe he was waiting till the morning.

But she knew somewhere deep inside that she had decided the same thing last night and for several nights before.

Dropping the curtains, she turned away dispiritedly. The old lady in the other bed was awake now, muttering to herself, plucking at the coverlet with both hands and staring, round-eyed, blinking very slowly, at the ceiling. The bed had metal bars around it like a child's crib. Mary stared down at her. Her chin looked quite sore. Her teeth, Mary saw, were on the bedside table in a jar. Her hair was a snowy white, but she'd lost a lot of it; you could see her pink scalp glistening through in patches. "Hello."

Mollie, he'd said her name was. She touched the woman's arm. "Hello, Mollie." There was no response. She drew her hand away.

She was very thirsty. There was a tumbler on her bedside table, but it was empty. She glanced around. This room they'd put her in was very small, but it was better than the one she'd been in before when she had woken up. There was more privacy, and the windows were big and not high up and barred and there was a washbasin in the corner. A washbasin! Relieved, she fetched the tumbler from the bedside table and took it over to the basin and filled it from the tap. It didn't taste very nice, not like the water at the cottage, but she drained the glass and then refilled it and carried it over to Mollie. "Would you like a drink, lovey?"

The old lady's dribble had run down her chin and onto her nightgown, leaving a soggy patch. Setting the tumbler down on the locker beside the bed, Mary went back to the washbasin and brought over the towel, drying the old lady's chin carefully. Tucking the towel carefully under her chin, she slipped an arm under her head and reached for the glass. "Sit up a bit, let me help you ..."

The old lady seemed frightened. She seemed to struggle a little. Her lips stretched and she made odd, throaty, gobbling sounds. She was very heavy, but Mary managed to get her sufficiently upright to press the glass to her lips. "There we are," she murmured softly, "have a nice sip. That's right!"

Most of the water went onto her nightie and into the towel, but Mary managed to get at least a little into the old lady's mouth. Putting down the empty glass, she laid her back down again against the pillow and gently stroked her thinning hair. "Did you have a bad dream, then, lovey? Oh, dear, never mind, close your eyes now, I'm here." Sitting by her on the bed, she began to croon.

She was still stroking and crooning softly to the old lady some time later when the door opened and the man strode in. He came to an abrupt halt, anxious for a moment. "Mary? What are you doing with Mollie? What have you been up to?" He crossed to the washbasin, picking his way angrily across puddled linoleum.

"There's water all over the floor! What have you been trying to do? You've left the taps running, look! Both of them!" Turning them off quickly, he strode back to her side, taking her by the arm. "Now that's a naughty girl, Mary! I'll have to get the floor mopped now. Let's have you back to bed."

Mary resisted as he forcibly led her towards her bed. "Don't treat me like a child! I don't want to go to bed!"

"I need you with your feet up if I'm going to mop the floor." He pushed her down onto the bed. "Stay there, now, till I've finished." He crossed grumpily towards the door and was back in a moment with a mop and bucket. The old lady made whimpering noises. He glanced over, squeezing out the mop. "And you've upset Mollie."

"No I haven't, she was thirsty! I just wanted to give her some water!"

He glanced anxiously at the washbasin. "You haven't been drinking out of that tap? It's not drinking water, Mary! I told you yesterday."

If he had, she couldn't remember. She felt huge anger welling up inside and smacked her fists down on the mattress. "I don't like this place! I want Jim!" Tears began rolling down her face. "I want to see Patsy! There must be something wrong. Why are you keeping me a prisoner? Oh, why don't you just let me go home!"

"Come on, Mary. You know why." He finished what he was doing and then carried the mop and bucket back to the door. When he looked back, his voice was kinder. "Be suppertime before too long, love. If you're good, I'll come back in a while and take you down to have it in the day room; you can watch a bit of telly. Harry Worth'll still be on. You might like him."

As soon as he had gone, she went straight back to the window, tucking the curtains right out of the way this time, but it was darker than ever and though she cupped her eyes and strained, nothing could be seen. All that could be seen, as she backed away, dispirited, was the reflection of the room she was in. Warning messages flashed inside her brain. Don't look. She made to turn away quickly, but it was too late, the image had caught her. Rooted to the spot, transfixed, she stared at the small, grey-haired, scraggy woman in a shapeless floral print dress and cardigan who was staring back at her from the glass.

Her thin, fuzzy grey hair straggled from beneath a white bandage worn pinned across the forehead like a Red Indian, like Geronimo. Her face too was thin, the eyes, shadowed below by dark circles, staring.

She stepped closer; so did the woman, peering back at her. The face, she could see now she was closer, had drawn, tired lines. Tram tracks ran across the forehead. The flesh of the cheeks and beneath the jaw was sagging. She raised her hand and touched the window lightly. So did the old woman, bringing her fingertips slowly up at the same time to meet hers.

Slightly and slowly the woman shook her head, and somewhere, from inside Mary's head or from her throat or from somewhere in the room, she didn't know which, came a strange, plaintive, humming sound, barely audible – a faint, long, high whimpering sound made on a single note. Dropping her hand, she fell silent. The old warrior woman had dropped her hand, too, and now she was raising it again and touching Mary's fingertips as she lifted her arm and rested them lightly on the glass. Somewhere, more strongly this time, the faint, eerie, terrible sound began again.

Cathy tried, but he wouldn't speak, wouldn't say what was wrong. He just drove grimly on, the streetlights shining through the rain-swept windscreen casting a moving pattern on his face so it was difficult to see if he was still crying. He didn't make a sound.

She gave up asking him after a while, and subsided in her seat, ruminating. He'd tell her when he felt like it, when he'd snapped out of his mood. Worse, this time, though. He had never actually cried before, not for a long, long time.

Staring out of the side window, she sighed. Why didn't men like to talk about things? It always made you feel so much better.

The rain seemed to be stopping. The houses on this street, as far as she could see them in the gloom, were very nice ones, detached, mostly, and quite big. If they did move, they'd need a new sofa. The one they'd got had stains all over from when the children were small and the springs were going. Something nice. A G-Plan, maybe. Ooh, and a fitted shag pile carpet! A new bed would be nice, too, something with a properly sprung mattress, and maybe a wardrobe and dressing table set instead of the old, heavy, scratched and mismatched ones they were using at the moment.

They were coming into Corscombe now, the point at which they would turn off onto the road for Chatstock and Anstey St Michael, and she was still staring idly though the window when Jim suddenly slammed on the brakes. Thrown forward unexpectedly, her body jarred, she clutched the dashboard with a cry. "Jim?!"

Fortunately, the road was relatively clear, or they would have had a nasty accident. Wordlessly, he executed a violent three-point turn and accelerated, heading back the way they had come. She stared at him, bewildered. "Where are you going? What are you doing? Jim?!"

It seemed he was heading for the hospital. They drove fast through the well-lit streets and then into the deepening darkness, all the way they had come, and finally into the car park with a squeal of the brakes. Pulling the car to a halt with a jerk, he threw open his door. Half out, he turned to Cathy, and, reaching over, took her hand. She could tell he was trying to be patient, but was really in a rush.

"Cathy, love, I've got something to tell you, but it'll have to wait. I have to go somewhere now. Bear with me, will you, pet? I'll tell you when I come back."

With a squeeze of her fingers, he was off. The car door slammed and, open-mouthed, Cathy watched as he strode almost at a run up towards the entrance. Winding down her window, she called after him, bewildered: "Jim!" – but either he didn't hear her, or he took no notice.

There was still rain in the wind here, and it blew in uncomfortably at her open window. Grimacing, she quickly wound up the window again and strained to peer through the glass at his disappearing figure.

She frowned crossly. What *was* he up to now?

The receptionist's desk was empty. Panting, he studied the notice board; seemed to be all outpatients and examining rooms and day rooms down here. She'd got to be upstairs, unless she was in some sort of an annexe. He looked around; no one in the entrance area to ask. He set off at a swift pace up the nearest stairs.

All the doors on the next landing seemed to be locked. Some had reinforced glass panels, through which he tried to peer. Most seemed to be wards; he could see various activities going on inside. It was getting towards suppertime. There was a distant clattering of crockery and a faint whiff of something like sausages. In a few rooms, a long table was being set.

At last, seeing a man who appeared to be in some kind of nursing uniform inside a room near the door, he rapped hard on the pane. The man turned his head. Mouthing at him, Jim rattled the door. The man approached very slowly with a suspicious frown. Jim itched with impatience. *Oh, come on, come on!*

He mouthed at the man again, trying to pantomime disorientation.

Going to think I'm a dangerous inmate ...

There was a rattling of keys and the male nurse, or whoever he was, opened the door warily. "Can I help you?"

Jim's voice was strained. "Sorry, sorry ... I'm looking for Mrs Mary Norris. Any idea which way I should go?"

"Mary Norris?"

"Yes, I'm her – was her – I'm Jim Norris."

The man shook his head. "Visiting hours are over, mate."

Jim ran his fingers through his hair. "I know, I know! Look, I was talking to the Big White Chief earlier –"

"Dr Hoffman?"

Jim frowned. "No, don't think that was his name." His mind had gone blank. "Began with a K ..."

"Kenning? Dr Kenning?"

He was relieved. "Yes, that's him. He was telling me about Mary and her operation." He didn't know how to put it. "And her difficulty, with her memory, like."

The male nurse was being infuriatingly unhurried. He stroked his chin, and then a flicker of enlightenment passed across his face. "Norris, you say? Hang on a tick ..."

He disappeared inside the room and emerged a moment later, stepping out into the corridor and locking the door behind him. "Thought I knew the name. Need to make a phone call. Come with me."

He led Jim to a small staff room, where he scuffed at the linoleum, desperate with impatience until the man came out again. "Right, I've established it's okay for you to see her. She's on the fourth floor. I'll have to get back to the ward, but if you hang on, someone will be here in a few minutes to take you up there. Just stay put, okay?" He set off at a rapid pace back along the corridor.

"What's the number of her ward?" Jim called after him. "The name?"

The male nurse didn't glance back. He was engrossed in sorting through his keys.

The fourth floor. Not seeing a lift, Jim set out along the corridor. He found a flight of stairs, and then another. Panting, occasionally taking the wrong turning, correcting himself impatiently he hurried on upstairs until the signs told him that at last, he was on the fourth floor, labelled *Butterfield Wing.*

The doors, though, were unlabelled, and few of them had panels in the doors. The second door he tried opened, and he found himself confronted by some sort of day room, with patients sitting around in chairs arranged in rows in front of a large television set. It was turned up very loud. He couldn't see Mary. Some of the people were slumped in their chairs, looking half asleep, but a number stared at him with curiosity as he stepped in. One man snarled and emitted a loud barking shout that sounded like a warning. Alerted, a woman in nurse's uniform sitting amongst them turned around.

His chest was heaving. "Looking for Mary Norris." The nurse stood up, but one of the female patients clutched her skirt, and she bent over the woman, murmuring.

He heard her call after him as he hurried back into the corridor, but he took no notice. He was close, now; he knew it. He would find her.

Halfway along the green-painted corridor, a door opened abruptly and a young, balding man wearing the uniform and a badge saying 'Charge Nurse' stepped out, blocking his way. There was a pause as they stared at each other, the man challenging, Jim exhausted and breathless.

"I'm Jim Norris," he gasped.

The Charge Nurse gazed at him a few moments longer, as if to gauge his state of mind, then nodded curtly at one of the closed doors. Leading Jim to it, he took out his keys, turned a key in the lock, and stood back, waiting. Softly, Jim opened the door.

It was a small room, brightly lit by two overhead bulbs. He could see two narrow white-painted, iron-framed bedsteads, one occupied, though not by Mary, and two lockers, a small washbasin in the corner; a couple of small pictures on the wall opposite the door and brightly patterned curtains at a tall window, pushed clumsily back, the room reflected in the panes. A small, fragile, grey-haired figure was standing motionless in front of the glass.

He was almost voiceless. "Mary?" His throat was dry. He tried again. The little figure didn't look at him or move. He took a step towards her. His voice was a little stronger now. "Mary."

Now that he was closer, he could see some kind of faint tremor running through her frail body. Following the direction of her eyes to the reflection in the windowpane, his heart clenched. *Oh, Mary, this must be so hard.*

"It's Jim, Mary."

Nothing.

He spoke very softly. "It's only old age, Mary, we're getting on, love. It's the way we go. See? Look at me." Moving behind her, very gently he put his arms about her, staring with her into the mirror. How many years since he'd held her? He'd forgotten how feather-light she was.

Fixing his eyes on their reflection, he slowly drew her gently against him. She made no response at first, but then, at last, after a long while, she seemed to heave a sigh, and from somewhere within her came a faint, strange, humming sound like the singing of the wind in telephone wires.

Softly, he pressed his lips to her hair. No Pink Lilac or chicken bran now; it smelled of some kind of antiseptic.

Very slowly, so slowly that he hardly knew he was moving, he began to rock with her. There was a huge lump in his throat. Softly, uncertainly and brokenly, he began to sing.

All the world am sad and weary ... eberywhere I go ...

He swallowed. It was a struggle to keep going.

I hear dem angel voices calling ...

He couldn't make out their reflection any more; his eyes were too blurry. He pressed his lips once more to her hair. Ah, Mary ...

Poor Old Joe ...

Epilogue

1975

S he's watching *The Magic Roundabout* again."

"She likes *The Magic Roundabout* – that and *Clangers*. Always watching the television. She's going to get square eyes."

He sighed. "Oh, leave her alone, pet. She's not doing any harm."

"I know she's not."

"Well, then." He glanced at the door. "Shall I ask if she wants a cuppa?"

Her lips twitched and the iron went down on the shirt with an irritated thump. "Tea'll be ready in a minute. Ten minutes."

He nodded amenably. "I won't ask her, then. What are we having?"

She was pleased with herself. "Nice bit of gammon with some pineapple slices."

That worried him a bit. "Not sure about pineapple. Gets my stomach."

"I'll have yours, then." She peeked slyly at him under her lashes. There was a tempting glint in her eyes. "Treacle pudding for after."

He knew she was watching for a positive response and he didn't disappoint her. "Treacle pudding, eh? Good, good!" The thought made his stomach rumble. "Ten minutes, did you say? I've got time, then, to pop out and water my tomatoes."

She nodded. "Bring a couple in with you, eh? They'll go nicely with the gammon."

"Will do."

Before nipping out at the back, he opened the door to

287

the front room just a crack. She was still sitting there, back straight, leaning forward a little, smiling as Zebedee bounced along, *boing, boing, boing* on his coiled spring.

"You all right, lovey?" She didn't answer. "Are you getting hungry? Cath says it won't be long."

She cocked her head without dragging her eyes from the television screen. "I'm sorry, Jim, I'll get your supper ready when this finishes."

His stomach gave a bit of a twist. "No, lovey, I've said, Cathy's getting it."

She shook her head stubbornly. "No, no, no, it's my turn. I'm going to make Welsh Rarebit." She had that bit of ribbon in her hair again today. It looked daft at her age; he wished she wouldn't.

"Tomorrow, Mary, lovey. You make it tomorrow."

She turned her head and threw a hurt frown at him, her tired blue eyes puzzled. "But you like Welsh Rarebit!"

He sighed. "I do like a little bit of gammon, too."

T H E   E N D

ABOUT THE AUTHOR

Jenny Piper lives with her husband in rural Hampshire. She has been variously an actress, an artist, a teacher and a psychologist, but has had a lifelong love of books and nowadays spends much of her time writing.

Watch for her next book, *Moving On*.

Visit Jenny at www.jennypiper.moonfruit.com or join her on Twitter: @jennypiper6.

DON'T PASS ME BY

Julie McGowan

1.

First, there was the blast. Then... silence. A complete and disturbing absence of any sound. No reassuring ticking of the clock that had kept Lydia company through many long evenings spent alone at the fireside. No creaking of floorboards. No whining of the cupboard door in the scullery as it swung back and forth on its hinges because it wouldn't close properly. Nothing.

As the first shock of the explosion began to recede, Lydia struggled to make sense of what had happened. She knew she had to move, although for the moment her brain felt too fuddled to work out why. There was just a need, an urgency that she couldn't identify. Tentatively she opened her eyes into the eerie quiet, forcing them to stay open against the grittiness of the brick dust that was swirling through the air as haphazardly as the confused thoughts swirling through her brain.

A huge orange halo lit the room from where the window, indeed the whole back wall, had been. It highlighted strange mounds of rubble and timber. Cold night air rushed in through the hole, aiding her return to consciousness. Into the silence came a thin, reedy, wail. Rescue workers, ambulances, perhaps.

She eased herself into a sitting position, wincing as her head made contact with the kitchen table. That must have been what saved her – she must have landed under the table as she fell. She winced again as she tried to push away some of the rubble around her feet. The wailing sound was increasing now, more insistent... more recognisable...

Grace! Grace was alive!

Suddenly Lydia was completely awake as the wailing turned into outraged howls. Her baby's need helped to push the pain away as she struggled to her feet, wincing this time from the sharp pain down her side.

She remembered now. It had nothing to do with the explosion.

"I'm coming!" she called, her voice croaky from the brick dust which had settled on the back of her throat. "I'm coming!"

As she began to clamber towards the front of the house, she found Billy lying immobile just a yard away from her, part of his body covered by fallen masonry. Perhaps he was dead.

The thought triggered no emotion. She forced her way into the hall.

The front part of the house seemed untouched apart from the layer of dust which had already penetrated everywhere. Grace was in her pram, unharmed, her limbs flailing in indignation that her demands were not being met with her mother's usual swiftness. *"Thank God,"* Lydia said of a deity she no longer believed in. *"Thank God."*

She lifted the crying infant into her arms, wiping her reddened distressed face with the edge of her cot sheet. "Sssh, ssh, you must be quiet while I think what to do."

She lowered herself onto the bottom part of the staircase, the weight of the baby sending spasms of pain shooting from her side round to her back. The child's crying ended abruptly as she latched desperately onto the breast Lydia offered her, and while Grace sucked, Lydia tried to force her foggy brain to work.

It couldn't have been a bomb – there had been no air raid warning. She could only think of the gasworks in the next street. The surrounding houses would have taken the brunt of it, with the back of this house catching the tail end. Strange to think that they had all been waiting for the day when Hitler would send his bombs over and now their house – possibly their street – had been destroyed by what appeared to be an explosion at the gasworks.

The earlier part of the evening came back to her. Billy's anger. His army boots against her body as she writhed on the floor, crawling towards the shelter of the table for protection minutes before the blast. Ironically, it was that which must have saved her from further injury.

They must go, now, she knew, before the rescue workers arrived to deal not just with them, but with Billy also. But what if he was dead? Then there'd be no need for them to get away in a hurry. She had to check.

Soothed by her feed and tired from her prolonged bout of crying, the baby soon fell asleep. Lydia settled her in the pram and steeled herself to return to the back room, from where there had so far not been a sound.

Billy was lying in the same position. Very quietly Lydia moved towards him, stepping carefully so as not to dislodge the remnants of their home, lest she disturb him. There was a trickle of blood on his forehead, but otherwise his face was unharmed. Grey with dust, as was his hair, his relaxed features gave him an innocent, boyish look, belying her last sight of his face, contorted with fury. He looked as handsome as when they first met, when he had swept her off her feet.

She gave herself a mental shake. No time now for remembering. His left arm was lying free of the masonry which pinned his body to the floor. Gingerly she slid her hand around his wrist. There was a pulse. Faint, but steady.

At the same moment she thought she could hear voices shouting and she knew it wouldn't be long before helpers arrived, calling out for survivors, with torch-light playing around the desolation.

"Goodbye Billy," she whispered.

She made her way back past the sleeping baby and climbed the stairs. Her movements were deliberate, almost trance-like, as she forced to herself to think only of the immediate need to get away with Grace. What had gone before and where their future lay could not, for the moment, be considered.

As below, the rear bedroom was devastated, but the bag she had already packed was sitting on the double bed at the front. She picked it up and tiptoed back down the stairs. Lifting the baby up and wrapping her in a shawl, she quietly stepped out through the front door into the night.

2.

"They're coming! The car's just turned in at the gate!"

Rhian left her vantage point in the front porch and flew into the kitchen, where her older sister was buttering bread.

"How many?" Bronwen asked as she wiped her hands on an old towel.

"I couldn't see. *Come on.*"

The two girls stood on the porch steps as the car pulled up. In the front were their parents and in the back sat a thin, dark-haired figure.

"It's a boy!" Rhian exclaimed. "Mam said we'd have girls!"

Mam got out of the car. "Don't gawp, you two – he's feeling shy enough already. I hope that kettle's not boiling dry."

Bronwen scuttled back into the house, but Rhian stayed to watch her Dad pull forward the passenger seat and the young boy climb out. Her heart began to beat more rapidly. *A boy! I wonder if he'll play with me. Climb trees and make dams in the brook. And Dad will be pleased to have a boy around.*

"Alright lad?" Dad was asking in his firm voice as the boy straightened up and surveyed the girl as openly as she was looking at him. He was several inches taller than Rhian, wearing a crumpled school uniform with a cap which sat askew as if not strong enough to subdue the thatch of dark hair upon which it perched.

"This is my daughter Rhian, who's nine," Dad went on, "and the other girl, who's just gone inside is Bronwen, who's thirteen – so you see, you'll fit in very nicely with us."

Rhian said "Hallo" shyly, but he simply nodded slightly and looked about him as Dad lifted a battered cardboard suitcase and a gas mask out of the boot.

"Come on," he said, removing the cap and pressing it into the boy's hands. "You'll feel better when you get some of Mam's food inside you."

Rhian ran on ahead into the kitchen. Mam was talking to Bronwen as she bustled round the kitchen with her usual swift movements.

"Mr. Owain Owen had said he'd try and make sure we'd have a girl – it would just be easier with the two of you – but

Mrs. Owain Owen said that was all that was left – the girls had all been accounted for. I don't know why *Mister* Owain Owen is the Billeting Officer – he doesn't get a word in when that wife of his is around..."

Rhian and Bronwen exchanged quick glances at this, because their own Dad rarely said a word when his wife was in full flow, but that was because she was chatty in a friendly way, not downright bossy like Mrs. Owain Owen. Aware of footsteps behind her, Rhian said loudly, "Dad told us to come through."

She moved further into the stone flagged kitchen and indicated the boy standing in the doorway. Mam's eyes swept over him. Rhian hoped he didn't see the pity in Mam's eyes as she surveyed his bedraggled state.

"Why don't you show Arthur where he is upstairs," she told Rhian, in the kind voice she used when her children were feeling poorly. "Bronwen, tell your Dad that he'd better come in for his supper now as well, before he starts seeing to the animals, because I won't be doing it twice."

The boy followed Rhian up the steep staircase, his feet clattering on the polished wooden steps.

"You'd better wash your hands, Mam always checks," she said, showing him the small bathroom. She coloured slightly. "The... er... lavatory's next door, if you need to go first."

But the boy washed his hands quickly under the cold tap, dried them skimpily on the towel Rhian proffered and then turned to her.

"I'm not stopping," he said.

"I think you have to," she replied. "Look, this is your room – you can see right across the farm from here."

She opened a door opposite the bathroom. Inside was a bed with a candlewick cover, a narrow wardrobe and a dressing table. The boy followed her in, looked through the window and then sat on the bed. Rhian felt hot all over again; would he be able to tell that there was a rubber sheet underneath the cotton one? Mam had been to a talk on evacuees at the Red Shed. "They all wet the bed, apparently," she'd said on her return.

"What's your name?" Rhian asked the boy now.

"Arfur," he said. "But I'm not stopping – not once me Mum's better, anyway."

"What's wrong with her?'

"She got hurt in the black-out. Broke her leg. There was no-one else for me to stay with, but I'm going back soon as she's better."

She wondered if she should say sorry about his Mam, but he didn't look as if he wanted her sympathy.

"You sound odd," was all she said instead. "Where are you from?"

"Bermondsey," he answered. "That's in London," he went on when he saw the blank look on her face. "But it's not me that talks funny, it's you lot."

He looked out of the window again.

"Where's all the other houses?"

"In the village – you'll have passed them in the car. We're at the end. Because we're a farm. Only a small one though. Cows in the flat fields and some sheep on the high ones. And we've got a pig."

He didn't seem to be listening to her chatter, but continued to stare out of the window.

"Will you climb trees with me?" Rhian asked after a few moments.

He turned quickly back to her then.

"Girls don't climb trees!" he scoffed. "'Specially not little puny girls."

"Yes they do!" she cried hotly. "And I'm not puny! I'll show you!"

"No point," he said, "'cos I'm not gonna be stopping."

Bronwen was calling them from downstairs. But Rhian didn't hurry him out of the room. She surveyed him steadily instead, taking in his dark, hostile eyes, the hair that was now flopping over his forehead and the shabby pullover that looked too small for him.

Oh yes you are staying, she thought, with the same certainty that her Auntie Ginnie, once she had a small sherry and a Marie biscuit inside her, claimed to know things. One way or another, she knew he was going to stay in her life forever.

3.

The car bounced and bumped along the rutted road, but thankfully the baby still slept in Lydia's arms.

"It seems a bit of a long way in the car," the Billeting Officer's wife said from the front seat, as the road began to rise steeply on leaving the main street, "but it's easy by foot if you go through Amos's field – that's what the doctor usually does – on his bike most likely, whatever the weather – how he hasn't caught a chill I don't know..."

The woman talked on, whilst her husband concentrated on the lane which was taking them to goodness knows where. Lydia had little idea of where she was, except that it was hilly and remote, and at the moment she didn't care. She leaned her head on the back of the seat and hoped there would be time for a decent cup of tea before the baby woke demanding a feed. And perhaps something to eat – the sandwiches on the train seemed a long time ago.

It had been a long day. She had listened to the dawn chorus from a bench on the scruffy bit of waste ground which pretended to be a park some streets away from the night's devastation, before making her way to Sebastapol Street where the public baths thankfully opened early. The lady on the door had watched over the baby for an extra tuppence while Lydia bathed and changed into clean clothes. Then there had just been time for tea and a bun in a café before inveigling her way through the straggling lines of evacuees at the station and climbing unnoticed onto the train.

It had taken forever to reach Bridgend and then there'd been a wait for the change to a narrow branch line. Children were dropped off at various unpronounceable stops along the line, but Lydia had stayed put until they had reached this place and it was evident they were going no further.

The welcoming committee, consisting of a number of well-meaning ladies with sing-song voices, had put on quite a spread in the schoolroom, but the children had dived onto that, and Lydia had only managed a small piece of cake and a cup that was more milk than tea.

She was brought back to the present by the Billeting Officer, who rejoiced in the name of Owain Owen, clearing his throat

297

preparatory to using a voice which probably didn't get much exercise when he was at home. He'd been efficient enough at the village school, though, dispatching the motley collection of children and the occasional mother to various houses and farms, ticking them off carefully on his clipboard. Until he came to Lydia, that is.

Then he'd resorted to checking through myriad forms and pieces of paper, muttering a few "I don't knows" before rifling through the papers again in the vain hope that they would, after all, throw up a solution for what to do with this young woman and her baby who were two bodies more than he'd been led to expect.

"I hope he's at home," he said now.

"He's at home," Mrs. Owain Owen said, with the satisfaction of one who knew the whereabouts of most of the locals at any given time. "Olwen Hughes saw him leaving the Matthews' house not half-an-hour since."

She swivelled her bulk around in the seat to address Lydia. "Terrible time Mrs. Matthews has been having with her old Dad – but the doctor's wonderful with him. Well, he's got a way with him – with almost everyone, the doctor has. Works ever so hard, he does – the only one here, now, see – even though he's got a dicky heart. That's what's kept him here, instead of joining up, but we're not complaining. He'll be very pleased that I've found him someone so soon – bit of a shock it was when his last housekeeper up and left. None of us knew she'd been at all close to her sister, but when the call came that she was sick, well, off she went, just like that. But then they do say blood's thicker than water, don't they? Chapel, are you?"

Lydia started at this abrupt non sequitur. "Er... no... um... C of E – I was brought up C of E."

Now was probably not the time to tell the woman that she never wanted to see the inside of a church again.

Mrs. Owain Owen sniffed and turned back in her seat.

"Ebenezer Baptist chapel most of us go to round here – but there's one or two that go to St. Paul's." The last two words were uttered in a way that gave a clear indication of the low opinion she had of those few foolhardy souls. Her voice brightened again as they pulled up in front of a square, stone-built house.

"There you are, Owain," she nodded at the light shining from a front window. "Told you he was in. Quiet man, he is – keeps himself to himself," she told Lydia. "Except when he's with his patients, that is. Different man, then."

"No blackout," her husband said as he opened the car door. "He'll have to be told, doctor or no."

"It's nowhere near dark yet, man, there's no need to be such a stickler – 'specially out here – who's to see?"

Lydia eased herself and the baby out of the back seat as they continued to bicker. A cool wind whipped through her thin summer dress, making her instinctively hold the baby closer. The light was just beginning to fade, and there was little sign up on this hillside of the hot sunny day through which they had travelled. She looked around at the raw beauty of the mountains which surrounded the village. There was a bleak majesty about their rounded tops rising above wooded areas here and there and fields which looked far too steep for man or beast to cope with. Barely a sound could be heard apart from the shushing of the wind through the trees at the side of the house. She shivered slightly and followed the Owens up the steps to the front door...

END OF SAMPLE CHAPTERS

"Don't Pass Me By" by Julie McGowan
can be purchased from all good online stores,
or better still, ask for it from your local independent
or chain book store.

SUNPENNY
PUBLISHING
GROUP

ROSE & CROWN, BLUE JEANS, BOATHOOKS, SUNBERRY, CHRISTLIGHT, and EPTA Books

MORE BOOKS FROM the SUNPENNY GROUP
www.sunpenny.com

A Little Book of Pleasures, by William Wood
Blackbirds Baked in a Pie, by Eugene Barter
Breaking the Circle, by Althea Barr
Dance of Eagles, by JS Holloway
Don't Pass Me By, by Julie McGowan
Far Out, by Corinna Weyreter
Going Astray, by Christine Moore
If Horses Were Wishes, by Elizabeth Sellers
Just One More Summer, by Julie McGowan
Loyalty & Disloyalty, by Dag Heward-Mills
My Sea is Wide (Illustrated), by Rowland Evans
Sudoku for Christmas (full colour illustrated gift book)
The Mountains Between, by Julie McGowan
The Perfect Will of God, by Dag Heward-Mills
Those Who Accuse You, by Dag Heward-Mills
Trouble Rides a Fast Horse, by Elizabeth Sellers

COMING SOON:

A Whisper On The Mediterranean, by Tonia Parronchi
Fish Soup, by Michelle Heatley
Moving On, by Jenny Piper
Raglands, by JS Holloway
The Stangreen Experiment, by Christine Moore
Sudoku for Sailors (full colour illustrated gift book)
Sudoku for Bird Lovers (full colour illustrated gift book)
Sudoku for Horse Lovers (full colour illustrated gift book)

Rose&Crown
Inspirational Romance
www.roseandcrownbooks.com

BLUE JEANS BOOKS

(Romance imprints of the SUNPENNY PUBLISHING GROUP)

BOOKS FROM ROSE & CROWN, and BLUE JEANS BOOKS

Uncharted Waters, by Sara DuBose
Bridge to Nowhere, by Stephanie Parker McKean
Embracing Change, by Debbie Roome
Blue Freedom, by Sandra Peut
A Flight Delayed, by KC Lemmer

COMING SOON:

30 Days to Take-off, by KC Lemmer
A Devil's Ransom, by Adele Jones
Brandy Butter on Christmas Canal, by Shae O'Brien
Redemption on the Red River, by Cheryl R. Cain
Bridge Beyond Betrayal, by Stephanie Parker McKean
Heart of the Hobo, by Shae O'Brien

Lightning Source UK Ltd.
Milton Keynes UK
UKOW05f0156251113

221684UK00002B/9/P